Trance and Transformation of the Actor in Japanese Noh and Balinese Masked Dance-Drama

This book has been awarded
The Adèle Mellen Prize
for its distinguished contribution to scholarship.

Trance and Transformation of the Actor in Japanese Noh and Balinese Masked Dance-Drama

Margaret Coldiron

Studies in Theatre Arts
Volume 30

The Edwin Mellen Press
Lewiston•Queenston•Lampeter

Library of Congress Cataloging-in-Publication Data

Coldiron, Margaret.
 Trance and transformation of the actor in Japanese Noh and Balinese masked dance-drama / Margaret Coldiron.
   p. cm. -- (Studies in theatre arts ; v. 30)
 Includes bibliographical references and index.
 ISBN 0-7734-6341-0
  1. Acting--Psychological aspects. 2. Masks. 3. Nå. 4. Topeng Sunda. 5. Calonarang. I. Title. II. Series.

PN2058.C65 2004
792.02'8'019--dc22

2004054145

This is volume 30 in the continuing series
Studies in Theatre Arts
Volume 30 ISBN 0-7734-6341-0
STA Series ISBN 0-7734-9721-8

A CIP catalog record for this book is available from the British Library

Copyright © 2004 Margaret Coldiron

All rights reserved. For information contact

>The Edwin Mellen Press   The Edwin Mellen Press
>Box 450   Box 67
>Lewiston, New York   Queenston, Ontario
>USA 14092-0450   CANADA L0S 1L0

>The Edwin Mellen Press, Ltd.
>Lampeter, Ceredigion, Wales
>UNITED KINGDOM SA48 8LT

Printed in the United States of America

To my father,
William H. Coldiron, J.D.

Contents

List of Illustrations — xi
Foreword — xiii
Preface (Professor John Emigh, Brown University) — xv
Acknowledgements — xxiii

Chapter 1 Orientation — 1
  'Transformation' and 'Trance' — 2
  Why Masks? — 3
  Why THESE Masks? — 6
  The Influence of Noh and Balinese Dance-Drama
    upon Western Theoreticians — 9
    Gordon Craig and the Übermarionette — 10
    Artaud and the 'animated hieroglyphs' — 12
    Jacques Copeau's 'Mask Work' — 13
    The Rise of 'Intercultural Theatre' — 17
  The Actor's Consciousness and Noh and Balinese Masks — 17
    Trance and Transformation of the Actor — 19
    Scope of the Study — 20

**Chapter 2 The Mask: Art Object, Pedagogical Tool
or Transformational Mechanism?** — 21
  Influences on the Current Study — 21
  On Masks — 23
    Mask as Object — 23
    Pedagogy: Mask as Tool — 26
  Performance Theory and the Theatre-Ritual Nexus — 29
    The Efficacy-Entertainment Braid — 31
    Performance and Cultural Context — 34
  The Actor's Consciousness — 35
    The Process of Transformation — 37
    Transformation vs. Transportation — 37

Transformational Mechanisms	40
A Framework for Examining the Performer's Process	42
Ritual Trance	46
Conclusion	47

Chapter 3 Masks and Balinese Culture   49
A Labyrinth of Complexities	49
An Embattled Paradise	52
Agama Hindu-Bali	57
Ritual and the Arts	59
Caste	62
Traditional Balinese Masked Drama	65
Topeng	68
Sidha Karya	70
Calonarang	72
Tenget	76
The Mask Making Process	78
Ritual Preparations	79
Carving	82
Painting and Completion	83
Dance Training	85
Pedagogy	86
Ritual Requirements	89
Taksu	92
Summary	100

Chapter 4 Japanese Mask Tradition and Noh Drama   101
A Foreign Country, An Obscure Art	101
Folk Mask Traditions	103
The Development of Noh Drama	105
Raising Status	107
Court Dances and Popular Entertainments	108
The *Sanjo*	110
A Sacred Performance Art	113
Noh and Religious Ritual	116
Shinto	117
Buddhism	122
Esoteric Buddhism	124
Zen	126
Noh, Spirituality and the Reconciliation of Opposites	127
The Noh Stage	129
Noh Plays	133
Music	135
Hierarchy	136
Noh Masks	139

Maskmaking	144
Carver-actors	150
Training	152
Becoming a *shite*	152
The Way of Noh	156
The Noh Aesthetic	157
Jo-Ha-Kyû	158
Monomane	160
Hana	162
Yûgen	164
Kokoro	165
Chapter 5 Balinese Masks in Practice	**169**
A Performance of Topeng Pajegan	170
Waiting for the *Pedanda*	171
Preparation	175
Topeng Keras	177
Topeng Tua	177
The Speaking Masks	178
Sidha Karya	184
Aftermath	187
The Performer's Process: A Surrender of the Self	188
Training	189
Music	191
Costume	193
Masks	193
Carver-dancers	195
Marrying the Masks	197
The Topeng Performance State	199
Magic Masks: Barong and Rangda	201
A Question of Identity	201
The Play	208
The Masks	210
The Performers	213
The Costumes	214
Calonarang at the Pura Dalem, Bona Village, Gianyar	218
The Setting	218
The Performance	219
Preliminary Dances	219
The Drama	221
Rangda	225
Completion	226
Trance and The Masked Performer	228
Conclusion	239

Chapter 6 Noh Masks in Performance	**241**
Takigi Noh at the *Suwa-Jin-Ja*, Sado Island	242
The Rehearsal	244
The Costumes	247
The Masks	250
The Performance	253
Secular Entertainment or Sacred Art?	260
Hagoromo and Tôru in Matsuyama	261
Preparation	262
Hagoromo	264
Transition	270
Tôru, Part One	271
Transformation	272
Tôru, Part Two	274
Post-performance	278
Performing in the Noh Mask	279
The Noh Performer as Medium	283
Chapter 7 The Consciousness of the Masked Actor	**287**
Transformation, Consciousness and the Mask	288
Elements of the Transformation Process	289
Ritual, Theatre and Consciousness	290
Altered States	294
What is Trance?	296
The Physiology of Trance	300
Driving Mechanisms and Mediating Elements	307
Sensory Deprivation	308
Charting the Trance Process	310
Body, Mind and Mask	310
Sacred Masks	313
Conclusion	316
Chapter 8 The Mask and Transformation	**319**
The Path Ahead	322
The Power of the Mask	323
Glossary 1 Balinese Terms	**325**
Glossary 2 Japanese Terms	**329**
Works Consulted	**335**
Books	335
Films	344
Index	**345**

List of Illustrations

Table 1	Periods in Japanese History
Diagram 1	The Efficacy-Entertainment Braid
Diagram 2	The Noh Stage
Figure 1	*Penasar Kelihan*
Figure 2	*Penasar Cenikan*
Figure 3	*Patih* (Topeng Keras)
Figure 4	*Topeng Tua*
Figure 5	*Patih Lucu* (comic Patih)
Figure 6	*Dalem* (refined King)
Figure 7	*Sidha Karya*
Figure 8	*Okina*
Figure 9	*Rangda*
Figure 10	*Barong Ket*
Figure 11	*Leyak*
Figure 12	Balinese carving tools
Figure 13	Anak Agung Gede Ngurah measuring a *Dalem* mask
Figure 14	Children's *Barong Macan* (Tiger Barong)
Figure 15	One of Barong's attendants
Figure 16a	*Jauk Manis* ("sweet")
Figure 16b	*Jauk Keras* ("rough")
Figure 17	*Aku-Jo* mask in *Kurama Tengu*
Figure 18	Folk mask of *Shi-Shi*

Figure 19	*Ko-omote*, carved by Hiroyuki Yamamoto
Figure 20	*Hannya*, carved by Hiroyuki Yamamoto
Figure 21	*Shi-shi Guchi*
Figure 22	A goblin disguised as a Yamabushi priest in *Kurama Zoh*
Figure 23	Goblin in *O-Beshemi* mask
Figure 24	Templates for Noh masks
Figure 25	Using a template
Figure 26	Noh mask carving tools
Figures 27a & b	Deliberate damage to new masks
Figure 28	Ida Bagus Alit recites mantras
Figure 29	*Gajah Mada* created by Ida Bagus Alit
Figure 30	I Wayan Balik as Patih Jelantik
Figure 31	*Patih Demung Bues* ("Lucu")
Figure 32	*Topeng Tua* by Ida Bagus Alit
Figure 33	Cristina Wistara as *Dalem*
Figure 34	Ida Bagus Alit as *Pedanda*
Figure 35	Balinese high priest
Figure 36	Widow witch in *Calonarang*
Figure 37	*Telek* or *Sandaran*
Figure 38	Rehearsal at *Suwa-jin-ja* on Sado Island
Figure 39	Hôshô School masks of *Ko-omote* and *Chujo*
Figure 40	Haori Tadao in *Kiyotsune*
Figure 41	Fujima Satomi in *Hagoromo* at the Kanze Noh Theatre
Figure 42	Kongô Hisanori as the Heavenly Maiden
Figure 43	Attendants dress the Heavenly Maiden
Figure 44	Udaka Michishige prepares for *Tôru*
Figure 45	The Old Man, *Tôru*, Act I
Figure 46	The young Minamoto no Tôru
Figure 47a and b	*Chûjo* masks carved by Udaka Michishige (Photograph of Figure 47a by Rebecca Teele)

Foreword

After a substantial period of background research investigating published material concerning these two performance genres and the cultures from which they have developed, primary data for this study was collected during eight months of fieldwork in Bali and Japan in 1997 and 1998 (generously sponsored by the British Academy). I gathered the material as a participant observer attending lessons in dancing and mask carving and observing performances and backstage preparations. I also conducted interviews with a number of Japanese and Balinese performers and mask-makers and, on my return to the UK, led workshops with Western performers using Noh and Balinese masks. Additional information was collected through correspondence and interviews in Europe and the United States. All interviews were transcribed by me and all photographs of masks and performances, unless otherwise attributed, are my own.

Orthography

The book makes use of terminology in Balinese, Indonesian and romanised Japanese. Determining correct spelling in each of these cases is somewhat problematic. Insofar as Japanese is concerned, I have largely followed the system used in Kenkyû-sha's *New Japanese-English Dictionary*. Indonesian, on the other hand, is a relatively new language and constantly developing, but spellings used here are consistent with contemporary usage. A major shift in accepted spelling occurred in the 1960s when colonial Dutch spellings were replaced, thus: *dj* became *j; tj* became *c* (pronounced 'ch'); *oe* became *u*. Older sources quoted in this paper tend use the earlier spellings. Balinese is primarily a spoken language which, in its written form (*tulisan Bali*), employs non-roman script. The spelling of Balinese words rendered in roman letters has never been regularised, but I have tried to remain consistent using, as far as possible, the simplest and most generally accepted spellings of most terms. In all three languages, however, spelling used by quoted sources has been retained.

Methodology

Data collection in a field such as this, where the data in question is fundamentally concerned with personal 'feelings' (that is, the thoughts, emotions and sensations of individual performers), resists statistical quantification. Much of the evidence provided here is thus necessarily anecdotal which, in the case of these cultures, should be regarded as a particular strength. As will be discussed in subsequent chapters, the Western linear, analytical, logocentric approach ultimately fails as a means of understanding Eastern cultures, which tend toward the cyclical, holistic and intuitive. The world of masks by its very nature is concerned with allegory, magic, myth and legend and nowhere more so than in Bali and Japan where mask use is still bound up with religious practice and mediumship. Throughout my research I have encountered stories used to illustrate or explain various aspects of mask use. Although stories are not necessarily 'facts' they can provide a means of understanding things that cannot always be explained by logic or reduced to statistics. In the liminal world that lies between apparent, 'factual' reality and inwardly perceived spiritual experience, the mask itself is concrete, and its unmistakable power remains a constant in a fluid realm of fluctuating perceptions and fleeting sensations.

Preface

This is a brave and admirable book that makes a unique contribution to our understanding of masked performance. It does so by focusing on a vexingly difficult subject to write about: the experience of the performer while performing. More specifically, Margaret Coldiron focuses her attention on the relationship of the performer to the mask in three specific traditions of masked performance: the venerable Noh theatre of Japan and the Topeng and Calonarang traditions of Bali. While the focus is kept tight and the discussion admirably pinned to specifics, there are very large questions involved here: the mutability of identity, the stability of consciousness, the power of myth and image, the relationship of the dancer to the dance. Paradoxically, it is precisely by keeping the focus trained on the relationship between performers and their masks in these very specific traditions that useful vantage points for the contemplation of these metaphysical black holes begin to emerge.

Ethnographic and historical accounts of performance have understandably focused on the conventions that define traditions of drama, theatre, and ritual and on the social, theological, and philosophical constructs that support and are in turn shaped by embodiments of these conventions. It is, ultimately, the audience's experience of performance and the relationship of that experience to social structures which is at issue in these accounts. Coldiron is clearly interested in such matters as well, and the contexts that give specific cultural meaning to the traditions she has studied are admirably presented here, with a minimum of jargon. By shifting the focus onto the experience of the performer, however, a different perspective is achieved; and that, it turns out, is our considerable gain.

As she herself points out, at first glance the traditions chosen seem an odd assortment. All use masks, but Noh and Topeng masks cover either slightly less than the full face or – for the storytelling and clown masks of Topeng – the upper part of the face only. Calonarang uses far larger masks, often covering the entire head and, by extension, the whole body. Noh is now a 'purely secular' form with a relatively fixed dramatic repertoire and set of *kata*, or patterns of enactment, that, over the past 600 plus years, have hardened into a repertoire known for its conservative approach to form and content. The origins of Topeng and of Calonarang, while venerable enough, are far more difficult to pin down; neither depends on definitive scripts and both, depending on time, place, and circumstance, can take on ritual significance or be performed for relatively secular occasions. Thus, the constraints and conventions of these Balinese traditions are far more dynamic and in flux than those of Noh; humor and improvisation mix freely with tales based on semi-historical chronicles and the fulfillment of ritual obligations. Noh is noted for its gravity and slowness, Topeng for its quicksilver speed, its energy and (in the hands of some of its most valued practitioners) its humor. Topeng and Noh are both traditions which prize training and artistry, while Calonarang draws much of its appeal and its power from the use or (sometimes, depending on the circumstances) the pretended use of trance possession – a mode of performance posited as being beyond artistic control.

These very differences, though, provide Coldiron with the ability to take in a range of approaches to the mask while remaining focused on the specifics of performance within two very particular cultures with strong but indirect historical and religious affinities, both Bali and Japan having absorbed strong Chinese and Indic influences and both having powerful indigenous traditions of ancestor worship. There is enough that is shared to make for a valid basis of comparison and to allow concrete hypotheses to emerge from cross-cultural fertilization; there is enough that is different to put the brakes on glib generalizations. Moving back and forth between cultures, she is able to raise generic issues about the use of masks while maintaining a high degree of specificity. By restricting the range of focus to these two cultural centers, she avoids the sort of 'daisy picking' of instances to prove a point that more broad-based studies are prone to encourage.

Balinese and Japanese performing traditions have both given rise to a considerable body of critical literature; yet, to my knowledge, no one before has ever seriously taken up their practices in tandem. In doing this, Coldiron makes admirable and judicious use of previous texts, especially where they shed light on the performers' practices and experiences 'under the mask'. One of the considerable pleasures of this book is to see how previous work has been taken up and considered in fresh contexts. She also incorporates many interviews from her own field research, admirably using her own multiple perspectives as a director, teacher, performer, and scholar to focus the issues addressed. Both in quoting those artists with whom she has had direct contact and in citing the testimony of others, she shows an admirable honesty in presenting seemingly contradictory accounts into the record, and the rare ability to then weave these disparate accounts into a coherent narrative of paradoxes and ambiguities appropriate to a study of masking; and she does this while eschewing obfuscation and unnecessary mysticism. Einstein is said to have remarked once that 'Things should be made as simple as possible, and no simpler!' Not to push the comparison too far, but Coldiron would seem to agree.

There are some surprising benefits that arise from looking at Balinese and Japanese traditions together. Balinese practice has only recently been historicized, and that history is still emerging. While Balinese masked dances are recorded in the 10th century and there is reason to believe that current practices in Topeng date back to the 18th Century, there was never a Balinese Zeami to set down for all time the logic that went into its genesis. It is fascinating, then, to note how often the words of Balinese practitioners echo Zeami's extraordinary 14th Century writings and/or later commentaries within the tradition of Noh. Thus, Topeng performer and scholar I Wayan Dibia talks of visualizing himself as a masked character while in the act of performing in a way which strongly parallels Zeami's principle of *riken-no-ken* – the double consciousness of the performer as both puppet and puppeteer. Thus, Topeng performer I Made Djimat tells how he creates an intimate 'marriage' between himself and his masks in ways that provide a practical approach to the Japanese observation that 'the mask is not put on the face, but the face should be thought of as being pulled into and clinging to the mask'. Time and again in reading the manuscript, I was reminded of ways in which Zeami's remarkable articulation of the issues involved in Noh translates into the practices of Balinese performers. Examples include the use of extremely economical movements of the head and hands to indicate extreme states of energy and attention, the use of preparatory rituals which, in effect, free the actor from 'the limitations of identity and selfhood', the technique of using an alteration of breath to lag slightly behind the beat in order to indicate old age, and the need to find the grace of the ideal king within oneself in order to transcend the role of imitator.

Conversely, an imperfect window onto the variability of practice in the earlier years of Noh is given by the accounts of Balinese Topeng performers moving back and forth between the varying demands of ritual and secular circumstances. Of particular value is the contemplation of the trance possessions at the heart of the Calonarang tradition. This is the most divergent of the traditions studied, and it would have been far safer to exclude it altogether. Its inclusion, though, encourages not only a rethinking of the continuum of neuro-psychological states that may be involved in Balinese masked dances, but of the relationship of Noh to Kagura and other ritual forms and the ways in which this heritage still operates as a part of the 'meaning' of Noh – for performers and audience members alike.

Matching this rich testimonial base against the growing literature on alternate states of consciousness, Coldiron comes to the perhaps inevitable conclusion that the successful masked performer of Noh or Topeng, though not ordinarily 'possessed', experiences a form of 'dissociation' that involves the surrendering and reclaiming of self in a way that alienates the performer from his own body as experienced in everyday life, and that it does this while freeing that performer to embody the 'character' nascent in the mask. The resulting charismatic effect is labeled 'Peerless Charm' by Zeami, 'Taksu' by the Balinese. As I Nyoman Kakul is quoted as saying, this state, for the performer, is marked by a 'total receptivity'; it is also marked by a hyper-awareness of oneself as performer/character – a consciousness that stands apart from but does not hinder the 'flow' of the performance itself.

How close this state is to its seeming opposite – the loss of consciousness and memory experienced in such traditions as Calonarang – is a matter of considerable interest. As the performers themselves frequently testify, the experience of these states is radically different, yet both are marked by 'dissociation' and a loss of 'selfhood'. What is it that triggers the more radical loss of consciousness that characterizes trance possession, and how close is the hyper-aware and focused state of the masked dancer in Noh or Topeng to such a state? While definitive answers to these questions are not possible, the range of evidence and the interpretive tools that Coldiron brings to the analysis considerably advances the contemplation of these topics.

Another issue emerges from reading the manuscript. How close is the state of hyper-awareness and 'dissociated' identity experienced by the masked dancers of Noh or Topeng to that experienced by a 'character actor' in non-masked theatre? A few years ago, using D.W. Winnecott's work as a guide, I attempted to lay down a continuum of performance modalities from the point of view of the performer. Coldiron has suggested some modifications in this schema, based in part on what she persuasively argues are the particularities of masked performance – particularities that include the restriction of vision and breathing, the reshaping of the body in relation to the mask, and the 'symbolic penetration' of the image itself. Her case is convincing. Yet the mark of a good book is often its ability to open up a dialogue against the grain of its intent. If, as Coldiron notes, maskwork in one form or another is now a standard part of the curriculum even in the most realistically oriented graduate programs of acting, what, if anything, is being taught by that work which can be transferred to non-masked performance? Claims generally include a greater sense of the importance of the body in performance, a widening of the range encompassed by the actor's sense of self, and a greater ability to invest in the remodeling of self as character during the concentrated, 'flow' experience of acting. Coldiron's work invites us to ask if what is being 'learned' by 'maskwork' is a more clearly experienced sense of 'dissociation' that, if the standard claims are true, may then be applied to non-masked acting, in whatever style.

Following Viktor Schklovsky and Brecht, the mask is often referred to as a device for the 'estrangement' of theatrical action, used to pique the audience's attention. Coldiron's work allows us to see the benefits of such estrangement for the performer, as well. And not only in masked theatre. I am not only thinking here of the masks of Greek tragedy or of Commedia dell'Arte, but of techniques commonly used in the teaching and practice of acting in the West over the past hundred plus years. I am thinking of Delsarte's gestural index for emotions and of Meyerhold's plastiques, of Meisner's hyper-attention to other performers, of Michael Chekhov's imaginary bodies and redeployed centers of energy, of Olivier's or Weigel's searches for the perfect prop, of Anna Deavere Smith's use of the exact phrasing and tonal variations of those that she interviews, and perhaps even of Stanislavsky's system of objectives and actions for the 'character' transferred onto the body of the performer and, sometimes, especially in rehearsal, yoked to his or her affective memory. All of these techniques, in one way or another, serve to make the strange familiar, the familiar strange. Do all these techniques, then, serve as tools for dissociation, as ways of surrendering and reclaiming the self as other and the other as self in the face of an alien text? It has often struck me as a teacher that such techniques are, in themselves, a bit like the 'magic feather' that Dumbo was given that 'allowed' him to fly. Any of the techniques can 'work' as long as they engage and recommit the energy of the performer to the logic of the performed. Expert performers in masked traditions, of course, know how to do this very well, for the mask demands such a process. Perhaps the clarity of this paradigm in masked performance, even for the novice, is so clear that it has a residual benefit for the nonmasked actor. And perhaps it is because of this paradigmatic clarity that the mask remains emblematic of the theatre, even in cultures that have long ago abandoned and even disparaged its use.

One of the cognitive scientists that Margaret Coldiron cites is the late Eugene d'Aquili. In two recent posthumous publications, d'Aquili and his partner Andrew Newberg examine the evidence from detailed studies involving SPECT scans of meditators using Tibetan techniques and of Franciscan nuns at prayer[1]. The results are quite similar and seem germane. Among other things, there is a marked rise of activity in the areas of the brain dedicated to attention and arousal, and a significant 'disafferentation' of the orientation center of the left side of the brain. In extreme cases there seems to be a shutting down of all inputs to this area, leading to the experience of an 'oceanic oneness' with the world. This is the area of the brain which monitors the body's orientation in space and, one which, many believe, contributes greatly to the consciousness of a distinct and separate 'self' with its own physical and psychological integrity. Though meditation and prayer are quite different as activities from the physically as well as psychologically engaged performances of Topeng or Noh, it is likely that variants of such changes also mark the refashioning of the self by masked (and unmasked?) actors.

While Coldiron's book resolutely focuses on the actor, I would like to shift attention back to the audience for a second. I have often noticed that when most deeply moved by a performance, there is a reluctance to move, to find one's feet and to get up. A marked 'disafferentation' in the spatial orientation areas of the left brain could help to explain this phenomenon. As in the studies of religious experience by d'Aquili and his associates, the distinction between self and other

---

[1] Eugene d'Aquili and Andrew B. Newberg, *The Mystical Mind: Probing the Biology of Religious Experience*. Minneapolis: Fortress Press, 1999; Andrew Newberg, Eugene d'Aquili, and Vince Rause, *Why God Won't Go Away: Brain Science and the Biology of Belief*. New York: Ballantine Books, 2001.

would be weakened, while at the same time attention is heightened and information reaching the emotion-associated limbic system increased: a neurophysiological recipe for 'empathy'. It may not be only the actor who experiences an altered state of consciousness in the theatre.

The masked performer embodies images and myths that bind societies together or give them focal points for marking difference. The actor/dancer gives force to form and, perhaps no less important, offers an exemplary lesson in how the paradoxes and ambiguities that haunt our tenuous hold on identity, selfhood, and empathy can be reconciled. Margaret Coldiron's admirable work clarifies the evidence at hand as to what the actor experiences during this process and opens up new lines of thought as to how the mask may function as metaphor and paradigm for the enduring power of the theatre. Her work, she states 'has been to examine the relationship of the actor to the mask in order to come to an understanding of the nature of this process of transformation and what effect, if any, the use of the mask has upon the actor and the process'. While no one can provide definitive answers, she succeeds admirably in bringing into far sharper focus the ambiguities and paradoxes attending the masked performer's experience.

Professor John Emigh
Brown University

Acknowledgements

My thanks go first to the British Academy who generously funded this project with both a three-year research grant and a very generous travel award for my fieldwork. I am also deeply grateful to my supervisor, Dr. Poh Sim Plowright, whose constant support and encouragement kept the project going.

In addition, I have had the great good fortune to have the help of a number of other individuals who have guided me and contributed to my research. In Bali, I Madé Badra, his wife Ni Madé Kerti and their children gave me a place in their home and support throughout my work and I Wayan Susila was very helpful as a guide and translator. Anak Agung Gede Ngurah and all the members of his household patiently taught me about woodcarving and made me a part of their family. Ida Bagus Alit, my teacher and friend, guided my efforts with patience, good humour and gave generously of his time, talent and vast knowledge. I am particularly grateful to Emily Readett-Bailey who introduced me to all of these people. Rucina Ballinger shared her extensive knowledge of Balinese culture and performance and helped me to make a number of contacts in Bali while her husband, Anak Agung Gede Dewi Putra, was of invaluable assistance as translator and interpreter. Many thanks go to all of my informants including Cristina Wistara, Dr. I Wayan Dibia, Dr. I Made Bandem, I Madé Djimat, I Nyoman Budi Artha, I Wayan Balik, I Nyoman Catra, Ida Bagus Anom, Ikranagara and Pino Cofessa. Special thanks go to Fred Eiseman, who has given me the benefit of his vast expertise and good sense and to my friend Margurite Lambert who joined me in attending temple ceremonies and encouraged me in my research. I am also hugely grateful to Laurie Billington for her wonderful library and resource centre, 'Pondok Pekak' in Ubud.

In Japan, the late Chifumi Shimazaki took me under her wing and provided careful guidance, helpful friendship and excellent scholarship. Rebecca Teele has given very generously her time and provided her unique insights as both performer and mask carver. She introduced me to her teacher, the carver and leading actor Udaka Michishige, and to the Nagoya carving group, who kindly allowed me to photograph their work. I am especially grateful to Iemoto of the Kongô school in Kyoto, Kongô Hisanori, and to Udaka Michishige who both allowed me to photograph their preparation and performance and discussed their work with me. My thanks too, to Kenji Matsuda of the Kanze school who allowed me to observe his private lessons and backstage preparations. Dr. Haruo Nishino, Dr. Naohiko Umewaka, Monica Bethe and Dr. Mae Smethurst have all been very helpful in providing information and sharing their thoughts. I am also grateful to Mr. Kozo Yamaji, who very kindly provided me with his book on *Okina*. Kaori Nakayama has given me tremendous help and support organising my research on Sado Island and also arranging for me to attend conferences of the Japanese Institute for Theatre Research. On Sado I was provided with every possible assistance by Mr. Shibuya of the Ryotsu City Cultural Office and his assistant Shigeki Takahashi as well as Ms. Setsuko Siatô and members of the Hôshô Noh school. I am also grateful to Mrs. Yasuko Ishagura, Arnoud Rauws, and Jon Brokering who took me to plays, allowed me to observe their lessons in Noh, provided translations and made sure I was looked after in every way. Mr. Hideo Shimazu and Ms. Chio Tomomatsu of Meien Kaikan looked after me in Nagoya and were very helpful in gathering information on mask exhibitions and providing me with additional materials. My thanks, too, to Yuka Goto, my translator, guide and friend in Kyoto.

Dr. James Brandon and the East-West Center at University of Hawaii, Manoa were also very helpful in providing me with additional materials and information as was Professor Kathy Foley of the University of California at Santa Cruz.

Others who have provided information and stimulation in this work are Dr. David Bradby, Dr. Angela Hobart and Dr. David Wiles of the University of London and 'Baliologists' Beth Young, Ron Jenkins, Judy Slattum and the late Dr. Fritz de Boer. I am particularly grateful to colleagues and friends who have read and discussed my work with me and given me very useful advice, most especially to Yana Zarifi whose constant curiosity, encouragement and intellectual rigor has kept me inspired.

My folks, Bill and Becky Coldiron, have been very supportive of this work and I am grateful to them for their faith in me. Finally and most importantly I would like to thank my dear friend and companion, John White, whose patience, unstinting support and perfect goodness have seen me through. Without his help and encouragement, none of this would have been possible.

Chapter 1: Orientation

The first question that might be asked about a study such as this one is why it should be embarked upon at all. What relevance can these two utterly foreign and rather esoteric theatre forms have for academics and practitioners of theatre in the West? As a performer, director and teacher of acting, I have been involved with the processes of dramatic transformation and performance for many years. I am familiar with a number of techniques for achieving transformation, yet what actually happens in the process remains a mystery. It is a continuing curiosity about this process, which lies at the heart of my work, that led me to embark upon this research. Perhaps more importantly, however, through my work using masks in actor training, I have noted that a special and particular process seems to be set in motion when an actor wears a mask and that in working with masks an actor may enter a trance-like state. I am not the first to have made this observation, but most others have done little more than marvel at the phenomenon. I set out on this work wanting to know more precisely what happens and why. In Western civilisation notions of the mask as a sacred or spiritually powerful object have long since been rejected as mere superstition, but in many of the theatres of the East the mask has retained its potency as both a theatrical tool and a spiritual object. These cultures do not fear the potentially mediumistic nature of the mask; instead, notions of visitation or mediumship appear to co-exist with the idea of the mask in a theatrical context. It is therefore possible that an investigation of the relationship between actor and mask in these cultures might shed light upon the secular but nonetheless somewhat mystical process of transformation in masked actors in the West. Although many studies exist of masks and mask use in various cultures, nearly all are primarily concerned with the mask as perceived by audience or observers. By directly investigating the responses of those who wear the masks, this exploration seeks to redirect the focus of mask study to the experiences of the masked performer.

'Transformation' and 'Trance'

It is important at the outset that the term 'transformation', which has come to have such a varied constellation of meanings in both Performance Studies and Anthropology, is clearly defined. By transformation I do not refer to the profound social alteration that may occur, for example, through rites of passage and other social or religious rituals in which masks may be used. Rather, I shall examine the more particular transformation of the actor into character within a specifically theatrical/dramatic context. Richard Schechner, a pioneer in the field of Performance Theory, has termed this process 'transportation' because the state is consciously evoked and temporary but, taking the performer's point of view, I believe 'transformation' is a more accurate term. The notion of transformation encompasses both the outward, visible change effected by donning a costume and mask and the inward, less obviously visible alteration in consciousness triggered partly by this outward transformation and partly by physical and psychological preparation activities.

The term 'trance' may be viewed by many as even more problematic and this shall be dealt with in detail in Chapter 7. For now, suffice it to say that the term 'trance' as I shall use it here refers to an altered state of consciousness freely entered into by the performer, rather than an aberrant mental state imposed by external forces.

Why Masks?

> *A Mask is a device for driving the personality out of the body and allowing a spirit to take possession of it.*[1]

Instantly recognisable as a symbol of the traditional theatres of the East, the mask is also a powerful image in the iconography of Western theatre. The familiar faces of comedy and tragedy adorn proscenium curtains, company stationary and countless items of souvenir tat sold by various theatrical organisations. It seems odd, then, that masks are almost never used in what is generally regarded as 'conventional' Western theatre, not even the genres in which, historically, they are known to have played an integral part, such as the classical plays of Greece and Rome. An exception might be made for the *Commedia dell'Arte* of Italy, which featured stock characters in masks (the miser Pantelone, the fool Zanni and the trickster Arlecchino, for example). For a time, because of the popularity of this form, masks became a feature of some other European theatres of the sixteenth and seventeenth centuries, albeit in a rather limited way. The fashion faded, however, and not least because of the prevailing attitude of the Church towards the mask, which was regarded as a dangerous tool of the Devil. As Marco De Marinis has observed:

> Christian and, later, Reformation and Counter Reformation Europe found in the mask . . . one of the incontrovertible proofs of the diabolical nature of theatre and of its irremediable baseness. From Tertullian to medieval theorists such as Thomas of Chobam to those such as Saint Charles Borromeo, the argument persists with an insistent, implacable monotony: The mask is wicked and diabolical and therefore to be condemned, because with the mask 'it seems as if people not only attempt to transform themselves, but, in a certain way, are denying the form which God has given

---

[1] Keith Johnstone, *Impro! Improvisation and the Theatre* (London: Methuen, 1981).

them' (Borromeo) and which has its central focus in the human face which mirrors the soul.[2]

This viewpoint condemns not only the mask object, but also the process of transformation with which it is associated, an implicit condemnation of theatrical representation itself. Masks are still identified with paganism, witchcraft and the dangerous anarchy of Halloween and the Carnival. Even now, in spite of the waning power of the Church and the increasing secularisation of Western society, we still mistrust the mask. This is exemplified first of all in the way in which the word is defined: "a covering worn on the face either as a disguise or for protection . . . a cloak, disguise, pretence . . . a face having a blank, fixed or enigmatic expression . . . something which covers or hides from view".[3] It is believed to have come from the Arabic *maskharah,* for 'buffoon' via *maschera* in Italian and *masque* in French.[4] So, although there is an association with entertainment, the word 'mask' also implies deceit, danger and foolishness. Verb forms, for example the activity of 'masking', are similarly concerned with concealment, inhibition and protection. It is a commonplace that the mask not only conceals, but also reveals. However, it might also be asserted that the mask conceals *in order* to reveal.

These ideas of disguise, concealment and revelation were taken up in the early twentieth century when masked drama enjoyed a brief revival in Europe and America. Two of the most prominent exponents, Bertolt Brecht in Germany and

---

[2] Marco De Marinis, 'The Mask and Corporeal Expression in 20th-Century Theatre' translated by Betsy K Emerick in *Incorporated Knowledge,* Mime Journal 1995, Thomas Leabhart, ed. (Claremont, CA: Pomona College Theatre Department, 1995) p. 14. Borromeo quoted from Ferdinando Taviani, *La commedia dell'Arte e la società baroca. La fascinazione del teatro* (Rome: Bulzoni, 1969) p. 29. In this regard see also David A. Napier, *Masks, Transformation and Paradox* (London: University of California Press, 1986). Napier argues persuasively that monotheistic Christianity cannot cope with the ambiguity of masks whereas polytheism, with its 'complex personae' whose appearance is mutable, is a world view which is more naturally inclined to notions of transformation (pp. 4–15).

[3] *Oxford English Dictionary*, 2nd ed. J. A. Simpson and E. S. C. Weiner, editors, Vol. IX (Oxford: Clarendon Press, 1989), p. 425.

[4] See John Ayoto, *Dictionary of Word Origins (*New York: Arcade Publishing, 1990), p. 340.

Eugene O'Neill in the United States, were influenced by Eastern theatre, especially by Japanese Noh, and experimented with masks in a number of different applications—Expressionist (or pseudo-Expressionist), didactic and neo-classical plays. Brecht's productions of *The Caucasian Chalk Circle* and *Die Massnahme* (*The Measures Taken*), for example, made particular use of masks and *Der Jasager* (*He Who Says Yes*) is virtually a translation of the Noh play *Taniko*.[5] O'Neill, whose use of masks in works like *The Great God Brown* marked a shift in American theatre away from established models, felt strongly that the use of masks represented the future of Western theatre:

> For I hold more and more surely to the conviction that the use of masks will be discovered eventually to be the freest solution of the modern dramatic problem as to how—with the greatest possible dramatic clarity and economy of means—he can express the profound hidden conflicts of the human mind which the probings of psychology continue to disclose to us. . . . [T]he mask *is* dramatic in itself, *has always* been dramatic in itself, *is* a proven weapon of attack. At its best, it is more subtly, imaginatively, suggestively dramatic than any actor's face can ever be. Let anyone who doubts this study the Japanese Noh masks.[6]

However, the use of masks for 'mainstream' theatre never really caught on and even O'Neill eventually abandoned masked plays. Rejected as too esoteric, the Mask fell victim to the shibboleth of theatrical 'realism'.

Since those experiments of the nineteen twenties and thirties, some mask-based theatre companies have appeared on the theatrical scene but they remain on the periphery, regarded as eccentric and of minority interest. Mainstream directors have occasionally made use of masks, perhaps most notably Sir Peter

---

[5] John Willett, *The Theatre of Bertolt Brecht*, rev. ed. (London: Methuen, 1977), p. 37.

[6] 'Memoranda on Masks' (*American Spectator* November, 1932 p. 3) in *Playwrights on Playwriting* Toby Cole, ed. (NY: Hill & Wang, 1960), pp. 65–66.

Hall in his productions of Greek classics, but this has been met with a certain amount of hostility from actors and bewilderment from audiences.[7] Yet, in spite of centuries of antagonism, the mask persists in the West as an image that at once symbolises 'Theatre' or 'Drama', even for those who have never seen a play. Why should this be? I suggest that this is not simply a matter of habit or 'trademark' but that the object represents a function. The mask remains an important symbol because the notion of masking is the very essence of theatrical play. The mask is an object that effects transformation and therefore, even in a culture which for the most part eschews the use of masks on the stage, it remains symbolic of the mysterious process which lies at the heart of making theatre.

My work has been to examine the relationship of the actor to the mask in order to come to an understanding of the nature of this process of transformation and what effect, if any, the use of the mask itself has upon the actor and that process.

Why THESE Masks?

There are traditions of masking in various cultures, but few are suited to this kind of examination. Many mask performance traditions are associated primarily with religious ritual and are not, strictly speaking, theatrical while others are ancient court entertainments, distinct from religious ritual, that have fallen out of use or have only recently been revived as historical documents or for the benefit of tourists. Both Japanese Noh and Balinese dance-drama, however, are living theatrical forms that have their roots in religious ritual but function equally as entertainment. Although they are very different, this dual role links them as theatres that manage to bridge the sacred and the secular.

---

[7] According to Peter Hall's casting director, Gillian Diamond, 93 actresses turned down the title role in Hall's 1993 production of *Lysistrata* primarily because the role required wearing a mask (personal communication).

Noh is a theatre of restraint. The plays are fixed texts, highly poetic and often based on well-known ancient epics, most particularly Murasaki's courtly medieval novel *The Tale of Genji (Genji Monogatari)* and *The Tale of the Heike*, legends of the rivalry between the samurai families of Minamoto and Taira. The central characters of Noh plays are usually unquiet souls—defeated warriors, jealous women, pining lovers, even the spirits of trees and flowers—who tell their stories and may, through an encounter with a sympathetic observer, come to terms with their fate. The 'salvation' which the protagonists may achieve is consistent with the Zen Buddhist philosophy that underpins much of Noh drama. Although today it is frequently presented in what appears to be a secular context, that is, in purpose-built, apparently commercial theatres, Noh drama is essentially spiritual. This is especially evident in *Takigi* (torchlight) Noh, in which plays are presented within the temple precincts in conjunction with a religious ceremony.

Balinese masked dramas, on the other hand, do not have set texts and are largely improvised on the basis of historical chronicles. The plays are lively enactments of mythological stories about gods and deified ancestors, usually performed in conjunction with temple ceremonies and are considered to be entertainment for both gods and human beings. Even when excerpts from these plays are performed in a purely secular context for tourists in Bali or on foreign tours, the same elaborate rituals are used to prepare, sanctify and purify both the performers and their tools, including, of course, the masks.

Because of the inextricable link between sacred and secular in both Noh and Balinese drama, an examination of the function of the mask and its effect upon the actor in these two particular genres makes it possible to come to some sort of understanding of the process of transformation as both a spiritual and a practical achievement. In addition, it is hoped that this study will help to illuminate certain aspects of the relationship between religious ritual, spirituality and theatre, most particularly because the masks in each genre can function as both sacred objects and as practical theatrical tools.

Noh and Balinese masks differ both in style and function. Balinese masks present idealised archetypes of heroes, kings and ministers, apotropaic gods and demons and physically deformed comic types. Even the most 'realistic' masks have exaggerated features and use colours to denote rank and character. Since Balinese masked drama has no scripts as such, the masks generally represent types rather than specific characters.[8] Noh masks, by comparison, appear to be more refined and, although stylised, may seem more recognisably 'human' than Balinese masks. Whereas there may be no more than fifty types among Balinese masks, there are over four hundred different Noh masks. These are sometimes so specific that Noh masks have been created for particular characters in individual plays. When no specific mask has been indicated, the interpretation of a given text may be substantially altered by the choice of one particular mask over another. For all of these substantial differences, however, the iconography of some masks in the two genres is remarkably similar and evidence indicates that those masks may have developed from common sources.

Another consideration which is significant for Western scholars is that both Noh and Balinese dance-drama, virtually unknown outside their own countries until the early twentieth century, have had a profound influence upon modern theatre practitioners and theoreticians in the West seeking new approaches to the problems of the acting process. One of the results of this influence has been that masks have become important tools in the training of actors in Europe and America. Moreover, the masks created for this work were based, at least partly, upon Eastern models. Given this, an examination of the way in which practitioners of these Oriental masked theatre forms interact with the transformational object—that is, the mask—may cast light on the transformation process as experienced by contemporary performers in the West who use masks. Finally, the interchange of ideas, methods and styles between Eastern and

---

[8] There are, however, some notable exceptions. Among the various genres of Balinese masked drama there are a number of masks that represent quite specific characters and make very particular demands. Some of these will be discussed in detail later.

Western theatre artists is an increasingly important aspect of contemporary theatre and one which threatens to blur the boundaries that define and differentiate cultures. An exploration which can reveal attitudes about the use of masks and their effect from the point of view of Noh and Balinese artists themselves may allow a clearer perspective from which to confront the issues raised by 'interculturalism' in the theatre.

At the heart of this study is an investigation into the element of spirituality that is associated with mask use both East and West. This phenomenon will be explored in both philosophical and psycho-physiological terms in order to gain a greater understanding of how masks work, effectively and affectively as transformational objects.

The Influence of Noh and Balinese Dance-Drama upon Western Theoreticians

These theatrical genres, which seem most alien to Western naturalistic/realistic theatrical sensibilities, have nonetheless held a great fascination for European and American theoreticians and practitioners of theatre since they were first 'discovered' by the West at the turn of the century. Moreover, the element that has attracted some of the greatest interest is also their most distinctively anti-realist feature—the Mask. Everything that the Mask represents seems to be at odds with the notion of 'Truth', the goal of the Stanislavsky-based acting techniques that have been most influential among practitioners and teachers. Those techniques were developed to answer the demands of nineteenth century realist works by playwrights like Ibsen and Chekhov, which called for a detailed verisimilitude on the part of performers. It was a theatre 'just like real life' in which ordinary people wrestled with ordinary human problems, passions and desires. This 'social realism' was revolutionary enough in its time, making the theatre not merely a place of entertainment, but also of education and social enlightenment. There were those, however, who sought a different, perhaps more transcendent theatre.

Gordon Craig and the Übermarionette

Edward Gordon Craig (1872–1966) was the inheritor of an acting tradition that valued a lively, vigorous, tangible human presence on the stage. He was the son of Ellen Terry[9] and had acted with the great actor-manager Henry Irving; he was born and bred in the realist tradition of Occidental theatre, yet he rejected it. He sought a new kind of theatre that would not merely imitate reality but would instead present a magnificent artifice:

> . . . the aim of the Theatre as a whole is to restore its art, and it should commence by banishing from the Theatre this idea of impersonation, this idea of reproducing Nature; for, while impersonation is in the Theatre, the Theatre can never become free.[10]

More radical still, he suggested that the actor should look beyond his humanity and find an imaginative, symbolic and spiritual means of expression:

> The perfect actor would be he whose brain could conceive and could show us the perfect symbols of all which his nature contains . . . he would tell his brain to inquire into the depths, to learn all that lies there, and then to remove itself to another sphere, the sphere of the imagination, and there fashion certain symbols which, without exhibiting the bare passions, would none the less tell us clearly about them.[11]

He suggested that the actor be transformed into an 'Übermarionette' a life-sized puppet, unemotional, 'alienated', and able to act in a simple and spiritual manner, distant from everyday life.

---

[9] Born to a theatrical family in 1847, she died in 1928 and was a leading actress of her day.
[10] Edward Gordon Craig, *On the Art of the Theatre* (London: William Heinemann, Ltd., 1911) p. 75.
[11] *Ibid.*, p. 13.

> The über-marionette will not compete with life—rather it will go beyond it. Its ideal will not be the flesh and blood but rather the body in trance—it will aim to clothe itself with a death-like beauty while exhaling a living spirit.[12]

This 'death-like beauty' of 'the body in trance' is a revolutionary idea for an actor brought up in a theatre that placed highest value on the truthful representation of human experience. Whence had this notion sprung? According to Christopher Innes, it seems likely that the concept of the übermarionette was inspired by seeing a Japanese Noh company that visited London in 1900:

> . . . one reviewer complained, 'The players . . . all have the appearance to the western eye of grotesque mechanical toys. None of their movements resemble ours, their faces seem bizarre masks. . . . ' [*The Times* 24 May, 1900] . . . In fact it was precisely those elements of the No [sic] that the public had found incomprehensible in 1900 that Craig wanted for his Übermarionette; and the qualities he singled out were the apparent absence of violent passion in the No; its clear significance; its distance from everyday life, or its 'unnaturalness'; and its simplicity and spiritual suggestion.[13]

Even more than the idea of actor-as-puppet, Craig was fascinated by the mask; he chose that name as the title of the periodical he created to expound his ideas about a new theatre and suggested that the mask was "the visible expression of the mind. . . the only right medium of portraying the expressions of the soul as shown through the expression of the face".[14] The masked actor could, perhaps, be the ideal solution to the problem of 'impersonation' and realism in the theatre. These

---

[12] *Ibid.*, pp. 84–85.

[13] Christopher Innes, *Directors in Perspective: Edward Gordon Craig* (Carbondale: Southern Illinois University Press, 1982) p. 122.

[14] *Ibid.*, p. 13.

ideas had a profound influence on a number of playwrights, designers and directors, most notably Yeats, who soon began to create masked dramas inspired by Noh.

> A mask will enable me to substitute for the face of some commonplace player, or for that face repainted to suit his own vulgar fancy, the fine invention of a sculptor, and to bring the audience close enough to the play to hear every inflection of the voice. A mask never seems but a dirty face, and no matter how close you go is still a work of art; nor shall we lose by staying the movement of the features, for deep feeling is expressed by a movement of the whole body.[15]

The astonishing theatrical effect of the body made more expressive by the fixed expression of the mask or a mask-like visage made a deep impression on another poet and artist who was to inspire a later generation.

Artaud and the 'animated hieroglyphs'
Antonin Artaud (1896–1948), another actor-turned-visionary, also rejected the realist bias of conventional European theatre and felt that:

> the theater . . . must break with actuality. Its object is not to resolve social or psychological conflicts, to serve as a battlefield for moral passions, but to express objectively certain secret truths, to bring into the light of day by means of active gestures certain aspects of truth that have been buried under forms in their encounters with Becoming.[16]

---

[15] Introduction by William Butler Yeats to *Certain Noble Plays of Japan* by Pound and Fenollosa, quoted in Ezra Pound and Ernest Fenollosa, *The Classic Noh Theatre of Japan* (New York: New Directions, 1959 [1917]), p. 155.

[16] Antonin Artaud, 'Oriental and Occidental Theatre' in *The Theatre and Its Double* translated by Mary Caroline Richards (NY: Grove Press, 1958) p. 70.

He sought a theatre of liminality, beyond the mundane, beyond the merely human and found its perfect embodiment in the Balinese dance drama which he encountered in a performance at the Exposition Coloniale in Paris in 1931:

> The spectacle of the Balinese theater, which draws upon dance, song, pantomime—and a little of the theater as we understand it in the Occident—restores the theater, by means of ceremonies of indubitable age and well-tried efficacity, to its original destiny which it presents as a combination of all these elements fused together in a perspective of hallucination and fear.[17]

This appeared to Artaud to be a theatre liberated from language, which possessed the affective power of spectacular ritual. He was particularly excited by the seemingly unemotional, gestural language of the performers.

> What is curious about these gestures . . . these dances of animated manikins, is this: that through the labyrinth of their gestures, attitudes, and sudden cries, through the gyrations and turns which leave no portion of the stage space unutilized, the sense of a new physical language, based upon signs and no longer upon words, is liberated. These actors with their geometric robes seem to be animated hieroglyphs.[18]

This de-humanisation of the actor, which Artaud finds so attractive (similar to the puppet-like quality that attracted Craig to Noh), seems to place the action on a higher plane in which universal and transcendent matters could be dramatised.

Jacques Copeau's 'Mask Work'

These theoreticians are linked in their association with Jacques Copeau (1878–1949), an actor, director, and playwright who lectured on matters theatrical throughout Europe and the United States. He cited his influences as "Gordon

---

[17] 'On the Balinese Theatre', *ibid.*, p. 53.
[18] *Ibid.*, p. 54.

Craig, Max Reinhardt and Granville Barker . . . Appia, Meyerhold and Stanislavsky".[19] He established the Vieux Colombier Theatre (where Artaud appeared as an actor with Charles Dullin's Atelier company), but his most important and enduring contribution to the theatre may be the many schools he established for training actors and the influence he thus has had upon actor training in both Europe and America.

Gordon Craig and his vision of a new theatre were a profound influence upon Copeau in the development of both his school and company. Through Craig he was introduced to Arthur Waley's *The Nô Plays of Japan* and, although he had never seen a Noh play, he (and his collaborator, Suzanne Bing,) prepared a production of the Noh drama *Kantan* that was performed by his students for an invited audience, which included Harley Granville-Barker and André Gide.[20] Because of this fascination with Noh and his devotion to the classical principles of Greek theatre he began to make use of masks in the training of actors:

> in order to loosen up my people at the School, I masked them. Immediately, I was able to observe a transformation of the young actor. You understand that the face, for us, is tormenting; the mask saves our dignity, our freedom. The mask protects the soul from grimaces. Thence, by a series of very explainable consequences, the wearer of the mask acutely feels his possibilities of corporeal expression.[21]

This 'Mask Work' is regarded as an important tool for helping actors find a fluent physical expressivity and is used in many of the most dogmatically Stanislavsky-based training programmes for professional actors. Begun by Copeau himself, it

---

[19] *Copeau: Texts on Theatre*, edited and translated by John Rudlin and Norman H. Paul (London: Routledge, 1990) p. 13.

[20] *Ibid.*, pp. 47–48, 256–258. See also Tom Leabhart, *Modern and Post-Modern Mime* (London: Macmillan, 1989) p. 31.

[21] Copeau, p. 50.

was continued and developed by his nephew, the teacher and director Michel Saint-Denis, and formed part of the curriculum of schools he established in France, Britain and the United States. In this work the actor is required to transform his 'inner state' and physical characteristics in harmony with the character suggested by the mask. Although it seems utterly contradictory to use such an obviously exterior means to engage what is held to be an 'inner' process, it is used with startling success. The mask, it would seem, functions as a kind of 'transitional object' in the actor's process of transformation, bridging the gap between actor and character, helping the actor to become something 'other'. Saint-Denis explained how this should work:

> A mask is a tangible object. It is a presence which encounters one's own—face to face. By the imposition of such an external object on one's face, one will actually feel possessed by a foreign presence, without, however, being dispossessed of one's own self. When one puts a mask on one's face, one receives a strong impulse from it which one must learn how to obey naturally . . . the mask is the energising force.[22]

It is interesting to note the language he uses in referring to the actor-mask relationship: 'a presence', 'possessed', and 'energising force'. These charged words imply an extra element, something beyond the tangible object of the mask with which the actor must come to terms. This almost mystical attitude toward the mask, ascribing to it certain powers which can act upon the performer, echoes Artaud and indicates that in rediscovering the mask as a theatrical tool, practitioners may also seek a return to the theatre's spiritual roots.[23] Thomas Leabhart has referred to Copeau's use of the mask as "a shamanic tool in theatre

---

[22] Michel Saint-Denis, *Training for the Theatre* (London: Heinemann, 1982), p.171.

[23] Artaud's ideal theatre was one in which 'enormous masks . . . [would] participate directly and symbolically . . . [to] enforce the concrete aspect of every image and every expression'. Artaud, pp. 94 and 97.

training" and contends that "Copeau's mask was a tool for altered consciousness in the actor".[24] It is this element of 'shamanistic' spirituality that is of particular interest, especially given that it should be the mask that is seen as the key to the actor's 'altered consciousness'.

Copeau, having begun with only a handkerchief to cover the actor's face, soon developed a mask with 'neutral' features, which is likely to have been modelled, to some extent, on the Japanese Noh mask known as *Ko-omote*. One of Copeau's early students, Jean Dorcy, describes how it evolved:

> We had to find this instrument, the mask. In the beginning we fumbled about. We first covered our faces with a handkerchief. Then, from cloth, we moved on to cardboard, raffia, etc., in short all pliable materials. Finally, with the help of our sculpture teacher, Albert Marque, we found the desirable material as well as the necessary modifications to the form of this new instrument. . . . A good mask must always be neutral: its expression depends on your movements.[25]

So, through this so-called 'Neutral Mask' a means had been discovered by which actors could be trained to be physically expressive and free from self-consciousness. Copeau's pedagogical descendants, Etienne Decroux and Jacques Lecoq, took his work further into the realm of corporeal expression and improvised mask plays. While Saint-Denis insisted that Mask work was strictly a tool for actor training, some followers of Decroux and Lecoq have gone further and established mask-based theatre companies.

---

[24] Thomas Leabhart, 'The Mask as a Shamanic Tool in the Theatre Training of Jacques Copeau' in *Incorporated Knowledge*, pp. 82 and 111.

[25] Jean Dorcy, from *A la rencontre de la Mime* (Neuilly: Les Cahiers de Danse et de la Culture, 1958) trans. Robert Speller Jr. and Marcel Marceau, *The Mime* (New York: Speller, 1961), quoted in Rudlin and Paul, *ibid.* p. 240.

The Rise of 'Intercultural Theatre'

In recent years, as international travel and touring have become commonplace, a fascination with so-called 'World Theatre' has developed. This has led some contemporary theatrical performers and mask specialists from the West to seek out the traditional mask theatre cultures (particularly in Japan and Bali where these traditions are still active) in order to extend their skills and deepen their understanding of mask use. Conversely, a number of Eastern mask practitioners have come to the West to teach and to study, documenting for international scholarship that which had, for generations, been passed down through oral tradition. In the course of this interaction, some cross-fertilisation has taken place with, for example, Noh masters and Balinese dancers trying their hand at Shakespeare and Greek tragedy and Western performers using Noh and Balinese techniques in their own work.[26] The 'interculturalism' which has thus developed has begun to create new theatrical performance styles, perhaps even new genres as is evidenced in the work of directors Peter Brook, Ariane Mnouchkine and Eugenio Barba, among others. Thus, the interaction of East and West now moves in both directions. For this reason an investigation of the attitudes of performers towards the mask, the fundamental tool of theatrical transformation, is essential.

The Actor's Consciousness and Noh and Balinese Masks

This brings us to the heart of the matter to be explored in this book. In what way does the mask influence the masked performer? Getting an answer to this question is, unfortunately, exceedingly difficult because the special and particular relationship between actor and character, though the very basis of theatre, is rarely articulated. Performers resist analysis of this most delicate and fundamental process for fear of divesting it of its 'magic', thus interviews with actors can

---

[26] Recent incidences include Noh master Naohiko Umewaka's recent *King Lear* in Singapore, Nyoman Catra's Caliban in a production of *The Tempest* at Emerson College, the Odyssey Theatre Company's 1989 production of *Macbeth* (which was rehearsed in Bali under the tutelage of various Balinese dancers), I Wayan Dibia's production of *Hippolytus,* and some of the performance work of John Emigh, Richard Emmert, Jonah Salz and others.

provide only a partial understanding about what goes on between actor and mask. This must be augmented by observation of the entire performance process from preparation through packing up and also through subjective personal experience of the masked state. Some information can be gleaned from the place of masks in a given culture and the way in which they are treated. In the West this is somewhat problematic; with the relatively recent revival of theatrical mask use in this century, practitioners have only begun developing methodologies for working with masks in the last twenty-five years or so. Each practitioner has his or her own particular philosophy and there is no real consensus among them about exactly how the masks should be designed or handled, nor any overriding aesthetic which unites these theories.[27] Moreover, these practitioners are primarily concerned with the use of the mask as a training tool rather than as an expressive instrument in its own right. On the other hand, both Noh and Balinese theatre possess highly developed techniques for using the mask effectively and each has a complex and precise aesthetic that underpins the work. It is interesting to note that the language of Western mask practitioners regarding the use of the mask is often highly mystical, in spite of the practical, thoroughly secular use to which the masks are put. In contrast, the practitioners of Noh and Balinese masked drama, in spite of the often intensely spiritual nature of their work, tend to discuss working with masks in purely technical, even mundanely practical terms. Could it be that Western practitioners and theorists are fumbling for a deeper significance, a spiritual dimension for the mask which has been lost through centuries of disapproval from Christian theologians? It is difficult to say, but certainly in Noh and Balinese masked drama the links to the spiritual realm are well established

---

[27] See, for example, Bari Rolfe, *Behind The Mask* (San Francisco: Persona Products, 1977); Michel Saint-Denis, *Training for the Theatre* (London: Heinemann, 1982); Keith Johnstone, *Impro! Improvisation and the Theatre* (London: Methuen, 1981); Libby Appel, *Mask Characterization: An Acting Process* (Carbondale: Southern Illinois University Press, 1982); and Sears Atwood Eldredge, *Mask Improvisation for Actor Training and Performance: The Compelling Image* (Evanston, Ill: Northwestern University Press, 1996).

and perhaps it is this secure knowledge of spirituality that allows such a practical, down-to earth attitude towards the use of masks.

Trance and Transformation of the Actor

My research indicates that the masked actor in Balinese dance-drama and Japanese Noh theatre performs in an altered state of consciousness. This might be described as a kind of trance state, although it is perhaps more precisely characterised as a form of dissociation. This occurs as a direct result of certain elements of performance shared by both genres, but most particularly because of the peculiar relationship of the actor to the mask. The masked performer does not 'interpret' a character through the face and body as unmasked actors do. Rather, the masked actor is given the task of bringing to life an exterior object, the mask, which obliterates the actor's own face and determines the physical characterisation. Thus, masked performance requires a particular sort of 'subjective objectivity' in which the actor must not only embody a character, but must do so by subjecting him or herself to the mask, a character whose expression has already been determined. Masked actors must inhabit, rather than interpret, and must bend themselves to the mask's character, rather than revealing themselves through their rendition of a role. To don a mask is, in some ways, to lose one's self. This could be regarded as a kind of metaphorical death that is required in order to bring the mask to life. This act of self-abnegation dissociates the actor from him or herself, and this dissociation represents a kind of trance. However, the state which is entered into is neither somnambulistic nor the sort of uncontrolled frenzy which is sometimes associated with the term, rather it is a state in which the actor both is and is not himself. In this state the performer is active and able to operate both subjectively and objectively achieving simultaneously a sense of unity with the mask and an exteriorised perception of his performance in it.

Scope of the Study

Accounts of both observers and participants in these masked dance-drama genres indicate that the mask has a perceptible effect upon the performer who uses it. The purpose of my investigations has been to try to determine why this should be and to explore the influence of the mask and its consequences for the performer. I suggest that the perceived transformational power of the mask and its effect on the actor's consciousness are due, in part, to psychophysiological processes which are engaged by particular elements essential to these masked performance genres. After a review of the literature relevant to this study, I shall provide a broad overview of the place of masks and masked drama in each of these cultures, including an examination of the maskmaking process, systems of performer training and the aesthetic philosophies which have developed in each performance genre at least in part as a result of the focus on the mask. Individual performances and performers, selected to serve as case studies, are then discussed and analysed in detail. Making use of recent research regarding consciousness and the actor and the relationship between ritual, music, dance and altered states of consciousness, I will explore the psychophysiological processes which come into play in masked drama. This will demonstrate the ways in which outward, observable physical aspects of the performer's work engage inner, organic processes of mind and brain in the act of theatrical transformation in these masked dance-drama genres. My focus is on the particular experience of the masked performer which, because of the mask, is subtly different from that of the performer who does not wear a mask.

Chapter 2: The Mask: Art Object, Pedagogical Tool or Transformational Mechanism?

Questions about the nature of consciousness, the relationship between ritual and theatre, the precise mechanism of the acting process and cross-cultural similarities in theatre practice and aesthetic have become matter for much current academic debate. Inspired and supported by the work of anthropologist Victor Turner and psychologist D.W. Winnicott, new approaches in the study of drama (Schechner's Performance Theory and Barba's Theatre Anthropology, for example) have emerged in the course of the last ten or twenty years in an attempt to create a critical and theoretical framework for these inquiries. Yet, in spite of the evident interest in these subjects, none has directly addressed the subjective experience of the masked actor or linked these two theatrical traditions.

Influences on the Current Study

Separately, both Noh and Balinese dance-drama have interested a wide range of scholars. General anthropological works by Mead and Bateson, Geertz, Lansing, Picard, Vickers and others, as well as less academic works by Eiseman, McPhee, Covarrubias, Coast and Daniel, provide perspectives on the place of masked drama within Balinese culture. Studies by Belo, Thong and Suriyani and Jensen explore the phenomenon of trance and its place and function in Balinese society. A few significant works, such as de Zoete and Spies' *Dance and Drama in Bali*,

Bandem and de Boer's *Kaja and Kelod: Balinese Dance in Transition* and Christian Racki's *The Sacred Dances of Bali*, have examined the various dance-drama forms in Bali, their historical development and contemporary practice. In addition, unpublished dissertations by scholars Deborah Dunn and Elizabeth Young have provided detailed analysis of Balinese *Topeng* (masked) dance drama. None of these works, however, focused on the use of the mask.

In recent years there has been a great deal of scholarship available in English on Noh theatre. Benito Ortolani's excellent survey, *Japanese Theatre: From Shamanistic Ritual to Contemporary Pluralism,* usefully links contemporary Noh and its shamanistic roots, while works by Bethe, Brazell, Komparu, Sekine, Brandon, Nearman and Rimer, clarify the complexities of the Noh aesthetic and illuminate important aspects of Noh practice including training methods, choreography, dramaturgy and costume. Most significantly, however, a 1984 edition of *Mime Journal* (titled *Nô/Kyôgen Masks and Performance*), edited by Noh performer Rebecca Teele, provides some interesting insights into the actor's experience of Noh masks. Because the world of Noh is intensely secretive and inward-looking, it is exceptionally difficult for outsiders (even other Japanese) to penetrate. However, through interviews with several prominent Noh actors and mask makers, Teele and her colleagues are able to cast light on a great deal of Noh performance practice and its philosophical and religious underpinnings. Contributions from Western scholars and performers of Noh, including Monica Bethe, Mark Nearman, Richard Emmert and Jonah Saltz, attempt with some success to interpret the rather arcane and culturally remote aspects of Noh in a manner sensitive to Occidental perspectives and understanding. Although this is in some ways helpful, it can also be rather misleading for those unfamiliar with Noh in its own cultural context. The Zen ideal of profound simplicity, which lies at the heart of Noh drama, resists Western analytical inquiry and to presume the existence of a high degree of psychological introspection on the part of Noh performers is not only a grave error but also rather misses the point.

The work most relevant to the present study is Professor John Emigh's recent book on *Masked Performance*, which examines the use of masks in both sacred and secular contexts relating this to "the play of self and other in ritual and theatre". However, Emigh's primary concern is the inner process of the actor–whether masked or unmasked–rather than the special qualities of the mask itself and the way in which it affects the actor's process. The book provides detailed discussion of some important Balinese masked dances, but does not venture into the world of Noh drama, choosing instead to concentrate upon practice in India, Southeast Asia and Oceania. Still, Emigh's insights into the nature of masked performance, gained in part from his own experience as a performer, are invaluable for a study of this kind.

Apart from Emigh and Teele, a wide range of material has influenced the current study. Some of this material is directly concerned with masks and mask use; some has to do with current theory regarding the study of ritual and performance, the consciousness of the actor and the transformation process. Drawing all of this together is a varied array of anthropological, psychological and neurophysiological research concerning the phenomenon of ritual trance.

On Masks

The literature in the area of masks and masked performance falls roughly into two categories: 1) that which looks at the mask objectively, having in mind the qualities of the mask as an art object and the effect of the mask upon the viewer or audience, or 2) pedagogical works, largely geared towards actor training, which focus on using masks for acting technique, personal development or therapy.

Mask as Object

The first category is comprised primarily of art and popular anthropology books that deal with the mask as object rather than theatrical tool. Among these are a number of very beautiful books about Noh masks, many of which hardly acknowledge that the masks pictured have had any purpose except as art objects. However, Solrun Hoass Pulvers' unpublished 1978 thesis on *The Noh Mask and the Mask Making Tradition* is probably the most thorough treatment of this subject in English. She discusses mask use and the maskmaking process in practical terms with detailed descriptions of the various mask types taking note of the spiritual significance ascribed to certain masks. In addition, Judy Slattum's *Masks of Bali*, the first specific treatment of Balinese masks, illustrates most of the major mask types, places them within their religious and theatrical context and gives a fairly detailed description of maskmaking methods. Both studies are useful in establishing the fundamental connection between maskmaking and masked performance. In both genres the artist, whether carver or actor, must subject himself to the requirements and the special discipline of the mask. In both cases the artist, Pygmalion-like, brings an inanimate piece of wood to life and it is no coincidence that some of the most gifted masked performers in both genres are also mask carvers.

A British Museum publication edited by John Mack, *Masks: The Art of Expression*, Andreas Lommel's *Masks: Their Meaning and Function*, and *Masks: Faces of Culture*, by John Nunley and Cara McCarty, are all sumptuously illustrated books of the 'coffee-table' variety and, though beautiful, are essentially descriptive rather than analytical. Surprisingly, Mack and his colleagues deal only briefly with Noh masks and not at all with any of the Southeast Asian mask traditions. Lommel, on the other hand, though still very general, makes some most interesting connections between the mask traditions of Southeast Asia, specifically Indonesia, and Noh masks:

> Japanese masks seem to have been influenced by Indonesia, above all by Java—at least it appears to be so when a purely visual comparison of masks is made. Historically this cannot be proved; the Japanese philosopher Kitayama tried to do so, but failed to publish his findings before his death. When the influence of Indonesia is taken into consideration and examined in detail,

Japanese theatre traditions do, in fact, seem to spring more from Indonesian and South East Asian sources than from China.[1]

Lommel cites Java as the chief influence upon Japanese masked theatre and, significantly, Java is also the source the Balinese claim for their own mask tradition. Emigh also notes similarities between the mask traditions of Indonesia (specifically Bali) and Japan and traces both to sources in Eastern India. As Lommel indicates, these connections are difficult to prove in historical and archaeological terms, but striking similarities between Japanese and Balinese masks are apparent, both in the iconography of the masks themselves and the way in which they are used.

Works by Susan Harris, Walter Sorell, David Wiles and others are general studies about the use of masks primarily from a Western perspective and the approach tends to be literary rather than practical. Wiles does address the problems of the actor to a certain extent and draws some interesting comparisons between Greek and Noh masks. David Napier's *Masks, Transformation and Paradox* is another work which considers Eastern and Western mask traditions together and in relation to one another, particularly in connection with the apotropaic image of *Kirtimukha* which is a feature of much Hindu architecture in both India and Bali. He relates this image on the one hand to the Greek Gorgon and, on the other, to the Balinese Barong and Rangda masks (among others). Napier notes "the anthropological problem of accounting for the supposed special states of mask wearers, and in the predominance in the anthropological literature of statements about such states in conjunction with the act of wearing masks"[2] but does not attempt to tackle the phenomenon in relation to actual performers and their practical experience. However, his recognition of the ambivalent and

---

[1] Andreas Lommel, *Masks: Their Meaning and Function,* translated by Nadia Fowler (London: Ferndale Editions, 1981), p. 180.

[2] David A. Napier, *Masks, Transformation and Paradox* (London: University of California Press, 1986), p. 16.

paradoxical nature of masks through which they simultaneously reveal and conceal, protect and endanger, linking the visible world with another magical and unseen realm, articulates precisely the circumstances of the masked performer in Balinese and Noh theatre.

Pedagogy: Mask as Tool

The followers of Copeau, Saint-Denis and Lecoq, inspired by the apparent power of the mask to stimulate the actor's imagination and to initiate extraordinary transformations in the wearer, have produced a number of books about using masks and it is these which make up the second category. These are practical texts in which the mask is viewed as a tool, but only as a tool, to be employed towards improving the actor's physical expressivity and stimulating the imagination. Saint-Denis himself, as well as the American practitioners Rolfe, Appel and Eldredge and Briton Keith Johnstone have all produced influential handbooks for teachers of acting who seek to make use of masks in actor training. These works are of interest because, while utterly secular and practical in their intent, they attempt to address the process of the actor and acknowledge the peculiar alchemy wrought by the mask. Saint-Denis notes that "the mask absorbs the actor's personality, on which it feeds. . . . Submission to the lesson of the mask helps an actor of talent to master a broad, inspired and objective way of acting".[3] It is as if the mask were a kind of parasite able to separate the actor from his own personality and which demands 'submission' yet, paradoxically, it is through this submission that the actor gains objectivity. He later instructs: "The student must look at the mask until he feels permeated by its expression"[4] indicating that the actor must seek to be completely overtaken by the mask in what would seem to be an act of trance-possession. The parallels here with Noh and Balinese practice are striking. Yet, although he mentions the 'magic' of the mask, he nowhere implies that the power of the mask is in any way supernatural.

---

[3] *Training for the Theatre,* edited by Suria Saint-Denis (London: Heinemann, 1982). p. 171.
[4] *Ibid.*, p. 174.

Its chief advantage, he says, is that "such work is anti-psychological"[5] by which he means that it resists analysis and personal self-expression on the part of the actor.

Sears Eldredge, in his 1975 doctoral thesis, made a study of the use of masks in actor training programmes, which was undoubtedly the starting point for his book on *Mask Improvisation* outlining his own method for "actor training and performance" based firmly on the Copeau/Saint-Denis model. However, in an introductory chapter he gives a brief overview of five perceived 'functions of masks' in theatre and ritual (as frame, mirror, mediator, catalyst and transformer[6]) acknowledging the mask's sacred dimension. He also addresses the matter of the paradoxical consciousness of the masked actor (possibly entranced yet fully conscious), suggesting that it "should be understood not through a bi-polar 'either/or' construct but as an experience of convergence—a 'both/and' duality of divided consciousness".[7] Although he provides a number of striking anecdotes demonstrating mediumistic behaviour on the part of his masked actors, the phenomenon is not analysed further. Among the practitioners interviewed for his earlier thesis was Bari Rolfe whose handbook, *Behind the Mask*, seeks to discover "what happens *behind* the mask? What effect does it have on the actor?"[8] She observes that the actor feels "the impulse to identify physically" with the mask and, like Copeau, she recognises that "When the face is hidden the . . . body is left free to respond expressively, unself-consciously".[9] She mentions in passing the influence of ancient mask traditions and instances of ritual mask use but this work is essentially a handbook for acting teachers using the 'neutral' or 'universal' mask and follows the Copeau/Saint-Denis philosophy. Another, similar, manual

---

[5] *Ibid.*, p. 175.

[6] Sears Eldredge, *Mask Improvisation for ActorTraining and Performance: the Compelling Image* (Evanston, Ill : Northwestern University Press, 1996) pp. 4–5.

[7] *Ibid.*, p. 8.

[8] Rolfe, p. 2.

[9] *Ibid.*, p. 5.

is Libby Appel's *Mask Characterization: An Acting Process,* which suggests a different, rather more exaggerated design for full-faced 'character' masks to help the student explore and extend his/her 'creative impulse' and "the development of the actor's confidence in trusting personal experience and resources to make decisions".[10] This use of masks for an exploration of personal psychological states and self-expression could not be further removed from the approach of the practitioners of Noh and Balinese dance-drama but it is typical of the Western, Stanislavskian tradition which conveys a secular 'sacredness' upon the subjective experience of the individual.

Keith Johnstone's *Impro,* another handbook for acting teachers, dedicates a chapter to 'Masks and Trance' and contrasts sharply with Rolfe and Appel's approaches. Johnstone, who had received no training in mask use before he began working with masks at the Royal Court Theatre in the late nineteen-fifties, "saw the masks as astounding performers, as offering a new form of theatre". He encouraged his actors to enter what he refers to as the 'Mask State' in which they might be 'possessed'.[11] This notion of the mask as a medium for visitation, a means of evoking mysterious, unseen 'spirits' is controversial, particularly in contemporary Western theatre. Johnstone's philosophy of mask work would seem instead to be more in keeping with the traditions of the East where mask use is still closely allied with religious ritual. Yet he too is an advocate of 'self-expression', although in this instance it appears to be the *mask* which must express itself.

> The manipulated Mask is hardly worth having and is easy to drive out of the theatre. The Mask begins as a sacred object, and then becomes secular and is used in festivals and in the theatre. Finally it is remembered only in the feeble imitations of Masks sold in the

---

[10] Appel, pp. 6–7.

[11] Johnstone, p. 148.

tourist shops. The Mask dies when it is subjected to the will of the performer.[12]

Johnstone cannot come to terms with the idea that masks may be sacred and at the same time theatrical and festive. Moreover, his opposition to 'manipulation' is in stark contrast to the traditions of Noh and Balinese performance. In these traditions it is felt that in order to be expressive masks must be manipulated, but with skill developed through years of focused study. When the manipulation is successful what is expressed is neither the personal emotion nor the psychology of the performer, nor is it a slick and cynical side-show trick; rather, the actor brings the mask to life. Instead of possession, the Noh or Balinese performer achieves a quite different sort of mediumship, which is the result of focused study, practice and the use of acknowledged technique. The mask is subjected to the will of the performer, certainly, but it is the mask that guides the manipulation.

Performance Theory and the Theatre-Ritual Nexus

Already difficult issues relating to the performer's process of transformation have been rendered even more complex in recent years because of a growing interest in the performance practices of 'non-Western' cultures on the part of both practitioners and scholars of theatre. Richard Schechner (inspired by and often working in conjunction with the late Victor Turner, an anthropologist) has, over the last thirty years or so, formulated a series of models for analysis of performance which have come to form the nucleus of what is known as 'Performance Theory'. As a result of trends in anthropology and psychology, which refer to many aspects of human activity not previously so-termed as 'performance', and the development in the nineteen-sixties of 'experimental' theatre and 'performance art', the necessity arose among scholars to establish a system for analysis of all kinds of 'performance'. The system may be applied to

---

[12] *Ibid.*, p. 149.

non-theatrical human activity and experimental performance as well as the more conventionally recognised 'performing arts' of drama, dance and music. However, the continuing problem of Performance Theory and its elaboration, the nascent academic discipline of Performance Studies, has been to define precisely what is meant by this by now very complex term: 'performance'. Schechner attempts such a definition in his groundbreaking work, which has become the handbook of the movement, *Performance Theory*. In a footnote to an essay titled 'Approaches' he points out:

> Performance is an extremely difficult concept to define. From one point of view—clearly stated by Erving Goffman in *The Presentation of Self in Everyday Life* (1959)—performing is a mode of behavior that may characterize *any* activity. Thus performance is a 'quality' that can occur in any situation rather than a fenced-off genre. . . . However, in this writing I mean something much more limited: a performance is an activity done by an individual or group in the presence of and for another individual or group. ... I thought it best to center my definition of performance on certain acknowledged qualities of live theater, the most stable being the audience-performer interaction. Even where audiences do not exist as such—some happenings, rituals, and play—the function of the audience persists: part of the performing group watches—is meant to watch—other parts of the performing group; or, as in some rituals, the implied audience is God or some transcendent Other(s).[13]

This definition, which would seem to cover most contingencies, appears to be workable as a starting place for analysis of performance, yet it continues to be a matter for discussion and debate among performance theorists, including

---

[13] Schechner, 1988, p. 30.

Professor Schechner. The performance genres that are the focus of the present analysis are avowedly 'theatrical' and clearly fulfil the definition's requirement of 'audience-performer interaction'. However, even within the realm of consciously 'theatrical' performance there are still other elements that need to be taken into consideration.

The Efficacy-Entertainment Braid

With the definition of performance itself so problematic, the way in which various types and modes of performance are classified becomes similarly complex. Schechner's experience and research interests are wide-ranging—from conventional theatrical performance to religious and social rituals of various tribal peoples (which, significantly, may not be regarded as 'performance' at all by the societies which practice them.) By the above definition, both tribal ritual practices and Broadway shows may be seen as 'performance', though clearly they are not the same. Nonetheless, they may be seen to share certain characteristics. To elucidate this problem of classification, Schechner has posited a model called 'The Efficacy-Entertainment Braid', which he explains thus:

> The basic polarity is between efficacy and entertainment, not between ritual and theater. Whether one calls a specific performance 'ritual' or 'theater' depends mostly on context and function. A performance is called theater or ritual because of where it is performed, by whom, and under what circumstances.
>
> | EFFICACY | ENTERTAINMENT |
> |---|---|
> | *Ritual* | *Theater* |
> | results | fun |
> | link to an absent Other | only for those here |
> | symbolic time | emphasis now |
> | performer possessed, in trance | performer knows what s/he's doing |
> | audience participates | audience watches |
> | audience believes | audience appreciates |
> | criticism discouraged | criticism flourishes |
> | collective creativity | individual creativity[14] |

---

[14] 'From Ritual to Theatre and Back' in Schechner, 1988, p. 120.

With regard to the classifications in the table above, Schechner points out that "no performance is pure efficacy or pure entertainment",[15] so different modes of performance will combine elements of each category in varying degrees of intensity. While it is useful to have characteristics of each performance mode spelled out in this way, it is apparent that all varieties of performance will mix elements from each category. How then, is the model to be meaningfully applied? Certainly the 'braid' analogy goes some way towards illustrating the interweavings of the various strands among these characteristics and takes into account the fact that a variety of combinations of these elements is possible. Applied to the genres that are the subject of this study, a graphic rendering of the 'braid' might look something like Diagram 1. Noh drama is for 'fun' rather than 'results'; it is performed both for an absent other and for a present audience; it emphasises symbolic time and the performer knows what s/he is doing. The audience watches and does not participate; there is a certain degree of belief in the staged proceedings, at least on a metaphorical level, but appreciation of the players' expertise is central. Criticism flourishes and the performance demonstrates both collective and individual creativity. Balinese Topeng, on the other hand, seeks both 'fun' and 'results'; it is performed both for an absent other and the present audience; it is linked both to symbolic time and 'now' and, though the performer knows what s/he is doing, s/he might also be in trance. The audience watches and does not participate, believes and appreciates, though criticism of the performance is not encouraged. By and large, individual rather than collective creativity is demonstrated. What does the model tell us? At first glance one might imagine Balinese masked performance to be more associated with the elements of efficacious ritual, since it seems to fulfil most of the criteria in the first column of the table, and that Noh drama would fall more strongly into the 'entertainment' category—but it all depends upon one's perspective. If one looks at the definition that Schechner provides for ritual ("a stereotyped series of

---

[15] *Ibid.*

simple complementary transactions programmed by external social forces"[16]) it would seem to apply more directly to the practices of Noh theatre, which has a strict protocol of fixed behaviours, than to Balinese masked drama, which tends to be more improvisational. In the end, neither the definition nor the 'braid' is wholly relevant for examining these masked dance-drama genres. The interweavings of efficacy and entertainment (in these as in other types of masked dance-drama) are even more complex than the categories given in the model would indicate. Moreover, they may be evaluated very differently when viewed from different perspectives: the perspective of the performer versus that of the observer from within the tradition, for example, or even the perspective of the observer within the culture versus that of the observer from outside the culture. In each of these instances the qualities and characteristics of the genre might be assessed differently.

This is the fundamental problem with the model, which Schechner himself recognises when he points out that "one can look at specific performances from several vantages; changing perspectives changes classification".[17] The way in which a performance practice is evaluated in terms of the characteristics outlined will differ from person to person, culture to culture and era to era. So, while it may be universally applicable, it is also subject to infinite interpretation. The 'Efficacy-Entertainment Braid' appears to demonstrate that, in the realm of performance certainly, there are no absolutes and that classifications will inevitably vary depending upon the perspective taken. Ronald Grimes (whose *Beginnings in Ritual Studies* is to that discipline what *Performance Theory* is to Performance Studies) cites Schechner's 'Braid' as just one among about twenty possible theoretical options for analysis and interpretation of ritual and

---

[16] Quoting psychologist Eric Berne (*Transactional Analysis in Psychotherapy*, New York: Grove Press, 1964, p. 36) in notes to 'Approaches' in Schechner, 1988, p. 33.

[17] *Ibid.*

performance.[18] With such a varied array of potential perspectives from which to view performance practices, a researcher in this field must determine which theory, model or methodology will be the most useful for the task in hand.

Performance and Cultural Context

Rather than taking a general approach, my research has led me to believe that performance genres and the performer's experience need to be considered individually, each in the light of its own particular culture and characteristics and should be observed (as far as possible) from the inside as well as from the outside before theories are applied which seek to define them. The preoccupation of Western scholars with universalist theoretical constructs which are inevitably biased towards a Euro-American, logocentric, objectivist viewpoint has been an increasing source of frustration for those who seek to examine performance practices within their own cultural contexts. Rustom Bharucha, one of Schechner's most articulate critics, suggests "that we (in the West and the East) need to develop a clearer, more precise, and historical awareness of the particularities of specific cultures" and criticises Schechner for "attempting to locate the particulars of 'Indian, Japanese, Southeast Asian, Native American and Euro-American performance', within a single performance theory".[19] While humankind is linked in its common humanity, there are important differences that define our various cultures that need to be taken into account, especially in the realm of performance. Theoretical models exist which, while acknowledging cultural differences, also address those shared aspects of human biology and physiology which transcend culture. For example, biogenetic analysis of human

---

[18] Models are grouped under 7 headings: phenomenology (Eliade, Van Gennep); underlying structures (Geertz, Birdwhistell, Bateson, Austin, Langer, Levi-Strauss etc.); social functions and processes (Durkheim, Douglas, Turner, Goffman and Schechner); psychology (Jung, Freud, Wallace, Huizinga, Neale etc.); ecological/biogenic (Rappaport and d'Aquili); historical/theological (Bouyer, Jungmann); and "imaginative, sympathetic participation" (Ricour, Tillich, etc.). Roland L. Grimes, *Beginnings in Ritual Studies* (Lanham, MD: University Press of America, 1982) p. 32.

[19] Rustom Bharucha, *Theatre and The World* (London & NY: Routledge, 1993), pp. 40–41.

response to myth, ritual and performance, pioneered in the work of d'Aquili and Laughlin (discussed below), has proved very useful for understanding the correlations between the experiences of masked actors in these occasionally similar, but nonetheless distinct, cultures. In this study, the experience of the masked performer will be examined within the specific cultural milieu of each genre, rather than as an illustration of a larger theoretical construct. However, it shall become apparent that culturally specific aspects of performance practice may have neurophysiological implications for masked performance across a range of cultures.

The Actor's Consciousness

Since Diderot in the eighteenth century, there have been all manner of studies on the subject of the actor and the processes by which the apparent transformation into a character is achieved. The requirements of the acting process are paradoxical: on the one hand the actor must portray the emotions and sensations of the character; on the other hand he/she must retain a separate, critical awareness which allows him/her to execute the technical requirements of the role (moves, lines and so forth). Should the actor subjectively 'feel' the emotions of the character or, rather, seek to remain distanced and objective in order to render those sensations skilfully through artifice? Is it possible to do both? What is the state of mind that enables an actor to achieve the 'dual consciousness' which theatrical transformation requires? Daniel Meyer-Dinkgräfe's examination of *Consciousness and the Actor* (1994) explores the numerous theories concerning the actor's involvement or identification with the character he portrays, from Diderot through Stanislavski to Grotowski and other contemporary scholars and practitioners. He observes that actor's consciousness must encompass a 'unity of opposites' and it is the interplay of self and other, central to the actor's work, which demands the capacity to exist consciously as both actor and character simultaneously. Meyer-Dinkgräfe relates this phenomenon to a state of "pure consciousness *(samadhi)*"[20] as defined in Vedic psychology. Schechner (borrowing from and elaborating on the work of psychologist D.W. Winnicott) has referred to the state of mind permitting simultaneity of self and other as 'not-not-me:'

> All effective performances share this 'not-not not' quality: Olivier is not Hamlet, but also he is not not Hamlet: his performance is between a denial of being another (=I am me) and a denial of not being another (=I am Hamlet). Performer training focuses its techniques not on making one person into another but on permitting the performer to act in between identities; in this sense performing is a paradigm of liminality.[21]

This liminal state in which the actor both is and is not himself is a state beyond normal consciousness in which the performer may be seen to be 'inhabited' by the character. Is this altered state of consciousness in any way related to Johnstone's 'Mask State'? This is possible, and it may be that the experience of the *masked* actor is even more complex, more intense than that of the actor who does not use a mask because the masked actor does not merely embody and interpret the character but must animate the inanimate mask. Indeed, since the face (which is the seat of identity) is covered by the mask, it follows that the ego is also, to some degree, obliterated. Thus, the consciousness of the masked actor may require a greater 'dis-association' from self while requiring an even more intensive identification with the mask character, as well as a high degree of technical expertise. As we shall see in the following chapters, the necessity for self-abnegation constitutes an important element of the aesthetic of both of these mask genres.

---

[20] Daniel Meyer-Dinkgräfe, *Consciousness and the Actor*, European University Studies; Series 30, Theatre, Film and Television; Vol. 67 (Frankfurt am Main: Peter Lang, 1996), pp. 123–127.

[21] Schechner, 1985, p. 123.

The Process of Transformation

The relationship between the actor and the mask is fundamentally concerned with the process of transformation and, in the genres examined here, the mask functions as both the symbol and the agent of theatrical transformation. However, as noted in the previous chapter, the term 'transformation' has become somewhat problematic, especially given the development of hybrid schools of study (Theatre Anthropology, Ritual Studies and Performance Studies, for example) which have occasion to focus their analysis upon aspects of theatrical performance but apply to this study certain criteria which may be seen as alien or 'non-theatrical' from the viewpoint of the traditional theatrical performer.

Transformation vs. Transportation

Schechner's definitions of the processes he refers to as 'transformation' and 'transportation' are a case in point. These terms, while perhaps useful for anthropological investigations, are not entirely appropriate for the current analysis because they define the experience of performer from the point of view of the audience. This is evident in the illustrations he provides of performers who are seen to have been 'transformed'. In the first instance these are individuals who have become identified with their roles in the public's perception, often because of repeated performances in the same role.

> "At the Ramlila of Ramnagar, India, one of the best actors is the man who plays the semidivine sage, Narad-muni. When Narad-muni speaks or sings, the audience—sometimes of more than twenty-five thousand—listens with special care; many believe the performer playing Narad-muni has powers linking him to the sage/character he plays. This man is no longer called by his birth name, not even by himself. Over the thirty-five years he has

performed Narad-muni he has increasingly been identified with the legendary figure.[22]

Schechner makes it clear that the performer himself does not claim to *be* the character with whom he has become so associated, or that he is in any way personally altered by his performance ('possessed' by the character). The 'transformation' has to do with the way in which the performer is perceived by those who have observed the performance. Schechner cites film stars John Wayne (in his public persona as 'The Duke') and Bela Lugosi (unhappily associated with his role as Dracula) as further examples of such 'transformations'. Within this category he also places ritual initiates in a Papua New Guinea coming-of-age ceremony through which they are 'transformed' (in the society's perception) from children to adults.[23] This is, of course, a rather different sort of transformation, one which is acknowledged and sanctioned, even required, by society. During the course of such initiation rites an individual might well experience a number of sensations similar to those of the actor who performs a masked character. Indeed, the initiate may even be required to give a masked performance as part of the initiation ritual. However, the 'transformation' to which Schechner refers here is a change in the initiate's status in the community, which may or may not include an alteration of the individual's perception of himself. Such a change is, of course, a transformation of sorts but it has little to do with the fundamental relationship of actor to character in a theatrical performance, a relationship that may develop quite separately from the perceptions and assumptions of the audience. A definition of transformation which reflects the experience of the performer must be taken from a perspective that encompasses the physical and psychological changes that a performer undergoes in taking on a character. These include outwardly manifested changes which come with donning costume and mask as well as inward psychological and neurophysiological changes which are

---

[22] *Ibid.*

[23] *Ibid.*, pp.126–129.

experienced by the performer but which may not be perceived by the audience. By and large, in *theatrical* transformation (as opposed to *social* transformation), both audience and performer are aware of the performer's dual identity as both performer and character, person and persona.

Schechner addresses the experience of the performer in his discussion of a process he calls 'transportation'. This term takes in several elements of the performance process including preparation, performance and 'cooling down'.

> ...during the performance the performers are 'taken somewhere' but at the end, often assisted by others, they are 'cooled down' and reenter ordinary life just about where they went in. The performer goes from the 'ordinary world' to the 'performative world', from one time/space reference to another, from one personality to one or more others. He plays a character, battles demons, goes into trance, travels to the sky or under the sea or earth: he is transformed, enabled to do things 'in performance' he cannot do ordinarily. But when the performance is over, or even as a final phase of the performance, he returns to where he started.[24]

Although this account acknowledges that the performer is 'transformed' (that is, *changed*) in the course of the performance process, the implication remains that it is a process in which the performer is (literally or metaphorically) taken from one place to another ('transported'). Here again, it is the audience's perception of the process that is being described rather than the experience of the performer. Moreover, as noted in the previous chapter, the notion of the performer 'transported' suggests not only a kind of 'enchantment' or 'rapture' but also that the process of transformation is somehow outside the performer's control. The process to which I refer is one that is consciously entered into and cannot be wholly perceived by the audience because it is experienced subjectively

---

[24] *Ibid.*, p. 126.

by the performer. It is a change in *state* rather than place and a good deal more complex than the description above (of 'transportation') would seem to allow. The process and method of change from 'ordinary life' to living as the character is influenced by a number of factors including training, aesthetic philosophy, circumstances of performance and specific techniques or mechanisms for shifting to the liminal state.

Transformational Mechanisms
In the succeeding chapters, it shall be demonstrated that aspects of the outward process of change often function as a 'trigger' for alterations in the performer's consciousness. The transformational process is set in train by a number of elements which, working in concert, help the masked actor to attain the subjective-objective duality which his work requires. In Balinese dance-drama and Japanese Noh this process begins with the performer's training which is essentially kinaesthetic and imitative and can lead to habitual dissociation in performance. It is further aided by the performer's special relationship with the mask, an exterior object that acts as both a link and a division between actor and character. Here I turn to D.W. Winnicott who first posited the notion of the 'transitional object' and is the source of Schechner's 'not-not me' model. Winnicott, a child psychiatrist, coined the term when he observed the way in which the weaning infant adjusted to the loss of the mother's breast, which it was accustomed to possessing 'on demand'. With this loss, the infant was made aware of a world outside itself, seemingly beyond its control. As a coping mechanism Winnicott noted that a child will often adopt a substitute, a 'transitional object' (a blanket or toy, for example) which helps it to bridge the gap between its own perception and external reality. Through the transitional object, inner and outer realities are reconciled. This observation led Winnicott to link this fundamental behaviour with adult human response to certain aspects of culture:

> Transitional objects and transitional phenomena belong to the realm of illusion, which is the basis of initiation of experience.

> This early stage in development is made possible by the mother's special capacity for making adaptation to the needs of her infant thus allowing the infant the illusion that what the infant creates (imagines) really exists. This intermediate area of experience, unchallenged in respect of its belonging to inner or external (shared) reality, constitutes the greater part of the infant's experience and throughout life is retained in the intense experiencing that belongs to the arts, to religion and to imaginative living and to creative scientific work.[25]

The actor's process of transformation into a character, which requires simultaneous acknowledgement and abnegation of self, is achieved through a concentrated effort of imagination. This is aided by rigorous training, performance elements (such as rhythmic music and preparatory rituals) and by the aesthetic and spiritual ethos of the performance genre. In the case of the masked performer, the process is further aided by the mask, which acts as a transitional object defining, delineating and reconciling the real and the illusory worlds that the performer must inhabit.

The process of transformation, then, consists of both outward changes in appearance (donning the costume and mask) and inward changes in consciousness that are, in part, triggered by these outward changes. The mask acts as a 'transformational mechanism' to initiate these changes. Like Schechner's model of 'transportation', this can be a process that the performer enters to re-emerge 'just about where they went in'[26] but it is nonetheless a change (transformation)—a physical, psychological and neurophysiological alteration in the state of the performer.

---

[25] D.W. Winnicott, *Playing and Reality* (London: Tavistock Publications, 1971) p. 14.
[26] Schechner, 1985, p. 126.

A Framework for Examining the Performer's Process

Where, then, is one to find a model for articulating the process of transformation from the point of view of the masked performer? The only reliable source must be from performers themselves but, unfortunately, performers rarely become theoreticians. However, a fourteenth century performer called Zeami (widely regarded as the 'father' of what is now known as Noh theatre) left behind a rich legacy of theoretical writings on the nature and method of Noh performance.[27] These works provide an important insight into the masked performer's process of transformation and, significantly, present a distinctly Eastern point of view. A more detailed analysis of Zeami's writings will be presented in later chapters but it may be useful at this point to highlight some key concepts that relate particularly to the process of transformation. These concepts derive from strands of Buddhist and Hindu philosophies fundamental to both Japanese and Balinese cultures and apply directly to performance practice in both genres discussed here. The relevance of these concepts to contemporary practice is affirmed by evidence from interviews and my own experience of masked performance.

The process of transformation is a learned skill that is honed over time and through experience. It begins with the actor's training and is aided in performance by transformational mechanisms such as the costume and mask and additional elements including rhythmic music and dancing. Equally important are preparatory rituals that are underpinned by an aesthetic and spiritual ethos. To achieve transformation, however, two essentials are required: first, the abnegation of the self and, second, a simultaneous subjectivity and objectivity within the performance. In discussing these two essentials, Zeami invoked the terms *mushin* and *riken no ken,* derived from Buddhist philosophy. The Zen philosopher D. T. Suzuki has provided one of the most comprehensive definitions of *mushin*:

---

[27] Although the treatises rarely refer directly to the mask, they are designed as instructions for the central *masked* actor in Noh, the *shite*. Because his vision is severely restricted by the mask, the treatises provide strategies for effective movement for the masked actor on the stage.

In Japan, perhaps as in other countries too, mere technical knowledge of an art is not enough to make a man really its master; he ought to have delved deeply into the inner spirit of it. This spirit is grasped only when his mind is in complete harmony with the principle of life itself, that is, when he attains to a certain state of mind known as *mushin* (*wu-hsin* in Chinese), 'no-mind'. In Buddhist phraseology, it means going beyond the dualism of all forms of life and death, good and evil, being and non-being. This is where all arts merge into Zen.[28]

The state is analogous to the Vedic principle of 'pure consciousness' (*samadhi*). In striving for *mushin,* the actor seeks to achieve the creative emptiness that allows for transformation since, within this aesthetic, "emptiness is the source of phenomenal change".[29] As the Noh master Umewaka Naohiko put it: "everything emerges from nothing, from silence, from the void".[30] To achieve this 'no-mind' state the actor is required to subjugate, even to deny his own ego and to submit himself wholly to the requirements of the character. In the genres at issue here, this behaviour is learned very early, from the first moments of the performer's training. As shall be demonstrated in the coming chapters, this training is entirely kinaesthetic and mimetic rather than theoretical, and consists, essentially, of unquestioning repetition of the teacher's movements. This denial of the self within the art becomes habitual and is essential to the performer's development. The masked performer is further aided in this process by the mask, which covers the face and thus, both symbolically and actually, erases the separate identity, the 'I-ness', of the performer. Yet while the mask erases one identity, it provides

---

[28] Daisetz T. Suzuki, *Zen and Japanese Culture* (Princeton: Princeton University Press/Bollingen Foundation, 1993 [1959]) p. 94.

[29] Minoru Kiyota, *Kendô: The History and Means to Personal Growth* (New York: Kegan Paul International, 1995) p. 21.

[30] Umewaka, Naohiko. The Inner World of the Noh, *Contemporary Theatre Review, 1992*, Vol. 1, 1, p. 33.

another. Kanze Hisao (considered one of the greatest Noh actors of the 20th century) described how the mask can function as a transformational mechanism:

> A Noh actor is something like a soul, always drifting between this world and the other world. He therefore needs something in which he can believe in order to give him the power of a confidence to give the feeling of the character he is representing. That thing is the Noh mask.[31]

While the mask serves to further alienate the performer from his own identity, at the same time it provides the means whereby he may take on the identity of the character. It becomes the mechanism both for the external transformation, which is visible to the audience, and an internal transformation of the performer's consciousness.

    Having donned the mask, the performer encounters a new phenomenon finding that, while denying 'self', he must still manipulate the mask and costume. This calls into play the second important concept relating to the performer's transformation, which Zeami called *riken no ken*. The term, often translated as 'the Detached Eye', refers to the necessity for the masked performer to imagine his performance from an objective viewpoint while at the same time subjectively personifying the character depicted in the mask. In this he functions in a manner not unlike Craig's ideal of the Übermarionette, as both 'puppet' and 'puppeteer'. Zeami describes the process in this way:

> The appearance of the actor, seen from the spectator in the seating area, produces a different image than the actor can have of himself. What the spectator sees is the outer image of the actor. What an actor himself sees, on the other hand, forms his own internal image of himself. He must make still another effort in order to grasp his

---

[31] Kanze Hisao, *Chosaku Shu* Vol. 2 (Tokyo: Heibonshe, 1981) p. 271, translated by Chiaki Yamase, unpublished MS, 1995, p. 8.

own internalized outer image, a step possible only through assiduous training. Once he obtains this, the actor and the spectator can share the same image. Only then can it actually be said that an actor has truly grasped the nature of his appearance. ... Therefore, an actor must look at himself using his internalized outer image, come to share the same view as the audience, examine his appearance with his spiritual eyes and so maintain a graceful appearance with his entire body.[32]

Yamazaki Masakazu has pointed out that the psychological state required for such activity is not analytical but rather "seems to be a matter of dealing intuitively in an instant with the entire flow of one's movements".[33] This notion of *flow,* a "surrender to the flow of action"[34] or "merging of action and awareness"[35] is cited by Schechner and others as a special heightened state achieved through intense concentration. Like Johnstone's 'Mask State', it is an altered state of consciousness that is the objective of the process of transformation. This performance state is recognised and acknowledged in the aesthetic of both of these performance genres—in Noh as *hana*[36] and in Balinese dance-drama as *Taksu.*[37] Its effect may be perceived by the audience, but it is experienced, physically and spiritually, by the performer.

---

[32] *On the Art of Nô Drama: The Major Treatises of Zeami,* translated by J. Thomas Rimer and Yamazaki Masakazu (Princeton: Princeton University Press, 1984), p. 81.

[33] 'The Aesthetics of Transformation: Zeami's Dramatic Theories', translated by Susan Matisoff, *Journal of Japanese Studies,* Summer, 1981, p. 246.

[34] Schechner 1985, p. 124.

[35] Mihalyi Csikszentmihalyi, *Beyond Boredom and Anxiety* (San Francisco: Jossey-Bass, 1975) p. 38.

[36] The term literally means 'flower', as in the flowering of the performer's art. See Rimer and Yamazaki, especially pp. 121–125. The whole of Zeami's treatise titled *Kyûi* deals with the nine levels of accomplishment in Noh performance of which the highest is called *myo* or 'the flower of peerless charm'.

[37] A complex term which takes in aspects of trance, mediumship and performance charisma. Both *hana* and *Taksu* will be discussed in detail in succeeding chapters.

The process of transformation seen from the performer's point of view, then, consists of a denial of ego along with the cultivation of a simultaneous subjective and objective awareness of the performance allowing for a 'self-less', 'intuitive' enactment of the character. This model, derived from the theoretical treatises of Zeami and supported by the observations of Schechner and others, shall serve as a framework for examining the activities of these masked performance genres.

Ritual Trance

If the performance state of the masked actor represents an actual neurophysiological phenomenon, it follows that science might be able to provide a method and language by which the process and development of this altered state of consciousness could be measured and described. In the nineteen-seventies, work appeared by Eugene d'Aquili, Charles Laughlin, John McManus and Barbara Lex exploring the neurophysiology of ritual trance. This work, which has come to be termed 'biogenetic structural analysis', has evolved methods by which altered states of consciousness can be examined both neurophysiologically and as cultural phenomena. Laughlin, McManus and d'Aquili have been particularly interested in the functions and effects of ritual and theatre upon observers and participants.

> Much ritual drama involves the expression of a society's cosmology via enactment of elements and relations making up the cosmology (Eliade 1963:19). Participation in the drama may induce alternate phases of consciousness (dreaming, as well as so-called ecstatic states, trances, visions, etc.) in which experiences arise that are interpreted so that they verify the cosmology. We have already examined several principles and mechanisms by which ritual drama may achieve remarkable influence over experience. These steps include control of cognitive complexity, orientation response, and autonomic tuning. Another means to

attain this control is by incorporating symbols as penetrating agents: symbols [...] that can penetrate to the deepest levels of neurocognitive organization and produce changes in their entrainment.[38]

Put simply, the enactment of ritual drama and the ritual activities associated with it (including those I have termed 'transformational mechanisms'), combined with the religio-aesthetic ethos of a given performance genre, affect performers not only on the ideational level but also on a deeper, neurobiological level. Biogenetic structural analysis has been particularly influential in the realm of Performance and Ritual Studies as well as in Theatre Anthropology. This is because all three disciplines have an interest in connections between shamanism, ritual and theatre, and seek to understand the function of the actor as shaman and as entertainer. My research has also benefited from the work of Felicitas Goodman and Susannah Bloch, whose clinical experiments in inducing trance and emotional states in neutral performer-subjects through purely physical stimuli point strongly towards a neurophysiological explanation for the special performance state of the actor. Both Noh and Balinese masked dance-drama are highly ritualised, accompanied by music and rhythmic drumming, and require a period of focused meditation on the part of the performer before entering the stage. Since each of these is an element of ritual trance induction, it would therefore appear that a connection between ritual trance and the performance state of the masked actor is highly probable.

Conclusion

A critical examination of the available literature on masks, actor training and performance illuminates some pathways by which questions regarding the state of

---

[38] Charles D. Laughlin, Eugene d'Aquili, John McManus. *Brain, Symbol and Experience: Towards a Phenomenology of Consciousness* (Boston and Shaftsbury: New Science Library Shambhala, 1990), p. 212.

the masked actor may be explored. The attitudes of Western teachers and performers towards masks and mask use are revealed in the writings of Copeau and his followers. Although they are few, studies of Noh and Balinese maskmaking and performance give some indication of the place of masks in each culture and the attitudes of performers in these genres towards the masks that they use. Studies of the psychophysiology of ritual trance provide important insights into aspects of the subjective experience of the masked performer in sacred ritual dramas. Some of these findings point toward a neurobiological explanation for the heretofore seemingly ineffable experience of the masked performer. Moreover, in examining the literature, some clear parallels emerge between these two genres in terms of mask iconography, elements of performance and aesthetic philosophy which, in their turn, cast light upon the actor-mask relationship.

Chapter 3:   Masks and Balinese Culture

A Labyrinth of Complexities

To understand the mask tradition of Bali, it is important to know something of the social, political, economic and cultural environment in which it exists. However, the organisation of Balinese society, which is in every element suffused with the Balinese-Hindu religion, is so complex as to make any attempt at explanation necessarily incomplete. Much damage has been done by those who would take the particular for the general and by those who seek to make aspects of Balinese culture fit neatly into pre-conceived, Occidentally-biased theories.

In the course of my work, sifting through available scholarship, observing performances, conducting interviews, and working with Balinese carvers, performers, teachers and scholars, I have found that information, often accepted as established fact, has turned out to be incomplete, even erroneous.[1] Part of the problem is the difference in perception between Eastern practitioners and Western observers. Whereas the West perceives time and history as linear and truth to be 'provable' through established and ascertainable 'facts' and 'statistics', the

---

[1] Anthropologist Mark Hobart has pointed out: "Despite—or even because of—the amount of research on Bali, it is becoming clear how little we know. The plethora of unexamined, but relevant, indigenous treatises and the degree of local variation alone suggest that generalizations are rather dubious. Much of the material has reported assertions in particular situations as facts, and facts as truth." In 'Thinker, thespian, soldier, slave? Assumptions about human nature in the study of Balinese society' in *Context, Meaning and Power in Southeast Asia*, eds Mark Hobart and R.H. Taylor (Ithaca: Cornell Southeast Asia Program. 1986) p. 151.

Eastern view is rather different. The perception of time in the East, particularly in Bali, is cyclical, almost amorphous. This is reflected in the languages (both Balinese and Indonesian) which acknowledge only the present tense, with even past and future expressed only in relation to 'now:'

> There is no conjugation of verbs. Other time markers abound: I go to the river today, I go to the river yesterday (perhaps in the early morning), I go to the river the day after tomorrow. Linguistically, though, the act is the same: I. . . always go to the river, regardless of when the going takes place. This enforced use of the narrative present acts as a powerful solvent on temporal barriers.[2]

In this tropical climate where rain, vegetation and insects soon wear away even the most robust stone carvings, the notion of permanence has more to do with recapitulation and reassessment than immutability. Records of historical incidents, religious ritual and performance methods are etched on the leaves of the *lontar* palm which, though carefully kept, must still be replaced by each generation. With each re-writing, new material is added and old material is modified so that what may appear to be established 'facts' and fixed rules are actually always in flux. Most important aspects of Balinese culture are passed on orally, through stories, epic poetry, dance-drama and shadow plays telling tales of gods, heroes and supernatural events. These fictions form the basis of cultural understanding for the Balinese. In this environment, facts and statistics are rather alien and 'truth' must be discerned through the mediating veil of fiction. The *wayang kulit* shadow puppets provide a useful analogy. These puppets are intricately carved from leather and each is carefully painted in astonishing detail, yet none of that detail is apparent to the audience. Instead, they see the drama played out on a backlit screen where the puppets cast their shadows, a reflection of the action rather than the action itself. This is a physical manifestation of the

---

[2] John Emigh, *Masked Performance: The Play of Self and Other in Ritual and Theatre* (Philadelphia: University of Pennsylvania Press, 1996), p. 136.

Hindu religious principle that reality cannot be perceived directly by human beings, and that all earthly life is only *Maya*, illusion. In this philosophical universe:

> That which ordinary people regard as a normal experience, such as a body, is an illusion, because it will decay tomorrow. Only the eternal is genuine and the eternal is one. . . . This world is illusion, Maya . . . according to this philosophy, the gods create illusions which we see as matter, but in reality even the gods themselves are illusions, a beautiful world of light playing with sound which we take for real. The true reality is the concentrated unity of divine will unencumbered by matter or other sensory impressions.[3]

In a world in which perceived reality is conceived of as merely illusory, the contradictions and inconsistencies which frustrate the Western scholar seeking fixed and measurable data must instead be seen as part of an ever-changing whole, a greater reality, a larger truth.

The brief historical and cultural overview which follows will provide some of the fundamental information necessary to give the reader an understanding of the context in which Balinese masked performance comes about, but it is not by any means a comprehensive view of Balinese life. Moreover it should be noted that the ethnographic findings which appear here and in subsequent chapters are based upon research among performers and mask-makers in the Gianyar[4] and Badung regencies only, and specifically from the

---

[3] Jan Knappert, *Indian Mythology: An Encyclopedia of Myth and Legend* (London: Diamond Books, 1995) pp. 170 and 265.

[4] Gianyar is generally held to be the centre of the arts in Bali and dancers from this area are reputed to be the best on the island to the extent that dancers from Gianyar are hired by temples elsewhere on the island to perform for particularly important ceremonies. For a thoroughgoing account of the development of masked dance in Bali and the significance of Gianyar see Deborah Dunn, *Topeng Pajegan: The Masked Dance of Bali* (PhD dissertation, 1983. Ann Arbor: University Microfilms International, 1987) pp. 19–48; also Bandem and de Boer *Kaja and Kelod: Balinese Dance in Transition* (Kuala Lumpur: Oxford University Press, 1981,

villages of Lodtunduh, Mas, Batuan and Singapadu. These areas were chosen because they are acknowledged, even among the Balinese, as important centres of culture. It should be understood, however, that local practice varies from village to village, family to family and even among members of the same family. Nonetheless, above any seeming inconsistencies in minor matters, the larger truth of the significance of the mask in Balinese culture and the function of the masked performer as mediator between the illusory world of present reality and the unseen, timeless world of the spirit will be apparent.

An Embattled Paradise

Bali is a small island in the Indonesian archipelago east of Java, a last remnant of Hinduism in what is now a predominantly Islamic country (though distinctly different from Arabist Islamic states). The Hindu religion may have come to Bali as early as the second century of the Current Era through contact with traders from the Indian subcontinent, and inscriptions in Sanskrit and Old Balinese dating from the late ninth or early tenth century indicate that it was well-established on the island by that time.[5] Bali was conquered by Java, which was then also Hindu, in the late tenth century, establishing a powerful religious and cultural connection between the two islands. Firmer links were established with the ascendancy of the Javanese Majapahit dynasty from 1293 and it was to Bali that the Majapahit court fled when its empire collapsed with the advance of the Muslim Mataram empire in 1515. The period which followed was a kind of 'Golden Age' for Bali in which the powerful kingdom of Gelgel extended its influence over East Java and the

---

1995) and Adrian Vickers, *Bali: A Paradise Created* (Hong Kong: Periplus Editions, 1996), pp. 140–146.

[5] J. L. Swellengrebel, *Bali: Studies in Life, Thought and Ritual*, edited by W.F. Wertheim et al. (The Hague and Bandung: W. van Hoeve) p. 18. See also Mary Zurbuchen, *The Language of Balinese Shadow Theatre* (Princeton, New Jersey: Princeton University Press, 1987) pp. 10–20.

neighbouring islands of Lombok and Sumbawa.[6] A great many of the Topeng masked dramas derive from the chronicles of these times with stories featuring great warriors, powerful kings and miraculous priests.[7] By the seventeenth century, European influence began to be felt in Bali as Dutch, English and Portuguese traders discovered the 'Spice Islands'. The kingdom of Gelgel gradually disintegrated and, by the end of the eighteenth century, Bali had divided

> into nine small warring kingdoms, each in competition with the other, each its own special cultural centre. The kingdom of Gelgel, which preceded the nine kingdoms, laid the foundations for the development of modern Balinese culture. The subsequent increase in the number of courts, each elaborating and extending the varieties of ritual, art, theatre and music on the island, deepened that culture.[8]

The Dutch laid claim to Bali as part of the Dutch East Indies, but Bali paid little attention and kept up an active trade with a number of nations including England and China.[9] The island remained relatively undisturbed until the mid-nineteenth century when the heretofore benign colonial government began to seek military control. After several bloody battles in the northern and eastern kingdoms, a kind of peace was achieved and, for a time, the various Balinese rajadoms managed to continue functioning in traditional fashion, though considered by the Dutch to be part of their empire. Between 1904 and 1908, however, a trivial dispute caused the Dutch to mount another significant invasion. This led to an event which

---

[6] Anthony Mason and Felicity Goulden with Richard Overton, *Bali* (London: Cadogan Books, 1989) pp. 76–77; also Swellengrebel, pp. 21–24. For more detail see Geoffrey Robinson, *The Dark Side of Paradise* (Ithaca: Cornell University Press, 1995) and Vickers, pp. 41–58.

[7] Elizabeth F. Young, *Topeng in Bali: Change and Continuity in a Traditional Drama Genre* (PhD dissertation, University of California at San Diego, 1980) p. 20.

[8] Vickers, p. 9.

[9] *Ibid.*, pp. 12–28.

indicates something of the intensity that lies beneath the seemingly placid demeanour of the Balinese:

> On the morning of 20 September the king, his family, and thousands of armed followers, all dressed in white and ready to meet death in battle, marched out to meet the Dutch. Each of the leading royal warriors ran amuk in turn, marching on as if bullets would bounce off their bodies. The Dutch opened fire on "women with weapons in their hands, lance or *kris*[10] [ceremonial dagger], and children in their arms", who "advanced fearlessly upon the troops and sought death". The Dutch found that this *puputan* could only be settled in death; surrender was impossible: 'where an attempt was made to disarm them this only led to an increase in our losses. The survivors were repeatedly called on to lay down arms and surrender, but in vain'. The king, his family and followers advanced relentlessly, killing themselves and any Dutch troops who came within range as they went. The Dutch later tried to cover up the death toll, but while it was fairly light on the Dutch side, well over 1000 Balinese were killed.[11]

---

[10] ". . . short sword that possess considerable magical power and must be treated with great respect; some have wavy blades; almost always worn by male dancers slung across the back, handle to the right; an important part of Balinese traditional dress for such events as weddings, tooth filings and so on". Eiseman, 1997a, p K-18.

[11] Vickers, p. 35, quoting from a participant's report of the chief of staff of the expedition quoted in Henk Schulte Nordholt, *Bali: Colonial Conceptions and Political Change 1700–1940, From Shifting Hierarchies to 'Fixed Order'* (Rotterdam: Comparative Asian Studies Programme 15, 1986) p. 5; see also Vicki Baum, *A Tale From Bali* (Singapore: Oxford University Press, 1973) a fictionalised account of the events leading to the *Puputan* and its aftermath. Vickers points out that this was not the first time the Dutch colonisers had encountered a *puputan,* that other incidents had been well documented during earlier conflicts in Bali and Lombok. This spectacular mass suicide (and that which followed in the kingdom of Klungkung) was, however, deeply shocking for the Dutch whose colonial activities were thereby made to look less benign. Michel Picard in *Bali: Cultural Tourism and Touristic Culture* (translated by Diana Darling , Singapore: Archipelago Press, 1996) contends (as does Vickers) that Dutch remorse over the *puputan* contributed to its determination to preserve Balinese culture at all costs.

Ritual suicide had long been a part of Balinese culture, not only in the form of *suttee,* the widow sacrifice known in other Hindu cultures (notably India), but also as a heroic gesture in the face of defeat in which the members of a royal household would offer themselves to the gods.[12] The gesture, if not the actual act of ritual self-sacrifice remains a strong element in Balinese culture, evidenced in particular by the so-called '*Kris* dancers' of the exorcistic dramas which feature the apotropaic figures of Rangda and Barong. In these plays, individuals fall into trance and endeavour to stab themselves with ceremonial daggers, but are magically protected from harm by the power of the gods embodied in the sacred masks.

The '*puputan*'[13] described above occurred in Badung near the modern capital of Denpasar, and these horrifying events were later repeated in the kingdom of Klungkung. The kingdom of Tabanan surrendered, but its raja committed suicide in prison and his family was exiled to Lombok. The canny rajas of Gianyar, however, had been wise enough to submit to the Dutch well before their powerful neighbours in Badung and Klungkung and were officially 'regents' for the occupying imperial power. By this means the royal families of Gianyar maintained their courts, their wealth and their troupes of performing artists.[14]

Appalled by the bloody human sacrifice which they had unwittingly instigated, the Dutch took care to try to preserve the island's unique culture. In a gesture of cynical irony or perhaps genuine remorse they built the Bali Hotel in the place where the royal household of Badung had made its *puputan,* and it was here that the first tourists were able to see Balinese dance-drama in performances

---

[12] See Vickers pp. 13–14 and 34.

[13] Literally 'conclusion, bringing to an end.' Fred Eiseman, *Balinese-English Dictionary,* second edition (Jimbaran, Bali: Fred B. Eiseman, 1997), p. P-29.

[14] See Dunn, pp. 38–40.

especially created for them.[15] By the nineteen-twenties and thirties, Bali had become a fashionable tourist destination that drew a number of artists and scholars seeking to document the extraordinary spiritual and artistic life of the islanders.[16] With the outbreak of the Second World War, however, the Westerners retreated and the Japanese occupied the archipelago virtually unopposed by the Dutch. After the Japanese defeat came the struggle for Indonesian independence, which was eventually won, and Bali is now a province of the Republic of Indonesia.[17]

Until the recent economic collapse, Indonesia was regarded as one of the powerful 'Tiger economies' in Asia, but most ordinary Indonesians are still desperately poor. Thus, in spite of the fact that Bali is advertised elsewhere as a glamorous, exotic vacation paradise, the island's native population mostly survive on subsistence farming as they have done for thousands of years. It is a cause for concern that the ever-increasing number of tourists and tourist facilities on the island are rapidly changing Balinese life, undermining the agrarian economy and bringing alien values into a hitherto relatively homogeneous culture.[18] Although it is a matter of some dispute, the tourist industry has probably, on balance, been something of a boon for Balinese performing arts, providing more opportunities

---

[15] Vickers, p. 97; see also Picard 1996, pp. 25–26.

[16] The painter Walter Spies maintained a house in Campuhan near Ubud (now converted to a hotel) and played host to a variety of Western visitors including Margaret Mead and Gregory Bateson and Jane Belo and Colin McPhee whose anthropological, cultural and musical studies on the island have become fundamental texts. The American dancer Katherine Mershon lived in the coastal village of Sanur and contributed to Mead, Bateson and Belo's work. See Vickers, Picard, 1996, and Tessel Pollman, 'Margaret Mead's Balinese: The Fitting Symbols of the American Dream', *Indonesia* (No. 49, April 1990) Cornell: Cornell Southeast Asia Program.

[17] For a detailed analysis of Balinese history, particularly the period leading to independence and the upheavals following the fall of Sukarno in 1966, see Robinson, 1995.

[18] Sadly, even subsistence farming is becoming less a feature of Balinese economic life as the burgeoning tourist industry converts rice fields into golf courses and elegant hotels. The Balinese remain poor, however, because the industry is controlled by and tends to employ non-Balinese Indonesians, mostly Javanese. The religious obligations imposed by traditional Balinese culture is one reason for this. These developments are documented in fascinating detail by Picard, 1996.

for performances, greater remuneration for artists and fuelling international interest in these ancient art forms. In any case, the island's unique culture has survived a number of more obviously dangerous upheavals including occupation by both the Dutch and the Japanese, revolution, political turbulence, volcanic eruptions and famine. The stability of the culture is partly, if not entirely, due to the intensity with which the inhabitants dedicate themselves to the complex cosmology of Balinese Hinduism.

Agama Hindu-Bali

Religion is deeply ingrained into every aspect of Balinese life to a degree that is almost inconceivable in the West; no element is untouched by it. A unique variant of the Indian faith, Balinese Hinduism incorporates animistic practices and ancestor worship that predate the advent of religious influences that are presumed to have come through trade with the subcontinent. Worship of the Hindu trinity of Brahma, Shiva and Vishnu (*Siwa* and *Wisnu* to the Balinese) is central to both religions, but in Bali the Hindu pantheon is augmented by innumerable local spirits and deified ancestors,[19] all of whom require prayers and offerings. For example, each morning and evening as many as twenty or more offerings are prepared and placed at various shrines and spiritually important places throughout each individual Balinese-Hindu household in order to placate the potentially

---

[19] The situation is further complicated by a figure that is meant to represent the central godhead for Balinese Hindus called Sanghyang Widi Wasa. In fact this 'god', which might be understood to be a unity of all of the Bali-Hindu gods as a single, all-powerful figure (corresponding, perhaps, to the Hindu concept of Brahman, 'the unmoved mover' of the universe or Surya, the sun god), is a political, rather than a theological invention. With the establishment of the independent Republic of Indonesia came the 'Pancasila' or Five Principles upon which the government of Indonesia is based. The first of these principles is the belief in 'one, all-powerful god' – clearly a problem for Balinese Hindus. In order to have the island's religion recognised by the Indonesian authorities, the figure of Sanghyang Widi Wasa was invented, the name having been derived from a word for 'God' created by Protestant missionaries who hoped to translate the Bible into the Balinese language in an ill-fated attempt to convert the islanders. See Fred Eiseman, *Bali: Sekala and Niskala*, Vol. 1: *Essays on Religion and Art.* (Singapore: Periplus Editions, 1990) pp. 10–24 and 38–50.

disruptive spirits called '*butakala*'.[20] On certain holy days these offerings may be quite elaborate. Any new appliance or building, whether a new motorbike or a shrine in the family temple, must have particular ceremonies performed to protect both the object and its user. No important activity (beginning dancing lessons, for example, or carving a significant mask) may be undertaken until an appropriately auspicious day has been determined, perhaps with the help of a *pedanda*, a high-caste priest. In fact all activities, from major religious rites to market days, must be carefully scheduled in conjunction with one or more of the three different calendars[21] which govern Balinese life. This life is an unceasing round of religious obligations, which are undertaken without question, for to neglect them is to court disaster. The Balinese world view acknowledges both *sekala* (seen) and *niskala* (unseen) forces at work in a universe that consists of *bhuana agung* (macrocosm, the larger universe, of which human beings are a only part) and *bhuana alit* (microcosm, the world of human beings as related to the macrocosm). What is essential in life is not to choose between 'good' and 'evil', as in the Judeo-Christian world-view, but to keep all the elements of the universe in balance.

> Evil is a part of the whole and good is a part of the whole. Neither can exist without the other. Instead, the life of any Balinese is devoted to maintaining a balance between these opposing forces—maintaining an equilibrium so that neither gets the upper hand.[22]

---

[20] "However butakala can be enlisted to help people, or at least leave them alone, if regular offerings and prayers are made to them. So it is really wrong to call butakala 'demons' or 'evil spirits'. They are capable of doing harm, but do not necessarily do so unless provoked or neglected. Butakala are particularly active on particular days, at certain known times of the day, and in certain locations, most of which are well known to practically all Balinese people." Eiseman, 1997a, p. B-20.

[21] These are: the standard, Western Gregorian calendar, the old Javanese 210-day *Pawukon* calendar and the Hindu lunar calendar known as *Saka* or *Çaka*. See Eiseman, 1990a pp. 172–192; also Lansing, 1995, pp. 28–31.

[22] Eiseman, 1990a, p. 2.

The function of much of Balinese masked drama is to help maintain this balance between the powerful forces of the universe, especially the forces of 'black' and 'white' magic. It should be noted that the term 'black magic' is used here within the context and frames of reference of Balinese cosmology and does not refer, as in Western Judeo-Christian cosmology, to anti-social or negative spirituality, since such interpretations do not reflect the Balinese-Hindu belief system. Indeed, whereas the term 'magic' in Western usage carries with it connotations of deceit and trickery and an implied falseness or pretence, 'magic' in Bali is a potent spiritual force which, significantly (and this cannot be too strongly emphasised), is *morally ambivalent*. It is a tangible power that may be used by those possessed of particular training and expertise to the benefit or detriment of themselves or others. Thus, 'magic' in Bali is a specific religious/spiritual, effective and affective practice, often associated with both physical and psychic healing. Practitioners of magic are conversant with both 'white' and 'black' applications of the skills and materials they use. Those possessed of magical powers (whether priests, healers, performers or lay persons) are called *sakti*, a term referring to spiritual power that does not carry with it connotations of either good or evil. This supernatural power represents neither divine benevolence, nor demonic malevolence, but is rather an ambivalent force to be feared, respected and desired in equal measure.

Ritual and the Arts

Devotion to ritual manifests itself not only in elaborate temple ceremonies (which may be observed somewhere on the island every day) but also in the attitude of the Balinese towards the work that they do, particularly with regard to traditional arts and crafts. That attitude is communal, rather than individualistic, and concerned with detail and the steady carrying out of fixed tasks in a familiar pattern. This ritualisation may partly account for the apparent detachment of the Balinese dancer who appears to be, as Artaud put it, 'an animated hieroglyph' and for the patient diligence of Balinese carvers, whether they are creating wooden ornaments for the Western handicrafts market or sacred masks for a temple ceremony. This is not to say that there is a stultifying uniformity to all that is created, but, rather, that repetition is accepted as a necessary part of life and work and that within the context of ritualised activity something higher is achieved. The Western stereotype of the maverick artist alone in his garret creating a unique work of genius is diametrically opposed to the Balinese way of working. Of course there are individual artists and notions of authorship are not unknown (Bali has its share of swaggering egomaniacs just as 'difficult' as their counterparts in the West). However, there is no equivalent word for the Western concept of 'art' in the Balinese language, instead there is a deeply ingrained attitude of mind that links these endeavours to religious duty, which is a matter of necessity rather than choice.[23] These activities, which in the West might be considered 'artistic' pursuits performed by a gifted minority for a coterie of connoisseurs are, in Bali, common skills engaged in by a broad spectrum of the population. They include dancing, acting, woodcarving and making music. Nor are the practitioners narrow specialists, rather they may be adept at all of these skills as well as many others, for example painting or the recitation and interpretation of ancient epic poetry, not to mention the preparation of the often magnificent and elaborate offerings that are created (principally by women) for temple festivals and domestic ritual occasions.[24]

Unsurprisingly, ritual and religion determine much of the way in which social institutions function in Bali:

> Balinese society is remarkable for the complexity of its organizational forms, at once diverse and fluctuating. . . . The 'village' *(desa)* is not so much a socio-political group nor, strictly speaking, a territorial unit, although of course it occupies territorial space. It is, rather, a religious congregation composed of a group

---

[23] Lansing, 1995, provides interesting insights into the question of authorship in Balinese poetry, painting and music, pp. 51–57.

[24] See Lansing 1995, pp. 63–66.

of people collectively responsible for the three temples associated with the *desa,* and comprising . . . the 'Navel Temple' *(pura puseh)* where the village's guardian deities and founding ancestors are venerated; the 'Village Temple' *(pura desa)* where the village council meets, and which is associated with fertility rites; and the 'Temple of the Interior' *(pura dalem)* where the disruptive influence of the not-yet-purified dead are placated and the deity of death is honored. Village membership is in this way defined by vertical relationships to a temple network rather than by horizontal relationships among the members of a community.[25]

Social and religious responsibilities towards these temples are significant in relation to the present analysis because it is the *odalan* (temple anniversary) which is among the most important occasions requiring masked performances.[26] Sometimes performers will be brought from another village (and paid) to perform at an *odalan*; however, if sufficiently skilled performers are among those who owe obligations to the temple, they may perform unremunerated as *ngayah*— "contributing one's help, work or service in connection with a temple ceremony".[27] In addition to these village temples, an individual may owe obligations to caste or clan temples, temples associated with the *banjar* (the basic traditional civic governmental unit) or with the *subak* (rice field irrigation society) as well as to the household and family temples. Then, of course, there is the 'mother' temple of Besakih, venerated by all Balinese Hindus, which stands

---

[25] Picard, *op. cit.* p. 12.

[26] "The drama is a necessary ingredient of temple festivals and other religious ceremonies as part of the offering to the gods. Also, the performances constitute a traditional communication network to disseminate religious doctrine to the village community." Young, p. xix. See also Emigh 1996, pp. 107–108.

[27] Eiseman, 1997a, p. N-12.

just below the summit of the holy mountain, Gunung Agung.[28] Each of these temples also has an *odalan*.

Caste

Social relationships are further affected by the caste system, which is another outgrowth of Hindu cosmology. There are four castes or *warna* (literally, 'colours') which are, in order of rank: *Brahmana* (priests and scholars); *Satria* (kings, warriors and officials); *Wesia* (civil servants and merchants) and *Sudra* ("persons without caste"[29]), there are no 'untouchables'. The *Brahmana, Satria* and *Wesia* make up the *Triwangsa,* the 'twice born' at the top of the social and religious hierarchy who represent only about ten percent of the population.[30] Caste is determined by birth and strict taboos still remain for those who would marry out of their caste. Should this happen (as it sometimes does) a high caste man may raise the status of a lower caste wife, but a high caste woman will lose her status should she marry 'beneath' her. A *pedanda* or high priest may come only from the highest, *Brahmana,* caste but village priests, called *pemangku,* are most often *Sudra*. The difference between the two is important because only the *pedanda* may make holy water and this function brings his status close to that of the gods:

> because the Supreme God Siwa incarnates himself in them during their liturgy. . . . As manifestations of Surya/Siwa they can then

---

[28] Gunung Agung is an active volcano that last had a serious eruption in 1963 during preparations for the *Esa Deka Rudra* ceremony, a ritual which may be held once in a hundred years (by the *Saka* calendar) for the purification of the universe. The devastation that it caused, wiping out whole villages and destroying farmland, meant that the ceremony had to be cancelled. That such a ceremony should be instigated at all gives some idea of the 'Balicentricity' of the islanders—for them it is Bali, the island of the gods, which is responsible for the survival of the universe. The eruption is said to have occurred because the date chosen for the ceremony was incorrect – chosen for political expediency to please then-president Sukarno. The gods' displeasure is further attested to (for the Balinese) by Sukarno's subsequent fall from power and the brutal and bloody anti-Communist crackdown, which followed.

[29] *Sudra* are sometimes also called '*jaba*', literally 'outsiders'. See Eiseman, 1990a, pp. 25–50.

[30] Mason et al., p. 103.

produce their supremely valued *tirta prande*, (holy water from pedanda), which removes pollution in connection with life crisis rituals.[31]

On the other hand, it is the *pemangku* who is most in evidence in temple performances involving trance, reviving those who require assistance and generally keeping the proceedings under some sort of control. A *pemangku* is also responsible for ceremonies before and after performances to purify the performance space, musical instruments, costumes, masks and performers.

In Balinese society, caste distinctions manifest themselves in many ways, perhaps the most far-reaching of which is language. Balinese is a language of three or four levels, each of which is distinctive enough to be almost linguistically separate.[32] Persons of high caste must be addressed in *alus* or high Balinese, those of low caste in *rendah*, low Balinese, and, conveniently, there is a 'middle' Balinese, which is used to communicate when caste status has not been established. The high caste *pedanda*, however, must be addressed in what amounts to a completely separate language, called *Basa Singgih*. Today many Balinese must use an interpreter when they visit a *pedanda* because so few are

---

[31] "...some very few high priests, called *rsi* if *Satria* or *Wesia* by descent and *mpu* if they are *Sudra*, have similar functions, but these belong to very special lines, vested with holy scriptures and holy water from ancient times." Fredrik Barth, *Balinese Worlds*. (Chicago and London: The University of Chicago Press, 1993), pp. 196–198. Holy water is an absolute essential in Balinese life and every household will have its own supply. The water is, for example, sprinkled on all the daily household offerings. In conjunction with masked drama (either sacred or secular), holy water is necessary to prepare all the elements before the performance begins and is sprinkled on masks, costumes, gamelan, musicians and dancers either by a *pemangku* or a member of the company appointed to this responsibility. For fascinating insights into the development of the caste system and the rise of the development of the caste system in Bali and the rise of the *Brahmana* caste see Vickers, pp. 49–53.

[32] Mason et. al. pp. 35–38. Eiseman, however, acknowledges only three levels (Eiseman, 1990b, pp. 130–146), low, medium and high, but this is arguable, especially since Balinese is primarily a spoken rather than written language with considerable local variations. The question of 'levels' in the Balinese language is extremely complex and beyond the scope of this paper, but Zurbuchen (pp. 63–81) provides precise detail about how levels of language are applied in practice. See also Emigh 1996, pp. 127–131.

conversant with this ancient, very formal language.[33] These linguistic caste distinctions are reflected in the Topeng masked dramas in which performers may speak as many as seven languages in the course of a performance.[34] The high caste characters usually speak *Kawi*, the poetic language of the ancient Javanese court, and must be addressed in high Balinese. The conversations are translated (with commentary) by servant characters into low or middle Balinese for the audience. Ancient Sanskrit, Modern Indonesian and even English may also feature.

There is a certain amount of disagreement among the Balinese about whether caste status is an important consideration when determining the aptitude of performing artists and mask makers. Among some of the high caste practitioners with whom I spoke it was felt to be so. However, not surprisingly, *Sudra* practitioners did not agree and felt that training and talent, rather than caste status, was the chief determinant of ability.[35] In practice, Topeng performers come

---

[33] Fred Eiseman, personal communication.

[34] See I Made Bandem and John Emigh, 'Jelantik Goes to Blambangan: A *Topeng Pajegan* Performance by I Nyoman Kakul (as recorded at Tusan, Klungkung, Bali on February 6, 1975)' *The Drama Review*, 23, number 2, June 1979, pp. 37–48. The article consists primarily of a transcription and translation of an actual *Topeng Pajegan* performance and gives an excellent impression of the way the spoken 'text' of a Topeng performance works. It is also reproduced in Emigh 1996, pp. 157–170.

[35] Dunn (pp. 87–88) had similar findings and Belo (1949) contended that "artistic skill and ability override caste divisions" (p. 6). Emigh 1996 (pp. 147-148) makes a strong point of the status reversals and relaxation of caste barriers in the case of performers, citing the example of the late I Nyoman Kakul, a highly respected *Sudra* Topeng master. In the course of my investigations I found that practitioners from the *Brahmana* caste in particular believe that a thorough understanding of the historical records (*Babad*) as well as the theological implications of particular ceremonies is essential to Topeng performance and that *Sudra* performers generally do not have access to materials necessary for the breadth and depth of study required. To some extent this may be true, since much material is etched on sacred *lontars* passed through families from father to son and members of the *Brahmana* caste are traditionally the keepers of information regarding theological matters. But *Sudra* families may also have a collection of *lontars*. The father of I Made Bandem, for example, as well as being an accomplished and highly regarded Topeng and Arja performer, was also a *balian usada*(traditional healer who uses information from *lontars* in his work). Bandem has inherited his collection of *lontars* (interview, 30 April, 1997).

from all levels of Balinese society and there are no restrictions with regard to which persons may study Topeng.

Traditional Balinese Masked Drama

Available sources indicate that masked dances have been a feature of Balinese culture since at least the ninth century,[36] perhaps as a result of Javanese influence or more direct contact with the Indian subcontinent.[37] Masked dances from the 'Bali Aga'[38] villages may be older still, but these are primarily ritualistic rather than dramatic. Traditional masked dramas performed in contemporary Bali fall broadly into three types:

Topeng: a generic term for masked dramas based on chronicles of Balinese history. The word *'topeng'* is synonymous with 'mask' and means, 'something pressed against the face'.[39] Sometimes, however, a distinction is made between *tapel,* the mask object, and *Topeng,* the masked play genre. *Topeng Sidha Karya,* also called *Topeng Wali,* is the term for Topeng performed in a sacred, ritual context and may use one to three performers. In *Topeng Pajegan,* which will be described at length in Chapter 5, a single performer takes all the parts and there may be as many as 20 different mask characters to perform. *Topeng Panca* is performed by a company of five (or sometimes more), and *Topeng Prembon,* a secular version, is a hybrid form which incorporates

---

[36] Bandem and de Boer, p. 45.

[37] See J. Stephen Lansing, *Rama's Kingdoms: Social Supportive Mechanisms for the Arts in Bali* (PhD dissertation, Ann Arbor, Michigan: University Microfilms International, 1977) pp. 8–10 and, more especially, Emigh, 1996 pp. 74–99.

[38] "People considered by the Balinese to be the original inhabitants of the island. Living in certain more or less remote villages, Bali Aga people differ from their more 'Javanized' neighbours with respect to burial practices, composition of the priesthood, calendar, etc." Bandem and de Boer, p. 144.

[39] "The word *topeng* comes from the root *tup,* meaning 'cover', and refers to something pressed against the face, that is, a mask." *Ibid.*, p. 46.

unmasked performers from other genres.[40] Important collections of ancient, sacred Topeng masks may be found in the villages of Blahbatuh and Ketewel. The Blahbatuh masks are said to have been brought from Java in the fourteenth century.[41] According to legend, they were brought as spoils of war to the King of Gelgel after the successful conquest of the East Javanese kingdom of Blambangan.[42] The Ketewel masks represent "the nine celestial maidens of Hindu mythology"[43] and are used in a sacred dance called *Sang Hyang Legong*, performed by young girls in a special ceremony. Both collections are very old and are not allowed to be photographed.[44] Some of the masks are considered to possess exceptional, even curative, powers.[45] These masks are rarely used for dramatic performances[46] but some certainly have served as models for masks used by contemporary performers.[47]

Calonarang: also referred to as 'Barong Dance' and sometimes '*Kris* Dance', this is an exorcistic play often performed at the *odalan* of a *Pura*

---

[40] "During the troubled 1940s, the King of Gianyar, I Déwa Mangis VIII, called together the dancers attached to his palace and asked them to create a Prembon (Combination). He asked that favourite type-characters be taken from Gambuh, Baris, Arja, Topeng and Parwa and a single story presented in which they all appeared. ...Once again, the Topeng repertoire, dealing with the historical kings and priests of Bali, was the source of subject-matter." Bandem and de Boer, pp. 84–85.

[41] Young, p. 154. This date is disputed, however. The masks were said to have been captured during the reign of Dalem Baturenggong, which would have brought them to Bali in the 16th century and Vickers suggests that they may date from the 18th century (Vickers, p. 70).

[42] Interestingly, the story of this conquest is a popular subject for Topeng drama. See Bandem and de Boer p. 47 and Bandem and Emigh, 1979.

[43] Bandem and de Boer, p. 71.

[44] A photograph of the Blahbatuh masks appears in T. Statke, *Camera Pictures of Sumatra, Java, Bali* (Middlesborough: Hood, 1935) and is reproduced in Vickers, figure 12 between pages 84 and 85.

[45] Young, p. 161.

[46] Performances with each of these sets of sacred masks are described in some detail by Dr. I Wayan Dibia in 'Nopeng atau Napel dalam Seni Patopengan Bali' *WRETA Cita*, Nomor 4, 11 Juni, 1995 pp. 2–3.

[47] For example, some of the masks now used by I Made Djimat, which were made by master mask-maker I Wayan Tangguh in 1969 or 1970, are copies of the ancient Blahbatuh collection (interview, 27 April, 1997).

Dalem.[48] There are two principal masked figures: Barong and Rangda. Barong, (usually *Barong Ket*[49]) is a large, shaggy creature operated by two dancers; he has a lion or dog-like face with fangs, bulging eyes and a goatee beard of human hair. Both coat and beard are believed to have magical or healing powers. Rangda, also fanged, has bulging eyes, a huge tongue decorated with gold markings, long, spiky hair and pendulous breasts and is almost invariably played by a man. In Calonarang, Barong represents the forces of 'white magic', against the 'black magic' of the demonic female witch, Rangda.

Wayang Wong: derived from the shadow-puppet tradition *(Wayang Kulit)*, this version of the *Ramayana* epic is performed rarely and in only a few villages. It is a very ancient form and the masks used are revered both for their age and their association with the sacred story. However, because it is a relatively rare form in which most of the masked performers are less likely to be 'trained professionals', it has not been included in this analysis.[50] The masked figures include, among others, Hanoman and Sugriwa, the monkey generals, and Garuda, a magical bird. Although masks exist for the characters of Rama and Sita in some collections (and, indeed, such masks are still made), those characters are now usually played by *Arja*[51] performers who sing their roles and do not wear masks.

---

[48] Jane Belo in her study *Rangda and Barong* (Monographs of the American Ethnological Society, New York: J.J. Augustin, 1949 pp. 7–8) refers to the *Pura Dalem* as the 'Temple of Death', presumably because it is located near the cemetery, a place of powerful supernatural forces. However, the term *'dalem'* means not death, but rather *'interior'* and may also refer to the king or *'raja'*. Belo points out that the Pura Dalem is "the only ancestral temple of the ruling radja's ancestors [...] or the ancestors of some former king." (p. 8).

[49] There are a number of different Barong masks in various animal shapes including tiger, wild boar, elephant, lion, cow, dog and goat, among others. This will be discussed in more detail in Chapter 5.

[50] It is called 'Wayang' because it was based upon the famous shadow-puppet (wayang) version of the story. The Balinese Wayang Wong is distinct from the Central Javanese dance-drama of the same name. See Bandem and de Boer, pp. 58–68. See also Bandem, *Wayang Wong in Contemporary Bali*, PhD dissertation, Wesleyan University, 1980.

[51] A sung dance-drama that developed in the nineteenth century, sometimes referred to as 'Balinese opera'. See Bandem and de Boer, pp. 79–82.

Topeng

Of the several variants of Topeng drama, I shall focus on the ritually significant *Topeng Wali*, since this is the source for the other versions and is most significant in terms of mask use. Also known as *Topeng Sidha Karya*, it is performed at most important ceremonies, both domestic and communal, generally in the outer courtyard of the temple in order to distract and entertain the *butakala* who might seek to disrupt the ritual. In it the dancer or dancers present a story based on the chronicles of Balinese history *(Babad)* which will have been specially chosen for the occasion. There is no 'script' as such, rather the performer(s) improvise on the basis of the appropriate *Babad* (some have been published but many others exist only in hand-copied versions inscribed on leaves of the *lontar* palm) inserting material which relates to the ritual or to the family or clan group for whom the Topeng is being performed. It is interesting to note that, as some family groups have become financially more prosperous, they occasionally arrange to have *lontars* created that trace their family history to one of the famous heroes of Bali's royal past. The connection may be tenuous, even dubious but, having been committed to the *lontar*, such an invented 'history' acquires the force of 'verifiable historical fact', however fanciful or far-fetched.[52]

The story is related through words and gesture by various characters and the performer may also insert contemporary references as he sees fit. The full-face Topeng masks represent idealised archetypal figures of *Patih* (prime minister), *Topeng Tua* (an elderly courtier), and *Dalem* (the king). These masks do not speak but convey their stories and character through gesture. They are high-caste characters who fall into two types: *alus,* 'refined, soft or delicate'[53] or *keras,* 'strong, rough, forceful'.[54] Among the half-masked characters (who do

---

[52] This is not to say that such genealogies are necessarily false, but certainly historical accuracy is less important in such instances than family prestige and poetic viability. See Bandem and de Boer, p. 56.

[53] Bandem and de Boer, p. 143.

[54] *Ibid.*, p. 148.

speak) are the comic servant/storytellers, a pair of brothers known as *Penasar Kelihan,* and *Penasar Cenikan.* The elder, *Penasar Kelihan,* is swaggering and pedantic and the younger, *Cenikan,* plays innocent but is a wily trickster (see Figures 1 and 2).[55] A performance begins with the *Penglembar,* two or three silent, full-face masks (normally *Patih* and *Topeng Tua* and, occasionally, another version of *Patih,* often comic, see Figures 3–5), after which the *Penasar* enters and begins to relate the story. When the *Dalem* (Figure 6) appears, his words are spoken in Kawi by the half-masked *Penasar,* who responds in his own character in Balinese translating the King's words. In the solo *Topeng Pajegan* one first sees the *Dalem,* delivering his instructions through mime, and then the *Penasar* speaking the King's words and making his responses. This presents an extraordinary picture:

> Occasional dissociation of voice and body is a striking and exotic aspect of the story-telling mode: at times, the dancer will bend his body in cringing subordination in keeping with his role as palace servant, while from his lips come the imperious commands, in Kawi, of his invisible master.[56]

In addition, there are a number of other half-masked characters that are comic villager types, often with grotesque deformities, called *Bondres.*[57] There are also two full-faced masks who speak: one is the high priest *(Pedanda)* who serves a storytelling function and has an open mouth, the other is the sacred *Sidha Karya.*

---

[55] For discussion and analysis of the characters of Topeng see also Young, p. 104–121, Emigh 1996, pp. 127–136, Dunn, pp. 56–63.

[56] Bandem and de Boer, p. 50.

[57] In recent years a new popular entertainment genre has begun to emerge which utilises these characters exclusively and is called Bondres.

Sidha Karya

Sidha Karya is the final mask which must appear in this sacred Topeng (see Figure 7), but his character is not related to the story which has been enacted. The name means 'one who completes the ceremony' and is, as the name suggests, essential for the completion of the ritual. It is the Sidha Karya mask itself, which makes this Topeng play sacred, and, as Bandem and de Boer explain: "When he is wearing this mask, and only then, the dancer serves a specifically priestly function". Unlike the other masks of the Topeng drama, Sidha Karya is considered to be sacred by its very nature, representing as it does a holy person, a spokesman for the god, perhaps even the god himself. Indeed, some Sidha Karya masks are felt to be especially magically powerful and therefore potentially dangerous for the wearer. The character represented is rather mysterious. The most prevalent explanation, among the performers whom I consulted,[58] is that Sidha Karya represents the legendary figure of '*Brahmana Kling*' or '*Keling*'. Here is how the story was related to me by the dancer Ida Bagus Alit:

> It's a long story, based on a myth of a Buddhist Brahman priest from Java; *Sidha Karya* is this Brahman priest. At that time there was a Brahman king in Bali, but the kingdom was not stable, all bad, very bad. So, the Buddhist Brahman priest comes here to restore harmony. At that time the *Dalem*, the prince in Bali, was holding a big ritual for all this distortion that was happening. Sidha Karya comes to Bali, he is filthy, he's come walking a long way from Java, and finally when he comes to Besakih [the 'Mother Temple' of Balinese Hinduism]) he meets all the community here holding the ritual, . . . including the Prince and one of his prime ministers, [who] . . . refuses to allow the priest to enter: "You look dirty. I don't believe you are a Brahman person. Why don't you go

---

[58] Dr. I Made Bandem, Dr. I Wayan Dibia (both of Singapadu), Ida Bagus Alit (of Lodtunduh), Ida Bagus Anom (of Mas) and I Made Djimat (of Batuan).

somewhere South?" [towards the sea, regarded as ritually unclean]. So that Brahman priest from Java is put in the south part of the island somewhere [and] . . . curses the ritual. Everything is a mess; the ritual doesn't go properly, many people die, trees die and it's very dry, the grass dies and the chickens, all the animals die. The Yadnya [ritual] doesn't happen because the people got sick. Finally . . . the prime minister, . . . finds out that this priest from Java has cursed the ritual, so he goes to fetch him "Please come, forgive us; I'd like to know who you are". And the priest says, "I am the Brahman, I've come here to find my family, the *Dalem* here is our relative from the same generation—a Buddhist Brahman". So he took the curse back, since he was accepted as a Brahman person from Java and a relative of the prince. So the *Yadnya* goes quite well and they complete the ceremony. That is why he then is called '*Sidha Karya*'—*Topeng Sidha Karya*— which means the job is done perfectly, completely. It's done well. So Sidha Karya, the one who came here from Java, made the ritual complete.[59]

This story, with some variations, is also cited by Bandem, Emigh, Slattum and Dunn, but it is by no means the only presumed identity of this important figure.[60] However, in all cases he is an ancestral figure with magical or divine powers. I shall consider this mask in more detail later and compare it to a similarly sacred mask from Noh theatre, called *Okina,* to which it bears a striking resemblance (see Figure 8).

---

[59] Interview, 5 April, 1997 translated by Anak Agung Gede Dwiputra. Emigh, 1996, posits some interesting connections between the legend of *Brahmana Kling* and perceived parallels in iconography and masked performance in Bali and Orissa, a province of eastern India (pp. 74–99).

[60] Of all, Dunn gives the most thoroughgoing account of *Sidha Karya,* his possible identities and symbolic significance. See pp. 71–80.

It is interesting to note that in Topeng drama the most 'important' masked characters are either silent or speak in Kawi,[61] a language incomprehensible to virtually all of the audience. In these cases it is really the mask itself that communicates all of the essential information about the character and it is the movement of the mask that 'tells' the story. These characters represent the past, the deified ancestors who are believed to be invisibly present and observing the ceremony, thus the masks render these invisible spirits visible and tangible. The mask belongs to the language of signs and the mask drama is a series of signs that communicate, not through written or spoken language, but directly via vision to thought. The viewer reads the mask and the gesture so that the text becomes secondary, perhaps completely unimportant. Even in Noh, which is, admittedly, a highly developed literary form, the text (also in archaic language) is less narrative than aesthetic, since it is sung or chanted at an unnaturally slow pace that is not readily comprehensible. Thus, the real 'meat' of the play is communicated by gesture, costume and, most importantly, the mask.

Calonarang

This has become a generic title for a number of broadly exorcistic plays in which the apotropaic figures of Rangda and Barong (Figures 9 and 10) are pitted against one another. Belo gives an accurate, if somewhat light-hearted, impression of how these plays work:

> The battle is enacted and re-enacted. No one ever wins. What happens is that dozens of villagers, aroused by the excitement held incarnate in these two figures and by the stylized interplay between them, go into trance, go through patterned behaviour in a somnambulistic state, attack the Witch with their krisses, are revived by the Barong, attack their own chests with their krisses,

---

[61] Kawi is a "literary language, old Javanese, based upon Sanskrit, that evolved in South India and was transmitted to Java; many sacred Balinese *lontars* are written in Kawi, which is unintelligible to the average person and must be interpreted; the heroes and heroines of the epic poems speak in Kawi", Eiseman, 1997a, p.K-10.

and preferably work themselves to a climax, a true convulsive seizure of hysterical order. After such a performance everyone goes home feeling perfectly great and at peace with the world.[62]

Dramatic versions of the story differ from village to village and even from temple to temple but at least one story upon which it is based may have some basis in historical fact, since the central character is believed to be the widow of a Balinese king:

> At the beginning of the second millennium AD . . . a Balinese Hindu prince named Airlangga ruled (from 1011–1049 AD) over both his native island and eastern Java. . . . Intriguingly, the entire story of the widow-witch shadows and parallels the history of Airlangga's mother, Mahendradatta—a Javanese princess . . . who married the Balinese prince, Udayana, and who seems to have been a worshipper of Durga...left with an unmarriageable daughter after she becomes a widow (the literal meaning of 'rangda'), she carries on a war of black magic against her son's kingdom.[63]

A full version of this drama generally begins with a group of young women (including the 'unmarriageable' daughter), who are acolytes of the witch, practising their black rites. The witch appears and sends them to spread pestilence throughout the land. Scenes follow in which one or more of the acolytes, now transformed into *Leyak* (see Figure 11),[64] are seen in the cemetery digging up or even eating corpses (sometimes a straw mannequin representing an infant). A horrifying but often comic scene follows in which a funeral procession, lamenting the misery of the epidemics, brings a dead body to the cemetery. After a good deal of scatological by-play, the members of the funeral party are frightened away

---

[62] Belo, 1949, p. 12.

[63] Emigh, 1996 pp. 79–81. See also Belo 1949, p. 18.

[64] Purveyors of magic who have the power to transform themselves into spirits or demons.

by the *Leyak*. Next, an emissary of the King appears with his attendants (they are equivalent to the two *Penasar* in Topeng) and he challenges the witch to appear. In some versions, this emissary is a *Patih*, or prime minister, but in others he is a powerful priest. According to Belo, a published version of the play in Dutch, *De Calon Arang,* apparently based upon an ancient *lontar,* identifies this character as "Mpu Bharada, the holy man... advisor to Erlangga [Airlangga] and the champion of right who matches his supernatural powers against those of Rangda".[65] The widow-witch, initially presented as a human character, transforms herself into the demon, Rangda, and the priest (Mpu Bharada) becomes Barong. The confrontation is not resolved in the defeat of Rangda, however. Followers of Barong may appear and, when they attempt to attack Rangda with their *kris*, some or all may fall into trance and turn the knives on themselves. The blades cannot penetrate their flesh, however violent their efforts and, protected by the power of Barong or Rangda, injuries almost never occur.[66] The Barong then appears, accompanied by the village priest (*pemangku*), and the entranced are revived with holy water and a touch of Barong's beard. In versions of the story performed for tourists, the graveyard scene is usually much foreshortened; there is sometimes a confrontation between the King's emissary and the witch in human form before she transforms into Rangda and, at the end, Barong will appear to drive Rangda away. When performed in a ceremonial context, however, the conclusion is rather more ambivalent; Rangda may turn away Barong's *kris*-wielding followers, who then turn the knives on themselves while she leaves the stage unscathed. Sometimes Barong will not even appear. Often, having defeated the king's emissary, Rangda dances for a time around the stage, shouting challenges to the audience and any practitioners of black magic who may be present (in physical form or in spirit) and then, sometimes in a frenzy, she runs to the cemetery where

---

[65] Belo, 1949, p. 30.

[66] Should there be an injury it usually ascribed to some ritual impurity on the part of the injured party. For a detailed account of one such incident, see Jane Belo, *Trance in Bali* (New York: Columbia University Press, 1960) pp. 124–179.

a special ceremony is performed. When Rangda returns to the temple, she may remain in trance for minutes or hours, speaking to the priests and the people until the mask is removed and the wearer revived with holy water.

To imagine that the angry widow-witch Rangda is simply a theatrical version of an historical character is to vastly underestimate the power and significance of this figure, because both Rangda and Barong are manifestations of the creative and destructive aspects of the gods. Many sources claim that the Barong mask represents an incarnation of the god Siwa and that Rangda represents his consort, Uma Dewi, in her furious manifestation as Durga.[67] There appear to be two different but not necessarily contradictory interpretations regarding the relationship between these characters. On the one hand in Bali "male and female together, as an entity, is the idea which runs through the whole culture"[68] so Barong and Rangda, although different, may be seen to represent two aspects of a single entity. The idea of the unity of god and consort (his female aspect) is a concept consistent with mainstream Hindu belief. On the other hand, Belo suggests "a possibility . . . that the masked figure of the Rangda was elaborated out of the Durga worship belonging to the Sivaite tradition, while that of the Barong developed in a parallel line from some form of the Buddhist worship".[69] As with some of the origin stories of Sidha Karya it appears to have been particularly important at some stage in Balinese history that these figures represent a unification or peaceful coexistence of the two philosophies. Evidence of Barong-like lion masks in the Buddhist cultures of China and Japan seems to lend some weight to the argument for a Buddhist connection.[70]

---

[67] Interviews with Dr. I Wayan Dibia (11 March, 1997) and Ida Bagus Alit (6 April, 1998). Sometimes, however, Barong may represent a local god who may or may not be associated with Siwa. The Barong in Jimbaran, for example is known locally as '*Dewa Ayu*' see Eiseman, 1990a, pp. 292–321. See also Belo 1949, pp. 18–39 regarding the identities of these masks.

[68] Belo 1949, p. 16.

[69] *Ibid.*, p. 32.

[70] The lion mask dance (Shi-Shi Mai) of Japan is particularly striking in its similarity to Barong, both in the features of the mask and aspects of choreography. Versions of the Shi-Shi mask are

Tenget

'*Tenget*' is defined by Bandem and de Boer as 'sacral power',[71] by Lansing as 'magically dangerous'[72] and by Eiseman as "having the ability to influence humans in a supernatural way; supernaturally powerful, mysterious, scary".[73] This is the power that is invested in sacred masks. So great is the power of some Rangda and Barong masks that, in connection with temple rituals and sometimes even in completely secular circumstances, the entire performance may seem to simply fall apart as a result of the havoc unleashed by the supernatural forces held within them. For example, the King's emissary may fall into trance as he approaches Rangda with his kris and will have to be carried away to the inner precincts of the temple to be revived. The wearer of the Rangda mask may also be debilitated by trance and require the assistance of temple priests. When the Barong appears, those who animate this mask, too, may fall into trance and have to be replaced.[74] The followers of the Barong, unmasked men who are not 'dancers' (that is, not trained performers), rush to attack Rangda with their daggers but fall to the ground insensate or in convulsions when she waves her magic cloth at them and then, in frustration, turn the daggers on themselves. To an outside observer it frequently appears that the demonic, apparently 'bad' character, Rangda, is the 'winner'. It must be remembered, however, that the Balinese moral universe requires not the defeat of apparent 'evil', but, rather, a balance of supernatural forces. The figures of Rangda and Barong, although fierce representations of dangerous power, are both seen as protective and their confrontation is staged in order to cleanse the community. Emigh observes:

---

used in both Noh and Kabuki. Belo, 1949, speculates a connection between Barong and the "Chinese dragon . . . who runs around town at New Year's time and clears space of evil influence" (p. 33). Interestingly she too notes a possible connection between the "mask dragon . . . called ChiChi Mai" [sic] and Barong.

[71] p. 175.

[72] Lansing 1995, p. 136.

[73] 1997a, p. T-10.

[74] Descriptions of such incidents may be found in de Zoete and Spies; Belo 1949; Bandem and de Boer; Lansing 1995 and Emigh 1996.

> More often than not, when these sacred masks are grafted onto a play they manifest a strength too explosive for the fictive world to bear. This is quite acceptable to Balinese audiences. A story may work its way to its own conclusion, or it may yield to ritual procedures needed to contain forces far too powerful to be dealt with by ordinary theatrical means. The resulting pandemonium is deemed both theatrically exciting and ritually effective.[75]

The power of these figures resides in the masks themselves and these are venerated as gods, kept in special areas of the temple, displayed on ritually appropriate days and used as conduits for the gods' instructions when consultation is deemed necessary. Frequently, Barong and Rangda masks from one temple will be taken to 'visit' their 'relatives' (other Rangda or Barong masks made of wood from the same tree) in another temple accompanied by the entire congregation. A ceremony such as the *Pengrebongan* (held every 210 days at Kesiman on the outskirts of Denpasar) is particularly striking. At least a dozen Rangda masks and nearly as many Barongs are brought together and, after a period of preparation in the inner precincts of the temple, are paraded around the outer courtyard in a massive procession. Most of those wearing the masks are in trance and they are accompanied by other trancers (many of whom engage in self-stabbing) as well as village priests and assistants who, when activity becomes particularly frenzied, sprinkle the participants with holy water to calm them. It is an extraordinary sight. During the procession (which lasts for about two hours) some of the hundreds who are watching also become entranced and join the procession. Finally, all are taken into the inner courtyard of the temple where the masks are at last removed and put on display while the trancers are revived.[76]

---

[75] Emigh, 1996, p. 66.

[76] For a detailed description see de Zoete and Spies, pp. 267–268.

The mask that is *tenget* is powerful in itself and can provoke trance behaviour whether or not it is animated. Barong, Rangda and Sidha Karya masks, all of which represent gods, are especially sacred in this regard. The persons who wear these masks must themselves be spiritually powerful *(sakti)* in order to cope with these dangerous supernatural forces.

The Mask Making Process

The power of these masks begins to be accrued even before they have been carved because the wood for sacred masks, like Rangda, Barong and Sidha Karya, must be acquired from particular trees growing in spiritually significant locations, for example a cemetery, cross-roads, or within the precincts of a temple. *Kayu Pulé*[77] is the wood used to create these masks; it is light in colour and weight and relatively soft for carving purposes. These practical considerations are, however, of secondary importance to the Balinese. *Kayu Pulé* is essential for making sacred masks because the tree is said to have been created from a drop of semen from the god Siwa who is, ultimately, the force represented by all of these characters. The story runs like this: Siwa, wishing to test the fidelity of his wife, Uma Dewi, feigned illness and said he could only be restored to health by drinking cow's milk acquired through ordinary rather than devious or supernatural means. Uma Dewi went to earth in search of this curative elixir and found a herd of cattle tended by a young man who, unknown to her, was Siwa in disguise. He said that he would only allow her to take the milk if she submitted to his amorous desires. At first she refused but, when she realised that this was the only means by which she could acquire the milk, she relented. Returning to heaven, she gave the milk

---

[77] "*Alstonia scholaris (Apocynaceae)*; white cheese wood, milky pine; medium to large tree that has fairly hard, strong wood of low density; used widely to make masks...bark has a very bitter alkaloid that is used in making traditional medicines." Eiseman, 1997a, p. P-27. The milky, latex-like sap, known as *rasa* in Sanskrit, means, literally flavour, sensation or taste but carries with it an association with lifeblood, elixir of life essence. Knappert defines it as "Sap of a tree, essence, distilled liquor, also a symbolism for honey, mead, *soma, amrita,* milk, rain and even sperm. It is the liquid which contains the vital energy, the essence of life by which all creatures are born and grow up." Knappert, p. 207.

to Siwa who immediately recovered. Saying he wished to discover how Uma Dewi had come by his cure, *Siwa* called on his son, Bhatara Guna, who had the gift of *unung,* being able to 'see the unseen'. When he revealed her infidelity and Siwa's complicity in the event, Uma Dewi's anger transformed her into Panca Durga—Durga of the five forms, who could be in many places at once. She then descended to earth and began to cause all manner of problems. Siwa, wishing to make it up with his wife, asked her to meet him at a crossroads at midnight. She was there, but he was late and her anger transformed her once again into Rangda. When *Siwa* finally arrived, full of desire, he was disappointed to find the horrific Rangda in place of his beautiful Uma Dewi, and his sperm fell to the ground. Since the sperm of Siwa must engender life and cannot be destroyed, Siwa laid a curse upon this drop of sperm so that, rather than becoming a human being, it became *Kayu Pulé,* forever after emblematic of the failure of love between Siwa and Durga.[78] Thus, the wood holds within it a magical potential for both the creative and destructive capabilities of Siwa/Durga. Masks carved from this sacred and powerful wood must retain something of the essence of Siwa/Durga, and the characters depicted must therefore possess aspects of this mystical life force. All Topeng masks are made from *Pulé* wood, including those which are less sacred but nonetheless significant, depicting historical figures (who are also deified ancestors) or archetypal characters. Although in these cases it is not so important for the wood to have been acquired from a significant location, all must possess this magical potential. This is perhaps why a piece of wood, carved with a fixed expression, can seem to be alive when animated by the actor-dancer.

Ritual Preparations

Once a tree has been selected, an auspicious day must be determined on which the wood may be cut. (The Balinese calendar, which incorporates an enormous

---

[78] Interview with I B Alit 6 April, 1998. This is similar to a number of stories related to the origins of the Rangda and Barong masks which refer to the amorous interactions of *Siwa* and *Uma Dewi* and her transformation into the angry and vengeful *Durga* or Rangda. See de Zoete and Spies, pp. 105–109, also Eiseman, 1990a, pp. 315–321.

amount of information regarding all of the relevant calendrical systems, lists the days in each month which are auspicious for various tasks such as cutting wood, beginning study, building temples or kitchens, even for making beer.) Before the wood is cut, in all cases certain ceremonies must be performed:

> Two offerings are made, one to the god of the place where the tree grows...and the second to the spirit of the tree. If the tree is especially *tenget,* or filled with divine natural energy, the process is perilous, particularly for the priest.[79]

A small offering, suitable for ordinary Topeng masks, would consist of an egg, a young coconut, some cooked rice and a *canang*.[80] The large offering required for a very sacred mask like Rangda or Barong (called *sorohang*[81]) might consist of four eggs, four young coconuts, four kilos of rice and a small chicken.[82] The wood is cut from a living tree and some of those growing in temple precincts are large enough to remain essentially undamaged by the removal of a section of 25 centimetres by 50 centimetres, which is about the size required for a Barong mask. According to some sources,[83] the green wood is soaked in water and must then be allowed to dry for several months before the carver can begin his work, but this has not been my experience. Among the carvers with whom I have worked[84] the wood is often used within days of having been cut, because when the wood is still 'wet' it is easier to carve, more resilient and more responsive. It is

---

[79] Judy Slattum, *Masks of Bali: Spirits of an Ancient Drama* (San Francisco: Chronicle Books, 1993), p. 124.

[80] "common type of small offering in the shape of a square or round tray made of immature coconut leaf; it contains various flowers below a topping of kembang rampé (shredded pandandus leaf), slices of fruit such as banana and sugar cane, and tiny bits of the ingredients of the betel chew." Eiseman, 1997a, p. C-2.

[81] "Complete set of offerings for a particular ceremony." *Ibid.*, p. S-22.

[82] Interview with Ida Bagus Alit, 6 April, 1998. Like everything else in Bali, the components of the offering are likely to vary somewhat depending upon local practice.

[83] See Slattum, pp. 124–125.

[84] Anak Agung Gede Ngurah and Ida Bagus Alit of Lodtunduh village in Gianyar.

significant that the wood is cut from a living tree in which the essential life force, *rasa*, still flows. Moreover, the sticky, latex-like white sap of the Pulé tree resembles semen, perhaps the most significant manifestation of *rasa*.

> *Rasa,* feeling, is the essence of everything, the embryo of the waters that is also the source of individual sensation. As the great permeator of all things *rasa* is not only the vital sap of plants, semen, *madhu* [honey], and so on; its essential character is so powerful that all important symbolic complexes in one way or another relate to it. ...*Pulé* is one of the sacred trees that, because of its milky sap, has extraordinary *rasa;* it possesses so much of this powerful life force that it may, as may other milky trees in both Bali and India, become the residence of a demonic spirit.[85]

The *rasa* of the tree, therefore, imbues the mask with life and the animated mask brings to life the gods and deified ancestors whom the masks represent. As if to emphasise this point, wood that has been soaked in water often takes on an unpleasant, rotten smell, but *Pulé* wood which is wet from the sap smells sweet and fresh. The most important practical reason for curing the wood is to ensure it is not afflicted with destructive insects. However, it is the belief of some carvers that if the proper ceremony is held prior to cutting the tree, no insects will be present because 'the god will make it perfect'.[86] Another consideration may be that, in Bali's tropical climate, insects are likely to invade newly cut wood unless it can be stored off the ground and away from vegetation.

Before carving begins (on an auspicious day of course) more offerings must be made:

> one to Bhatara Surya, the Sun God as witness of the work, and one to *Taksu*, the spirit of inspiration or 'talent,' asking a blessing for

---

[85] Napier, pp. 207, 210.
[86] Ida Bagus Alit, 18/4/98.

success. Holy water is sprinkled on the wood and the carver's instruments, and the carving process, the same for both sacred and tourist masks, begins.[87]

The carver must be both physically and spiritually 'clean' before embarking on a holy mask and this entails meditation, bathing and fasting[88] as well as dressing in a newly clean *kamben* (waistcloth)[89] and the ceremonial *udeng* headdress for the work.[90] Some carvers choose to work only in the household temple when making sacred masks, both for inspiration and for protection, since creating a sacred mask means putting oneself at risk from the magic of any number of spirits both benign and dangerous.[91]

Carving

The work of carving a Topeng mask might be completed in a day or two with several hours of concentrated effort, though it is more usual to take three or four days. The larger, sacred masks of Rangda or Barong take longer, perhaps a month or more. Balinese carvers use a variety of different sized chisels *(pahat)*, both flat and curved, to create the general shape and later, using some of the tiniest of these, to pick out the ornate detail of intricate crowns and hair decorations. Fine shaping is done with *mutik* knives and curved *pangot* tools (see Figure 12). The carver works seated on a woven palm mat on the floor of an open *balé* (a raised pavilion), holding the mask with his feet. With a hand-axe and large chisels he

---

[87] Slattum, p. 125.

[88] The level of fasting depends very much upon the individual. Ida Bagus Alit, who likes his food, explained that an appropriate fast would disallow pork, chicken or beef but would allow duck or fish. According to Alit, the fast should continue for forty-two days.

[89] Balinese waistcloth, standard dress for men and women, Eiseman, 1990a, p. 355.

[90] *Sarong* and *udeng* (*dastar* in high Balinese) are part of *pakaian adat*, the customary dress worn for temple ceremonies.

[91] Carver Ida Bagus Oka, of Mas, said that when he makes a Rangda mask he must work every day in the family temple until the mask is finished. He often feels compelled to work obsessively for hours without stopping and often finds that the mask invades his dreams. If a mask is brought to him for repair or repainting, he must make offerings daily. (Interview, 14 April, 1997).

roughs out the features, giving them more refined shape with the knives (Figure 13). Once the basic size and shape of the face have been established, he will begin to hollow out the back, leaving it rather thick at first to allow for problems and mistakes. Gradually the shape is refined and the back of the mask is hollowed out further to accommodate the actor's features. If a mask is being created for a particular actor, he may have a 'fitting' to ensure that the mask is properly proportioned for his own face. Teeth, made of mother-of-pearl for the Dalem mask or (occasionally) of boar's teeth for Sidha Karya or King Bedahulu,[92] are added to the mask when carving is completed.

Painting and Completion

The complex process of painting the mask varies depending upon the type of mask and its likely use. Today acrylic paints are commonly used for many masks, but sacred masks still require traditional paints made from natural substances:

> ground calcified pig jaw or deer bone must be used as a base. Colour comes from various sources: yellow from clay, black from carbon, gold from gold leaf, and red imported from China.[93]

A single mask may require hundreds of thin coats of paint which are finally sealed with clear acrylic or *ancur*, a glue-like substance made of 'milk and water

---

[92] The name means 'Different Head' and the legend tells of a Balinese king of such spiritual power (sakti) that his head would leave his body during meditation. "And while he sat in meditation his head mounted up to Svarga [heaven] leaving his body behind." One day the head stayed away so long that the King's servant "became anxious. And while he stood there in his perplexity a man came by carrying a pig...he bought the pig for fifty kepings and cut off its head and stuck it on the raja's body." When the king awoke from his meditation and saw his reflection "he wept bitterly and refused to return to Bedoeloe . . . At last [his servant] persuaded him, promising to build him a pavilion so high that no one should be able to see him from below. So the king always sat up aloft in his high pavilion, and if anyone looked up he shot an arrow and killed him." De Zoete and Spies, pp. 295–296. Emigh used this story as the basis for a contemporary Topeng play *The Pig-Headed King*, which toured in the Eastern United States in the 1970s. See Emigh 1996, pp. 257–259.

[93] Slattum, p. 126.

buffalo skin'[94] that must be dissolved in water. *Ancur* is also the adhesive component of traditional paints.

> Facial hair (usually goat's hair) is applied after painting, attached with tiny bamboo nails and at this point holes are made for a strap of string and rubber to hold the mask in place when worn. Ceremonial masks must then be purified in a ceremony called *pengambean*,[95] since the mask has been held by the mask maker's feet while being carved and the Balinese feel that this part of the body is spiritually unclean. Sacred Sidha Karya, Barong and Rangda masks must undergo a further ceremony in which they are invested with spiritual power.
>
> Ceremonies, held at night during the dark of the moon on a prescribed day, invite the deities to enter the mask. . . . If the ceremony is successful, around midnight when spiritual contact is made, the priest wears the mask and goes into trance, dancing or running about the graveyard, but is magically protected and unharmed. The graveyard is considered to be electrified by magic and very dangerous at this time. Those who are watching surround the Rangda or Barong. Capturing the priest, they make offerings to release him from the trance. Numerous Balinese have witnessed such a ceremony, after which the priest wraps the mask in a white cloth and places it in the temple. Now it belongs to the village and is their protector as long as rituals are followed to appease its spirit.[96]

---

[94] Eiseman, 1990b, p. 216. Eiseman gives a detailed description of the making of a sacred Sidha Karya mask by the master mask maker I Wayan Tangguh of Singapadu, pp. 207–219.

[95] "to clean up all the impurities and improper treatment and restore the mask, if not to sacredness, at least to a state where one could feel good about it." Eiseman, 1990b, p. 218.

[96] Slattum, p. 127. Although Slattum refers to this ceremony as *pasupati*, one of my informants (Ida Bagus Alit) draws a distinction between pasupati, the penultimate ceremony which makes

Barong and Rangda masks which are not intended for temple performances may not require this ceremony of dedication to the gods, but they will be brought together with their costumes in the course of another purification ritual, called *ngatep*,[97] which unites the face (mask) and body (costume).

Subsequently, the masks will be honoured by the mask maker or the dancer on various occasions such as full and new moon, *Kajeng Keliwon*[98] and, most particularly, on *Tumpek Wayang*, when all paraphernalia of theatrical performance are given special offerings. A Topeng performer will also make offerings and prayers for the masks before and after a performance.

Dance Training

Children in Bali see dance in temple ceremonies from infancy and are able to hum, whistle and sing the complex patterns of the gamelan from an early age. Dancing becomes part of children's play and it is startling to see how easily even very young Balinese children can follow complex dance movements with seemingly effortless skill.[99] In theory, anyone can begin training as a masked performer at any age. In practice, skills are often passed down through families and one is unlikely to see a Topeng performer under the age of ten.[100] Boys may join a children's Barong club *(Seka Barong)* from the age of five or six and can

---

a mask *tenget* (spiritually powerful) and the separate ceremony, *ngerehan*, dedicating the mask to the god. Slattum's description which she refers to as 'pasupati' is probably ngrerehan. A pasupati ceremony takes place in the temple 'where the mask lives' whether that is the Pura Desa, Pura Puseh or Pura Dalem. The ngerehan ceremony takes place in the cemetery. (Interview, 18 April, 1998).

[97] *Ibid.*, p. 126. "... ngatep: join, put close together, put something back together, as, for example, joining the Barong mask to the Barong or the rangda mask to its body." Eiseman, 1997a, p N-11.

[98] "... coincidence day between Kajeng, the third day of the Triwara (3-day week), and Keliwon, the fifth day of the Pancawara (5-day week); occurs every 15 days and is especially important for making offerings to butakala." Eiseman, 1997a, p. K-2.

[99] For some interesting photographic evidence of how dance movement is made a part of a Balinese child's life see Gregory Bateson and Margaret Mead, *Balinese Character: A Photographic Analysis*. (New York: New York Academy of Sciences, 1942) pp. 85–88.

[100] Dunn, pp. 87–88.

learn to manipulate a small version of the Barong outfit or dance in masks of the monkeys or demons who sometimes accompany Barong (see Figures 14–15).[101] One who wishes to become a dancer, if from a dancing family, "needs only express his desire to his father, uncle or cousin".[102] Otherwise he must seek out a teacher and, if he lives in another village, the student may become a member of the teacher's household during the period of study, returning home only occasionally for ceremonial obligations. The relationship between teacher and student in traditional training is not a commercial transaction and money rarely changes hands, but "symbolic debts accrue".[103] On the first visit to a teacher, the student will bring a gift of, perhaps, coffee and sugar, a few kilos of rice or some material for a *kamben* as a gesture of respect. Thereafter, if the student lives with his teacher, he will be given room and board and be expected to help with household chores.

Pedagogy

Earlier generations of dancers, like Dunn's chief informant I Ketut Rinda, began by learning the elements of *Gambuh*, an ancient, courtly dance drama based on the Prince Panji stories of the *Malat*.[104] However, young dancers today usually begin with the non-masked *Baris* (Warrior) dance, either in the form of *Baris Gedé*, (performed by a group of six to ten boys or men as a welcome to the gods during a temple ceremony), or solo *Baris*, a spectacularly virtuosic, non-narrative

---

[101] The 'goblin' mask shown in Figure 15 looks very much like one from *Wayang Wong*, perhaps the clown-servant figure of *Sangut*.

[102] *Ibid.*, p. 109.

[103] "A teacher could expect special support and aid from these families [of students] when circumstances arise that require help." *Ibid.*, p. 109.

[104] Dunn points out that the advantages for the Topeng performer learning from the Gambuh model include "a broad dramatic and dance base, as well as vocal and linguistic familiarity with epic literature." At the time of her writing, Gambuh seemed to be dying out, but it is now undergoing something of a revival due to the efforts of the Society for the Preservation of the Ancient Dance in Bali and the staff of STSI (now ISI) (Sekolah Tinggi Seni Indonesia), the university-level performing arts academy in Denpasar. For additional information on this genre, see Bandem and de Boer, pp. 27–43; de Zoete and Spies, pp. 134–142; Racki, pp. 50–54.

dance which displays the skill and bravery of a medieval Balinese warrior. [105] Children may also begin training with *Jauk,* a masked dance of a rather benign demon sometimes associated with Barong and Rangda (see Figures 16a and b). The movement vocabulary of the dance is similar in style to *Baris* but also includes some comic improvisation.[106]

As well as learning dance movement, an important part of a student's education is assisting his teacher in performances, carrying the baskets of masks and costumes, helping with costume changes and assisting in the rituals. The lessons themselves are hardly private; other members of the household or visitors may watch and other children, not yet students, may observe and imitate. Because of this the student quickly learns to maintain concentration and ignore any distractions.

Training is entirely practical rather than theoretical, exemplary and physical rather than verbal. Choreography and characterisation are demonstrated by the teacher and copied by the student. Corrections are made physically rather than verbally and, in the early stages, a teacher may dance behind the student manipulating head, arms, hands, body and feet into the correct positions while 'singing' the tune or rhythms of the gamelan accompaniment. There is certainly no discussion of concept, interpretation or matters of psychology. Choreography, style, and meaning are communicated almost subconsciously:

---

[105] See Dunn, pp. 112–113. There are a number of dances for girls as well, including the well-known Legong Kraton in which young girls dance both male and female roles. Although there is no specific prohibition, female Topeng performers are very rare and female Barong dancers are virtually unknown. Rucina Ballinger, an American trained in Topeng, has been told by Balinese performers that "women are not strong enough" for Topeng or Barong. It is also extremely rare for a woman to play the part of Rangda. A story is told in Bali that a daughter of former president Sukarno who had studied Balinese dance was to play Rangda in conjunction with a festival of Indonesian Arts in Europe in 1963, but before she could perform she became seriously ill. This is still used as 'evidence' of the danger for women who seek to wear the Rangda mask (interview with Rucina Ballinger, 22 April, 1997).

[106] See Young, p. 85; Bandem and de Boer, pp. 106–107; de Zoete and Spies, pp. 174–177; also Eiseman, 1990a, pp. 296–297, on Omang and Jauk characters who appear in the Jimbaran Rangda-Barong confrontation.

> After many hours of the teacher's manipulations, the movements are said to have 'entered' the student. The Balinese word for this is *ngaresep,* meaning 'understood' in both a mental and kinetic sense, *i.e.,* the mind as well as the body has fully grasped the form. . . . Thus, dance is learned first by imitation of the teacher's movements and then by the manipulation of limbs. Both of these methods apply even to accomplished dancers. . . . During a dance lesson, the child is thoroughly engrossed in learning. The face registers no emotion. . . . The teacher transmits the 'mask-like' quality of classical Balinese dance by executing it himself. . . . The child remains receptive to the required mood by subduing any personal feelings.[107]

This non-verbal, physical method of training is an important aspect of the performer's development and means that, from the outset, the Balinese performer is dissociated from his 'personal feelings' and led to express a form which is exterior. Dancers in training are manipulated like puppets and seem utterly 'ego-less', a quality that Belo referred to as 'the puppet complex'.[108] The masked performer in particular may be seen as both puppet and puppeteer, animating an exterior form that he also inhabits. Self-expression, motive and psychology are unimportant, whereas technical skill and physical understanding are essential. This non-analytical self-abnegation leads to the apparently detached, objective style of playing that so enchanted Artaud.

---

[107] Rucina Ballinger, 'Dance in Bali: The Passing on of a Tradition' in *Dance as a Cultural Heritage,* Vol. 2, edited by Betty True Jones. Selected Papers from the ADG-CORD Conference 1978 (New York: Congress on Research in Dance, 1985) p. 251–252.

[108] "It was not only in Java, but in Bali also, that the dancers themselves were trained to resemble puppets. In Bali the puppetlike mimicry was less strictly carried out, but the stylised gesture, the expressionless face of the traditional dance, the complete lack of a personal quality in the performance of the serious roles were there all the same. The effect was enhanced when, as in many theatrical forms the actors wore masks. . . . The puppet complex, then, could be summed up thus: A puppet is that which represents a spirit. Plays are originally representations of non-

The level of concentration, even in very young performers, is impressive but the circumstances of performance make such disciplined focus absolutely essential. Dogs, chickens, unruly children and religious processions can and do invade the performance space as a matter of course, but the Balinese performer must continue undeterred. In order to achieve this, the choreography must be completely assimilated so that it can be performed without conscious thought. The masked performer has several tasks: his body must be at one with the music *(kawinan dengen musik* or 'married with the music'); he must bring the mask to life *(menghidupkan topeng);* he must perform precisely within the prescribed style for the mask *(halus, manis* or *keras*—refined, sweet or strong); and he must be alive to any potential hazards or opportunities for comic play within the performance space. In speaking parts he must also impart the story clearly while keeping the interest of the audience—not an easy job in the noisy, busy atmosphere of a temple ceremony.

Ritual Requirements

Not surprisingly, just as there are rituals for the preparation and dedication of materials used in Balinese dance drama, the performers, too, must fulfil certain ritual obligations. An aspiring performer may have already consulted the gods regarding his vocation before beginning training. As he approaches his first performance, more formal gestures may be made:

> Another ceremony, *ngundung taksu*, 'inviting the ancestors' or 'inviting the spirit of the dance,' is done on the day of the first performance. The student brings a gift (such as a pair of gilded temple umbrellas) for the temple, along with offerings, which are blessed by the *pemangku* or village priest. The pupil prays to

---

human spirits. By dramatic connotation, actors and dancers are like puppets, for they behave in accordance with a spirit which is not their own." Belo, 1960, p. 12.

Dewa Pregina (the deity of the dance) requesting guidance and blessings.[109]

Masked performers, particularly those who animate the ritually significant masks of Sidha Karya, Rangda and Barong, must complete a special ceremony of purification "to protect them from error and from the power of the masks".[110] The ceremony, called *mawinten,* varies according to local practice with regard to the number of times and the particular places where it must be performed; however, in all cases it must be held on an auspicious day and presided over by a *pedanda*.[111] One informant described a *mawinten gedé* ('great *mawinten*') ceremony:

> **Nyoman Catra**: "All of the family members who take the ceremony stay in the temple for three days, wearing white clothes. Sleep, eat, study in the temple. Every day we have to take bath, the total I think for three days is eleven times of *pancoran* [bathing in holy spring water]. . . . Every day we are holding the incense and we cannot drop it down until the incense is finished. Several ceremonies we have to do" [sic].[112]

Mawinten requires discipline and a high degree of spiritual purity, so some actors will not perform with these more significant masks until they feel they are prepared for the restrictions that they impose.[113] Unmarried performers, for

---

[109] Ballinger, p. 252.

[110] Dunn, p. 116. According to one of my informants, anyone who uses the sacred *Kawi* language, including Arja performers and those who read aloud the *Kawi* epics, must undergo this purification ceremony.

[111] For some dancers the ceremony involves spending the night in meditation in the temple, other practice requires that it be performed in the dancer's home and the house temples of both Buddhist and Sivite high priests. Interviews with I Made Djimat, Ida Bagus Anom, I Made Bandem; see also Dunn, pp. 116–117.

[112] Interview with I Nyoman Catra, 24 March, 1997.

[113] Dunn cites Bandem "that after *mawinten*, one shouldn't walk under a sleeping place, or under a clothes line, or ever be guilty of using abusive language to another person" (p. 128). Ida Bagus Alit indicated that a performer of *Topeng Pajegan* (who is required submit to the *mawinten*

example, may wait until after they have 'settled down' before submitting to *mawinten*. If necessary, the ceremony can be repeated, according to Bandem, if the performer "believes that his purity has been disturbed".[114]

Offerings are made before and after any performance as a matter of course "to please the gods, ward off rain, and insure the general 'welfare' of the performance".[115] All performers, costumes and equipment (the gamelan, for example) will be ritually purified with incense and holy water before the performance. In the case of masked performers, a document called *Dharma Petopengan* contains information regarding the mantras and offerings required of them. Significantly, most Topeng performers perform a ritual and recite mantras for opening and closing the basket of masks.[116] The opening mantras call upon spirits of the ancestors and the god of *Taksu* to enter the masks and the body of the performer and the closing mantras bid the spirits "to return to their heavenly homes".[117] Clearly the use of such mantras implies a notion of visitation or mediumship associated with Topeng performance. Dunn points out that "these particular mantras are directly related to the basket of masks, implying that the masks themselves might be the vessels for these spirits during a performance".[118] Indeed, one of Young's informants "could tell when the god came into his body

---

ceremony) must fast and abstain from sex before a performance. I Made Djimat's son who is unmarried, in his early twenties but already an accomplished Topeng performer, told me that he has not undergone the ceremony because he feels that he is 'not ready', and *belum bersih*–not yet clean. Thus he does not perform *Sidha Karya*.

[114] Dunn, p. 116.

[115] Young, p. 90. There are several types of pre- and post-performance offerings which vary in size depending upon the circumstances of performance; see Young, pp. 91–92 for details regarding names and contents of these offerings.

[116] The content of these mantras may differ from performer to performer but are, according to Zurbuchen: "clearly similar to the formulas and invocations used by other ritual practitioners in Bali. They are partially composed of Sanskrit and Sanskrit-like elements.... They make use of power syllables *(modre bijaksara)* such as *ang, ung, mang,* and close with familiar incantory phrases such as *poma, poma, poma.*" Zurbuchen, p. 191. *Poma, poma, poma* means 'let it be so'.

[117] Dunn, p. 119.

[118] *Ibid.*

because he would feel cold and get goose bumps".[119] The questions which then arise are: to what extent might the Balinese masked performer be 'possessed' by the spirits of the masks, and what might this indicate about the performance states observable in Balinese masked performance?

Taksu

> *To explain what is taksu . . . What's taksu? Many definition of that—many people try to describe but they all have different explanations because everyone has different feelings, different experiences. And how to get taksu, nobody can explain it. Sometimes you get it, sometimes you don't.* [sic][120]

Often translated simply as 'charisma', the complex concept of *Taksu* is central to understanding Balinese attitudes regarding performance yet, as the comment above indicates, it is a concept which is difficult to pin down. Various scholars have wrestled with the problem; Bandem and de Boer call it 'magical power, inspiration',[121] Eiseman says that "it can be taken as the spirit of one's profession or talent".[122] Elizabeth Young goes further:

> *Taksu* is a kind of power or inspiration, which is derived from the divine presence, and radiates from within. If a performer has *taksu*, what he says, how he acts, what he does, is funny and compelling for the audience. He is inspired beyond his own mundane capabilities to perform in such a way that he will be exceptionally good, pleasing for the gods and the audience. He is powerful and

---

[119] Young, p. 91.

[120] Ida Bagus Anom, interview, 14 April, 1997.

[121] Bandem and de Boer, p. 175.

[122] Eiseman, 1997a, p T-2.

> compelling because his artistry has divine inspiration, not because
> he has performed out of some sense of grim duty to his god.[123]

By this definition, the performer's inspiration comes from the gods and it provides him with a charismatic power beyond that of the individual performer. More than just magical inspiration, it is palpably connected to the gods who, it would seem, empower the performer to enthral the audience. Ana Daniel, in a reminiscence about her time training as a Topeng dancer in Bali, gives a more poetic definition which indicates the performer's own participation in the process:

> A special state of receptivity to the mysterious powers of the gods who will manifest in some form during ritual performance; the place where light, spirit, life enter; a beneficent spirit that can be controlled.[124]

Here, in addition to talent augmented by 'divine inspiration', *taksu* also requires 'a special state of receptivity' on the part of the performer. It is also 'a beneficent spirit', implying again that some force outside the performer acts upon or in conjunction with him. In this regard it is important to note that the term '*taksu*' also refers to an important shrine in the family temple:

> where one's family ancestors are invited to alight on special holidays, to receive prayers and offerings from their descendants . . . As soon as someone begins to learn a particular art form they make offerings and ask for help at their *taksu* shrine[125]

So, although *taksu* refers to a performer's talent or charisma, there is also an association with ancestral spirits who are contacted through the *taksu* shrine. There is not a direct connection between the ancestors venerated at the *taksu* shrine and the *taksu* of the performer, but there exists some sort of association,

---

[123] Young, p. 79.

[124] Ana Daniel, *Bali Behind the Mask* (New York: Alfred A. Knopf, 1981) p. 165.

[125] Lansing 1995, p. 57.

most particularly in the case of masked performers who must call upon the deified ancestors to manifest themselves when the box of masks is opened.[126] Bearing in mind that the masks themselves are idealised portraits of some of the most significant of these deified ancestors, it is entirely possible that *taksu*, for the masked performer, may carry with it connotations of visitation or mediumship. In any case, *taksu* is clearly beyond mere individual charisma, stage 'presence' or 'star quality;' rather it seems to negate the individual, who becomes instead the vehicle for a greater power. Lansing explains:

> For us, artistic creations are often regarded as expressions of our 'deepest' selves, and their permanence is connected to our ideas about immortality. In Bali, it seems that immortality belongs to the *taksu*, and one's individual 'self' at any given moment is not regarded as an 'author' who spontaneously creates something completely new. To further complicate the picture, the verbal form of the word *taksu* is one of the terms used to describe going into trance possession.[127]

This suggests that achieving *taksu* might be something akin to being 'possessed' by the character. Several informants mentioned this sensation in connection with *taksu*:

> **Ida Bagus Anom**: "When you have *taksu* you don't know on the stage. It just comes and you are another person on the stage. When you finish dancing, to be yourself—because on the stage it's not you, you're another person—that's a difficulty."[128]
>
> **Ida Bagus Alit**: "It's as if you are possessed by a spirit, sometimes we forget what we have done, you have forgotten what you have

---

[126] Interview with Ida Bagus Alit, 5 April, 1997.

[127] Lansing 1995, p. 59.

[128] Interview, Ida Bagus Anom, 14 April, 1997.

said, you have forgotten where you have moved your hand. It's like being led, the movement of your fingers or your eyes or your head."[129]

Madé Bandem: "Oh yes, it's ecstasy. *Taksu* is on the level of unconsciousness."[130]

Yet this sensation is clearly distinct from the sort of convulsive trance-possession experience of, for example, those who engage in self-stabbing. Indeed, all of my informants vigorously denied that this heightened performance state was in any way equivalent or even similar to trance as understood in Balinese culture. Jane Belo, in her study of *Trance in Bali* had similar findings. She had filmed performances of the Rangda and Barong dances in 1931 and again in 1934 and, in the course of her analysis of the trance episodes, she questioned how much was genuine trance and how much was 'acting'. An interesting description is given of the trancer I Rena who also performed the comic role of a trance *balian* in the Calonarang play:

> There was not the least confusion in his mind between real trance and the one he put on in the play. One day when I was questioning him about his part and he thought I had misunderstood the significance of it, he said "But *that's* not going in trance, that's *acting!*"

The fine artistry of Rena's dramatic performances and the fact that, although not in very good health, he was able to sustain his scenes over an extended time place him in the front rank as an actor. His case constitutes some of the strongest evidence we have that the tendency to disassociation goes hand in hand with acting

---

[129] Interview, Ida Bagus Alit, 5 April, 1997.

[130] Interview, Dr. I Made Bandem, 30 April, 1997.

ability and that a predisposition to the one may include a predisposition to the other.[131]

This recognition of the heightened performance state as a form of dissociation distinct from trance possession is significant. Psychophysiological evidence which casts light on the nature and reasons for this state will be covered in greater depth in a later chapter. For the time being it is worth noting that indications of *taksu* correspond with indications of dissociation including a dislocated sense of time and an inability to remember details of the performance.

If *taksu* is not trance possession, in what way can it be associated with notions of visitation? As has been indicated earlier, the Rangda and Barong masks are certainly felt to be 'inhabited' by the gods in certain circumstances when the wearers of these masks, in a state of trance, act as spokespersons for the gods. In other circumstances, for example the Calonarang drama enacted for a temple festival or a tourist performance, the wearers of these masks strive for and may achieve *taksu*, still representing the god although not in trance-possession.[132] In the case of the Topeng performer, animation of the masks may also be seen as mediumship of a kind. Young states unequivocally that:

> The gods may also descend into the body of human beings. In order to prepare an appropriate space for the gods, men must purify themselves. When a Topeng performer makes ritual purifications, and presents offerings before a performance, it is an

---

[131] Belo, 1960, p. 108.

[132] Interviews with I Nyoman Catra 24 March, 1997 and I Wayan Dibia 11 March, 1997. Both performers spoke of the 'special feeling, good feeling' when performing Barong in a ceremonial context which is quite distinct from convulsive or debilitating trance. To be asked to animate a Barong from a local temple is a great honour and both dancers cited the respect and affection which they received from the audience for being the medium for the god's (Barong's) dance. The dancers of the Sadha Budaya Troupe of Ubud, who perform weekly for tourists at Ubud Palace, also perform regularly in Calonarang performances at temples in the Ubud area. Perhaps because the troupe's own Barong outfit is *tenget*, the dancers feel that the *taksu*, when achieved, is the same whether the performance is for tourists or the temple. Interview, with I Made Sadia 10 March, 1997.

invitation for the divine presence *(Dewa Taksu)* to enter his body. If the actor does the proper prayers and purification, a divine presence enters his body, and he is said to have *taksu*.[133]

By this it would appear that if the correct rituals are followed, the gods will 'descend into the body' and *taksu* will automatically ensue, but other sources indicate that this is not necessarily the case. As many of my informants pointed out, "Sometimes you get it, sometimes you don't". The ritual requirements must always be fulfilled, but clearly something more than the mere presentation of offerings and prayers is necessary; technical skill, study and meditation also figure. Dunn's investigation of *taksu* is probably the most exhaustive in the literature. Significantly, she found that the source of *taksu* is perceived differently by different individuals and different traditions. According to her informants, *taksu* may be any of the following:

1. A thoroughgoing dedication to one's art; the expertise gained through diligent study and practice.
2. A natural 'gift' which one might or might not choose to develop.
3. A gift of the god of *taksu (Dewa Taksu)*, also associated with trance.
4. Something inherited, passed on from generation to generation.
5. A heightened state of consciousness resulting from spiritual meditation.[134]

Her definition takes in all of these different interpretations:

Taksu, then, manifests itself in the relationship between the performer and the audience that is enchanting, magnetic, and larger than life. According to the various beliefs presented, it is either the result of the accumulated talents of a skilled and well-

---

[133] Young, p. 79.

[134] Dunn, pp. 123–132.

prepared performer or it is a special quality that one is either born with, inherits, receives as a divine gift or achieves through study and meditation. It is maintained as 1) a latent power, 2) through a certain purity of life style with ritual obligations, 3) through devotional practices either before the *pellingih taksu* or at special sacred places or 4) through study and remembering the *kanda mpat*.[135]

The majority of Dunn's informants considered the source of *taksu* to be 'supernatural'[136] but that achieving it also requires effort on the part of the individual performer. My informants, too, cited purity, correct ritual practice and study as essential to achieving *taksu*; technical skill is a given, but that alone is not sufficient. Prayers and mantras recited by the masked performer when opening the box of masks call on the god of *taksu* or upon the deified ancestors to make themselves present in the performance[137] and to empower both the masks and the performer. There are also mantras for individual masks asking that the qualities necessary for a particular character be made manifest in the performance (gentle beauty for the *Dalem*, for example, and strength of breath for *Topeng Keras*).[138] So as well as *Dewa Taksu*, there are individual personalities of the masked characters with which the performers seek to be endowed. It is not

---

[135] *Ibid.*, p. 132. Certain of Dunn's high-caste informants related *taksu* to marshalling the forces of the *Kanda Mpat*, the four 'sibling spirits' which "are materialized and become visible at a child's birth in the form of the amniotic fluid, the placenta, the blood and the umbilical cord". These spirits "correspond with colors, parts of the human body...and with the senses". They are called upon in the course of all of the major rites of passage in an individual's life and are considered to be guardians. "They symbolize the close relationship between the macrocosm, *buwana agung* and microcosm, *buwana alit* through which power is transmitted. . . .*Taksu* seems to be a gathering together of the powers of these four brothers." The relevance of the *Kanda Mpat* to the masked performer, particularly in relation to the Barong figure, will be discussed in greater detail in a later chapter.

[136] *Ibid.*, p. 123.

[137] See Dunn pp. 118–119; Daniel, p. 146; Emigh 1996, pp. 112–113.

[138] Interview with I Made Bandem 30 April, 1997; interview with Ida Bagus Alit 18 April, 1998.

surprising, then, that some performers contend that the mask itself is a medium for *taksu*:

> **Ida Bagus Alit**: "As soon as I put on the mask I feel I have a burden, so by having that burden automatically it changes my energy—I feel differently. That automatically changes me."[139]
>
> **Ida Bagus Anom**: "Mask I think is the medium to have *taksu* because you see the mask and the mask gives you the energy to become that character."[140]

The Topeng performer has the special responsibility to bring to life these images of the deified ancestors, the masks of the great warriors, divine kings and wise ministers of Balinese history. The concept of *menghidupkan topeng*—making the mask live—is an essential component of the *taksu* of the masked performer. The silent, full-faced masks of *Patih, Tua* and *Dalem* and the sacred Sanskrit and Kawi-speaking *Sidha Karya* do not tell the story of the drama, and yet are absolutely essential. They are representatives of the past made present through the *taksu* of the performer. The mask itself is an important element in this process of transformation first, because it suggests the nature of the character to the performer and acts as a source of inspiration and second, because the masks are a representations of the deified ancestors. For the masked performer, *taksu* is achieved only in conjunction with the mask and its spirit:

> You see the mask and the mask suggests, the mask tells you. That's one of the ways to get *taksu*, to make the mask alive. If you can feel that character of the mask and become one with the mask, and then the music, the story unite and when I come out [I'm] not Anom, I'm a king![141]

---

[139] Alit 5 April, 1997.

[140] Anom 14 April, 1997.

[141] *Ibid.*

Summary

There is much in the tradition of mask use in Bali which, taken together, leads the actor to a dissociative state in performance. The first evidence of this is seen in a general cultural bias towards the communal rather than the individual in all aspects of life and work. Behaviour is ritualised to a high degree and this is supported by a religious philosophy which pervades all activities. Life, work and art in Bali are at the service of the gods and directed by them. The maskmaking process itself is a ritualised, religious activity as much as a practical one and it invests the masks with supernatural power at every stage. The training of the masked performer also entails religious responsibilities in addition to mental and physical discipline. The pedagogy is essentially physical and non-analytical, leading to a visceral understanding that discourages individual expression. The aesthetic philosophy, too, calls for self-abnegation and carries with it associations of visitation and mediumship. The performer is encouraged to give himself up to the *taksu*, bringing the masks to life and allowing the gods and deified ancestors to reveal themselves through his performance.

Chapter 4: *Japanese Mask Tradition and Noh Drama*

A Foreign Country, An Obscure Art

Because it is now a modern industrialised country often at the forefront of technological innovation, one may be inclined to forget just how far removed the culture of Japan is from that of the West. It would seem (given the general tenor of books written about each place) that Balinese culture, however exotic, may be more accessible and comprehensible for the Western observer than that of Japan. A great part of this can undoubtedly be attributed to more than 250 years of self-imposed cultural and political isolation enforced in Japan during the Edo period (1600–1868), which ended only with Commodore Perry's arrival in 1853. During that period of isolation the Tokugawa shogunate[1] sought, with notable success, to regulate every aspect of Japanese life. Not only was foreign travel forbidden to the Japanese, but foreigners were also forbidden to enter Japan. Certain concessions were made for Chinese, Korean and Dutch traders, but their access to ordinary Japanese people was very limited.[2] It was a period of peace and relative prosperity in which many of the arts flourished, but their development was rigorously controlled by the shogunal government and its army of bureaucrats.

---

[1] Shogun was the title taken by the military dictators who ruled Japan from 1185–1868.

[2] R. H. P. Mason and J. G. Caiger, *A History of Japan,* revised edition (Singapore: Charles E. Tuttle Company, Inc., 1997) pp. 203–207.

Throughout Japanese society a strict hierarchy prevailed, with dress codes and prescribed behaviour for every social class, so that upward social mobility was virtually impossible. Patterns of behaviour established through hundreds of years of this authoritarian bureaucracy and the ethnocentricity engendered by cultural isolation can still be observed in contemporary Japanese life in elaborate social rituals, matters of etiquette, and attitudes towards culture, both foreign and domestic. The autocratic shoguns have long since passed away, but the Japanese people still adhere to strict codes of behaviour which may not be fully comprehended by or comprehensible to foreigners.

The world of Noh drama, the classical theatre of Japan, provides an extreme example of this highly coded and ritualised behaviour and it is also a world that is shrouded in secrecy, carefully protected from outsiders who might undermine or vulgarise this almost sacred national art. It is no coincidence that it was during the Tokugawa period that the Noh drama "achieved the form which has remained substantially unchanged to the present".[3] What remains today is a meticulously preserved model of late medieval performance practice, modified to suit seventeenth and eighteenth century aristocratic tastes. It may seem incomprehensible that a living theatre form could become so completely fixed in a performance style that is several hundred years old but, having become a court art under the protection of the military elite, Noh was forced to adopt the exacting standards that its patrons demanded. Change and development were not considered appropriate and Noh drama became more or less the exclusive property of "upper class initiates and connoisseurs".[4] Nonetheless, it survived and remains one of the most sophisticated of Eastern dance drama genres.

---

[3] Benito Ortolani, *The Japanese Theatre: From Shamanistic Ritual to Contemporary Pluralism*, revised edition (Princeton: Princeton University Press, 1995) p. 103.

[4] *Ibid.,* p. 104. However, recent scholarship has cast new light on 'popular' Noh performances during this period, some given by professionals for the general public and other 'private' performances given by amateurs, including women. See Gerald Groemer, 'Noh at the Crossroads: Commoner Performance During the Edo Period', *Asian Theatre Journal*, Vol. 15, number 1, Spring 1998, pp. 117–141 and 'Elite Culture for Common Audiences: *Machiiri Nô*

In this chapter I shall explore some of the sources of Noh, touching on the folk mask traditions, court and popular entertainments from which it emerged. I will also examine its association with religious ritual and the significance of the mask within this context. Discussion of elements of Noh performance, pedagogy and the maskmaking process will focus on practical considerations and the subjective experience of the performer.

Folk Mask Traditions

Japan has a long history of mask use in ritual and drama, remnants of which are still visible today although any records of the origins of these traditions have been lost. As in Bali, local practice differs from place to place and the history of many masks can only be discerned from legend, if at all. Among the colourful and arresting masks of the folk traditions are the *Oni* (demon), *Tengu* (goblin) and *Oto* (comic female) masks as well as the *Shi-Shi* 'lion' mask, which bears such a striking resemblance to the Balinese Barong.

The *Oni*[5] demon mask appears in various forms throughout Japan and is, in the north and particularly on Sado Island, associated with a trance dance with drumming called *Oni Daiko*. The function of these masked dances was once exorcistic but they are now seen primarily in festivals and performances for tourists, far removed from their original context.

The *Tengu* goblin, with its red face, fierce grimace, long nose and bulging brass eyes, is remarkably similar to Javanese masks of *Rawana* and other demon-gods and Tengu characters feature in several Noh plays, *Kurama Tengu* ('The

---

and *Kanjin Nô* in the City of Edo', *Asian Theatre Journal*, Vol. 15, Number 2, Fall 1998, pp. 230–252.

[5] "The *oni* are the most prolific and, in terms of significance and function, most diversified creatures in Japanese folk religion . . . they] can be highly paradoxical–both benevolent and vicious, both attacker and the subduer of evil spirits." Solrun Hoass Pulvers, *The Noh Mask and the Mask Making Tradition*. unpublished PhD dissertation (Australian National University, 1978) p. 53. Thus like the Barong, Rangda and the *Bhoma* figure in Bali, the *Oni* serves an apotropaic function protecting the community.

Goblin of Kurama'), for example. However, the masks used for these roles are usually *Beshemi* ('tight-lipped', Figure 23)[6] or, occasionally, *Aku-jo* ('ferocious old man' Figure 17), and these bear little resemblance to the folk mask. The character, which derives from folk and Shinto traditions of local deities, appears to be rather frightening but is generally benign. He tends to be mischievous rather than evil, not unlike the Balinese *Jauk*.

The popular comic female mask, *Oto*, appears in a number of contexts, particularly in street performances given in connection with religious festivals. Versions of the mask also occasionally appear in *Kyôgen*, the comic plays performed in conjunction with Noh dramas. Although there are a number of variations, the mask essentially presents 'an exceptionally ugly woman' but the character also has a good deal of charm: "a fresh and spirited girl bursting with vitality, giving the impression of a living woman's wholesome inner beauty".[7] The mask is likely to have derived from that used for ritual enactments of the bawdy dance of the goddess *Ama no Uzume* whose story is elaborated below. Today, however, these sacred associations seem to have been forgotten.

The *Shi-shi* dances are among the oldest masked performances in Japan and may have existed well before the 'lion' mask was imported from China. In ancient Japanese, the term *Shi-shi* "designated edible wild animals such as wild boars or deer"[8] and this may explain why there are so many variations in the *Shi-shi* folk mask (just as there are of the Balinese Barong, see Figure 18.) Thus, it entirely possible that the Japanese *Shi-shi* is an indigenous form which was only later influenced by a similar continental dance featuring a lion-like mask. Versions of the *Shi-shi* mask are found in several later theatrical forms including Noh, Kabuki and Bunraku. In the folk tradition, the creature has a purificatory

---

[6] Pulvers, 1978, p. 185.

[7] Iwasaki Kyôun, 'Kyôgen Masks', translated by Rebecca Teele in *Nô/Kyôgen Masks in Performance* (Claremont, California: Mime Journal, 1984) p. 189.

[8] Ortolani, p. 26.

and exorcistic function and in some communities *Shi-shi* masks are considered sacred and are worshipped as gods.[9]

The Development of Noh Drama

Noh drama has had a chequered history. In its earliest incarnation it consisted of itinerant entertainers at the bottom of the social scale who travelled from village to village performing magic tricks, acrobatics, juggling and, occasionally, sacred rituals or dances concerning local gods or spirits. Gradually these companies came under the protection of monasteries and then, in the middle of the fourteenth century, a certain child actor in a well-known company was seen by the young shogun Ashikaga Yoshimitsu (1358–1408) who immediately fell in love with the beautiful boy player.[10] Under the tutelage of his father, Kanami (who was by all accounts a phenomenally talented actor and a highly skilled playwright) and the poets and artists of Yoshimitsu's court, the boy Fujiwaka (renamed Zeami by his protector), transformed this vulgar popular entertainment into a court art of extraordinary sophistication. He wrote verse dramas based on classical epic poetry and Shinto legends and evolved an aesthetic (borrowed from court poetry) in which the measure of great artistry was neither spectacle nor emotional intensity, but *yûgen:* a profound grace, a mysterious elegance. Zeami's fortunes waned with the demise of Yoshimitsu and he spent the last years of his life in exile. Significantly, however, he left a series of secret treatises on the art of Noh

---

[9] In an interview with the author (10 June, 1997) Noh scholar Monica Bethe indicated that these beliefs persist. "In general, Japanese mask traditions are secular. Of course there are exceptions, for example there is a particular village in north-eastern Japan in Akita Prefecture where two *Shi-shi* masks are worshipped as deities. Their manipulators are 'chosen by the gods' and the dance is a blessing on the village. There are other instances, but always specific to particular places." See also Immoos, Thomas. *Japanese Theatre*, translated by Hugh Young (London: Cassell and Collier Macmillan Publishers Ltd., 1977) pp. 23–24.

[10] The novel *The House of Kanzê* (London: Century Publishing, 1985) by Nobuko Albery gives a fascinating fictionalised account of the life of Zeami and presents a vivid picture of the highly cultured court of Yoshimitsu.

drama, which were rediscovered and published in the twentieth century, and now stand as a kind of canon of Noh technique and aesthetics.[11]

In spite of Zeami's fall from favour, Noh drama continued to prosper as a court art and in the Tokugawa era became subject to regulations touching on every detail of performance, from the designation of companies authorised to perform Noh, to the speed of performance and the precise dimensions for each individual mask. Having traded poverty-ridden independence for courtly patronage and security, Noh drama largely lost touch with the common people. When the shogunate fell after the arrival of Commander Perry and various Europeans who sought trade and diplomatic links with the long-isolated island nation of Japan, Noh drama went into decline. It was only due to the efforts of certain powerful personalities, notably the Noh actor Umewaka Minoru, that Noh was able to survive.[12] Through Umewaka, Noh came to the attention of Ernest Fenollosa and, through him, Ezra Pound, Arthur Waley and W. B. Yeats, all of whom promoted Noh in the West. At the end of the Second World War, however, the occupation authorities believed Noh to be a dangerous relic of feudalism that should be wiped out. Fortunately, because of the efforts of enlightened foreigners like the American scholar Earl Ernst (who served in the Censorship Office during the American occupation), Noh was recognised as a unique and refined art of international importance.

A victim of its own success, Noh survives as a beautiful, rarefied and carefully preserved theatrical form, adored by a coterie of mostly elderly cognoscenti in Japan and by a small but passionate community of foreign

---

[11] Zeami's theoretical works have appeared in a number of English translations since they were first made available for publication in the early twentieth century. The translation by J. Thomas Rimer and Yamazaki Masakazu is highly regarded and widely available, but does not contain all of the treatises. Mark J. Nearman's translations have been published over a period of years in issues of *Monumenta Nipponica* and include material not covered by Rimer and Yamazaki. Nearman's translations are held by many to be more thorough and precise.

[12] See Ezra Pound and Ernest Fenollosa, *The Classic Noh Theatre of Japan* (New York: New Directions, 1959 [1917]) p. 5.

enthusiasts. It is as foreign to most contemporary Japanese as it is to the uninitiated Westerner, but this was not always so. Noh has its roots in religious rituals and folk performances that were a fundamental part of the lives of ordinary people, and, indeed, elements of this folk tradition are at the very heart of contemporary Noh. To understand why Noh developed in the way that it has, it is necessary to examine the social, political and religious forces that transformed the popular entertainment *sarugaku* (literally 'Monkey Music') into a venerated art of the aristocracy now referred to with deep respect as *nôgakudô* ('The Way of Accomplishment'). The interactions of two elements are chiefly responsible for this transformation: first, the desire among practitioners to raise their social status and, second, the association of performers with shamanistic and exorcistic religious rituals.

Raising Status

Strict social hierarchy was not new to the Tokugawa period; a fairly rigid class system had prevailed in Japan since at least the tenth century of the Current Era and probably earlier, as a result of the importation of Confucianism from China as early as the third century.[13] However, the Chinese Confucian system allowed individuals to rise in rank by merit through a complex system of examinations whereas, in the Japanese system, preferment was based upon family associations and wealth.[14] Thus, it was difficult for even the most talented individuals to improve their status unless they could make some kind of connection with those already in power. The effect of this hierarchical class system was fundamental to the emergence and development of Noh drama.

Although the precise origins of Noh drama are obscure, scholars "have established beyond any doubt a lineal connection between fourteenth-century *nô*

---

[13] Peter Nosco, *Confucianism and Tokugawa Culture* (Honolulu: University of Hawaii Press, 1987) p. 5.

[14] Mason and. Caiger, p. 57; see also H. Paul Varley, *Japanese Culture,* third edition (Honolulu: University of Hawaii Press, 1984) p. 50.

actors and many previous generations of *sangaku, dengaku* and *sarugaku* performers".[15] These performance genres, although very different from Noh as it is performed today, are acknowledged as the immediate precursors of *nôgaku*. As if to emphasise the point, the medieval actor, playwright and theorist Zeami (1363–1443)[16] and his performer-playwright father Kanami (1333–84), who are regarded as the founders of what is now known as Noh, referred to themselves as *sarugaku* rather than Noh performers.

Court dances and popular entertainments

The court arts of *gigaku* ('elegant entertainment') and *bugaku* ("dance entertainment"[17]), which were at their height of popularity during the Heian period (794–1192), derived from music and dances brought from mainland China and Korea between the sixth and eighth centuries.[18] *Gigaku,* a dance drama that promoted Buddhist philosophy, gave way to *bugaku* by the ninth century when the latter was made the official court entertainment.[19] Both used large wooden masks, which appear to have evolved from East Indian models. Though rather different in form and style, there is evidence that these relics of court art influenced the development of Noh masks,[20] and even a cursory examination

---

[15] Ortolani, p. 86. *Sangaku* is a term referring to a variety of entertainments imported from the Chinese mainland including acrobatics, juggling and magic acts; *dengaku* was 'rice-field entertainment', which grew out of fertility rituals and harvest celebrations performed by farmers. *Sarugaku* is generally seen as a development of *sangaku* incorporating the various entertainments of the older form with a new mimetic/dramatic element. See Ortolani pp. 54–93.

[16] These dates, although generally accepted, are approximate. For a detailed discussion on Zeami's dates of birth and death see Erika de Poorter, *Zeami's Talks on Sarugaku* (Amsterdam: J.C. Gieben, 1986) pp. 29–32.

[17] *Bugaku* is sometimes known by the name of its musical counterpart, *gagaku.*

[18] James R. Brandon, ed., *The Cambridge Guide to Asian Theatre* (Cambridge: Cambridge University Press, 1997) p. 144.

[19] Ortolani, p. 30.

[20] Ortolani, pp. 36–37. Gigaku masks covered the whole head, whereas *bugaku* masks generally covered only the face, but were still larger than Noh masks. See also Pulvers, 1978, pp. 34–36 and Heinz Lucas, *Japanische Kultmasken: Der Tanz der Kraniche* (Kassel: IM Erich Röth-Verlag, 1965) and Kyôtarô Nishikawa, *Bugaku Masks,* translated by Monica Bethe (Tokyo and New York: Kodansha International Ltd. and Shibundo, 1978).

reveals a number of similarities. Some *bugaku* masks, for example, feature a separate chin piece, attached to the upper part of the mask with string, in the manner of the Okina mask, which is still used in Noh.[21] Moreover, female *gigaku* masks possess ambiguous expressions not unlike Noh woman masks (Figure 19) while the *bugaku Kenjaraku* mask, with its fanged jaws and horns,[22] could almost be a prototype of the Noh *Hannya* mask (Figure 20). The *gigaku* mask of *Shi-Shi,* which bears an extraordinary resemblance to the Balinese Barong and was similarly associated with healing, purification and exorcism,[23] has been transmogrified in the Noh *Shi-shi Guchi* to a vaguely human though still demonic face (Figure 21).

During the same period, the popular performance genre of *sangaku* developed from entertainments imported from China, such as juggling, magic tricks and acrobatics, while *dengaku* evolved from native harvest and fertility rituals. *Sangaku* gradually gave way (or may have been the ancestor) to *sarugaku,* which placed less emphasis upon acrobatics and 'circus-like spectacle' and more upon *monomane* or 'imitation', something more akin to 'realistic' acting.[24] Sources indicate that a type of ceremonial *sarugaku* was performed by court musicians in conjunction with *gigaku* and *bugaku*, while the more lively and populist version was performed outside the capital.[25] The decline of the emperors at the end of the Heian period and the rise of the Samurai military class during the Kamakura period (1192–1333) saw the decline of the court arts. *Gigaku,* which was essentially a Chinese import, died out completely and the magnificent masks that remain are virtually the only evidence left of this art. *Bugaku,* which had assimilated many aspects of *gigaku,* evolved into something more clearly

---

[21] Ortolani, pp. 37, 48.
[22] See Lucas, *Japanische Kultmasken.*
[23] Ortolani, p. 31.
[24] *Ibid.,* p. 58.
[25] *Ibid.,* p. 59.

Japanese and continued to be performed, particularly in religious contexts, but gradually fell out of fashion. It did not disappear, however, and it may still be seen today, mostly in special performances in shrines, temples and Imperial palaces. *Sangaku* and *dengaku,* on the other hand, continued to prosper in the provinces during this period of transition, and became popular with the increasingly influential Samurai class. Performers, however, were at the very bottom of the social hierarchy.

The sanjo

In medieval times, and certainly during the Kamakura period, entertainers were social outcasts, forced to live in special ghettos *(sanjo)* with others of their class including butchers, undertakers and prostitutes who, because of the nature of their work, were considered 'impure' but whose activities were, nonetheless, necessary to the community.

> The restrictions imposed on the outcastes [sic] varied in different periods, but in general they were denied any social intercourse with the rest of the population and could hardly expect any protection of the law. The humiliations implied in the state of being an outcaste were many, and ranged from strict limitation of occupation, prohibition to circulate in public except at specific hours of the day, to strict regulations concerning clothing and place of residence, severe punishments for minor violations of the rules, and so on.[26]

A significant body of scholarly opinion holds that the gradual rise of *sangaku* and *sarugaku-nô* from popular spectacle to court entertainment may be attributed to the determined ambition of the outcast performers to escape from the *sanjo* and

---

[26] *Ibid.,* p. 80.

the social stigma with which it was associated.[27] The first step was to seek the protection of religious organisations, which were not only wealthy but often wielded significant political power as well.[28] Performances were a regular feature of religious festivals and evidence exists that entertainers utilised this association with temples and monasteries as a means of raising their status. For example, when ceremonial *sarugaku* fell out of favour, these court performers were required to seek their fortune elsewhere.

> *sarugaku* performers who had lost the protection of the court. . . formed groups of professional performers called *hôshibara* who donned the habit and wore the haircut of monks, but in reality did not belong to any monastery or temple; the habit and the exterior religious appearance were their way to escape high taxes and conscripted labor in the fields. They became responsible for the enormous increase in popularity of *sangaku* outside the capital and the main, official places of worship. For money, the *hôshibara* would perform anything, including religious services for the dead.[29]

So, as well as providing entertainment at temples during festival time, these proto-Noh performers also posed as monks and performed religious rituals. It has been suggested that Kanami and Zeami's family "belonged to a group of outcasts, the Asobi-be, who specialized in funeral rites".[30]

---

[27] Ortolani cites in particular the work of Gotô Hajime, *Nôgaku no kigen* (*The Origin of Nôgaku*), (Tokyo: Mokujisha, 1975). See also Ortolani 58–62.

[28] Mason and Caiger, pp. 98–100.

[29] Ortolani, p. 59.

[30] Ortolani, p. 86, cites Akima Toshio 'The Songs of the Dead: Poetry, Drama and Ancient Death Rituals of Japan', *Journal of Asian Studies*, Vol. 41 (May 1982): 485–509, and suggests that this association "provides a plausible explanation for Zeami's frequent use of ghosts as protagonists in his Nô plays".

As the ceremonial *sarugaku* of the court disappeared, a new, popular *sarugaku* appears to have grown out of the provincial *sangaku*. During this transitional period, the term *sangaku* gradually disappeared and the term *sarugaku* took its place in performance records. Perhaps because of the influence of court performers, this new *sarugaku* sought to become more refined and, to reflect this a new ideogram was brought into use.

> Originally it was represented by two Chinese characters, one meaning a monkey, the other meaning music. The monkey character was changed to a part of one denoting a god, so the meaning became 'divine music'. This alteration symbolized the change that the Noh actors sought in their status. While the monkey form was used, the art of *sarugaku* was crude; but by the time the god form was employed, the art had become much more refined. . . . The change in character also showed the close relationship between *sarugaku* and religion.[31]

This could be viewed as a cynical decision which allowed these outcast performers to improve their social status by implying a divine origin for their art, but the association of *sarugaku* and Noh with religion was and is taken very seriously by practitioners. It was, on the one hand, the key to the genre's legitimacy in a world in which performers had somehow to make the best of a precarious existence, and, on the other hand, it is a continuing source of enormous pride for those associated with Noh, affecting the attitudes of both players and audiences. Whatever the reasons for the genre's alliance with religious ritual it has, since Zeami's time, considered this connection to be part of its essential nature.

---

[31] Sekine, Masaru. *Ze-Ami and his Theories of Noh Drama* (Gerrards Cross: Colin Smythe, 1985) p. 24.

A Sacred Performance Art

Sarugaku-nô associated itself with the most fundamental myths of Japanese national history and spiritual life. In the *Fûshi-kaden,* Zeami claims that the origin of Noh is to be found in the dance of the Shinto goddess *Ama no Uzume:*

> The beginnings of *sarugaku* in the age of the gods, it is said, occurred when Amaterasu, the Sun Goddess, concealed herself in the heavenly rocky cave, and the whole earth fell under endless darkness. All the myriad deities gathered at the heavenly Kagu mountain, in order to find a way to calm her. They played sacred music to accompany their comic dances. In the midst of this Ama no Uzume came forward and . . . danced in front of a fire that had been lighted, she pounded out the rhythm of her dance with her feet and became possessed by divine inspiration as she sang and danced. The Sun Goddess, hearing the voice of Ama no Uzume, opened the rock door slightly. The land became light, and the faces of the gods could be seen again. It is said that such entertainments marked the beginning of *sarugaku*.[32]

Having established *sarugaku's* divine credentials in the Shinto religion, Zeami goes on to link his art to a Buddhist legend in which Gautama's followers "performed sixty-six entertainments" to distract a crowd of "unbelievers" so that the Buddha could complete his devotions. "Such were the beginnings of our art in India".[33] Finally, Zeami claimed that *sarugaku* was given to Japan by the legendary Hata no Kôkatsu[34] who performed masked entertainments in the court

---

[32] *On the Art of Nô Drama: The Major Treatises of Zeami,* translated by J. Thomas Rimer and Yamazaki Masakazu (Princeton: Princeton University Press, 1984) pp. 31–32.

[33] *Ibid.,* p. 32.

[34] Legend has it that Hata was found as an infant, floating on the Hatsuse river in a jar. This child was so beautiful that those who found him believed he must be divine and the event was reported to the emperor. The child appeared to the emperor in a dream that night and told him of his holy mission. Thereafter, he served in the emperor's court, apparently for several generations. Having passed the art of masked dancing on to his descendants he went to Harima

of Prince Shôtoku (574–622)[35] and magically pacified the warring factions in the land. It is significant that the semi-divine Hata used masks for his performance, and the legend holds that these sixty-six masks were especially made for him by the revered Prince Shôtoku.[36] The notion of Noh as a gift from the gods, and the association of masks with this divinity, is pervasive and has been reasserted in a number of legends and stories. For example, Umewaka Minoru, the 'saviour' of Noh in the late nineteenth century, traces the history of his family's connection with Noh to an ancestor's dream of a Noh mask:

> The twenty-eighth descendant was Hiogu no Kami Kagehisa. His mother dreamed that a Noh mask was given from heaven; she conceived, and Kagehisa was born. From his childhood Kagehisa liked music and dancing, and he was by nature very excellent in both of these arts. The Emperor Gotsuchi Mikado heard his name, and . . . he called him to his palace and made him perform the play Ashikari. Kagehisa was then sixteen years old. The Emperor admired him greatly and gave him the decoration . . . and the honorific ideograph 'waka' and thus made him change his name to Umewaka.[37]

Here, the Noh mask is symbolic of the divine gift of accomplishment (*nô* literally translated means 'accomplishment') which wins praise and favour from the emperor. The story demonstrates an ongoing perception of Noh as a sacred art and masks as magically powerful.

---

province on the Inland Sea where, in a changed form, he was worshipped as a god. See Rimer and Yamazaki, pp. 32–37. In adult life, Zeami used Hata as his family name, claiming descent from Hata no Kôkatsu. See de Poorter, p. 147.

[35] Venerated regent related to the imperial family as well as the powerful Soga family. He was instrumental in creating a centralised state in Japan and promoted both Confucian and Buddhist doctrines and practice. See Mason and Caiger, pp. 40–42; also Varley pp. 20–23.

[36] Rimer and Yamazaki, p. 33.

[37] Ezra Pound, and Ernest Fenollosa, *The Classic Noh Theatre of Japan.* (New York: New Directions, 1959) p. 5. Quoting from a programme note for a performance in March 1900.

The relationship of *sarugaku-nô* performers to religious ritual is not, however, merely anecdotal. Noh performance practice provides tantalising evidence of a strong connection between Noh and shamanistic possession in *kagura*, the "entertainment for the gods performed at Shinto shrines".[38] In these rituals, the shaman, usually a *miko* (a shrine priestess/medium, not always a woman), would become possessed by a god or a living or dead spirit and speak for them. E. T. Kirby has suggested a metaphorical connection between the story of *Amaterasu* in the cave and shamanistic trance-possession in *kagura:*

> The sun-within-a-cave image is . . . a body-consciousness metaphor in which Amaterasu represents the god who emerged and emanated as a voice from within the shaman. The 'light' she sheds on the world is that of the benefits which shamanism provided for society.[39]

In the same way, the actor who imitates a god or spirit has a similar function to that of a shaman; he is a medium through which the god communicates with the temporal world. Kirby goes on to make the case for a more concrete relationship between shamanism and Noh:

> The societal pressures which produced the noh play began, it would seem with the official decrees, issued in AD 780 and AD 807, which prohibited ecstasy outside the shrines, primarily as a means of combating the spread of Buddhism. These decrees created an outcast class of the *mikos* and related practitioners of shamanic trance, but had little effect upon their popularity other than directing them toward the performance of dances and songs as entertainment. . . . For those who had become outcasts but still sought to earn a living from their shamanistic abilities,

---

[38] Ortolani, p. 305.

[39] E. T. Kirby, *Ur-Drama: The Origins of Theatre.* (New York: New York University Press, 1975) p. 77.

dramatization of the rituals as entertainment, with function and trance eliminated, would likewise have been a logical response to the situation of proscription.[40]

The surviving canon of Noh plays lends weight to this hypothesis, since the vast majority of plays require the leading actor to appear in the guise of a god, a spirit, or an unhappy ghost and many feature scenes of exorcism. It may be argued that the plays are entertainments rather than rituals, but the striking feature of *sarugaku-nô,* which sets it apart from its antecedents like *sangaku,* is its use of masks. In the earlier court dance-dramas *(gigaku* and *bugaku),* the use of masks was reserved for monks and priests only,[41] but as popular *sangaku* developed into *sarugaku* and *sarugaku-no,* these lay performers donned masks in order to impersonate gods and spirits in shrine ceremonies. Moreover, in the case of *Okina,* which is regarded as the essence of Noh, the play is an acknowledged sacred ritual and, significantly, it is believed that at the moment the actor dons the Okina mask, he actually becomes the god. Just as in the *Topeng Sidha Karya* of Bali, it is the mask that provides the means for the actor's mediumship, and, while he wears it, the mask confers divinity upon the performer.

Noh and Religious Ritual

At this stage, it may be useful to examine the nature of religion in Japanese culture and its connection with Noh drama and its antecedents. Compared to Bali, contemporary Japanese culture appears to be a great deal more secular. Among the general populace and even among the Noh performers interviewed in the course of this research, questions about spirituality seemed to be regarded with the kind of dismissive, worldly cynicism with which one is familiar in the West. However, the religious belief systems of Japan are complex and, perhaps because of the legacy of Zen Buddhism (with which Noh drama has a fundamental

---

[40] *Ibid.,* p. 87.
[41] Ortolani, p. 90.

relationship,) the Japanese often appear to be determinedly non- or even anti-mystical and can rarely be drawn out when questioned about religious beliefs. Nonetheless, beneath the veil of modern cynicism, Japanese culture can be deeply spiritual and much of this spirituality is evidenced in Noh drama, particularly in the actor's relationship to the mask.

Shinto

Shinto, 'the way of the gods', is the indigenous faith of the Japanese people. It is essentially animistic and concerned with the worship of the *kami,* which may be gods or the spirits of people, places, plants or animals.[42] Having no canon of fixed doctrine, Shinto is not so much a philosophy as a practice. It is fundamentally and exclusively linked to the Japanese nation and culture; that is, its myths concern only the founding and development of Japan and are not concerned with, indeed hardly acknowledge, the rest of the world. According to Shinto belief, the emperors of Japan are direct descendants of *Amaterasu,* the sun goddess who heads the Shinto pantheon.[43]

> Subsequently, the grandson of the Sun Goddess, Ninigi-no-mikoto, received instructions to descend and rule Japan. To symbolize his authority he was given three divine treasures: a mirror, a sword, and a string of jewels. Moreover, he was accompanied on his

---

[42] "Fundamentally, the term is an honorific for noble, sacred spirits, which implies a sense of adoration for their virtues and authority. All beings have such spirits, so in a sense all beings can be called kami or be regarded as potential kami." Sokyo Ono, *Shinto: The Kami Way* (Rutland, Vermont and Tokyo, Japan: Charles E. Tuttle Company, 1962) p. 6.

[43] This, naturally, places the emperor in the position of true divine right and he must therefore, by nature, be a '*kami*'. It is thus not surprising that a particular condition of the surrender of Japan at the end of World War Two was that the emperor should renounce his divine status. Following the Meiji restoration in 1868, Shinto was established as the state religion and priests and temples were placed under state control. The Allies believed, with some justification, that Shinto had provided the spiritual and philosophical underpinnings for Japanese aggression and imperialism and, when Japan was defeated in 1945, the Allies saw to it that Shinto was disestablished, leaving priesthood and practitioners in disarray. See Ono, pp. 16–19.

journey by the kami that had participated in the entertainment outside the celestial cave.[44]

These three articles, the mirror, sword and jewels, have become the Imperial Regalia of Japan, handed down through generations of emperors and are kept in various Imperial shrines. The mirror, "symbolic of the spirit of the Sun Goddess",[45] is an important feature of Shinto worship, and a small circular mirror may be found in a place of honour in most shrines.

> A mirror has a clean light that reflects everything as it is. It symbolizes the stainless mind of the kami, and at the same time is regarded as a sacred symbolic embodiment of the fidelity of the worshipper towards the kami.
>
> In mythology the mirror is a mysterious object. In ancient society it was an object of ceremonial and religious significance rather than of daily use.[46]

It is not merely coincidental that the mirror is also of particular significance for Noh. An essential feature of the Noh stage is the *kagami-no-ma* or 'mirror room' where the actor, having donned his costume, sits before a full-length mirror to contemplate both his reflection and the mask he is to wear. After a time, the actor picks up the mask, salutes it (by bringing it close to his face and bowing) and then, with the help of assistants, he puts it on. Wearing the mask, he continues to sit before the mirror in which the image of the character is now reflected.

Shinto is concerned with matters of daily life and life-cycle rituals. Like Balinese Hinduism, Shinto worship seeks to keep the universe in balance and does so by attending to the needs and desires of the kami through *matsuri,* usually translated as 'festival', but literally, 'service to the *kami*'.

---

[44] *Ibid.,* p. 5.

[45] *Ibid.,* p. 13.

[46] *Ibid.,* p. 23.

All ceremonies, except the simple act of worship performed by an individual before a shrine, involve four elements: purification *(harai)*, an offering *(shinsen)*, prayer *(norito)*, and a symbolic feast *(naorai)*.[47]

Offerings are the essential ritual requirement in Shinto and may be made daily or even twice daily in order to keep the *kami* satisfied. "If this simple act is neglected, it is believed that the *kami*, particularly the ancestral spirits, will be unhappy and that misfortune will be experienced by individuals who are remiss in observing this duty".[48] The offerings may consist of food and drink, flowers, money, symbolic objects, even animals. Significantly, "various forms of entertainment such as the dances, drama, wrestling and archery"[49] may also serve as offerings to the *kami*. First among these is the tradition of *kagura,* and what is known of the earliest forms of this entertainment of the gods bears a striking resemblance to aspects of temple anniversary ceremonies in Bali. In early *kagura,* it is thought that a pillar *(kamukura)* was erected on which the *kami* were meant to alight to receive offerings and watch the entertainment presented for their benefit. This entertainment might consist of songs and dances but might also include *kamigakari*, "divine inspiration, divine possession or the person who is possessed by the god",[50] in other words, shamanistic trance possession. Honda Yasuji has asserted that in Noh plays in which the leading actor *(shite)* portrays a god, spirit or ghost, the role "derives from that of the *miko* in *kagura* who, while in a state of *kamigakari,* is overtaken by a spirit and utters the *takusen* (divine utterance)".[51] Indeed, *bugaku* (court masked dance entertainment) and later Noh and Kyôgen were eventually made part of the ceremonial entertainments. One

---

[47] *Ibid.,* pp. 50–51.
[48] *Ibid.,* p. 52.
[49] *Ibid.,* p. 55.
[50] Ortolani, p. 13–14.
[51] *Ibid.,* p. 91.

particular Shinto rite, which most clearly demonstrates the relationship of modern Noh to ancient *kagura*, is the annual *Onmatsuri* festival at Kasuga Wakamiya Shrine in Nara:

> On the first day, a special bow and arrow dance by Noh actors of the Komparu school and an old *furyû* dance by Kyôgen actors of the Ôkura school are performed beneath the ancient *yôgô* pine located on the south approach to the shrine. This is referred to as the 'ceremony under the pine' *(matsu-no-shita-no-shiki)*. The second day, a full formal program of five Noh and four Kyôgen is presented on a temporary low stage set up on the grass in front of the temporary shrine.[52]

This Yôgô pine is believed to have "provided a passage for the descent of Nô from the world of the gods to the world of 'men' . . . A 'spirit' descends through the 'vertical axis' of the tree to a dancer beneath, inducing trance and causing him to move 'at the will of a god as his creature, a medium possessed of the divine spirit.'"[53] The events on the first day are, in essence, a shamanistic ritual acknowledging the mediumistic function of the Noh actor. The events of the second day are ordinary Noh performances, some of which demonstrate the close relationship of Noh drama to shamanistic trance-possession.

This relationship is most clearly demonstrated in the first category of Noh plays, sometimes referred to as 'god Noh', which consists of a number of plays

---

[52] *Ibid.*, p. 1 . The term *furyû* refers to folk dances originally performed to avoid pestilence, it later came to refer to non-dramatic dance pieces in Noh and Kyôgen. See Ortolani, pp. 69–70 and p. 300.

[53] Donald Keene, *Nô: The Classical Theatre of Japan* (Tokyo and Palo Alto: Kodansha International, Ltd., 1966) p. 35. Kirby, 1975, points out that the pine tree at the back of the Noh stage is sometimes "said to have been inspired by this tree" but that this is not the case. It is rather "a representation of the principle of the tree as 'conductor' in shamanistic trance possession". Kirby, p. 78.

that have obviously developed from shrine dances. *Takasago* is a typical example:

> A priest from Kyushu makes a pilgrimage to Takasago Bay in Harima. Spring breezes whispering through the pine trees, and the sound of the waves as they beat against the shore, join to form a lovely symphony with the soft tones of the evening bell wafting down through the mist on a mountain top nearby. An old couple appears and they begin sweeping up the leaves, and purifying the sand on the shore. They answer with ancient poems which tell of the wedding of the pines at Sumiyoshi and Takasago. Pine trees symbolize eternal life. The old man explains that even though separated, the hearts of a married couple should always be together. He goes on to tell of the seasons and all living things, by means of old poems. The old man announces that he and his wife are the spirits of the pines of Sumiyoshi and Takasago. Then they board a boat and disappear into the mist over the bay.
>
> In Scene II the god of Sumiyoshi appears and dances, announcing prosperity and long life for all mankind.[54]

The priest character serves as a witness, an enabler who invites or incites the gods to speak; the leading actors are vessels for the gods who speak through them. The actors who represent the gods, whether in human or divine form, are masked throughout, whereas the witness is always unmasked. Thus, it appears that it is the masks themselves that are emblematic of the gods. It is noteworthy that all the masks have recognisably human characteristics, even when the god appears in divine aspect. So, while it is understandable that the couple who appear in the first part of the play wear the masks of an old man and woman, it is interesting that when *Sumiyoshi* returns as a god to perform his dance for prosperity and

---

[54] Daiji Maruoka and Tatsuo Yoshikoshi. *Noh*, translated by Don Kenny (Osaka: Hoikusha Publishing Co. Ltd., 1969) p. 9.

longevity, he is depicted with the *Kantan-otoko* mask, which resembles a young man. Perhaps the intention is not that the mask should show an abstract rendition of a non-human creature, but it should rather be a human conception of an abstraction. Not *the* face of the god, perhaps, but *a* face of the god.[55]

The god plays serve to demonstrate that the kami are ever present, that they may appear at any time and that they are benevolent towards humankind. Other moral lessons may be part of the text as well ("the hearts of a married couple should always be together", for example), but the plays are primarily celebratory in nature. God plays are given at the beginning of a Noh programme as an act of purification and dedication to the gods. Thus, the structure of the programme reflects Noh's roots in Shinto ritual by beginning with *matsuri,* service to the kami.

Buddhism
Buddhism originated in India around the fifth century before the Current Era. An outgrowth of Hindu philosophy, its chief divergence from Brahmanic teaching is "the denial of soul, of any enduring entity in man apart from temporary associations producing the illusion of a person, an ego".[56] Essentially, Buddhism contends that human beings are trapped by their desires and attachment to earthly things and so must suffer through an endless cycle of death and rebirth. In order to break this cycle, one must follow "the eightfold path (right views, right intention, right speech, right action, right livelihood, right effort, right mindfulness, and right concentration)"[57] and thereby achieve enlightenment, an

---

[55] Pulvers (1978) points out that the *Kantan-otoko* "has gradually displaced the earlier god masks [. . .] of a more static and strong expression in a number of plays. One reason may be that with the slowing down in tempo of performance a mask was preferred that appeared to change more with slow movement", p. 202.

[56] Ananda K. Coomaraswamy, *Hindus and Buddhists* (London: Senate, Studio Editions 1994) p. 249.

[57] Varley, p. 18.

end of suffering and Nirvana.[58] By the time it reached Japan in the sixth century, Buddhism had spread throughout most of Asia and had altered greatly from its original doctrines. It was introduced from the mainland, possibly from the Korean kingdom of Paekehe, at a time when both Japan and Korea were profoundly influenced by China, newly unified under the Sui Dynasty (589–618). By the beginning of the T'ang Dynasty (618–907), Buddhism in China had "come to be regarded as virtually essential to the institutional centralization of the country".[59] Prince Shôtoku, who sought to unify the warring clans of Japan, was a devout follower of Buddhism and its strongest proponent, but did not succeed in supplanting native Shinto with this new religion. Buddhism's pessimistic world view, that "all things are impermanent, suffering is universal, and man is a helpless victim of his fate",[60] was very much in opposition to the essentially optimistic world view of Shinto, that "the world is inherently good [and] gives promise of an unlimited development of life power".[61] By the seventh and eighth centuries, however, and in particular during the reign of emperor Temmu (673–686), Buddhism had come to be seen as representative of 'higher civilization'[62] (that is, of continental sophistication) and was adopted by the court. From this time the two faiths found the means to co-exist, albeit not always comfortably. A number of sects emerged, each of which made efforts to reconcile Shinto and Buddhist beliefs.

---

[58] "Even the word 'Nirvana' is common to Buddhism and Hinduism, and controversy turns upon whether Nirvana is or is not equivalent to extinction. The question is really improper, for the meaning of Nirvana is no more than a freeing from the fetters of individuality–as the space enclosed in an earthen pot is freed from its limitation and becomes one with infinite space when the pot is broken. Whether we call that infinite space a Void or a Whole is more a matter of temperament than of fact." Comaraswamy, p. 249.

[59] Varley, pp. 17–18.

[60] *Ibid.*, p. 19.

[61] Ono, pp. 102–103

[62] Varley, p. 20.

A syncretistic faith taught by Buddhists emerged which claimed that the buddhas were the prime noumenon, while the kami were their Japanese manifestations. In Shingon Buddhism for example, the Sun Goddess was said to be the avatar of the Cosmic Buddha. Thus in later centuries each major division of Buddhism developed its own special variety of syncretism to correspond to its sectarian doctrine.[63]

As a result, Buddhist temples were built in proximity to Shinto shrines, Shinto *kami* became synonymous with Buddhist deities and, since all activities associated with death are utterly repellent to Shinto, Buddhist priests were given the sole responsibility for death rites. Buddhist monasteries became great centres of learning, and Kûkai, the founder of the Shingon (True Word) sect, is credited with inventing the *kana* syllabary by which means Japanese became a written language. (Before the invention of *kana,* any Japanese historical records or literature were recorded in Chinese characters, in spite of the fact that Chinese and early Japanese were linguistically unrelated. The establishment of a written form for Japanese was the first step in establishing a truly Japanese culture independent of continental influence.)

Esoteric Buddhism

In relation to the present study, of all the early Japanese Buddhist sects, Shingon in particular warrants closer scrutiny. It represents a development of Tantrism, a practice that evolved in India around the year 600. Shrouded in mystery, Tantric Buddhism is regarded with some suspicion because of its association with magic rites and sexual practices.

---

[63] Ono, p. 86.

> Because of its stress on incantations, spells and primitive magic, Tantrism has been viewed by many outsiders as a corrupt and decadent phase of Buddhism.[64]

Many Balinese rituals, particularly the Calonarang dramas which feature witchcraft, magical incantations, sacrifices and death, have strongly Tantric overtones. However, Tantrism in the Far East was of a different order and is often referred to as 'esoteric Buddhism' since its characteristic feature is that its precepts are disseminated directly from master to pupil through secret teachings. The Shingon sect holds that the Cosmic Buddha *(Dainichi)* is a 'universal entity' and that all other 'transcendent beings' are merely manifestations of this cosmic force. Enlightenment is achieved through the proper execution of certain ritual activities.

> In order to enter into communion with Dainichi and realize the essential oneness of all existence, the supplicant must utilize the Three Mysteries of speech, body and mind. Proper ritual performance requires the coordinated practice of all three mysteries.[65]

These mysteries consist, in essence, of mantras, mudras and meditation and it is through the use of these tools that the worshipper may become one with the universal. Not only do these 'mysteries' correspond to the ritual activities of Balinese Topeng actors as they open the box of masks, but, as we shall see, they also come into play in Noh training and performance.

---

[64] Varley, p. 47.
[65] *Ibid.*, p. 48.

Zen

The other Buddhist sect that is particularly significant in relation to Noh is, of course, Zen. It was established in Japan during the Kamakura period, a time that also saw the rise of Noh's most ardent patrons, the Samurai warrior class.

> Because of its stress on self-discipline and control, Zen seemed particularly appropriate as a creed for the warriors of medieval Japan and no doubt it exerted a strong influence on the molding of the samurai way of life.[66]

Zen, literally, means 'meditation' and the sect maintains that personal enlightenment may be achieved through a discipline of quiet meditation. It emphasises a reverence for the ordinary and, significantly, rejects reasoning and intellectual effort as a means to enlightenment.

> Rationality must eventually give way to intuitive insight, which alone frees a person to live naturally and spontaneously. . . . Attachment to the commonplace and reliance on understanding things for oneself are two important principles of Zen's still-living philosophy. They also underlie Zen aesthetics, which frown on anything gaudy or elaborate, and emphasize, on the one hand, naturalness and, on the other, a kind of reflective restraint that deliberately leaves room for the imagination.[67]

Zeami's aesthetic principles are deeply influenced by Zen philosophy, particularly in his later writings.[68] Simplicity and restraint are the hallmarks of Zen-influenced art and behind it all is a profound mysticism that defies rational explication. For the Noh actor, this means an unquestioning dedication to the acquisition of skills and techniques of a highly coded performance practice. Real

---

[66] *Ibid.*, pp. 93–94.

[67] Mason and Caiger, pp. 169–170.

[68] It is generally accepted that Zeami spent some years as a Zen monk, perhaps from around 1422 when he was in his late fifties. See de Poorter, pp. 38–39 and Ortolani, p. 97.

understanding of the underlying meanings of the texts and movements, like spiritual enlightenment, comes only through disciplined application, not through explanations. The state of mind of the Noh actor while performing must be one of simultaneous concentration and 'mindlessness', and only in this state can he achieve true excellence in performance. Zen philosophy delights in this sort of apparent contradiction, as is evidenced in the *koan,* a kind of riddle used as a concentration device in Zen meditation (perhaps the most famous example of which is: 'What is the sound of one hand clapping?') The *koan* cannot be solved, it is not "a question that has a wordy answer. It is a *procedure* for exploring life's deepest existential issues".[69] That state of 'mindless concentration' is an altered state of consciousness in which seemingly paradoxical elements can be reconciled.

Noh, Spirituality and the Reconciliation of Opposites

The secular theatrical genre of Noh drama, which began as common street entertainments performed by outcasts at the bottom of the social scale, is also a highly spiritual and refined court art derived from ancient and sacred religious rituals. It is a living theatrical art that has, nonetheless, remained virtually unchanged for many generations—an animated artefact of an ancient aesthetic. It is a paradox and, like the *koan,* the more intensely this phenomenon is analysed, the more complex and paradoxical it appears. Yet this is entirely consistent with the culture from which it has sprung. Religious belief in Japan consists of a number of seemingly incongruous elements which co-exist in somewhat uneasy conjunction. Noh drama, having developed through association with various traditions in this milieu, has managed to incorporate several of these components into an art that somehow transcends any apparent contradictions.

---

[69] James H. Austin, MD, *Zen and the Brain: Toward an Understanding of Meditation and Consciousness* (Cambridge Massachusetts and London, England: The MIT Press, 1998) p.112.

Buddhism and Shinto, for example, would seem to be thoroughly incompatible, although they have managed to co-exist in Japan for many centuries, and Noh manages to address both optimistic Shinto polytheism and Buddhist moral philosophy. Indeed, it reflects Shinto traditions of shamanistic trance-possession as well as Buddhist meditative mysticism.

The Buddhist Shingon and Zen sects seem in many ways to be not vastly dissimilar in their fundamental principles, since both believe that enlightenment is achieved by becoming one with a universal cosmic force. However, the two differ significantly in methodology and aesthetic. Shingon, bound up with ritual incantatory magic and secret esoteric practices, inspired artists to create intricate and abstruse icons and mandalas to assist in meditation. The refinement of its art and its exclusivity appealed to the sophisticated and refined Heian courtiers. Zen, in contrast, places its emphasis upon simplicity, clarity, naturalness and self-realisation. It inspired a more restrained artistic expression in painting, flower arrangement, the tea ceremony and, perhaps most famously, the austere Zen 'garden' consisting of stones and raked gravel. This spartan, rustic simplicity appealed to the practical instincts of the rising warrior class. Yet, in spite of such obvious incongruities, one can see evidence of both philosophies in Noh. On the one hand, it is a closed world where secret teachings are passed from one generation to the next, and where a complex symbolic vocabulary is evident not only in its highly poetic texts but also in various elements of performance including costume, properties, stage architecture and movement. On the other hand, Noh features a determinedly non-analytical pedagogy and its performance has about it a simplicity and restraint in which all movement is pared down to absolute essentials so that each gesture is almost an abstraction. Noh is at once both simple and complex, austere and baroque.

The merging of seemingly contradictory elements is also evidenced in Noh masks. They are startlingly expressive, but the expression is often ambiguous; and it is this very ambiguity which lends each mask such a vast range of expression. Moreover, for all their realistic detail, Noh performance tradition dictates that the masks do not quite fit the human face, so that the audience is constantly reminded that the performer and character are separate entities. However, in spite of this apparent dichotomy, performance tradition also dictates that before each performance the actor must seek to become one with the mask in which he is to perform. Contradictory yet coincident, these apparently disparate components harmonise in Noh performance. One particularly fascinating incongruity is encountered in certain 'demon' plays, in which the leading actor performs the role of a demon in disguise. Zeami's *Kuruma-Zô (The Carriage Priest)* provides an excellent example. In this play a goblin, disguised as a *Yamabushi*[70] priest confronts the 'carriage priest' of the title (so called because he travels in an "old, broken carriage"[71]) and "engages him in a religious contest of words".[72] The goblin-in-disguise is defeated in this argument and departs, but he soon returns in his true form and makes an attempt "to overcome the other's holy power by his evil influence".[73] When performing as the goblin in disguise the Noh actor appears without a mask, but when the goblin appears in its 'true form' he is masked (see Figures 22 and 23). Thus, the face is a mask and the mask, the true face.

The Noh Stage

The modern Noh stage retains a number of elements which attest to the genre's association with shrine ceremonies held in the open air (see Diagram 2). The stage area is roofed, even in modern indoor theatres, and is surrounded by an area of white stones, which once served to reflect "the natural light of the sun to

---

[70] "Ascetics associated with an indigenous mountain worship *(shugendô)*. They used to spread their faith through performances of *yamabushi kagura,* a tradition rich in colorful rituals, acrobatics, sword dances, magic with fire, and masked plays." Ortolani, p. 324.

[71] P. G. O'Neill, *A Guide to Nô* (Tokyo: Hinoki Shoten, 1953) p. 93.

[72] *Ibid.*

[73] *Ibid.* The goblin, incidentally, is defeated a second time and "goes away acknowledging the superior power of the Buddhist priest".

illuminate the stage".[74] The large pine tree that is painted on the back wall of the stage (the *kagami-ita,* or 'mirror board', which serves as both backdrop and sounding board) is said by some commentators to represent the Yôgô pine at Kasuga shrine mentioned above

> It is said that a god descended to earth by way of the tree, took the form of an old man, and danced in celebration of the harmony between the gods and man.[75]

This association of the painted tree with the traditional abode of the observing god (the *kamukura*) is further reinforced by a continuing custom in which the performer sings the first words of verse in a Noh play to the pine on the back wall. That this gesture represents an offering to the gods is clearly apparent in ceremonial Noh performances given on stages specially constructed beside significant, sacred trees. The *Takigi* (torchlight) Noh performed every year beside an enormous thousand-year-old pine in the grounds of the Zôjô-ji shrine in Tokyo is a notable example. The bamboo painted on the side wall, which holds the low door *(kiri-do)* through which the chorus enters, is a relic of the bamboo canes that marked the four corners of the playing space in outdoor performances and also demarcated the area as sacred space.[76]

The three pines placed beside the bridgeway *(hashigakari)* are also reminiscent of outdoor performance, but they have a practical function as well, acting as markers by which actors may determine their placement. The four pillars supporting the stage roof (particularly the *metsuke-bashira,* or sighting pillar) serve this function too, and are especially significant for the masked actor who must use them to keep properly oriented in the stage space. In fact, much of

---

[74] Maruoka and Yoshikoshi, p. 101.

[75] Teele, p. 14. Ortolani cites this story too, but Kirby disputes it contending that "it is a generic image, a reference to the ritual sakaki tree in the myth of Uzume and Amaterasu, and a representation of the principle of the tree as 'conductor' in shamanistic trance possession." Kirby, p. 78.

[76] See Kirby, p. 78.

the design of the Noh stage may be attributable to the mask because of the restrictions it imposes on the leading actor's vision. So that the *shite* can have complete freedom of movement for the complex choreography that he must execute, it is necessary for unmasked members of the ensemble to be placed in such a way that there is no chance of a collision. Each member of the Noh ensemble has an assigned position: musicians and stage attendants at the rear of the stage; chorus and *waki* ('witness', the secondary character) at the side; Kyôgen player at the edge of the bridge and the *shite* (leading actor) up right, in the strongest stage position. Of course the *waki,* and the Kyôgen player do move in the central stage space, but these 'home' positions represent the position to which performers retire when the focus of the action is elsewhere, and act as choreographic markers. The stage itself is divided into nine imaginary, specially named areas, which indicate placement for dramatic action and dancing.

The dimensions of the Noh stage were made to conform to strict regulations created by the Tokugawa government during the eighteenth century "quite specific in all details of measurements, materials, ornamentations, orientation and so on"[77] and Noh stages built since that time conform to these measurements. Older examples of the Noh stage may still be seen in certain shrines and temples; on Sado Island, for example, where Zeami was once exiled, there are more than thirty different *nô-butai* scattered throughout the island, many still in use.

The stage floor is made of planed and polished Japanese cypress *(hinoki)* and beneath it are placed large jars or bowls which act as resonators (in modern theatres these are more likely to be made of shaped concrete). An important feature of Noh choreography is the rhythmic stamping performed by the leading actor, which not only acts as a signal to the musicians but also heightens the drama at particular moments in the play. The stage, then, is not only a place for

---

[77] Ortolani, p. 144.

dramatic action but also a percussion instrument that is 'played' by the *shite* as he dances.

> Five different sounds, which are the five standard notes in the Noh musical scale approximately corresponding to D, E, G, A and B, are produced with the *ashibyoshi* [stamps] at five different points on the stage, although they are hardly distinguishable even by the ordinary fan . . . These sounds represent, in the order named, midsummer or dog-days *(doyó)*, summer, spring, fall and winter, and in the *mai* [dance] when, for instance, spring is to be indicated, the dancing must take place on no other point on the stage but that which is designated as spring. The same rule goes with the other seasons.[78]

These rhythmic stamps corresponding to the seasons provides additional evidence of Noh's abiding connection to Shinto ritual and recalls the dance of *Uzume*, which lured the Sun Goddess from her cave.[79] In spite of hundreds of years of secular accretions, this resonating platform on which a performer sings and dances while wearing the mask of a god or spirit, retains its potency as a place of mediumship and divine revelation. The Noh stage is thus frequently characterised as:

> a sacred space where the meeting of our world with the other dimension is represented. The bridge becomes the passage through which gods become visible, restless or angry ghosts appear to haunt, or to implore the prayers that can give them salvation.[80]

---

[78] *The Noh Drama* (Tokyo: Kokusai Bunka Shinkokai, 1937) pp. 12–13

[79] *Ama no Uzume* danced on 'an upturned barrel' which resounded with the rhythmic stamping of her dance. See: Thomas Immoos, *Japanese Theatre*, translated by Hugh Young (London: Cassell and Collier Macmillan Publishers Ltd., 1977) pp. 39–40.

[80] *Ibid.*, p. 145.

Noh Plays

Noh plays are divided into five groups, loosely based upon their subject matter:

>**First group**: *Waki-nô,* sometimes also called *kami-mono,* are plays in which the leading actor represents a deity.
>
>**Second group**: *Asura-nô* or *Shura-mono,* plays about warriors.[81]
>
>**Third group**: *Katsura-mono,* or 'wig plays', in which the leading character is a woman.
>
>**Fourth group**: These are miscellaneous plays of varied subject matter, some of the most important of which are the *kyôran-mono,* mad-person plays, the *genzai-mono,* plays about the present (that is, medieval time) and *onryô-mono,* plays about vengeful ghosts.
>
>**Fifth group**: *Kiri-nô,* or final plays, many of which feature demons and goblins. These are lively and exciting plays that generally end a Noh programme.

A traditional full-length programme of Noh plays would present one or more plays of each group (interspersed with shorter, comic Kyôgen pieces), following the order above. However in contemporary Noh such an extensive programme is very unusual. Performance records clearly indicate that during Zeami's time Noh plays must have been much shorter than they are today. The longer playing time has come not as a result of additions to the text, but rather because of a gradual slowing of the pace of performance which took place over many years and was then fixed as standard during the Tokugawa period.[82] During the Muromachi

---

[81] The name comes from that of the Buddhist underworld to which it is believed that the spirits of warriors killed in battle must descend, wandering in misery until they can be redeemed. In *Shura-mono,* the protagonist is generally the ghost of a warrior who asks a priest (the *waki*) to perform the rites necessary for his salvation. See Ortolani, p. 133. See also Chifumi Shimazaki's excellent introduction in *The Noh, Volume II: Battle Noh* (Tokyo: Hinoki Shoten, 1987) pp. 1–26.

[82] Dr. Haruo Nishino, interview, 28 May, 1997; see also Ortolani pp. 103–104, who suggests that the pace slowed in order for players to better demonstrate qualities of *yûgen,* the mysterious grace which was the apogee of courtly skill and sophistication.

period, as many as ten Noh plays and Kyôgen comic pieces might be performed in a single day, whereas today a full programme (which can last as long as five or six hours) usually consists of no more than three Noh and two Kyôgen pieces.

Of the more than two thousand Noh plays which are known to have existed during the great flowering of Noh between the fourteenth and seventeenth centuries, only about two hundred and forty survive in the current repertory.[83] Since these plays were selected "according to the taste of the Tokugawa period",[84] they generally demonstrate the cultivated and refined sensibilities of courtiers of that time. However, many earlier Noh plays had enormous popular appeal and these spectacular plays drew huge crowds. Even among the stately masterpieces performed today, one can get a taste of what made Noh appeal to all social classes during the Muromachi period. The demon plays of the fifth group provide the most obvious examples with fast action, exciting dances and fabulous costumes and masks. Zeami warned his students against performing these pieces for the court, maintaining that their vulgarity would offend a sophisticated audience. Nonetheless, he was himself the author of a number of excellent fifth group plays, including *Kuruma Zô* mentioned above.

Most Noh plays are structured in two parts. In the first part the *waki* (often a priest) enters and introduces himself as a pilgrim or traveller; he may or may not have companions *(waki tsure)*. He describes his journey and the reasons for it and, perhaps after a few steps around the stage space to indicate travel, he describes the place at which he has arrived, where the 'action' of the play will occur. Following a sometimes lengthy prelude by the musicians, the *shite* enters and tells his or her story. After an exchange with the *waki,* during which additional information about the leading character is revealed, the *shite* may exit or simply retire to the back of the stage to change costume and, often, the mask. While the costume change is being effected, there is usually a comic interlude *(ai*

---

[83] Ortolani, p. 132.
[84] *Ibid.*

kyôgen) featuring a Kyôgen player. When the *shite* re-appears, the character generally has taken on another form (like the Sumiyoshi pine and the Tengu goblin mentioned above) in which the character's true nature is revealed. The second half of the play concludes with a lively dance at the end of which the *shite* gives a single, resounding stamp and then exits slowly along the bridgeway.

Music

Music is an essential feature of Noh drama, especially since all of the text is either chanted or sung and all of the movement is strictly rhythmical. To the Western ear, the music in Noh can seem even less melodic than the gamelan accompaniment for Balinese dance-drama and even more obviously related to the world of shamanism and mediumship. The instruments consist of the *fue,* a high-pitched flute; the *otsuzumi,* a drum held on the player's knee played with the hand; the *kotsuzumi,* a drum held against the player's shoulder also played with the finger tips; and, sometimes, the *taiko,* a slightly larger drum which sits in a low rack on the floor and is played with two sticks. The drums and flute not only set and maintain the tempo of the performance, they also summon the gods, ghosts and spirits whose stories are to be enacted. Perhaps the most striking element of the accompaniment is the *kakegoe,* weird cries made by the drummers, usually first heard in the musical interlude before the *shite* enters.

> Originally they were probably part of the conjuration for the descent of the spirits; they presently serve as [an] integral part of the *nô* music. The human voice, in this form of syllables which the drummers shout, hum, or moan, is considered as a fifth instrument, added to the flute and the three drums, with an essential function in the building of the unique atmosphere of the *nô*. There is no

improvisation, the *kakegoe* are strictly indicated as part of the score.[85]

The musicians 'summon' the *shite* with the flute, drums and, most importantly, with the *kakegoe*. These cries and the musical accompaniment continue throughout the drama and become quite frenzied during the final dance sequence, as if urging on the leading actor. After the *shite's* final stamp, there is one last cry, and a final drumbeat to end the play.

Noh musicians are trained specialists and, although Noh actors usually learn to play drums and sometimes flute in the course of their studies, the two types of performers do not exchange roles; which is to say that musicians do not act, and actors do not perform professionally as musicians.[86] Actors chant and sing the text and execute their rhythmic stamps, interacting seamlessly with the musicians who provide a separate rhythmic, melodic and atmospheric element.

Hierarchy

As is to be expected of any Japanese court art, a strict hierarchy prevails at every level in Noh. Groups of professional Noh performers are divided into five 'schools': the Kanze, Komparu, Kongô, Hôshô and Kita. The first four of these can trace their origins to the Muromachi period and even the 'youngest', the Kita school, was established by the early seventeenth century.[87] Since they were the only companies officially recognised by the Tokugawa government, these five groups subsumed some of the other Noh performing groups of the time, so that

---

[85] *Ibid.*, p. 306.

[86] The exception to this rule is the *rannô* "in which all performers exchange roles with, for example, musicians dancing, actors playing and *kyôgen* players chanting in the Noh chorus." "Such performances, sometimes done as end-of-the-year parties, add considerably to the performers' store of experience." Monica Bethe and Karen Brazell, 'The Practice Of Noh Theatre' in *By Means of Performance: Intercultural Studies of Theatre and Ritual* (Cambridge: Cambridge University Press, 1990) p. 178.

[87] These schools represent only those of the leading actors *(shite);* the musicians, *waki* and *kyôgen* players each have their own schools. See O'Neill, *A Guide to Nô,* pp. 5–6.

within an individual school there may be several separate sub-groups. (The Umewaka family, for example, is nominally part of the Kanze school, but maintains its own distinct performing traditions.[88]) The five schools are also ranked and the Kanze, founded by Kanami and Zeami is generally regarded as pre-eminent among them.[89]

Within the schools, too, the hierarchy persists, and the head of each school has the title of *iemoto*.

> a kind of teacher/king, immensely respected and faithfully served by his disciples, with the right of allowing or prohibiting a performance, deciding who would be the main performer among the many artists of the school, interpreting the correctness of a certain dance pattern, punishing and expelling individuals from the school, determining the use of the costumes, masks and theatrical equipment, handling the finances, awarding rank and diplomas, and, since the Meiji era, also holding the copyright for all textbooks and material published by the school.[90]

The power of the *iemoto* over all aspects of performance is significant in considering the relationship of the Noh actor to his mask, since it is most likely to be the head of the school, rather than the individual performer, who determines which mask will be worn for a particular character. This means that those moments in the *kagami-no-ma* may be an actor's first opportunity to see the mask

---

[88] See P. G. O'Neill, 'The Nô Schools and their Organisation' *Bulletin*, 73 (London: Japan Society of London, June 1974) pp. 2–6.

[89] The world of Noh is a very political one in which jealousies and intrigues abound. Any ranking of the five schools cannot be allowed to imply that any one is better than another. The Kanze school is, without question, the largest and most famous and it may well be the wealthiest. The school maintains large, beautifully appointed modern theatres in both Tokyo and Kyoto where performances are given regularly.

[90] Ortolani, p. 105

in which he is to perform and this can have a powerful effect upon the performance that is given.

> When I did,. . . . I practised with a Deigan [mask] that [my teacher had] made before, but when it was the day of the performance it was one of the Kongô school masks that was prepared for me. . . . I found, after putting on the mask and seeing this new face, that I felt a different kind of a relationship with the role, that Lady Rokujô was *that* person, *that* face. . . . Then, actually going out onto the *hashigakari*, [bridgeway] even before the curtain went up, and then going out on the stage, I really felt that I was different, that I was seeing through someone else's eyes. Or someone else was seeing through my eyes. I hadn't ever felt that so strongly before. I felt that there was an energy that the mask had.[91]

The mask chosen for this actor was a masterpiece from the Kongô school collection, used by actors for many generations. It did not differ greatly in appearance from the contemporary mask with which she had rehearsed, yet the performer felt strongly that this special mask generated a tangible power. The special qualities of certain Noh masks are acknowledged by their placement in yet another hierarchy. The masks in each school's collection are ranked by various criteria including the age of the mask, the person who made it and its particular performance history. *Kurai-dori* is the term used to describe the 'position' or 'level of quality' of a mask and it is the *kurai* of the mask that determines the interpretation of the role and the play.[92] In the course of an actor's career, he will graduate from one level to the next as his age and skill increase. During his early teenage years

---

[91] Interview with Rebecca Teele, 4 June, 1997. Ms. Teele is something of a rarity in that she is both non-Japanese and a woman, yet is accepted as a professional Noh performer.

[92] Nakamura Yasuo, *Noh: The Classical Theater*, translated by Don Kenny (New York: Weatherhill/Tankosha, 1971) pp. 158–159. This was also emphasised by the late Kongô Iwao, iemoto of the Kongô school: "In the past people used to ask before a performance, 'What will be the *kurai*, the level of dignity, of the performance?' and the answer would be 'the level of the mask. To really understand the level of a mask is difficult . . .The important point is that the actor should be able to perceive the character of the mask and use it accordingly". 'Recollections and Thoughts on Nô' in *No/Kyôgen Masks in Performance* , p. 90.

he may be permitted to play certain young god roles wearing a mask and later, with more experience, he may be allowed to wear a young woman mask as *tsure,* companion to the leading character. By the age of twenty, he will be allowed to perform as *shite* (leading actor) only in young woman or young man masks.

> Next he moves on to roles requiring the *heita* mask—the powerful, mature warriors of such plays as *Tamura* or *Yashima*. In his thirties he will study female *shite* roles of the fourth category, wearing the *shakumi* mask in *Fujito* or *Sakuragawa*. He may then progress to the roles of gods and demons, wearing the appropriate masks, to the great female *shite* roles of the third category, and, finally, when past sixty, to the parts of old women, wearing the *yase-onna* mask in such works as *Sotoba Komachi*.[93]

Thus, the plays, companies, personnel and even masks and costumes of Noh each have their place in an individual hierarchy. Among all these rankings, however, it is the level of the mask that determines the level of the performance, who may be allowed to play the role, the costume that may be worn, even the quality of the music and choral chant.[94] More than any other factor, it is the mask which has the greatest influence upon the interpretation of the play and all the elements of performance.

Noh Masks

According to Nakamura Yasuo, the ritual masks from which Noh masks developed were derived from Buddhist temple statues:

> The ancient Japanese believed that although the gods could not be seen, they would come immediately if prayers were offered, bearing blessings or ready to quell evil . . . .the introduction of

---

[93] Keene, 1966, p. 69.
[94] *Ibid.,* p. 70.

> Buddhism to Japan brought with it the practice of praying before Buddhist images called *butsu-zô*. Under this strong influence the native gods and goddesses which heretofore had not been envisioned, especially the ancestral gods, were given form for the first time in sculpture and painting as Shinto images.[95]

Since the static wooden sculptures did not convey the movement and vitality ascribed to the *kami*, the facial features of the statues were copied to create masks that allowed the images to be animated.[96] This may serve to explain why even the masks used to represent spirits of flowers, trees and mountains have human features (the spirit of the Sumiyoshi pine mentioned above, for example.) *Fudô*, a guardian figure from esoteric Buddhism who appears in the fifth group play *Chôbuku Soga*, is depicted with an elaborately carved mask that derives directly from temple statues. The mask is the subject of a famous legend that illustrates the supernatural power attributed to some masks in Noh. It concerns the sixteenth century Noh actor, Kongô Ujimasa, who was so impressed by a temple sculpture of *Fudô* that he secretly returned to the temple where it stood and removed the head from the statue. From this he cut away the face in order to create a mask for his performance at the emperor's court. When the performance ended, however, he found that the mask remained stuck fast to his face and could only be removed by tearing his flesh. This mask, called *Nikutsuki Fudô*, ('*Fudô* which sticks to the flesh') remains in the collection of the Kongô family.[97]

---

[95] Nakamura Yasuo, 'Nô Masks: Their History and Development', translated by Rebecca Teele, *ibid.*, p. 120. For a more detailed discussion, see Pulvers, 1978, pp. 37–44.

[96] One particular Shinto deity, which Nakamura cites as the model for the *Ko-omote* mask is *Tamayorihime*. The translation of her name ('divine spirit draws near young girl') indicates that the figure represents a *miko*, the shrine priestess who enters into trance-possession to speak for the god. Here again, one sees the association of the Noh mask with ritual and trance possession. Nakamura, *ibid.*, pp. 121–122.

[97] Pulvers, 1978, pp. 38–39

According to Nakamura, there are at least one hundred and fifty different types of masks in use in Noh,[98] which he divides roughly into six groups:

1. Okina

2. Kijin (Demon-God, *Beshemi,* for example)

3. Jô (Old Man)

4. Otoko (Man)

5. Onna (Woman)

6. Ryô (Spirit: *Hannya* and *Fudô* are two examples)

Of these only Okina is held to be sacred, although there are a number of specific masks of various types which are associated with legends of the supernatural, like the *Fudô* mentioned above. In *Sarugaku Dangi,*[99] Zeami tells of a mysteriously powerful *Tenjin* mask (used for heavenly spirits):

> Once someone borrowed the mask, but because they had a peculiar dream concerning it, they returned it. At that point the mask was retired from use and highly revered, but on the basis of a second dream it was restored to use and is still worn today.[100]

Another significant legend tells of a demon mask worn by Zeami himself during the time of his exile on Sado, when he performed a Noh play at Shôbô Temple:

> he is said to have performed . . . expressly for the purpose of relieving a severe drought. Immediately following this ritual performance, there was reportedly a torrential rain. The fierce

---

[98] Nakamura, 'Nô Masks', p.114. There are even more if one counts masks used only by individual schools of Noh; see Pulvers, 1978 pp. 162–216.

[99] Notes of Zeami's talks about his art to his son Motoyoshi.

[100] Rimer and Yamazaki, p. 238, see also de Poorter, pp. 123–124.

demonic mask that Zeami purportedly wore for the occasion remains today a treasured relic in the temple.[101]

It is not surprising that masks depicting gods and demons should inspire stories about their strange, otherworldly powers, but even quite simple, human masks are sometimes felt to have special resonances. This is not because they are possessed by some supernatural being, but rather because there is something in the inherent nature of the mask that gives it a quite separate life power. The Noh actor Kanze Hisao confessed:

> There are certain masks for which I have felt great love and adoration, and there are other superior masks that have given me such strength in performance that they made me seem to have much greater powers of expression than I actually possessed.[102]

Naturally, a performer is likely to feel a sense of awe when using a mask that is a masterpiece three or four hundred years old. As one actor put it:

> There is no difference between old and new masks, but perhaps the feeling is different in performance with the more valuable costume and special mask.[103]

Yet the Noh mask is more than just a beautiful and expensive prop. Zenchiku, an actor of the Komparu school to whom Zeami entrusted his secret writings, in his own theoretical writings on Noh aesthetics tried to deal with this question of the essence of the Noh mask's power.

> Zenchiku proposes that what is miraculous in art—which is concerned with the fashioning of images—is the creative force that is transfused into the image by the artist. The mask . . . is therefore

---

[101] Nearman, 'Behind the Mask of Nô' in *Nô/Kyôgen Masks in Performance*, p. 38.

[102] Kanze Hisao, 'Life with the Nô Mask', translated by Don Kenny in *ibid.*, p. 65.

[103] Interview with Matsuda Kenji (Noh master of the Kanze school) translated by Yasuko Igarashi, 30 May, 1997.

not simply a representation but as a creative manifestation may partake of the divine, and consequently will have some degree of beneficial spiritual efficacy.[104]

The spiritual power of the mask is seen here as inherent and tangible and comes to the mask in the act of its creation. Zenchiku writes of "the mask's organ of mind"[105] in a way that implies that it possesses an independent life force. By the Tokugawa period, this perception was acknowledged in the way that the ideogram used for 'mask' was interpreted:

In Zeami's time, it was read *men*, as an abbreviation for *kamen*, 'substitute or provisional face'. This character was now read *omote* in Nô circles to emphasise the notion that the object represented an actual face and was to be treated as such by the actor.[106]

For the actor Kanze Hisao, the use of the term *omote* indicates "the recognition of the mask as a companion that provides an entrance into the world the actor is attempting to create on the stage and through which the audience can also enter and join him in building that special world".[107] By this interpretation, the mask is the actual face of the character and functions as a bridge between the audience and the 'special world' of the play, inhabited by the character. The actor, then, is the medium, who both gives life to the mask and is himself imbued by the mask's divine 'creative force'.

Yet not all masks are equally powerful; performers make it quite clear that some masks are 'better' than others. What gives a 'good mask' that special quality? Some masks are highly regarded because of the person who carved them:

---

[104] Nearman, 'Behind the Mask of Nô', p. 43.

[105] *Ibid.*, p. 43.

[106] *Ibid.*, pp. 57–58. The ideogram for 'omote' is a combination two characters, 'omo' which means to recollect and 'te' a suffix form meaning 'many directions' thus 'omote' means not only 'face' or 'front' but also implies something recognised, recollected, from many directions (Dr. Poh Sim Plowright, personal communication).

[107] Kanze Hisao, 'Life with the Nô Mask', p. 66.

the masks of Zaken and Kawachi, master mask makers of the seventeenth century, for example, are priceless masterpieces. On the other hand, a mask may be equally highly regarded by a performer if it was made by a beloved relative or teacher[108] or simply because of its innate expressiveness, for no two masks are ever exactly alike.

Maskmaking

Although Noh maskmaking is not associated with elaborate religious ritual as it is in Bali, every element of the process is nonetheless regulated by hundreds of years of tradition.

> Noh masks are made according to specific measurements, which with the development of types for specific roles, gradually became prescribed down to the finest detail including length of eye, style of eyebrow or size and shape of eye-opening for a particular type.
>
> The size of a mask will vary according to type. The height (length) may vary from about 19 to 22cm., with most women's masks 20 to 21cm. This, according to the late mask maker, Susuki Keiun, was worked out on the basis of the Muromachi period [1336–1568] ideal of the relationship between mask and entire figure on stage as being one to eight. The ideal height of the male actor would have been about 1.65m.[109]

Cypress from the Kiso valley *(kiso hinoki)*, used for traditional Japanese architecture (including the Noh stage) is regarded as the ideal material for Noh mask-making, not only because of its associations but also because of its straight grain, lightness and strength. However, some early Noh masks were made from other woods including paulownia, Judas tree *(katsura)* and camphor wood *(kusu-*

---

[108] The Noh actor Umewaka Naohiko owns a few masks carved by his father, the late Umewaka Naoyoshi, and he made his debut in *Shakkyo*, wearing a *Shi-shi Guchi* mask made by the elder Umewaka. Not surprisingly these masks have a special resonance for this particular actor

[109] Pulvers, 1978, p. 5.

no-ki).[110] Contemporary mask makers sometimes use cheaper imported cypress or, "old building timber from shrines, temples or other buildings that have been torn down".[111] Although *kiso hinoki* is cured in salt water and dried for several years before it is carved, there is still a risk that some resin might remain in the wood and seep out to stain the face of the mask. For this reason, masks are sometimes boiled after carving to remove any remaining traces of resin.[112] The choice of wood for the mask is left to the maker and may be determined at least in part by financial considerations.

Pulvers points out that "as much as ninety per cent of the basic mask types were created by the end of the Muromachi period", but not all of the types correspond precisely to those used today.[113] Particularly excellent examples of these old masks have become *honmen* ("designated model masks of the old masters"[114]) and have served as models for later 'copies' called *utsushi-men,*[115] many of which are as valuable as the originals. Each of the five schools of Noh has its own collection of masks, some dating from the Muromachi period, which are of inestimable value simply as art objects. However, in Noh, as in other mask performing traditions, it is felt that a mask becomes more expressive with use; therefore old masks that have been used for generations are held to be most expressive. Many of these very ancient masks have been carefully preserved and may still be seen in performance. Sadly, however, when Noh fell on hard times during the Meiji era, a number of very valuable masks were sold by the schools

---

[110] A contemporary Noh mask-maker whom I interviewed has even established a workshop in Bali where Balinese carvers make creditable copies of Noh masks at a fraction of the Japanese price.

[111] Pulvers, 1978, p. 2.

[112] *Ibid.,* p. 26. Balinese masks may also be boiled to rid the wood of parasites.

[113] *Ibid.,* p.164.

[114] *Ibid.,* pp. 89–90.

[115] *Ibid.,* p. 55.

and have become part of the collections of certain temples and noble houses or are in the hands of private collectors.[116]

Contemporary carvers may become involved with the restoration of old masks, or might only create decorative pieces for the collector's market, but a few are able to specialise in making new masks for Noh actors. Each new mask is individually carved, but it must still be consistent with one of the existing types in every detail—there is really no room for innovation. This consistency is achieved by using paper templates, *kata-gami,* "cut-outs of the mask's profile and curve of the cheeks"[117] which allow carvers to measure their progress more or less precisely (Figures 24 and 25). Some experienced carvers with a keen eye can, of course, work from memory in roughing out the general shape, but most find the templates useful guides for getting exact proportions.[118] The carving is precise and subtly detailed, with great care and attention given to the expressive elements of the mask. For example, some of the seemingly impassive woman masks include slight indentations, virtually invisible until the mask is moved, which catch the light and give the impression of joy or sorrow as the mask angled up or down. To achieve this subtlety, the Noh mask carver has recourse to an enormous number and variety of specialised tools, including chisels and flat and curved knives of all sizes (Figure 26). The inside, that is, the back of the mask, is shaped in the last phase of carving and it is interesting that special concern is taken about the wearer's response to this part of the mask:

> The criterion is not only that the mask fit easily on to the face and give ample room for nose, mouth and chin or that it allow the wearer to see through at least some apertures, but also that the expression realized 'in inverse' on the back reflect something of the facial expression of the mask. The back is the last thing the

---

[116] Ortolani, p. 148.

[117] Pulvers, 1978, p. 6.

[118] See Teele, 'Interview with Udaka Michishige' in *Nô/Kyôgen Masks in Performance,* p. 137.

actor sees when putting on the mask. It must also be beautiful and not distract by being poorly carved. Some mask makers would take this one step further and say that the back of the mask is complete and comes alive only when the Noh actor puts it to his face.[119]

The back of the mask is where the mask maker can show his individuality and where he leaves the mark or signature, which indicates authorship. Some of the earliest Noh mask-makers left no signature, but the name of the carver, in the form of the *yake-in* (signature seal), is now an essential part of the mask, used to assess its value as an art object or antique.[120] Whereas a Balinese mask-maker may complete a mask in only a few days, a Noh mask can take weeks, even months to complete. This is partly because *hinoki* is a harder, drier, more difficult wood to work than *pulé,* but also because the carving on the face of the mask must be so fine that even smoothing the surface with sandpaper should be unnecessary.[121]

As meticulous as these *utushi-men* may be, the fact remains that no two masks, even those made by the same hand, will be exactly alike.

> From my experience, no one ever makes the same mask twice, even if they use the same templates. There is always some variation somewhere. For example, you always begin with the *Ko-omote*, they always look a little bit different. And they do tend to look like the carver, often, or someone close to the carver. . . .A

---

[119] Pulvers, 1978, pp. 10–11.

[120] This is important because even a new Noh mask used for decoration, if it is of good quality, will be priced at no less than ¥120,000 – ¥180,000 (approximately £600–£1000) and, according to Matsuda Kenji, a new mask for an actor may cost in excess of ¥500,000 (approximately £2500). Thus, individual actors rarely have their own collection of masks for performance.

[121] Jeanne Chizuko Nishimura, 'A Life-giving art: Traditional Art of Nô Mask Carving', in *Nô/Kyôgen Masks in Performance,* p. 144. Nishimura gives the impression that sandpaper is forbidden, but other carvers disagree. According to Rebecca Teele, one reason why sandpaper is avoided is that the fine dust it creates seems to "close the pores of the wood" and hinders the painting process. (Interview, 31 October, 1998).

> piece of wood has a personality of its own too, some kind of a quality of its own.[122]

While balance and proportion are important in creating a mask, an essential quality of the most expressive Noh masks is a subtle asymmetry that lends the mask vitality. This is not merely a matter of realistically capturing the natural imbalances of the human face, because the asymmetry of the mask works in conjunction with the structure of the Noh play and with the spiritual underpinnings of the genre itself.

> Noh masks are made asymmetrically so that the right eye seems to look downwards while the left eye seems to look forward. This is because most of the characters are ghosts who seek (or require) enlightenment. Therefore, with the asymmetry, the audience sees the character looking earthward (unenlightened and earthbound) on entering and walking along the *hashigakari,* but forward (enlightened) as he or she returns after the events of the play. Also the mouth should have a slight downward turn on the right side and upward on the left, more cheerful.[123]

This imbalance is the essential element in creating the renowned ambiguity of the Noh mask.

Only one element of the carving process is given over to something like a religious ritual, but it is an important moment: opening the eyes of the mask.

> A short prayer is said before boring open the eyeholes with an awl, for at this point life and spirit are given to the mask.[124]

With this ritual, derived from Buddhist practice,[125] the mask is symbolically endowed with life. It is at this moment that, as Zenchiku observed, "the creative

---

[122] Interview with Rebecca Teele 4 June, 1997.

[123] Interview with Udaka Michishige, 31 October, 1998.

[124] Jeanne Chizuko Nishimura, *Nô/Kyôgen Masks in Performance,* p. 144.

force is transfused into the image by the artist".[126] The actor, too, becomes a creative force which animates the mask because, unlike Balinese masks which have painted eyes with slits underneath through which the actor can see, the Noh mask quite literally requires the actor to see through the eyes of the character.

The painting process is, as with the Balinese masks, elaborate and complex and makes use of an array of natural substances including an element unique to Noh mask-making—*furubi,* "a brown soot-based liquid to bring out the nuances and add subtlety to the mask".[127] Because the *honmen* (model-masks) are hundreds of years old and are particularly venerated, *furubi* has come to be a necessary component of new Noh masks to soften their colours and give them the patina of age. Perhaps more surprisingly, some mask makers may even damage a new mask in order to make it look as though it has been used (Figures 27a and b):

> They may scratch away the paint in some areas after painting the masks: this is often done on the lips, where it helps subdue the brightness of the red. It is also done on the hair on women's masks, often leaving squiggly marks that suggest the mask has been eaten by bugs. Or the blackness of the hair may be subdued by running over it lightly with fine sandpaper, leaving tiny unpainted spots where there is any roughness in the surface. These are then touched up with *furubi*...
>
> Some masks, such as those for gods or demons or old people, may receive even rougher treatment. The paint on protruding areas such as the nose, chin or bones jutting out on emaciated faces. . . may be completely scratched off showing the bare wood beneath. Here

---

[125] One of the most important events for Buddhism in Japan was the eye-opening ceremony of the huge (53 feet tall) bronze statue of *daibutsu,* the great Buddha at Nara in 752. The eyes were painted by "a cleric from India" and there were some 10,000 Buddhist priests in attendance. See Varley pp. 35–36.

[126] Nearman, 'Behind the Mask of *Nō*' p. 43.

[127] Pulvers, 1978, p. 3.

> again, the damage is made to look as natural as possible, as if it were caused by accident or constant exposure.[128]

Ironically, after all of this calculated abuse, Noh masks are handled with the utmost care and kept in silk-lined bags, often padded with silk pillows, to prevent any possible damage. In a culture in which age alone may be the criterion for judging the value of an object, apparent age seems to be necessary—even if it is illusory—to lend credibility to a new object used in an ancient art form. In Western terms we might say that the new Noh mask itself wears a mask, a disguise indicating age and use.

Carver-actors

In the early days of Noh, masks were usually made by the actors who wore them. The Magojirô mask, for example, "is named after its maker Kongô Magojirô Hisatsugu (1537–1564), the earliest mask maker one can date with certainty"[129] and is said to have been modelled on his wife, who died young. Over time and with increased regulation, each aspect of Noh gradually became more specialised so that today it is rare to find a mask-maker who is also a professional performer. Yet, just as in Bali, the performer and the mask-maker have much to contribute to one another's work. Udaka Michishige, one of the very few contemporary actor-carvers and a leading member of the Kongô school comments:

> As a carver there are a number of technical points of which I am particularly aware because I am also an actor. For example, I am especially aware of the importance of studying the angles of the area around the mouth. It is important to discover what surfaces best reflect and resonate with the sound of the voice when the actor chants. If a mask is not carved out with this in mind, and the carving of the back of the mask kills or dampens the sound of the

---

[128] Pulvers, p. 23.

[129] *Ibid.*, p. 208.

chant that the actor has worked to perfect, then it is not a good mask.[130]

Similarly, the discipline of carving masks, becoming deeply familiar with each nuance of the mask, can inform the performance:

> There's a whole different kind of body awareness and sense for expression that you get when you realize what the rigors, the demands of the mask are. I think that informs the dancing.[131]

All of the performers interviewed felt strongly that some masks were better than others for performance, but those who had no experience of making masks were unable to articulate precisely what qualities made the difference. It is, perhaps, a matter of instinct. A performer tests a mask by looking at it, by moving it to see how it catches the light, by examining how the mask's eyes seem to see, but what is he looking for? One carver-actor, asked to describe what makes a good mask, replied: "It's the quality of reaching across space with something to say, a voice that's waiting".[132] A good mask, then, may be one that demands to be animated; one that requires the actor to give it life. The late Kongô Iwao pointed out: "The true value of a mask is revealed only when worn by a performer on the stage".[133]

For both mask-makers and actors, the value of a mask lies in its effectiveness as an expressive tool in performance, but when masks come to be viewed as 'art objects', a disheartening element of commercialism enters the frame. The carver who is simply a copyist, who is unfamiliar with the literature, the characters and the choreography, or does not intimately understand the physical needs of the performer may still be able to create a creditable copy. But, however attractive the object, it remains inferior to a mask which has been

---

[130] 'Interview with Udaka Michishige' in *Nô/Kyôgen Masks in Performance*, p. 136.

[131] Interview with Rebecca Teele, 4 June, 1997.

[132] *Ibid.*

[133] Quoted in Poh Sim Plowright, *The Classical Noh Theatre of Japan*. (London: Chadwyck-Healey, Ltd., 1991), p. 41.

created for performance. The mask that hangs in a museum with empty eyes is a sad shell, and the mask created as a souvenir, without reference to its real 'purpose' is a dead thing, without spirit, without life. In contrast, the mask that is brought to life, like Galatea, by a magical fusion of the human and the divine in performance is a miraculous object which gathers "resonance" through use.

Training

As with Balinese dance-drama, the training of performers for Noh is essentially an imitative, physical process. There are significant differences, of course. First of all, Noh plays are written texts (literary masterpieces, in some cases) which must be memorised perfectly—improvisation has no place in this performance tradition. Secondly, all aspects of the art are strictly regulated, including the pattern of instruction, precise details of style, and the measures of achievement. I shall deal here only with the training of the leading actors, since it is only they who are allowed to wear masks.

Becoming a *shite*

Traditionally, according to Zeami's *Fûshikaden*,[134] a child should begin training as a Noh actor at the age of six or seven. In fact, many actors begin much earlier: two of my informants started at the age of three, another began his training at five. Because the vocation is generally inherited, a child's first and perhaps only official teacher is most likely to be his father. As with Balinese dance-drama, the child learns by imitation and repetition:

> The father dances sections from a play with the child; the father singing the words while the child struggles to imitate his motions. Frequently the father manipulates the child's limbs, accustoming

---

[134] 'Teachings on Style and the Flower', generally held to be the first of Zeami's treatises.

> them to the proper positions. . . . Song is also learned by repeated imitation.[135]

There are no technical exercises, rather the child learns from the outset sections of plays that he will someday perform. At this early stage no attempt is made to give the child an understanding of the content of the material he is learning; rather, the focus is upon physical assimilation of the movements. He may make his stage debut very early in his training in any one of a number of non-speaking *kokata* (child actor) roles which only require him to walk on to the stage, take the appropriate position and remain still until told to move. (An adult actor, perhaps even his teacher, will be on stage as *koken,* a stage assistant, to be certain that the child performs properly.) Although he will be taught *utai* (Noh chant) from the outset, actual vocal training begins slightly later, around the age of ten when "the voice begins to achieve its proper pitch".[136] As the child grows older, gains skill and confidence and has mastered several pieces, he is encouraged to practice independently while continuing with his regular lessons.

> By the time I was in junior high school, I was expected to spend time practising by myself, and to watch practices and study the instruments of the ensemble. Often my father would give me instruction just two weeks before a performance.[137]

Because Noh plays follow the same basic structure, which falls into identifiable sections defined by tempo or verse style, once a student has mastered several examples of a particular type he is able to learn new scenes of a similar type very quickly. Still, the learning process is essentially physical: even learning the text (which is in an archaic, medieval Japanese not readily understood without specialised study) is a matter of learning sounds and rhythms rather than words

---

[135] Bethe and Brazell, 'The Practice of Noh Theatre', p. 169.

[136] Zeami, *Fushikaden* in Rimer and Yamazaki, p. 4

[137] Kongô Iwao, 'Recollections and Thoughts on Nô', p. 76.

and thoughts. The acting process, then, becomes completely instinctive and is not subject to analysis:

> In Japanese traditional theatre training there is little explanation of what or how (undoubtedly this is influenced by the Zen precept that intellectual knowledge of something is inferior to experiential 'knowing'). . . . The teacher and student are absorbed into the common entity, the art itself.[138]

At the age of eleven or twelve, the young actor will perform his first speaking roles and may exhibit a high degree of skill, though Zeami cautions: "this Flower is not the true Flower. It is only a temporary bloom".[139] In later adolescence, a difficult period of rapid physical growth during which his voice is also changing, Zeami suggests that the young actor be made to concentrate on practice until he outgrows his awkwardness. It is at this time, too, when he may take up residence with a master teacher or the head of the school *(iemoto)* for more intensive training. However, as in many Zen-influenced arts this 'training' may also involve spending many hours doing menial chores, which inculcate the virtues of humility and discipline.[140]

In these years, an actor has his first opportunity to perform with a mask and will begin to learn how to cope with the special difficulties it presents:

> When I first used a mask. . . . I was about 14 or 15 years old. [It was] *Ko-omote*. First, I was very glad that I was allowed to put on a mask, but I was also scared because when I put on the mask I couldn't see very much so I lost my balance, it was scary. . . . At first I practised the dance without the mask and then I put on the

---

[138] James R. Brandon, 'Performance Training in Japanese Nô and Kyôgen at the University of Hawaii', *Theatre Topics*, Vol. 3, number 2, 1993, pp. 106–107.

[139] Rimer and Yamazaki, p. 5.

[140] Bethe and Brazell, 'The Practice of Noh Theatre', p. 171.

mask and bit by bit I was told by my colleagues, the older actors, what were the good parts, what were the bad parts.[141]

The first masked role is an especially important hurdle representing an actor's first test as a 'full-grown' performer.[142] Each school has individual methods of grading degrees of proficiency, and when it has been determined that the student has reached a sufficient level (usually by his mid-twenties) he is allowed to move out of the teacher's house and begin teaching. (Giving lessons is the principle source of income for most Noh performers.) He will have the opportunity to perform in leading roles with the *yôseikai* (young artists group) of his school and will appear in *tsure* (companion) roles and in the chorus in professional performances. He will undoubtedly be required to assist in the complex business of dressing the leading performers backstage and may also have the important responsibility of serving as a stage attendant *(koken)*.[143] Even when he has reached this position, however, he will probably continue to train occasionally with his master teacher. The roles an actor is allowed to play are chosen carefully and depend upon the perceived level of his development, since "Noh plays are ranked according to difficulty, and an actor must have the permission of the head of the school to perform certain plays".[144] From the age of thirty-five until his mid-forties, according to *Fushikaden,* an actor should be at his peak, and able to perform the most challenging roles.

---

[141] Interview with Ryoichi Kano, translated by Arnoud Rauws, 12 June, 1997.

[142] Kanze Hisao, 'Life with a Nô Mask', pp. 65–66.

[143] The *koken* serves not only to place and remove props, adjust the *shite's* garments and help with costume changes, but must also act as prompter and, if the leading actor becomes incapacitated, must be prepared to step into the role immediately. The chief stage attendant is usually 'an actor of equal or superior ability to the *shite.*' Bethe and Brazell, 'The Practice of Noh Theatre', pp. 171–172.

[144] There are certain plays that serve as 'landmarks', or perhaps tests, of an actor's development. Bethe and Brazell name four of the most significant: *Shakkyo, Miidera, Okina* and *Dôjôji,* the last being perhaps the most challenging in the repertory. Bethe and Brazell, 'The Practice of Noh Theatre', p. 172. See also Tsumura Reijirô, '*Dôjôji:* Preparations for a Second Performance' in *Nô/Kyôgen Masks in Performance,* pp. 104–113.

The Way of Noh

The traditional training of a Noh actor begins before 'the age of reason' and is wholly experiential, imitative and non-analytical. The performance process is thus entirely instinctive. As a result, the performance of a Noh play requires almost no rehearsal. Actors, musicians and chorus, who might never have met before, will generally have only a single 'walk-through' rehearsal to verify cues and timings before giving a play for the public.[145] This style of training means that performers are rarely able to be articulate about method and process because these are so deeply ingrained.[146] As frustrating as this is for the Western researcher, it is in keeping with the philosophical underpinnings of the genre. Conscious, logical understanding is seen to be shallow and superficial compared with the deeper understanding that comes when the conscious mind is no longer in control. This is how Noh comes to be understood as something more than theatrical performance and may instead be seen as a means of achieving enlightenment.

> To follow a way is to immerse oneself in an activity, to practice it until one attains mastery. . . . Anyone who attains true mastery, even in a humble art, enters a sphere of consciousness unknown to the average person. This consciousness might be defined as enlightenment or as art, for the dichotomy between the sacred and

---

[145] The *shite* and *waki* will, of course, have studied their roles carefully, but will have done so alone The *shite* generally learns the play in its entirety and is able to sing all of the roles (except that of the *kyôgen)* and chorus parts.

[146] For those students of Noh who are not born into the traditional framework, this can prove frustrating. It is possible for individuals who have not been in a position to receive training from childhood to become professional Noh performers. Often an interest will have been engendered through amateur lessons or Noh clubs at school or university. In this case the aspiring professional (usually in their teens or early twenties) must find a Noh master willing to take them on and give themselves over to the intensive training which those born into the profession will have known for most of their lives. Bethe and Brazell, 'The Practice of Noh Theatre', pp. 172–173.

the profane has never been as well-defined in Japan as in the West, and aesthetic values have had as much force as moral ones.[147]

The principles of esoteric Buddhism which had a profound influence on the first theoreticians of Noh, Zeami and Zenchiku, "held that the universe manifests itself through art, and that artistic activity leads the mind to identification with universal truth".[148] The study and practice of Noh involves processes of voice, body, and mind and corresponds in this way to the 'three mysteries' of esoteric Buddhism: mantras, mudras and meditation.[149] The state of consciousness to which the performer aspires is not one in which personal feelings or emotion are expressed, but one that transcends the self. The physical and vocal elements of performance exist at a level of subconscious automaticity, as one performer put it, "While practising it is not my mind that remembers the movements, I remember with my body".[150] The Noh actor gives himself over to the performance of the role, its prescribed movements and sounds, and is not concerned with personal self-expression through the character. The performer is like a puppet, manipulated by the physical requirements of the role, following a set of commands that have been physically assimilated since childhood. What is important about this in relation to the present analysis is that, just like the pedagogy of Balinese masked dance-drama, this method of training creates circumstances which can lead to an altered state of consciousness, making the performer susceptible to dissociation and trance.

The Noh Aesthetic

There are certain principles, articulated by Zeami and very much products of his time, which have become fundamental to the Noh aesthetic. Some of the terms

---

[147] *Ibid.*, p. 185.

[148] *Ibid.*, p. 186.

[149] *Ibid.*

[150] Interview with Ryoichi Kano, 12 June, 1997.

derive from Buddhist philosophy or from the art of court poetry and seem superficially to have little to do with performance. Yet, understood in context, they provide a language by means of which quite complex matters regarding the structure, quality and perception of the performance as well as the mind, body and spirit of the performer may be discussed. The matrix of complex religious and aesthetic ideas which inform the art of Noh is a vast subject and has been examined at length elsewhere. However this brief overview of some of the most significant concepts may serve as a guide to the terminology and criteria by which a Noh performance is evaluated.

Jo-Ha-Kyû

The concept of *jo-ha-kyû*, which was first used in relation to *gagaku*, is essentially to do with structure and tempo of both play and performance. The term *'jo'* refers to the beginning, and is "sometimes translated as 'introduction' or 'prelude'".[151] It can indicate either the beginning or first phase of a Noh play or the first item of a programme of Noh plays, usually a *waki-nô*, first-group play. The term also indicates "the slow and stately tempo"[152] appropriate to plays concerning the gods, and the tempo appropriate for the beginning of a play, the exposition. The manner of presentation of these plays, Zeami instructs, should be "simple and straightforward".[153]

Ha is often translated as 'development' but the more precise translation, 'breaking,' "suggests the increased dramatic and musical level of energy after the more composed and stately *jo*".[154] Thus, *ha* represents a change, a shift in tempo and style, breaking the mood of *jo*. The plays which make up the *ha* portion of the programme are more complex than those which have gone before, and "form the

---

[151] Rimer and Yamazaki, p. 265.
[152] *Ibid.*
[153] *Ibid.*, p. 84.
[154] *Ibid.*, p. 264.

central element in the day's entertainment".[155] They present a greater challenge to the actor because they require *monomane,* the imitation of a human being, that is, the creation of a character.

Kyû, is taken to mean 'climax' or 'finale', but Rimer and Yamazaki contend that "a literal translation, 'rapid', conveys the quick tempo appropriate to the end of the *nô*".[156] Zeami insists that *kyû* has the same meaning as *agaku,* a term used in *renga* poetry[157] to indicate the final stanza, but also indicates that *kyû* represents a quick tempo and "strenuous movements".[158] The final play in a Noh programme should therefore be a lively and exciting piece, which concludes with a powerful and spectacular dance.

> The term *ha* requires breaking the mood of *jo,* and is an art that brings complexity and great artistic skill to the performance. *Kyû,* on the other hand, extends the art of *ha* in turn, in order to represent the final stage of the process. In this fashion *kyû* brings on powerful movements, rapid dance steps, as well as fierce and strong gestures, in order to dazzle the eyes of the spectators. Agitation characterizes this final stage of the *nô.* [159]

On the surface, it would appear that *jo-ha-kyû* is roughly equivalent to the notion of a beginning middle and end, but it is much more. *Jo-* a slow beginning; *ha-* a change in tempo and development; *kyû-* a final quick climax: these terms may be applied to many different aspects of performance. Thus *jo-ha-kyû* is not just a consideration in the planning of a programme of Noh plays, but can also be applied to the structure of an individual play and the structure, development and

---

[155] *Ibid.,* p. 84.

[156] *Ibid.,* p. 266.

[157] A popular courtly pastime in medieval Japan was the *renga* party at which the gathered nobles would compete in the creation of linked verses. See Rimer and Yamazaki, p. 84 and Varley, pp. 106–109.

[158] Rimer and Yamazaki, p. 21.

[159] *Ibid.,* p. 84.

tempo of the actor's performance. Within that performance there is a *jo-ha-kyû* of each dance sequence and a *jo-ha-kyû* of the individual gesture. Beyond the play, *jo-ha-kyû* is even used to refer to the atmosphere of the performance and the mood of the audience.[160]

Monomane

Monomane refers to imitation or *mimesis*. Rimer and Yamazaki translate the term as 'role playing' and contend that Zeami did not mean to suggest "the kind of naturalistic acting style suggested by the English word, . . . rather he stressed that the essential spirit of the role was to be the object of the actor's art".[161] Ortolani, on the other hand, holds that the term corresponds "to what we today would call realistic acting".[162] In a sense, both of these interpretations are correct. In *Fushikaden*, Zeami recommends careful study of those types of persons whom a Noh actor might be called upon to play: high officials, aristocrats and women of the court. "He must imitate down to the smallest detail the various things done by persons of high profession, especially those elements related to high artistic pursuits." However, he cautions against realistic portrayal of commoners: "they should be imitated in detail insofar as they have traditionally been found congenial as poetic subjects. . . . Thus the degree of imitation must vary, depending on the kind of role being performed".[163] A realistic portrayal of the medieval Japanese commoner, Zeami asserts, would be found vulgar and unpleasant by the aristocratic audience that Noh hoped to keep as enthusiastic patrons, thus *monomane* would, in this case, be modified to suit the sensibilities of the audience. 'Naturalistic' and 'realistic' are terms which prove problematic

---

[160] "If an actor begins to chant in an atmosphere of *jo* that matches the mood of his audience, he must begin his dance in an atmosphere of *jo* as well. When the atmosphere of the audience is at the level of *kyû*, however, he must begin at that level. On such an occasion, should the actor still insist on using the level of *jo*, as usual for an introduction, the results will inevitably be unsatisfactory." Zeami in *Sarugaku dangi*, Rimer and Yamazaki, p. 183.

[161] Rimer and Yamazaki, p. 262.

[162] Ortolani, p. 120.

when applied to acting style even in our own time, so it is not surprising that the term *monomane* is similarly contentious for Noh scholars. It must be understood that Zeami wrote of *monomane* within the context of the acting conventions of his own time when performance was generally an outdoor affair given for crowds at religious festivals. *Sarugaku-nô* was a spectacular entertainment that combined music, chant, dance and acrobatics in the presentation of plays about supernatural beings as well as 'real people'; it could hardly be considered comparable to, say, a contemporary television drama in terms of acting style. More particularly, the creation of character, both in Zeami's time and in contemporary Noh, is guided and achieved by means of the mask. Twentieth-century Occidental theorists of acting style who became enamoured of Noh drama (Gordon-Craig and Yeats, for example) hailed this ancient Japanese theatre precisely because of its lack of 'realism', and saw the mask as emblematic of Noh's symbolic reality, which they felt was artistically superior to 'naturalistic' Western drama. Perhaps what they saw was a theatre in which the outer accoutrements, however artificial, revealed the inner truth of the character, whereas the contemporary theatre that they decried, whatever its passionate pretensions to 'naturalness' and 'reality', seemed to reveal only the superficial skills of the performer. In Zeami's essay on the matter of *monomane* in *Fushikaden,* it is significant that he does not at any point discuss the use of masks, rather, he makes special note of the appropriate manner of performing without a mask:

> Although it is not possible to imitate any particular individual countenance in performance, actors sometimes alter their own ordinary facial expressions in an attempt to create some particular effect. The results are always without interest.[164]

In Zeami's theatre, the mask was a tool for *monomane;* it was a means by which the actor could give a 'realistic' portrayal of the character because he wore the

---

[163] Rimer and Yamazaki, p. 10.
[164] *Ibid.,* p. 12.

character's face. Using the principle of *monomane,* the unmasked actor may not use his own face to imitate the character, rather "the face must remain as expressionless as a mask".[165] Since it is the mask which defines the character, when no mask is used it is inappropriate for the actor to impersonate a face or to express with his own face what he imagines the character's feelings to be. Thus, among the most accomplished actors, *monomane* becomes something beyond 'imitation' through which the actor and character become one. Zeami observes:

> In the art of Role Playing *[monomane]*, there is a level at which imitation is no longer sought. When every technique of Role Playing is mastered and the actor has truly become the subject of his impersonation, then the reason for the desire to imitate can no longer exist. . . . For example, in imitating an old man, the psyche of a truly gifted player will become altogether like that of a real old man. . . . Now since the actor has already himself assumed the personality of an old man, he actually 'becomes' the old man and can have no wish to imitate one.[166]

The mask, of course, provides the means for this transformation. With the mask there is no necessity for mere impersonation because, when the actor puts it to his face, he obliterates his own identity and puts himself at the service of the character defined by the mask. It is the means by which the actor leaves himself behind to 'become' the character.

Hana

'The flower' is a term that is used throughout Zeami's writings in a variety of ways. Essentially, *hana* "represents a mastery of technique and thorough practice, achieved in order to create a feeling of novelty".[167] It is, on the one hand, the

---

[165] Zeami. *Kadensho* translated by Chûhie Sakurrai, Shûseki Hayashi, Rokurô Satoi, Bin Miyari. (Kyoto: Foundation of Sumiya-Shinobe Scholarship, 1970) p. 24.

[166] Rimer and Yamazaki, p. 55.

[167] *Ibid.,* p. 53.

highest degree of the actor's skill that can only be acquired through rigorous training and, on the other, a unique moment of inspiration in an actor's performance. In this it refers to what the audience perceives in the actor's performance, rather than to the actor's own perception of his work. An actor who possesses the flower has perfect communication with the audience through a performance that reveals moments of surprising novelty. In *Kyûi*, Zeami discusses the 'Nine Levels' of accomplishment in the actor's art, which range from "the art of crudeness and leadenness" to "the art of peerless charm".[168] The ideal is that the actor should begin at the middle of this range, "the art of broad mastery", and work his way through the highest levels before attempting the baser grades. The thoroughly accomplished actor would then possess all the skills necessary to play the entire range of characters, from the most elegant court lady to the grossest demon. Even in the performance of the crudest characters, this ideal actor would still possess the peerless charm of the highest level. This level of achievement coincides with the special state mentioned above, in which *monomane* becomes complete identification with the character:

> "The meaning of the phrase Peerless Charm surpasses any explanation in words and lies beyond the workings of consciousness."[169]

Thus, the ultimate aim of the Noh performer is to reach this altered state of consciousness "the moment of Feeling that Transcends Cognition".[170] It is a complete marriage of art and artist, in which the performer is able to fascinate the audience through his skill without self-consciousness. In this, the notion of *hana* is remarkably similar to the concept of *taksu* in the aesthetic of Balinese dance-drama.

---

[168] See *ibid.*, pp. 120–125; see also Nearman, 1978, Ortolani, pp. 115–119 and Sekine 120–128.
[169] Rimer and Yamazaki, p. 120.
[170] *Ibid.*

Yûgen

This term, which is regarded as central to the Noh aesthetic, is often translated simply as 'grace', but such a bald, elementary interpretation hardly begins to describe the complex nuances of meaning expressed in the concept of *yûgen*. According to Rimer and Yamazaki, the term, was "originally found in Chinese philosophical texts meaning 'dim, deep, mysterious'".[171] It was brought into the realm of the arts first in relation to *waka,* the dominant poetic form from the middle of the Nara Period (mid-eighth century) through medieval times.[172] In this context, *yûgen* referred to a mystery and depth achieved through "suggestion, imitation and nuance",[173] a poetic expression that left much unsaid, but communicated resonances of deeper meaning. The twelfth-century Buddhist priest Shun'e, writing about *yûgen* in relation to *waka* poetry, provides a useful description of how *yûgen* functions in Noh:

> It is only when many meanings are compressed into a single word, when the depths of feelings are exhausted yet not expressed, when an unseen world hovers in the atmosphere of the poem, when the mean and common are used to express the elegant, when a poetic conception of rare beauty is developed to the fullest extent in a style of surface simplicity—only then, when the conception is exalted to the highest degree and 'the words are too few', will the poem, by expressing one's feelings in this way, have the power of moving Heaven and Earth within the brief confines of thirty-one

---

[171] *Ibid.,* p. 260.

[172] Varley, p. 39. A *waka* poem consists of 31 syllables in the form: 5-7-5-7-7. In Zeami's time *waka* was the basis for a kind of linked verse, in which one poet would compose the first three lines (5-7-5) after which another poet would complete the last two (7-7). The creation of such linked verse was a popular pastime among courtiers in the Ashikaga Era. See Varley, pp. 106–109.

[173] Varley, p. 88.

syllables and be capable of softening the hearts of gods and demons.[174]

This definition might be applied to Noh texts since they consist mainly of verse, much of it in *waka* form, in which puns and multiple layers of meaning abound. Beyond the text, however, the Noh *kata* (the movements, gestures and patterns of performance) exhibit this capacity with depth of meaning communicated simply through spare, highly stylised movement and gesture. Above all, this quality of *yûgen* is especially evident in Noh masks. They are first of all objects with faces which, although immobile, express many subtle nuances of meaning through their seemingly ambiguous expressions. Secondly, they are tools used by the actor to communicate the action of the play and the thoughts, feelings and attributes of the character. In fact, the mask object cannot be considered separately from its function because in performance every movement and gesture is coloured by the mask, while the mask is characterised by each movement and gesture. *Yûgen,* deep, mysterious elegance, is observed in the actor not by the body alone, but by the combination of performance elements which create the stage figure represented by the *shite*. *Yûgen* is expressed through the way mask, costume, movement, rhythm and tempo interact with the mind-body-spirit of the performer. Any one of these elements alone cannot convey the complex nuances of meaning expressed by all of the elements working together. Thus *yûgen* may be said to be an expression of the deeply complex through the exquisitely simple.

Kokoro

With regard to the actor's relationship with the mask, the concept of *kokoro* is, perhaps, the most important principle of all those articulated by Zeami and might almost be seen as one which unites them all in its underlying implications. Like *yûgen,* the term comes from the world of *waka* poetry, but it takes on new

---

[174] Quoted in *ibid.,* p. 88, from Earl Miner, *An Introduction to Japanese Court Poetry* (Stanford: Stanford University Press, 1968) p. 102.

significance when applied to Noh performance. In poetry, *kokoro* is "the inner emotional 'heart' of a poem, its content, meaning, conception"[175] and it is coupled with the notion of *kotoba*, "the outer 'leaves of words', its diction, expression, style".[176] In Noh performance, *kokoro* has to do with the actor's consciousness and Zeami invokes the term when writing of the state of the actor in moments of apparent inaction:

> The actor must rise to a selfless level of art, imbued with a concentration that transcends his own consciousness, so that he can bind together the moments before and after that instant when 'nothing happens'. Such a process constitutes that inner force that can be termed "connecting all the arts through one intensity of mind".[177]

The actor's 'intensity of mind' is the essential element that is at the heart of the performance. Zeami uses the example of a puppet, able to give the illusion of life and action only when animated by its strings; without them, he collapses, lifeless. Similarly, in Noh performance the illusion of life on the stage can only be created by "the intensity of mind" of the actor whose concentration gives life to the character. This concentration must, however, be 'selfless', given over to the expression of the character, rather than the thoughts and desires of the performer. Zeami emphasises that the intensity of the actor's concentration must not be revealed to the audience, otherwise "it will merely become another ordinary skill or action".[178] *Kokoro* is thus more than merely focused attention; it is a consciously invoked altered state of consciousness. As the actor Kanze Hisao put it:

---

[175] Arthur Thornhill III, *Six Circles, One Dewdrop: The Religio-Aesthetic World of Komparu Zenchiku* (Princeton, New Jersey: Princeton University Press, 1993) p. 7.

[176] *Ibid.*

[177] Rimer and Yamazaki, p. 97.

[178] *Ibid.*, p. 97.

one must enter a condition of 'nothingness' sufficiently deep that one no longer has consciousness of the fact one is acting.[179]

This state of conscious unconsciousness is akin to the state of oneness with the cosmic consciousness that the esoteric Buddhist adept seeks to achieve through the three mysteries of voice, body and mind. In Noh performance, the voice chants the text of the play, the body performs the stylised choreography of the role while the mind is focused on a kind of creative 'nothingness'. Ortolani observes:

> The reality of *kokoro* is therefore rooted in the true essence of all things, or the all-encompassing, unchanging pure Buddha-nature. The various facets of *kokoro* appear and work in the artist at different levels: emotional, rational, pre-rational-intuitive-spontaneous-sublime. The reality remains the same; it is the artist who passes through phases or stages of skills and realizations, eventually becoming one with the heart of everything, unconsciously and spontaneously following the rhythms of the One, the Absolute, the primordial energy.[180]

This mystical reading of *kokoro* is consistent with medieval Japanese thought and is reflected elsewhere in the writings of Zeami as well as those of his successor, Zenchiku, the other great Noh theorist of the period.[181] It is the state that Zeami refers to in relation to *monomane,* when he writes of the actor who goes beyond impersonation to 'become' the character, and in relation to the *hana* of 'peerless charm' (*myô*), which is achieved at the highest level of acting skill. It is an identification with the role that some have characterised as a kind of possession.

---

[179] Hisao, 'Life with a Nô Mask' in *Nô/Kyôgen Masks in Performance,* p. 70.
[180] Ortolani, p. 124.
[181] See Thornhill, pp. 166–169 and 74–77.

The actor Kanze Hisao argues for a direct connection between this state and the mask:

> The donning of the mask is considered the most important element in evoking this phenomenon of possession. . . . It must be such that by simply donning it, one can metamorphose oneself into something quite different from one's everyday self, and it must give rise to a creative ability in the actor. This is the role of the Nô mask. The actor must be able to depend on it if he is to have sufficient profundity to provide such evocatory powers. . . . The covering and hiding of the face is a denial of both normal acting and of the very existence of the actor as an individual as well.[182]

Donning the mask is an act of self-abnegation that is both symbolic and real for the performer. It symbolises the actor's subjugation of his own identity to that of the mask, which obscures the actor's face and replaces it with another. The actor disappears behind the mask and allows his consciousness to become the animating force that brings the character to life. Every aspect of Noh performance is bent towards making this act of transformation, which is both physical and spiritual, possible. Kinaesthetic, non-verbal, non-logical physical training from early childhood, evocative, rhythmic music and aesthetic philosophy all combine to lead the actor into a dissociated state in which a kind of mediumship can take place with the mask as catalyst for this transformation.

---

[182] Kanze Hisao, 'Life with a Nô Mask', p. 70.

Chapter 5:   Balinese Masks in Practice

Masked performance takes place in a variety of milieux in Bali, from sacred temple ceremonies, to exhibitions at cultural centres, to dinner entertainments for tourists in international-style five-star hotels. As far as the performers are concerned, any of these performances, whatever the occasion, requires equivalent skill, care, attention and ritual preparation since both gods and demons are likely to be observing the work whatever the circumstances. However, the examples selected for consideration here are performances given in conjunction with temple ceremonies, since it is in these circumstances that Balinese masked dance-drama most often occurs and it is within this context that many complex aspects of the form become more readily comprehensible.

Temple ceremonies and life-cycle rituals occur somewhere on the island daily and nearly all require the performance of a masked dance-drama as part of the ritual. The ceremonies and accompanying performances are always well attended, though the atmosphere is quite informal and members of the audience come and go as they please throughout. These events, as both religious ritual and entertainment, are an integral part of people's daily lives. The stories and characters are well-known but, because of the improvisational nature of the dramas, each performance is unique. Whatever may serve as 'backstage' is open and accessible to anyone and both children and adults gather to watch the performers prepare. In spite of this accessibility, there seems no loss of mystique.

In this chapter I shall begin with an examination of a typical performance of *Topeng Pajegan,* one of many I have observed in the course of my research in Bali. Although no two Topeng performances are exactly alike, they all follow a similar pattern so this single example should give a fairly clear idea of how the genre works and what tasks are required of the masked actor. This case study will be followed by discussion and analysis of the experiences of several different performers, focusing on their response to the demands of the masks and elements of the performance process.

The second part of the chapter investigates the liminal world inhabited by the 'magic' masks of Rangda and Barong. While there is no 'typical' performance of Calonarang, most share certain characteristics, though these can vary greatly depending upon the circumstances of performance and the particular nature of the masks used. I will first discuss the complex of meanings associated with Rangda and Barong, their masks and the other components of these performances to establish a context within which to consider two different performances, which will be described in detail. The analysis will further investigate the experiences of the performers who are brave and skilled enough to take on the powerful supernatural forces represented by these masks.

A Performance of Topeng Pajegan

It is the *odalan*[1] of the house temple of a family belonging to the *Pasek*[2] clan. Two members of the family arrive at the dancer's home in Lodtunduh at about ten o'clock in the morning and are offered coffee and cigarettes as they wait for the dancer, Ida Bagus Alit, to bathe and change his clothes. Alit's assistant Gusti,

---

[1] Temple anniversary festival when the gods and deified ancestors are invited to descend.

[2] A large and important clan of the *Sudra* caste held to be the descendants of *Brahmanas* from East Java who were "invited to come to Bali in the tenth century to resolve religious disputes". See Eiseman, 1990a, pp. 35–36. Significantly, members of this clan are allowed to have cremation towers seven stories high (nearly as high as those for members of the *Ksatria* caste) in recognition of their high-caste ancestry.

who is training as a carver and dancer, loads two baskets with masks and headdresses into the back of the small truck that will transport us all to the site of the performance. Alit, *baru bersih* ('newly clean' as is required of anyone entering a Balinese temple and especially important for someone contributing to the ceremony), dressed in a fresh *kain* and *saput*, head tie and smart jacket, comes out of the house carrying a sacred *kris* and a large sports bag containing his costume. All attired in formal temple dress, we clamber into the truck for the fairly terrifying drive along the winding road to Mawang village, about five kilometres south.

Waiting for the *Pedanda*

Upon arrival, the dancer's party is led to an area adjacent to but outside the *sanggah* (house temple) where a small performance space has been created. A rectangular area of ground about thirty feet long and perhaps twelve feet wide has been covered with palm mats and blue plastic tarpaulins and roofed with bamboo struts and palm leaves. At the north end of the space the gamelan orchestra has been arranged around three sides; at the south end, facing the temple, a curtain of gold-painted coloured cloth *(prada)* has been hung and behind it is a small raised platform where the dancer's baskets and bags are set. A large basket of offerings is already in place on the platform where we are invited to sit. Presently, someone from the house brings dishes with the components of betel chew[3] and packets of cigarettes. A little later, glasses of hot, sweet Balinese coffee and palm leaf dishes of cooked rice and coconut sweetened with palm sugar are brought. Alit, who must fast before he performs *Topeng Pajegan,* sips the coffee but leaves the rest untouched. The host sits and chats with Alit and several members of the gamelan ensemble come to pay their respects or exchange gossip. Children begin to gather at the edge of the tarpaulin and we wait. The *pedanda* (Brahmana high priest) has

---

[3] "... the leaf of the betel pepper tree, a bit of lime, and a sliver of areca nut, the fruit of a tall, slender palm that grows all over lowland Asia". Eisman 1990a, p. 217. It is a mild narcotic now generally popular only with the older generation of Balinese.

not yet arrived and, since the *Topeng Pajegan* must be performed at the same time as the ritual, nothing can begin until the *pedanda* comes.

Topeng Pajegan is the version of the sacred masked dance-drama called *Topeng Wali* or *Topeng Sidha Karya*,[4] which is executed by a single performer. The word '*Pajegan*', which in this context means one who performs all of the roles, is etymologically related to another Balinese term meaning guardian.[5] The *Topeng Pajegan* performance frequently takes place outside the temple to help protect the ritual from 'uninvited guests' who might seek to disturb the priest's work. In larger ceremonies, a *Wayang Lemah* daylight shadow puppet performance also takes place at the same time, to serve as an entertainment for the deities and a distraction for the buta-kala.[6] In an interview, Alit described the way it works:

> There are 3 courtyards in a temple—the outer courtyard, the middle courtyard and the inner courtyard. When there is a ritual, the priest will be inside the inner courtyard and the performance of *Wayang Lemah*, the daylight puppeteer, will be in the inner courtyard, side-by-side with the priest. The Topeng dance, the masked dance, should be performed in the outer courtyard because

---

[4] The two terms are used interchangeably to refer to the same performance form. *Topeng Wali* means 'ritual Topeng' and *Topeng Sidha Karya* refers to the final mask character, Sidha Karya, which means literally 'completes the ceremony', it is the performance of this mask which is the essential ritual element in the performance.

[5] '*jaga*' and '*pajagaan*' see Eiseman, 1997b p. G-11. Bandem and de Boer fail to mention this connection saying only that the term "comes from an expression used in purchasing rice, when someone buys an entire crop of paddy, rather than by the kilo, he is said to *majeg* the crop, that is, he does the whole thing on his own". (Bandem and de Boer, p. 48). Balinese etymology is a difficult subject particularly because, being primarily a spoken language, spelling is very irregular. The argument for a relationship between *Topeng Pajegan*, sometimes spelled '*Pajagan*', and a notion of guardianship as evidenced by the protective function of the ceremonial performance is, however, compelling.

[6] Zurbuchen 1981, p. 179–180 gives an extended description and explanation of the *Wayang Lemah*. Interestingly, Lansing points out that the words of the characters in *Wayang Lemah* are not translated from Kawi as they are for the night-time shadow puppets *(Wayang Kulit)* nor is there a screen on which the images are projected. "The gods have no need for a screen since, unlike humans, they perceive reality directly. . . .And since the gods understand Kawi perfectly, there is no need for translations, and the entire performance occurs in Kawi, without any translations into Balinese." (Lansing 1995, p. 68).

the definition of *pajeguh* (from which *Pajegan* is derived) is 'guardian spirits', to guard against the evil spirits who could destroy the ritual. . . . During the climax of the ritual, the priest will be chanting, side by side with the shadow puppet. In case there are some *butas* who go through without the knowledge of the *Sidha Karya Topeng* performing, guarding outside, and go into the temple, the *buta-kala* will be distracted, counting the small holes in the shadow puppets. So while the *butakala* is counting all the holes he'll be too busy, and will ignore the priest doing the ritual.[7]

By this it appears that the distraction of potentially disruptive spirits is the primary function of the masked drama, however, equally importantly, it also provides entertainment and a socially binding affirmation of family and culture. It is the intrinsic nature of this masked drama to serve as a link between the spiritual world and the everyday lives of the people. Here the Balinese notions of *buana agung* and *buana alit* (macrocosmos and microcosmos), *sekala* and *niskala* (that which is seen and that which is unseen) are illustrated. The 'great world' *(buana agung)* of the gods and heroic ancestors is made visible by the performer for ordinary mortals of the 'small world' *(buana alit)*. The story told by the speaking masks (which is specially devised by the performer for the particular occasion of performance) not only entertains but also gives explanations and teaches spiritual lessons which relate directly to the ceremony being performed. The masks themselves make present the deified ancestors and the legendary past in tangible form making the unseen *(niskala)* spiritual world discernible. In the case of the *odalan*, then, not only are the gods and ancestors invited to visit the temple unseen, in spirit, but they are also revealed and embodied through the Topeng drama. The performer is the link between the two worlds, a human being who, through the mask, gives form to the gods.

---

[7] Interview, 5 April, 1997.

> The spirits of the real gods and heroes whose exploits form the basis of the stories have been invited into the inner sanctum, and it is assumed that they may be watching the performance. The separation between the audience and the actors, worshippers and gods, past and present, imagination and reality, and the inner and outer worlds can sometimes, startlingly, appear to vanish.[8]

Thus, in *Topeng Pajegan* not only does the performer entertain the guests, both human and divine, but his entire performance also protects the ritual from disruptive forces. Finally, and most important of all, he 'completes the ceremony' for the mortal world by entering into the spiritual realm as he embodies the god wearing the sacred Sidha Karya mask.

While we wait, more members of the family arrive with tall offerings of fruit, flowers and cakes; a little later a procession carrying offerings and *pratima* (the small figures which serve as seats for the visiting gods and ancestors) parades through the house compound and into the *sanggah* as the gamelan plays. Nearly three hours pass before the *pedanda* finally arrives. This delay is not unusual and, although there are plenty of ritual activities that can go on without the *pedanda*, the Topeng performer must simply wait. On an auspicious day like this one, a *pedanda* may have a number of ceremonies at which he must officiate and performers of *Topeng Pajegan* may also have three or four engagements in a single day. If one ceremony is delayed either for the actor or the priest, all the rest will be affected, which means that a performance scheduled for a morning or afternoon may not take place until late at night. Given this inclination to '*jam karet*' (literally, 'rubber time'), the actor must cultivate a calm and patient attitude of mind which will also allow him to be prepared at any moment to begin his performance.

---

[8] Lansing 1995, p. 69.

Preparation

When the *pedanda* arrives, things begin to happen very quickly. Alit removes his jacket and begins to put on his costume, a complex process that marks the first stage of the performer's entrance into the realm of historical legend and deified ancestors he must evoke for the audience. The first layer of costume consists of white trousers worn under a *kamben*[9] of white cotton. The *kamben* is secured to a holster apparatus worn over the dancer's shoulders in which his *kris* (ceremonial dagger) is carried; it is then held more firmly in place by a wide strip of canvas webbing wound tightly around the actor's body at the upper chest, just under the arms. This *sabuk* (belt) not only secures the *kamben*, but also restricts the expansion of the chest and forces the actor to breathe from the diaphragm, thus providing the breath support required for making himself heard over the noise of the gamelan orchestra, the chatter of the audience and the din of other ritual activities that may be going on simultaneously with the Topeng performance. Next come the *stewel*, black velvet leggings decorated with beads, spangles and tiny pearls, the *saput*, a cape decorated with gold leaf, the *baju*, a short black velvet jacket with decorated wristbands, and then several layers of fringed and beaded decorative panels and neck pieces. The transformation is impressive; the audience now sees an enormous and powerful figure dressed in the style of a fourteenth-century Balinese warrior. The effect upon the actor beneath this construction is also transformative. The costume is heavy and hot, particularly in Bali's equatorial climate. It also restricts movement, especially of the arms, shoulders, neck and head, but this restrictiveness works to the performer's advantage in that it corresponds with the physical shape that is required by the traditional movement vocabulary. In Balinese dance the shoulders and elbows are lifted and the torso generally moves as a unit, so that the primary expressive components of the dance are executed by feet, hands and small, sharp movements

---

[9] The Balinese term for *kain*, it is a strip of cloth worn as a garment generally tied at the waist or, in this case, at chest height. It is usually 2.5–3 meters in length and about a meter wide.

of the head. Donning the costume helps to focus the performer both physically and mentally upon the task at hand since any unnecessary activity is both difficult and uncomfortable.

It is now time to open the basket of masks. An offering has been prepared containing a coconut, an egg, some uncooked rice and a *canang*. Holding a burning stick of incense, whose smoke will waft the essence of the offering to the gods, Alit recites a mantra calling upon the Hindu trinity and the deified ancestors to be present (literally, to 'come and sit') in the offerings and to watch the performance (see Figure 28). He also calls upon the god of *Taksu* and the ancestral spirits to be present in his body and in the masks. Finally, he taps upon the basket three times saying '*poma, poma, poma*' ('let it be so') and the basket is opened. The lid of the basket is upturned to provide a shelf for the masks, which are laid out in the order in which they will be performed and the headdresses *(gelungan)* are hung around the edge of the basket. The gamelan orchestra, which has been playing intermittently for the last three hours, now strikes up the jangling theme of *Topeng Keras*, the music for the *Patih*, powerful warrior and chief minister to the king. Although his own hair is shoulder length, Alit puts a hairpiece of long black hair over his own, an indication that these elements of costume are not merely disguise, but are also sacred objects which serve to facilitate the inner transformation of the performer. The next item is the mask. There are a number of different versions of the *Patih* mask, some of which represent specific historical or mythological persons. In this case it is Gajah Mada, the great hero of the Majapahit era (see Figure 29). This powerful mask is unique, carved by Alit himself to his own design. The liveliness of its strong features and its penetrating gaze lend the mask such vigour that, when it is animated, the character is magnificent and imposing. Alit looks briefly at the mask while reciting a mantra to *bayu*, the god of wind and breath, to imbue him with strength. He then recites another to Gajah Mada himself, that he may be entered by his spirit. A headdress of gilded leather decorated with tiny mirrors and semi-precious stones comes next and, finally, flowers are placed over each ear so that the edge of the mask is not apparent. After briefly checking his appearance in the mirror held by his assistant, he sits at the edge of the platform behind the curtain and shakes it in time with the music.

Topeng Keras

The *Patih* is a highly energetic characterisation, the most prominent feature of which is an extreme physical tension, which is released briefly in furious movements then held again as the dancer strikes a pose, fingers quivering. As Deborah Dunn puts it, "The feeling of this dance is one of alertness, ferocity, strength and the prestige of the warrior hero."[10] It is the mask that determines the performer's level of energy in executing this choreography and the more powerful *(keras)* the mask's expression, the higher the level of energy required. '*Keras*-ness' is apparent in the iconography of the individual mask, in its colour and the quality of its features. All *Patih* masks use the colour red to some degree, therefore this mask, which is a very dark reddish-brown, is extremely *keras*. This is reflected, too, in the prominently bulging eyes, contracted brow and full lips as well as in the furiously concentrated expression. The performer who wears this mask must appear to be massive, powerful, sudden and intimidating. Yet, although the fundamental choreography and musical accompaniment remain the same, a performer wearing the *Patih* mask of Jelantik (Figure 30) would have a very different quality. While still *keras*, this character requires a refinement in movement which corresponds to the rather more *halus* or refined quality of the mask, with its light colour and calm expression. The *lucu* (funny) versions of Topeng Keras (Figures 5 and 31) call for different choreography within the same movement vocabulary, that is, quick, strong, direct and decisive.

Topeng Tua

Having established that the playing area is one to be inhabited by kings and warriors of the heroic past, the *Patih* departs. Behind the curtain, Alit removes the

---

[10] Dunn, p. 57; see also Emigh 1979 and 1996, Jenkins 1978 and 1979 and Daniel.

mask and headdress and trades them for those of *Topeng Tua* (literally 'old mask'). This is another very striking mask, also carved by Alit (see Figure 32), which is topped with a gilded headdress with long white horsehair. There is no pause of any significant length as the gamelan orchestra changes to the halting tune for *Topeng Tua*. The dancer has time for only a brief look at the mask before he puts it on, then he adds the headdress and side ornaments and takes his place behind the curtain. The character revealed when the curtains part is an elderly courtier of high status, indicated in part by the jewel in his brow.[11] Alit describes him as an old and distinguished former *Patih* who, although aged, possesses the power of an experienced warrior and the dignity of a statesman. Nonetheless, the movement vocabulary for *Topeng Tua* has a number of comic elements playing on the character's age and occasionally undermining his dignity. These elements include laboured breathing after exertion, (parting the curtain, for example), being overcome by dizziness and being troubled by body lice. Unlike the *Patih*, *Topeng Tua* may have a good deal of interaction with the audience and he is a character much beloved, especially by children. Here, again, the character of individual *Tua* masks may differ considerably and this will affect the quality of the performer's movement as well as the *mise en scène*. A younger mask, for example, may be more vigorous, while one with older features will be more enfeebled; the mask's expression may be warm or forbidding and this can determine how much interaction, if any, there will be with the audience. Alit's *Topeng Tua*, whose features seem kindly, is clearly of very high status and therefore does not interact with the audience a great deal. The tempo of the performance is therefore generally rather slow and measured.

The Speaking Masks

When the mask of the old man is removed, there is a significant change. Alit takes a long drink of the bottled drinking water provided for him and, as the

---

[11] This decoration, called *cudamani* is placed in the area of the 'third eye'and indicates high rank and spiritual power. See Dunn, p. 100.

gamelan begins the music for the *Penasar*, Alit begins to sing, bellowing a verse of classical *Kakawin* poetry that relates to the theme of today's story. Although most of the audience is unlikely to understand the words he sings, which are in Kawi, they recognise that the story is about to begin.

> The use of the ancestral language is more important than the content of the words used here. Most audience members would simply identify the language and style of singing as *ucapan gambuh*, speech of the courtly gambuh theatre. The audience would also be cognizant of the theatrical association of this mode of speech with the Majapahit Empire.[12]

Whereas contemporaries like Bandem and Djimat are primarily known as fine dancers, Alit is in great demand as a specialist in 'making the story'. The breadth and depth of his knowledge of the historical and religious documents like the *Weda* (Balinese versions of the Hindu Vedas) and *Babad* (historical chronicles) and his rigorous research to create stories appropriate to each particular occasion have begun to earn him a reputation throughout South Bali. He now has a number of students who, although they may already have trained with another traditional teacher or at the Academy of Performing Arts (STSI, now ISI), come to Alit to learn the stories and the special mantras that are necessary to the *Topeng Sidha Karya* performer. As he continues to sing, Alit dons the mask and headdress of *Penasar Kelihan*. Unlike those that have gone before, this is a half-mask with open eyeholes allowing the actor to speak and to see clearly. Earlier generations of dancers used a half-mask with prominent eyes more in the style of the full masks of the *Penglembar*, but this has gradually given way to the style seen in Figure 1.[13] The *Penasar Kelihan* is a servant to the king and very

---

[12] Emigh 1996, p. 129.

[13] See also Emigh 1996, pp. 127–128 and Dunn, p. 105. Their teacher, Kakul, used a Penasar mask with bulging eyes that was, even at that time (1975), unusual. My informants have indicated that the old-style Penasar mask with eyes is still used for particularly important sacred Topeng performances.

conceited. Alit makes his entrance around the side of the curtain rather than through it and interacts with the gamelan in his ambling, dance-like walk. His journey around the curtain and towards the audience seems to take him from the elevated world of the high-caste deified ancestors to the reality of the present day. He is a representative of the court of one of the great rajas of the past, yet he is also, somehow, at home in the contemporary world. "He is the story teller and interpreter for his lords, full masked roles who are too refined or too awesome to speak for themselves".[14] The character is almost parodically self-important and pretentious and delivers himself of the story in commanding tones, occasionally breaking into a passage of chanted Kawi which he then explains in Balinese. The kind of concentration required for this mask is very different from that of the silent, full-faced characters who express themselves exclusively through movement. First, because of the open eyeholes, the actor is more aware of the audience—an audience which, in the circumstances of a Topeng performance, is not always fully attentive and is rarely silent. Second, because his primary mode of expression now is through speech and verbal play, telling a story which involves the explanation of a complex genealogy which must be related to the family and the ceremony for which the Topeng is being performed. The 'text' is not scripted but, rather, improvised around the chronicle that Alit has chosen as most appropriate to this occasion. Into this must be woven contemporary references, moral lessons and plenty of jokes to keep the audience interested. After about twenty minutes of storytelling, the Penasar is called away by the commands of his unseen master and he exits. The actor, although still dressed as *Penasar*, sings the king's words in Kawi as he goes.

In theory, the next masked character to appear should be *Dalem*, the king, but Alit rarely performs with this mask and does not do so on this occasion. It may seem odd that such an important character, who could be a central figure in the story, may not necessarily appear on the stage. The question of whether to

---

[14] Dunn, p. 58.

include the *Dalem* is generally a matter decided by the individual dancer and, because he is quite stocky, Alit finds that he is physically better suited to the more robust roles of *Patih* and *Penasar Kelihan*. A dancer of more delicate stature, I Made Bandem, for example, is usually felt to be better suited to the role and indeed Bandem is regarded as one of the pre-eminent interpreters of the *Dalem*.[15] The movement of the *Dalem* character is graceful and sinuous, the character is very refined *(halus)* and beautiful, but not weak (see Figure 33). Geertz, in his analysis of *The Theatre-State in Nineteenth Century Bali* refers to the Balinese king as a 'human ideogram' and his description seems to sum up the character of this idealised monarch:

> Sitting for long hours at a stretch in a strictly formal pose, his face blank, his eyes blanker, stirring when he had to with a slow formality of balletic grace, and speaking when he had to in a murmur of reticent phrases . . . the icon king depicted outwardly for his subjects what he depicted inwardly to himself: the equanimous beauty of divinity ... the king as a sign conveyed not merely the quiet gentleness of a tranquil spirit, but also the blank severity of a just one.[16]

The *Dalem* is a full-faced mask and therefore doesn't speak, or, rather, doesn't speak for himself. In the forms of Topeng that involve more than one dancer, the *Penasar* will announce the king's approach. When the other dancer appears in the *Dalem* mask, the *Penasar* will speak both the king's words (in Kawi or middle Javanese) and his own replies (in Balinese) and those of the (invisible) counsellors who have gathered to confer with the king. Since the

---

[15] On the other hand, I Made Djimat, who is also quite stocky, identifies strongly with the Dalem mask in spite of his physique: "Because Topeng Dalem a little bit like man, little bit like woman and I am a little bit like man, like woman. It is sweet, not so strong, very sweet and that I like. And Gambuh, I like play Panji but my body not good Panji because now I am big, before I am small. But I like to play very much." Interview, 27 April 1997.

[16] Geertz, 1980, pp. 130–131.

Balinese audience generally do not understand Kawi, the *Penasar's* questions and responses (as well as his asides to the audience) will be structured so that the *Dalem's* words may be inferred. If the king does not appear at all, as in Alit's performance at Mawang, the actor may exit singing the words of the king (though still masked as the *Penasar*) and return as another character to report the results of the king's meeting.

Alit returns in the mask and headdress of *Bendesa Gereh,* known also as *Bondres Pasek Bendesa,*[17] the village religious leader—a character particularly significant for the *Pasek* clan who are held by tradition to be descendants of Brahmana holy men from Java.[18] It is a half-mask of an old man with a small nose and open eyes topped with the white *udeng* (headdress) appropriate to a *pemangku* (village priest). He enters slowly, sits and speaks quietly and respectfully about the king, his commands and their results. As Alit exits, still in the mask of the *Bendesa*, he sings in Kawi in the voice of the next character, the *Pedanda*. Offstage, he continues to sing as he exchanges the half-mask of *Bendesa* for the full-face mask of the *Pedanda*, which features an open mouth permitting speech (Figure 34). Once costumed, the high priest strides self-importantly onto the stage wearing his tall ceremonial crown and supported by an elegant walking stick, the handle of which is carved in the shape of a snake's head, the sacred *Naga*.[19] He is the final storyteller who ties up the loose ends of the plot and pontificates about the significance of the ceremony being performed by his 'counterpart', the real *pedanda* who sits among the offerings, ringing his bell and performing the mysterious mudras required by the ritual (see Figure 35). The action of the real priest is largely ignored; his work is with the gods. The

---

[17] See Slattum, p. 38. Alit's mask differs significantly from the mask pictured by Slattum, which was carved by Dewa Putu Bebes.

[18] See Eisman, 1997a, p. B-11 and Young p. 108.

[19] "Naga Basuki and Naga Anantaboga are the two dragon-snakes that attend the world-turtle Badawang [turtle on whose back the world is carried in Hindu mythology]; they symbolize man's earthly needs." Eiseman, 1990a, p. 359.

Topeng Pedanda, on the other hand, interprets the meaning and significance of the ritual for the ordinary human beings on whose behalf it is performed. However, there is a kind of a paradox here. The real *pedanda* is treated with highest respect—no one may sit higher than he. Those who would speak to him must clasp their right hand in the (unclean) left with the right thumb extended upwards when they are in his presence, and all must address him only in the highest, most formal Balinese language. The *pedanda*'s wife is of equal rank and may either assist her husband or perform ceremonies herself (and will continue to do so should he predecease her).[20] In a bizarre contrast, the *Topeng Pedanda* character is a comic figure, conceited and pretentious. The iconography of the mask, with its dark reddish brown colouring and coarse features, is distinctly *keras*, rather than *halus*. Dunn noted:

> It is very interesting that the mask for the padanda [sic] goes against expected rules for its iconography.... The features are not alus and the portrayal of the padanda is often not terribly refined ... possibly it reflects a kind of village point of view toward an unknown or distant character who exists in another world and whom they need to make familiar.[21]

In this particular instance, the *Pedanda* is not overtly comic, but he is something of an arrogant buffoon. Still, he is an important storyteller who inspires a certain amount of awe in spite of his pomposity. The combination of powerfully magic and mysterious elements with light-hearted comedy, satire and buffoonery, all within the context of a sacred ritual drama, may be a rather difficult concept for the contemporary Western observer to comprehend, since it violates time-honoured Aristotelian notions of what is appropriate for high

---

[20] Belo, 1949, p. 7.

[21] Dunn, p. 104.

theatrical art.[22] Yet the Balinese Topeng performer has no problem with these seeming contradictions; indeed, not only the performing tradition but also the religious philosophy of the culture insists that each of these elements has its place in a balanced dramatic universe.

As he concludes his remarks to the audience, the Topeng *Pedanda* announces the coming of *'Dalem Sidha Karya'*, the honoured god-king who is about to appear in order to complete the ceremony. As Alit removes the mask and crown of the *Pedanda*, he sings in the holiest of languages, ancient Sanskrit. It is a language spoken only by the gods and high priests in ceremonies, and is considered too sacred for ordinary people to use. Nonetheless, the Balinese audience can recognise words and phrases that are familiar from ritual formulae. He checks that the special offering, which *Sidha Karya* must dedicate, has been prepared and then he dons the mask.

Sidha Karya
The *Sidha Karya* mask (Figure 7) is quite different from all the masks that have preceded it. Although it is white, the colour that denotes the most refined characters, the features are distinctly not *halus*. The prominent teeth jut, feral and aggressive, from his grinning, open mouth. His eyes are curved slits which seem to denote laughter, but the stylised lines painted on his face might indicate otherworldliness as much as age or laughter. The *cudamani* jewel in his forehead shows his status as a high-caste individual and is emblematic of the mystical third eye, 'the inward eye of higher perception';[23] and at each temple there is a small, horn-like decoration, the significance of which is unknown. Taken together, the features appear to be demonic, but the iconography seems contradictory. If he is a beneficent god, why does he possess features that are associated with danger and

---

[22] The closest corollary might be the medieval mystery plays, but these ritualised enactments of sacred stories were for the benefit of sinful mortals rather than heavenly spirits and were not themselves part of a sacred ritual.

[23] Napier, p. 138.

evil? In interviews with performers, carvers and scholars, no clear explanation was given for the bizarre, paradoxical appearance of the *Sidha Karya* mask. Some assert convincingly that the fierceness of the mask is an indication of the character's divine nature.[24] But who is this *Sidha Karya,* the one who "completes the ceremony? Is he *Brahamana Keling,* King Batureggnog's mysterious kinsman from Java? Is he *Jayapangus*, the ancient Balinese king who was part-human, part-demon? Is he a powerful priest representing a unity of Buddhist and Sivite practice? Is he, perhaps, the physical manifestation of an aspect of Siwa or Wisnu? Any or all of these identities may be correct, depending upon the performer and local belief. In practice, it matters very little to the audience, who simply recognise the figure as one possessed of great *sakti,* loved, feared and respected, and who is essential to the successful completion of the ritual.

Alit has two different masks for *Sidha Karya,* one for ceremonies in which he performs outside the temple and another for ceremonies in which he performs in proximity to the *pedanda*. The latter, he says, is especially sacred to Siwa, the former, which he uses today, is associated with Rangda in her function as a guardian and "Queen of the Witches"[25] who controls the *buta-kala*. The Siwa-associated mask is the smaller of the two and belonged to Alit's grandfather; it has an animal-like, demonic ferocity, with pig's teeth and an encircling fringe of short black hair at the outer edge. The mask that he wears today is slightly larger and, although still undeniably demonic in character, it seems to grin with rather more geniality. The behaviour of the two masks, though within the same general

---

[24] Moerdowo (1977, p.15) for example, suggests that the mask represents "Wisnu in his demonic manifestation, *Wisnumurti*." (Dunn, p. 76). IB Alit contends: "*Sidha Karya* is Wisnu; Wisnu is dancing in Wisnu's form" (interview, 5 April, 1997) and Bandem, too, mentions *Wisnumurti* "Wisnu is god, beautiful god and very handsome god but when he is showing his power as *Wisnumurti*, he transforms himself becoming 9000 giants. Like transformation idea, showing his power" (30 April, 1997). It is interesting to note that a version of the mask, painted black instead of white, is often used as the face of *Jero Gedé*, one of the two gigantic '*Barong Landung*' puppets carried in processions in connection with various ceremonies in Bali. This mask is also used for meditation.

[25] Belo, 1949, 12; Suriyani and Jensen, 1993, p. 79.

movement vocabulary, is markedly different. As a general rule, the *Sidha Karya* character "bursts upon the scene and engages in running and jumping patterns that are accentuated by momentary fits of laughter and fingerpointing . . . threatening dashes toward the audience are mingled with a kind of delighted circling".[26] The individual qualities of a particular mask, however, may alter the manner in which these actions are performed. In Alit's case, the Siwa-related *Sidha Karya,* though full of laughter, is fierce and awe-inspiring but maintains a degree of dignified restraint in his physical characterisation. The Rangda-related mask, on the other hand, is wild and dangerous, yet playful, and displays elements of the rather effeminate, almost 'camp' quality often associated with Rangda.

While putting on the mask, Alit recites a protective mantra as he places himself at the service of the powerful supernatural forces that reside within it.

> As Sidha Karya [the actor] will alternately take on the functional roles of ancestral character, emissary of the gods, embodiment of the godhead itself, and intercessor for the assembled audience. In short, he is a mediating figure, adjusting his role within the ritualized proceedings so as to 'successfully' deliver the offerings of man to the gods and the blessings of gods to men.[27]

He dons the headdress of white horsehair (the same one he used for *Topeng Tua*), and then takes up the white cloth inscribed with sacred symbols in which the mask was wrapped. In the other hand he carries *Sidha Karya's* special offering as he walks to the centre of the playing area.

Sidha Karya laughs maniacally, as if privy to some great joke at the expense of the audience. He waves his white cloth, laughs, executes bird-like hops to the right and left, laughs again in the manner of Rangda and then rushes at the audience. The children, who have been sitting at the edge of the playing area

---

[26] Dunn, p. 61.
[27] Emigh 1996, p. 150.

(with the best view of the action), now scatter with excited screams and laughter, some hiding behind or clinging to their parents. The character is sometimes known as *pengejukan,* "One-who-takes-people-up-in-his-arms"[28] because a part of the ritual may involve catching a child from the audience and giving him a *keping*[29] from the offering. First, however, the offering must be given to the gods. Some rice and flowers are dropped from the offering basket to the ground at the centre of the playing area as Alit recites a mantra. He then tosses rice and coins to the four cardinal directions, calling upon the gods to forgive any imperfections in the ceremony: Brahma, in the South, Mahadewa in the West, Wisnu in the North, Iswara in the East and Siwa in the centre. He takes a single *keping* from the offering and, drawing a reluctant child from the audience, he presses the coin into his right hand, murmuring another mantra. After displaying the shy but proud and excited little boy to the audience, *Sidha Karya* sends him back and, with a wave of his white cloth, he leaves the stage. The ceremony is complete.

Aftermath

The audience rises to go and the *pedanda* is packing up his ritual paraphernalia, but the Topeng performer still has a few important tasks to complete. He removes the mask and headdress of *Sidha Karya,* which Gusti packs into their respective baskets. Alit takes holy water and the sticks of incense which have been left burning in the offerings on the platform throughout the performance. He prays, sprinkling the offerings and the baskets of masks and headdresses with holy water. With this mantra he thanks the gods and ancestors for their help and attention and bids them return to their 'heavenly homes'. Again he taps the baskets, stabs out the stick of incense in the offering and the baskets are closed.

---

[28] de Zoete and Spies, p. 184; Dunn, p. 72.

[29] *Keping,* also known as *pis bolong,* are old Chinese coins with a hole in the centre. They are no longer used as money but "used in offerings and for ceremonial purposes" (Eiseman, 1997a, p. P-24).

His work as performer finished, Alit quickly changes from his costume to his temple clothes. The sponsor offers a tray with a covered basket containing several high-denomination rupiah notes. Alit makes a show of refusal, then takes most of the money, giving a note to his assistant, Gusti, and leaves the remainder as a 'donation' to the temple. The 'fee' which Alit has collected may amount to as much as 100,000 rupiah per performance, which is a substantial amount in Balinese terms (a month's wage for an unskilled worker), but at the time of writing works out to roughly ten US dollars. He will also take home the large offering containing up to five kilos of rice as well as eggs, coconuts, onion, garlic and salt. After a few minutes of socialising with our hosts, Alit's baskets and bags are carried out to the waiting truck and we are driven back to Lodtunduh where Alit's wife will dismantle the offering so that it can be used later to feed the household.

The Performer's Process: A Surrender of the Self

> *"In Bali, it's like a process of entering a new world, the world of the mask. That means you have to sacrifice your own personality to be the new body of the mask. Giving up one's personality to enter the world of the mask, that is the only way for people to bring the mask alive, otherwise it will become only a piece of wood."*
> Dr. Wayan Dibia[30]

Much is demanded of the *Topeng Pajegan* performer. He must be prepared to wait for long periods, yet be ready to perform at a moment's notice. He must portray a number of different characters making the movement and words of each consistent with its archetypal mask. Once the performance has begun, there is no rest, no opportunity to assess the success of the last character or to contemplate the next. He must perform alone, without benefit of a script, telling a complex story that will keep his audience interested and entertained for more than an hour while fulfilling the requirements of the ritual. These are important responsibilities that leave no room for self-indulgence or self-expression. Indeed, it is this surrender of the self that makes the performance possible. The dancer, through the masks, becomes a conduit for the story and for the spirits of the gods and deified ancestors whom the masks portray. This capacity for self-surrender is absolutely necessary to the performance and is achieved partly as a result of the methods of training and partly because of the performer's particular relationship with his masks.

Training

As indicated earlier, the traditional training of a Balinese performer is, from the very beginning, entirely physical and without reference to interpretation or meaning. The dancer must simply assimilate the conventional movement vocabulary for each character through imitation and manipulation by the teacher and he must submit himself completely. Initially he is wholly preoccupied with the correct execution of the choreography, which is learned by repetition of the entire dance rather than through a series of technical exercises.[31] There are several aspects of this training method which are significant in terms of inducing a 'de-personalised' or dissociative performance state. First, of course, information is communicated kinaesthetically rather than verbally and therefore establishes from the outset a right-brain dominated relationship to the work. The movements must be performed with perfect skill and there are specific technical requirements that must be achieved. The elbows must always be lifted; the arms must not hang below the waist; knees must always be bent with legs turned out; the head must remain as still as possible unless effecting a specific choreographed movement, and so on. The movements are precise and stylised, with separate elements

---

[30] Interview, 11 March, 1997.

[31] Learning each piece as a whole is the pattern in other Balinese performing arts as well. See Edward Herbst *Voices in Bali: Energies and Perceptions in Vocal Music and Dance Theater* (Hanover and London: Wesleyan University Press, 1997) pp. 8–12, on his singing training with the Arja performer Ni Nyoman Candri and others.

executed by each part of the body—head, hands, shoulders, torso, legs and feet. All of this requires a high degree of concentration that is not concerned with analysis, but rather 'spatial perception' and 'recognition of patterns'[32] which are non-verbal, right-brain functions. Second, the elements of choreography are not learned separately as technical exercises, but as part of an integrated and organic whole. For example, a ballet dancer in the West may perfect his or her arabesque at the barre so that it can eventually be used within the context of any number of ballets to express joy, perhaps, or longing. A Balinese Topeng dancer, on the other hand, must learn an entire dance in every detail without breaking it up into individual exercises to be taken out of the dance and developed separately. The leg or hand movements are not transposed from one character into another because, although there are certain similarities, each character has its own particular movement vocabulary. Finally, the various elements of the choreography do not refer to anything outside the context of the dance. The sinuous walk of the *Dalem*, for example, expresses nothing in particular—it is simply the way the *Dalem* walks. Even complex movements of the hands, which are often compared, erroneously, to Indian *mudras*, are merely decorative and have no special significance; *nadab gelung*, for instance, means only to 'touch the headdress',[33] a gesture neither of pride nor of submission. The Topeng dancer learns the gesture as part of a choreographic whole in which all of the elements taken together constitute the characterisation.

In contrast to actors in the West, there is never any question of the Balinese performer identifying with the characters he portrays or expressing personal ideas or feelings through them; self-expression of that kind does not really figure in this work. It would be considered presumptuous for a performer to identify with these semi-divine characters, to imagine that he could be 'like' the

---

[32] Barbara Lex, 'The Neurobiology of Ritual Trance' in *The Spectrum of Ritual: A Biogenic Structural Analysis*, Charles D. Laughlin and Eugene d'Aquili, editors (New York: Columbia University Press, 1979) p. 125.

[33] Bandem and de Boer, p. 149.

Dalem, for example, or that through the *Dalem* ideas or feelings of the performer might be expressed. Certainly, individual Balinese performers may recognise and acknowledge an affinity with certain characters, but this a matter of physical aptitude or personal taste rather than assertion of self through the character. Individual styles do emerge of course, particularly in the performance of the speaking characters (the *Penasar* and *bondres*) in which skills in, for example, comedy or storytelling become more apparent. Indeed, the speaking masks are often the conduits for political and philosophical comment, making this 'traditional' theatre thoroughly contemporary. However, the kind of personal expression and identification with character that is associated with Euro-American concepts of 'method' acting do not figure in this aesthetic.

Music

Once he has begun to assimilate the movement vocabulary, the dancer must concentrate upon co-ordinating his movement with the music. Each character has a particular musical theme and, embedded within the complex of interlocking rhythms and melodies played by the gamelan orchestra, there are clear time markers which signal changes to the dancer. He must listen primarily for the sound of the large gong, which produces a deep sonority not always clearly discernible over the higher-pitched melodies of the metallophones. Having assimilated the character's movement, the dancer strives to become one with the music, surrendering himself to its rhythms and responding to its commands. Within the context of a performance the Topeng dancer takes a more authoritative role with the gamelan orchestra and the musicians rely upon the performer's signals for various musical gestures including sudden breaks called *angsel* and drum beats that accentuate sharp movements of the head or body. It is an essentially interactive relationship in which the performer is subject to the music's rhythms while he also signals changes in tempo and intensity through his movement. These signals are 'built-in' to the movement vocabulary of each character and are familiar to performers and audience.

The strongly rhythmic, rather than melodic, nature of the gamelan accompaniment functions as a 'driving' mechanism which, particularly within the context of a sacred ritual, is a powerful inducement to altered states of consciousness.[34] The gamelan usually used for Topeng is the Gamelan Gong Kebyar, a large orchestra with a particularly brilliant tone that may consist of as many as 30 or more players and instruments including metallophones, cymbals, drums and gongs.[35] The level of noise it produces is extraordinary and quite overwhelming for the observer, particularly within the walled space of a temple. For the dancer, who must move synchronously with the gamelan, the effect is, if anything, greater:

> **Ida Bagus Alit:** "Gamelan plays a very important part in getting the concentration. You have to be able to concentrate on your character by listening to the medium, the gamelan. The gamelan will actually help you to concentrate to do your job. The gamelan, for the *Sidha Karya* mask, for example, has already been married to a certain song. . . . So when you dance *Sidha Karya,* it has to be that song, and if you listen to that, concentrate to that, you will be able to do better dancing by listening to the gamelan."[36]

> **Ida Bagus Anom:** "And then you hear the music, the music starts and you feel the spirit of the music, what [sort of] energy [does] the music give you? Strong? Soft? In the middle level? . . . You hear the music and the music gives you the power to become that character."[37]

---

[34] Lex, pp. 122–124; Rouget, pp. 325–326.

[35] See Michael Tenzer, *Balinese Music* (Singapore: Periplus Editions, 1991) pp. 34–35, 77–81 for detailed information regarding the instruments of the Kebyar ensemble and their tuning.

[36] IB Alit, interview, 5 April, 1997.

[37] Anom 14 April, 1997.

The dancer must positively seek to be completely absorbed, allowing himself to become one with the accompaniment—*kawin dengan musik,* married with the music. This concentration upon rhythmic interaction with the musical accompaniment is an additional self-abnegation that can lead to dissociation and trance.

Costume
The performer's individuality is further diminished by the costume, which is not only a generalised indicator of the mythical past (rather than a specific reference to a particular person or time), but also distorts the actor's own body to conform with traditional iconography. There is little scope for action other than that prescribed by the choreography because the voluminous costume both disguises the body and restricts movement. The performer is completely engulfed. Thus, choreography, music, costume and mask work to create a single entity, the character, and to obscure the individual who renders the performance.

Masks
More than any other aspect of Topeng performance, it is the use of the mask which most clearly exemplifies the performer's self-abnegation. If an individual's personality is felt to reside in the face, then to cover one's face with a mask represents a most powerful act of self-surrender. Each mask in Topeng imposes upon the performer a particular movement vocabulary and collection of ritualised gestures that must be perfectly integrated with the musical accompaniment, thus it is the mask that fundamentally determines the performance. A remarkable quality of these masks is that, although they are carved from wood and their expressions are fixed, in performance they appear to move and register a broad range of emotion from warm kindliness to furious anger. How is this achieved? What is it that a performer does to produce this extraordinary effect?

It is important first of all to have some idea of the physical sensation of wearing the mask from the actor's point of view in order to understand the means by which a painted piece of wood can become so expressive. The inside of a

Balinese mask, unlike Noh masks, is left unpainted, though sometimes the bare wood may be sanded to leave a smooth surface. Until the earlier years of this century, Topeng masks were held to the face with a bar of wood or flap of leather that protruded from the back of the mask and was held in the dancer's teeth. (Javanese Topeng masks are still held this way.) Today, however, the mask is held firmly in place by a thick band of rubber attached to the mask with string. It fits tightly and, although the carved nostrils may provide some air, breathing through the mask is still restricted. The actor can see through thin slits carved below each eye, but vision is very limited. Headdresses, which in some cases fit over the top edge of the mask, are heavy and may press the mask painfully against the forehead or shift the mask lower on the face, further restricting vision and breathing. In order to make the eyes seem to see, the actor must imagine looking out through the painted eyes of the mask while actually using the slits below the eyes to see where he is going.

Given that the actor who wears the mask cannot see the mask's face and cannot be certain that the position of the mask's features corresponds with his own, the process by which a mask may be made to live in performance is more complex than it might first appear. A relationship must be developed with the mask that will enable the performer to imagine the mask's face and costumed body and then to move according to that image rather than his own body image. Dr. Wayan Dibia (a Topeng performer as well as a scholar) explained:

> I try to visualise the combination of myself with the mask to dancing with the character. So this kind of abstract reference for me to look at while I am dancing, that picture, comes again and again during the process of performance.[38]

Moreover, since each mask is unique, the dancer's movement must correspond to its particular attributes. Thus the performer's movement is directed

---

[38] 4 March, 1997.

not only by character type (*Dalem*, or *Patih*, for example) but also by the particular qualities of the specific mask.

> **Wayan Dibia:** "Yes, there's a set choreography, that's true, what kind of choreography, what kind of movement in that set choreography is different depending on the mask itself."[39]

> **Nyoman Catra:** "We have an image of what the character is. For instance, the old man with a very subtle and dignified mask, and when we work it we can use the body more straight and look more slow. Because the mask is very dignified, an old man with white moustache, white eyebrow, everything is white, very calm and strong. If we have another one with a smile and a slightly open mouth, we can use a harder breathing. We let our body drop down and let the mask have a short breathing cycle."[40]

The performer must direct his movement through the features of the masked character so that he sees, not with his own eyes, but with those of the mask. His body must conform to the physical type suggested by the character. Even the breath, that most fundamental activity, is directed by the individual characteristics of the mask. This complex process is a profoundly dissociative activity which alienates the performer from his own body as he imagines, from the outside, the figure that he must animate from the inside, using his now-alienated body. It is a process that would be quite impossible without the performer having already established a strong relationship with the masks that he is to use.

Carver-dancers
The powerful connection between a performer and his masks is especially strong when the dancer himself has carved the masks that he wears. Many Balinese

---

[39] Dibia, 4 March, 1997.
[40] I Nyoman Catra, 24 March, 1997.

performers feel that the two activities are so complementary that to do one successfully, one must do the other:

> **Ida Bagus Anom:** "My grandfather, mask maker and dancer, also my father. I'm like the third generation continuing mask making and dancing. In that time when I started to carve a mask, my father said, 'No, Anom, you must study movement'. Because in Bali if you make a mask you must also know how to do movement, also the story behind the mask, the music you must understand—not just make a mask. They help each other, need each other. For example, how can you make a good mask if you never put on a mask on the stage? You can't make a mask, because you never feel it. How to make a mask work with music, with the movement? This is why my father said to me, 'You must study dance.'"[41]

> **Ida Bagus Alit:** "In order to be a mask dancer, you have to master how to carve masks first, otherwise you wouldn't be able to transfer the knowledge and feelings you have from making a mask. . . . I feel I have to learn from maskmaking to dancing because they are one.[42]

The carver sees the face of the character emerge from the wood as he carves, thus the carver-dancer can develop that visage to project particular qualities, shaping the character. A carver, in the course of his work, comes to know each detail of a mask's expression intimately; thus the carver-dancer has the distinct advantage of knowing his masks well, even before they are finished.

> **Ida Bagus Anom:** "If you put on a mask you make by yourself, you see the mask during the process from the block of wood you carved yourself, you see the process of the mask. The mask

---

[41] IB Anom, 14 April, 1997.

[42] IB Alit 5 April, 1997.

already comes to you, you come to the mask. You don't need again the imagination of the mask from the outside because you see, you've made it, the mask."[43]

Not all dancers are carvers, however, nor all carvers dancers. Moreover, many carver-dancers, including those quoted here, use masks that were carved by others, often their fathers or grandfathers. Although such masks have a strong resonance for the dancer who inherits them, an intimacy must still be established between performer and mask.

Marrying the masks

A performer comes to know his masks through a process which, like learning the movement vocabulary of each character, is non-linear, non-verbal, non-analytical and engages "holistic, synthetic thought"[44] associated with right-brain function. In the course of my research I found a remarkable consistency among performers when they were questioned about this process:

> **Wayan Dibia:** "You study your mask carefully by moving it silently, just to look. I guess technically you just try to put more memory in your brain about the form and the expression through the mask, so that quality will transcend through your body when you move. That image will be allied to the entirety of your body. Although each artist will approach it slightly differently or would say it slightly differently, but the process is almost the same. People hold the mask and just look at it, look at it again and again. The idea is just to record it, what kind of expression."[45]

> **Madé Bandem:** "My father always teaching me, in a way he was guiding me how to use that mask by watching the mask all the

---

[43] Anom, 14 April, 1997.
[44] Lex, p. 125.
[45] Dibia, 3 April, 1997.

time. You sleep with the mask until you are able to dream about the mask and you get to try on the mask."[46]

Madé Djimat: "I must look first, long [time], then with the glass [mirror]. Long time coming to understand this mask; it's difficult when it's a new mask. . . . We sleep together always with my masks. I sleep here, my masks stay there, like sleep together. I think this is like husband and wife. This is important."[47]

Manipulation and contemplation of the mask allow the performer to form a clear mental image of the face he is to wear and provide the means by which he can test its expressiveness. Turning the mask this way and that, he can see how the mask catches the light and what is the most effective angle by which the mask's eyes can engage the eyes of the audience. He also gains a sense of the mask's 'personality', that is, whether it seems warm or aloof, demonic or playful, aggressive or thoughtful. John Emigh gives a vivid description of his teacher, the late Topeng master I Nyoman Kakul, trying out a new mask:

> Occasionally, when I would bring a new mask home, Kakul would take hold of it with his right hand, supporting it on his palm from behind so that it was fully visible to him. He would turn it first one way, then another, and make it look up and down. He would play with the movement, adjusting the speed and the sharpness of definition, until he was satisfied that he had found how the mask moved best; how it wanted to move. Only then would he put the mask on his face and begin to move his body, bringing the mask to life, making an amalgam of mask and self that, for lack of a better word, can be called character.[48]

---

[46] Bandem interview, 30 April, 1997.
[47] Djimat 27 April, 1997.
[48] Emigh, 1996, p. 116.

The performer's 'marriage' to his masks is not a single ritual act, but, rather, a long process of familiarisation and meditation, augmented by particular ritual activities. In the main, these consist of providing offerings in order to, as one informant put it, 'feed the masks'. Simple offerings of fruit, flowers, incense and holy water are provided for the masks (or for the gods related to masked performance, *Pasupati* or *Taksu*) at *purnama* (full moon), *tilem* (dark moon) and on *Kajeng Kliwon,* a day on which disruptive spirits are believed to be particularly active. Some performers place a new mask near their bed so that they can see it before they go to sleep and upon waking, and some assert that to be truly 'married' they must dream of the mask. If a performer believes he is 'married' to his masks, he is unlikely to share his masks with other performers:

> **Ida Bagus Alit:** "You can't loan your masks. It's just like getting married to your wife or your husband, you have to be able to commit yourself, it's a big commitment in your lifetime. You have to think first. You face a big responsibility as the wife or the husband of that mask."[49]

This 'marriage' is a physical and spiritual commitment in which the performer seeks ultimately to "become one with the mask".[50] In this relationship, the performer makes himself subject to the specific character represented, not simply the generalised archetype of king, warrior, or courtier but to the particular personality of a given mask. A performer may enter into this relationship with all of his masks or, as is more usual, with certain individual masks with which he feels a strong affinity.

The Topeng Performance State

Whether or not the Topeng performer considers himself to be 'married' to his masks, his relationship to them is powerful. Each mask calls for a particular

---

[49] Alit 5 April, 1997.

[50] Alit 5 April, 1997.

posture, movement vocabulary, breathing pattern and interaction with a specific musical accompaniment. In addition, the response to these requirements must be immediate and unthinking, since the nature of the genre does not allow for quiet contemplation or analysis between the appearance of one character and the next. The performance state of the masked actor in Balinese Topeng is one in which ego must be set aside so that the performer can allow himself to be subject to the requirements of each mask. This self-abnegation allows for a kind of self-hypnosis or suggestibility, freely entered into by the performer, through which the character of each mask may be manifested. In this state, engendered by a kinaesthetic, non-analytical relationship to the various elements of performance (music, movement, and mask), the performer seeks to be entered by the spirit of *Taksu* in order to give appropriate expression to the mask. Physiologically, the performer is subject to sensory deprivation (restricted vision), restricted breathing (resulting in reduced oxygen intake), and rhythmic auditory stimuli (from the music of the gamelan). These physiological manipulations, particularly in combination, can induce an altered state of consciousness in the performer. Bearing in mind that all of this takes place within the context of a religious ritual, in a society in which spiritual matters, including magic, are central to every aspect of everyday existence, it is difficult to see how this altered state could be avoided. The state is not, strictly speaking, shamanistic possession, nor is it 'trance' in the conventional sense of zombie-like somnambulism, since the performer retains consciousness and must actively take decisions during the course of the performance. Yet it is certainly a state of consciousness in which the performer is dissociated from his own body and ego. It shares with shamanistic trance-possession a sense of mediumship or visitation in that the performer, through the mask, brings to life legendary heroes, deified ancestors and gods. Without the mask, even though he may seek to create a similar relationship to a character, the performer cannot achieve the same state. Why? Because without the mask, the performer is not subject to the same combination of sensory stimuli and restrictions. The mask restricts vision and breathing, dissociates the actor from his body, and has, in itself, spiritual significance and recognised magical potential.

Magic Masks: Barong and Rangda

A Question of Identity

No other masks in the Balinese performing tradition are so much associated with trance, magic and the supernatural as those of Barong and Rangda. Moreover, in spite of the diverse analyses to which these images have been subjected by non-Balinese observers, they retain their mystery. Western scholars have attempted to apply various theories that seek to create some kind of comprehensive identification for these two figures. Bateson and Mead, for example, identify them as clear antagonists in a nightmarish Freudian scenario which features Rangda as the fearsome, evil, devouring Mother, and Barong as the gentle, benevolent Father. Belo, in her searching investigation, is diplomatically dubious about this rather simple construct, and recognises that any attempt at interpretation must come to terms with:

> a deeply complex, laminated structure, layers upon layers of meaning reaching down into the present out of a foggy or accurately recorded past, for the most part deeply comprehended but not articulately stated by the people whom it most directly concerns.[51]

She carefully traces the historical and theological links between the Balinese figure of Rangda and the Hindu goddess Durga,[52] as well as the previously-mentioned connection between Rangda and the legendary eleventh-century widow-witch Mahendradatta (see Chapter 3).[53] Parallels between Durga

---

[51] Belo, 1949, pp. 18–19.

[52] Another name for the Hindu goddess Kali who, in turn, represents "Devi-Uma in her ferocious and terrifying aspect", Knappert, p. 133.

[53] See also Belo 1949, pp. 20–29.

and Rangda are tantalising. Iconographic representations of the Hindu goddess on temples in India and Java show strong similarities to carvings of Rangda and to the Rangda mask; Durga, like Rangda, is a force of death and destruction, but she is also associated with fertility and Tantric rites.[54] This may serve to explain the overtly female aspects of the Rangda costume (her large, pendulous breasts, for example), and those which are more gruesome (like the mask's long jagged tongue and the dangling tubular attachments said to represent human entrails). Belo cites Dr. C. J. Grader who makes an explicit connection between Rangda and Durga based upon the carving of a Durga-like figure in the *Pura Meduwé Karang* in the Balinese village of Kubutambahan dating from the Middle Balinese period.[55] He further notes that the Calonarang stories share "a curious connection with the time of Erlangga".[56] Thus Belo links both Queen Mahendradatta and the goddess Durga with the mask of Rangda. Finally, however, she concedes that, for the Balinese themselves, neither of these models fully conveys the character's complex nature.

> She [Rangda] has the sort of authenticity which in our culture belongs to Santa Claus, to the Tax Collector, and to the Angel of Death—with the difference that we could not very well imagine all these figures rolled into one, while the Balinese seem to find no difficulty in attributing to Rangda such a multiplicity.[57]

Barong's identity is still more murky. Slattum proposes that "the animistic religion that might have preceded Bali Hinduism probably involved a variety of such creatures [protective animal spirits] which eventually formed the stable of

---

[54] Knappert, p. 243, Belo 1949, p. 28.

[55] See C. J. Grader 'De Poera Medoewé Karang te Koeboetambahan, een Nord-Balisch Agrarisch Heiligdon', *Djawa,* No. 6, pp. 1–34.

[56] Belo, p. 28.

[57] *Ibid.*, p. 19.

Barong characters".[58] This certainly serves to explain why there is such a diversity of Barong types in Bali, and why such an apparently demonic creature is seen as a protector, but fails to address Barong's darker side and transformational nature. In many Calonarang stories, the human agent who opposes the forces of black magic transforms into the Barong, so that the Barong is not really an animal at all, but a powerful spirit. Belo's argument that Barong may be associated with Buddhism and derived either from old Javanese Buddhist tradition or was imported directly from China is interesting but appears to depend entirely upon a coincidence of physical similarities and the questionable assumption that Chinese culture is older, more sophisticated and therefore more credible as a source than native traditions.[59] Napier, in a more recent study of Greek and Hindu iconography, links Rangda with Medusa and both Rangda and Barong with various leonine apotropaic images including the Indian *Kirtimukha* ('Face of Glory') and the *bhoma*[60] figure which is a feature of Balinese temple architecture.[61] Barbara Lovric cites references to Barong (as *Sang Kala Gede,* a figure related to *bhoma)* in the eleventh century manuscript *Usana Bali.*[62] Emigh, following on Napier,

---

[58] Slattum, p. 96.

[59] A number of scholars including Bandem and de Boer, Hanna and Picard cite the Chinese Lion or Chinese Dragon as the prototype for Barong. Interestingly, David George has suggested that the influence could have been in the opposite direction. He says about the Balinese Barong: "My own research reveals one tantalising possibility: etymologically, in Chinese transcript Barong would be Pai or Pah Long, namely White Dragon or even Java Dragon", David E. R. George, *Balinese Ritual Theatre*, Theatre in Focus Series (Cambridge and Alexandria Virginia: Chadwyck Healey, 1991) p.110.

[60] Also spelled 'Boma': "fanged face of whom appears above many gate-entrances to the inner courtyards of temples, its function being to prevent evil spirits from entering, according to some authorities. Alternatively, if a person tries to enter the temple with bad feeling, Bhoma is supposed to change those feelings. He blesses those with good feeling". Eiseman, 1997a, p. B-12. Eiseman cites a number of legends, the most apposite for Napier's purposes (in establishing the connection with the 'Face of Glory') is "A story from India has Boma as the son of Siwa, who was sent to defeat Kala Rahu, but who arrived too late. Siwa told him to eat himself, which he did, up to his neck. Siwa then sent him to guard temples and called him Kirti Muka." This story is also recounted in Emigh 1996, pp. 35–41.

[61] Napier, pp. 83–134 and 207–223.

[62] Barbara Lovric, *Rhetoric and Reality: The Hidden Nightmare. Myth and Magic as Representations and Reverberations of Morbid Realities,* unpublished PhD dissertation, University of Sydney, 1987, p. 310.

draws parallels with the Orissan mask of *Narasimha*, "the wrathful 'man-lion' avatar of Vishnu, who came to earth to destroy the blaspheming demon tyrant, *Hiranyakashipu*".[63] The limitation of these explanations, however fascinating and compelling, is that they fail to take into account the Balinese point of view.

Perhaps the most illuminating discussion of the identities of Barong and Rangda, and one which takes account of the Balinese belief system, appears in Katharine Mershon's reminiscence of her time on the island, *Seven Plus Seven: Mysterious Life-Rituals in Bali*. Mershon, a dancer from California, settled with her husband in the village of Sanur on the south coast of Bali and lived there for a number of years in the nineteen-twenties and thirties. During that time she took instruction in Balinese Hindu theology and religious practice from a learnéd *pedanda*, and later assisted Mead, Bateson and Belo in their research. In her account, 'Pedanda Madé' explains that Barong "is related to *Banaspati Radja* [sic], lord of graveyards, who guards bodies of those placed in his care at death".[64] He goes on to point out that *Banaspati Raja*, 'King of the Forest', is also the name given to the most powerful of the *kanda empat*, the four sibling spirits who accompany a newborn child into the temporal world. These are associated both with the gods *(dewa-dewi)* and the 'elemental' spirits *(buta-kala)*[65] and thus carry with them potential for both white and black magic. Because of this twofold supernatural power, my informants were exceedingly reluctant to speak about the *kanda empat*, since to do so would place them in spiritual danger. The sibling spirits are central to most of the *manusia yadnya*, the life-cycle rituals that are fundamental to Balinese religious practice and they have a special association with the concept of *Taksu*.[66] They are manifested at birth as the amniotic fluid *(yeh nyom)* called *Anggapati;* blood *(getih)*, called *Merajapati;* vernix caseosa

---

[63] Emigh, 1996, pp. 41–43.

[64] Mershon, Katherine Edson. *Seven Plus Seven: Mysterious Life-Rituals in Bali* (New York: Vantage Press, 1971) p. 40.

[65] Dunn, p. 130.

[66] Ibid., p. 131.

(lamad, the membrane covering the foetus' skin), called *Banaspati;* and the placenta *(ari-ari),* known as *Banispati Raja,* another name for Barong.[67] Pedanda Madé explained to Mershon that each spirit is associated with a particular god— water with Wisnu, red blood with Brahma (god of fire), the umbilical cord with 'the Earth-Mother' and the child's first breath with Iswara, so that the *kanda empat* also represent the four elements. The afterbirth has all these elements for he is them all. So Banaspati Radja, the placenta, is like Banaspati Radja, the *Barong,* for both are protectors. That is why the Barong has a shaggy body, stringy like the veins and arteries in an afterbirth. This is how the Barong is magically endowed, *sakti pisan.*[68]

From this it would appear that Barong is a personification of this protective sibling spirit, manifested in the placenta, but that is not quite accurate. This explanation outlines the character's overarching theological significance, but not his identity, for Barong is at once more universal and yet more particular. Lansing's chief informant points out:

> Banas Pati Raja...is the spirit that animates the Barong. However, the Banas Pati Raja who enters the Barong is not the birth spirit of a single person, but that of everyone in the village. ... Banas Pati Raja, in the Barong, comes from the kanda empat, the invisible spirit-brothers of all the children of the village.[69]

So, *Banaspati Raja* is 'the spirit that animates' the Barong, but each individual Barong mask has its own identity which derives, at least in part, from the all of the inhabitants of the village in which it resides. Another important aspect of this complex interrelationship between the *kanda empat, Banispati Raja*

---

[67] Eiseman, 1997a, p. K-6; see also Lovric, p. 311, Dunn, pp. 129–132, Lansing, 1995, pp. 34–35, 44–45. For a more detailed discussion of the *kanda empat,* see Eiseman, 1990a, pp. 100–107. Eiseman also points out elsewhere (1997a, pp. B12-13) that the *Boma* figure mentioned earlier is known as "Banispati in E. Java. Banaspati is god of the forest and the village in India".

[68] Mershon, p. 42.

[69] Lansing, 1995, p. 44.

and Barong is the association of *Banaspati Raja* with *Taksu*, which holds particular significance for "all sorts of entertainment [and] empowers people for trance".[70] This may serve to explain why Barong is so much associated with trance, both inducing trance in those who animate the mask and relieving those who are entranced (the so-called '*Kris* Dancers') in the battle with Rangda.

How then does Rangda fit into this matrix of meanings? In Indian Hindu belief, Durga (as the ferocious aspect of Uma Devi) is the *shakti*, or female counterpart/consort of Siva and it has been suggested that the Barong-Rangda partnership is a Balinese rendering of Siwa-Durga nexus,[71] a viewpoint which reflects the strong Sivite inclination of Balinese Hinduism. As Durga is the consort of Siwa, representing his female aspect, so Rangda is the counterpart of Barong. In other words, they are one. They are therefore not antagonists, but together represent a unity of 'good' and 'evil', or, more appropriately, white and black magic. Western Judeo-Christian observers, with an 'either-or' world-view, might find this contradictory, but it is exactly consistent with the Balinese Hindu belief system. This is why a confrontation between Barong and Rangda is inconclusive, since both are required in a balanced universe. Moreover, Rangda, like Barong, is seen by the Balinese as a protector.

> the strange thing is that any enactment of Rangda's role, . . . is considered a fortunate occurrence, if not an actual exorcism, certainly in the nature of a reassurance that the powers of evil, though forever with us, are under control and in such close communication with living humankind that they may be quite easily propitiated and kept in a favorable frame of mind.[72]

---

[70] Dunn, p. 131. According to Dr. Angela Hobart, whose current research investigates the use of Rangda and Barong masks in healing. The Barong Ket is also often used by traditional healers for its magical curative powers (personal communication).

[71] Dibia interview, 11 March, 1997. This is also mentioned in de Zoete and Spies, p. 95.

[72] Belo, 1949, p. 19.

So what have we? Barong and Rangda may be seen as aspects of Siwa and his consort, as creators and destroyers, opposed yet linked. They are both magical, associated with graveyards and death and are at the same time protective spirits, honoured and revered. These definitions remain generic, however and, although they may help to lend a deeper understanding of the significance of these figures, they fail to indicate the precise identity of the masks. What has emerged from my own investigations indicates that any attempts at a blanket identification for either of these figures falters when confronted by the multitudinous variations in local beliefs and customs. In practice, each Barong or Rangda mask, however it may adhere to a recognised archetype in iconographic terms, has a unique identity and significance for the village and temple to which it belongs and each has its own particular personality. There is a difficulty in determining precise details about individual masks since the masks themselves are regarded as supernaturally powerful, as are the *bhatara-bhatari* (gods) for whom they serve as tangible earthly representations. The Balinese believe that discussion of matters supernatural, especially those to do with chthonic magic (associated with both masks), is dangerous, and that to invoke the name of a god portrayed in these masks is to invite misfortune. Thus, the gods represented by the Rangda and Barong masks are known by generic names which reflect the esteem in which they are held by the community: *Dewa Ayu,* or *Ratu Ayu,* meaning beautiful god; *Jero Luh,* an honorific roughly equivalent to 'honoured lady'—this is how the masks might be addressed. They have other names as well, for example, *Anak Lingsir,* 'The Old One' or *Sane Barak,* 'The Red One' or *Auban,* meaning 'covered body', these essentially descriptive terms are ways in which they might be referred to in conversation.[73] Their real names, however, are

---

[73] Dewa Ayu is the name given to the Barong and Jero Luh, Anak Lingsir, Sane Barak and Auban are names given to the mask of Rangda and her attendants in the village of Jimbaran. See Eiseman, 1990a, pp. 293–321 for a detailed description of the Rangda-Barong confrontation in that village.

never spoken, perhaps they are not known, but the gods that inhabit the masks are very real and present to those who worship them.

The Play

> *"It would be possible to fill a whole book with descriptions of Barong performances, each differing in important details. How is one to compress so much variety into a small space, and to generalize what is so particular."*[74]

The so-called Calonarang[75] drama (which is not necessarily the story of Queen Mahendradatta) serves as an opportunity for certain local gods, represented by the Barong and Rangda masks, to display their power. However, unlike Topeng Pajegan, there is no 'typical' performance of Calonarang that can serve as a general example. The version that is presented for tourists every day in Batubulan is said to have been created in 1890. According to Bandem and de Boer:

> Like other Balinese creators, the makers of Calonarang drew from a general cultural pool of pre-established materials, some belonging specifically to 'the dance', others from far and wide in the heritage. . . .At the heart of the new creation was (as is so often the case in Balinese dance), an attempt to rework a *wali* [sacred] element in terms of classical Hindu-Balinese style and

---

[74] de Zoete and Spies, *Dance and Drama in Bali*, p. 86.

[75] The meaning of 'Calonarang', also spelled '*Calon Arang*', (in Balinese and Indonesian, 'c' is pronounced 'ch' so the term is pronounced *Chalonarang*, or, as in the former Dutch spelling, Tjalonarang) is difficult to pin down. In spite of the homophonic qualities of the term, it does not appear to be related etymologically to 'rangda', which means 'widow'. Slattum asserts that "The title of the drama translates as 'easy' *(calu)*, 'to eat or kill' *(arang)*". Eiseman views it rather differently and (1997a) defines 'calon' as 'candidate' (C-1) and 'arang', a High Balinese term, as 'rare, scarcely' (p. A-10). In correspondence with the author, Eiseman speculated: "*Arang* seems to mean 'unusual' or 'rare'. It seems reasonable to infer that this could refer to things that one unusually or rarely encounters, such as *leyaks*. Thus *Calon Arang* could mean 'head of the *leyaks*'". However, he went on to point out: "But that is just a Western interpretation and does not necessarily represent the meaning assigned to the term here". (e-mail 21 March, 1999) What is clear is that neither the term Calonarang nor the drama need refer to widows in general or to Mahendradatta in particular.

conventions. . . . In the Calonarang dance-drama, attempts were made to provide a frame in performance for the Rangda. A crucial difference is that the godhead manifesting in the mask can not be contained by any human agency, for Rangda can not be fully tamed.[76]

There are a number of ceremonial appearances of Barong and Rangda masks which, although dramatic and performative in a broad sense, are not, strictly speaking, theatrical. These include the *Pengrebongan* at Kesiman and the street performances in Jimbaran village. The story of the widow-witch of Girah or Dirah is only one of many stories which is referred to in a general way as 'Calonarang' and even this story differs from place to place. One of the other stories that provides an opportunity for Rangda and Barong masks to be used is *Balian Batur*,[77] a story about a male sorcerer who spreads pestilence and is opposed by a Buddhist high priest or, in some cases, by the Raja of Mengwi. Another is *Cupak*, the story of twin brothers, one virtuous and the other greedy, who vie for the love of a beautiful princess.[78] Sometimes stories from *Arja*,[79] such as *Basur* or the story of Prince Koripan, which are essentially romances, provide a framework for the appearance of Rangda or Barong.[80] Throughout the literature on this subject, it is asserted that the Calonarang is, above all, a battle between the two mask characters, but in practice this is often not so. In very many cases the two masks do not meet at all and there is no scene of confrontation between these two supposed antagonists. It would seem that many of the Western observers who have written about these masks cling to a fixed notion of a battle between 'Good'

---

[76] Bandem and de Boer, pp. 113–114.

[77] Observed in Bona, Gianyar 9 May, 1998 (discussed below) and in another version at Batubulan, Badung 21 May, 1998.

[78] The plot is given in detail in de Zoete and Spies, 143–149 (spelled in the old Dutch fashion as 'Tjoepak'); another version is described by Emigh 1996, pp. 61–66.

[79] A secular entertainment, which developed in the nineteenth century, it is sometimes referred to as 'Balinese Opera'.

[80] See de Zoete and Spies, pp. 202–210.

and 'Evil' without taking account of the much more complex Balinese conception of these figures, discussed above. Given that masks of both characters are venerated as protective gods, to set one against the other in some cases could be viewed as sacrilege. For example, according to my informant in Bona village, the *Pura Dalem* in which the sacred Rangda masks are housed does not possess a Barong mask and, although a Barong from a neighbouring temple often performs an introductory dance before the Calonarang, the Rangda masks are never confronted by a Barong in the course of the drama because it is 'too dangerous'. The Rangda masks are believed to possess tremendous magical power and it would be an insult to these gods to confront them with a Barong.

The Masks

The masks of Rangda and Barong are generally made from the wood of a tree growing in a spiritually powerful place, for example in a temple, graveyard or at a cross-roads. The wood must be cut on an auspicious day and special ceremonies must be performed before the wood is taken. Carvers of these masks are often specialists, or in any case will have been subject to purification ceremonies *(mawinten)* and are persons regarded as spiritually powerful enough to cope with the supernatural forces associated with the masks. They must fast for a period[81] before beginning and must bathe and dress in appropriate clothes (a clean *kain* and formal headdress) for the work.[82] Some carvers, whether carving a new mask or repairing an old one, will work only within the temple, where they can be protected from forces of black magic. If a mask is brought for repair or repainting, special offerings must be made daily and the work generally must begin on *Kajeng Kliwon*, a day when demonic spirits are particularly active. Some carvers report that vivid dreams come to them when they are carving a

---

[81] Usually forty-two days, one month and one week in the Balinese calendar.

[82] The fast requires abstaining from pork, beef and chicken; duck and fish–perhaps because they live in the water–are allowed. Interview with Ida Bagus Alit 6 April 1998.

sacred mask and one carver, Ida Bagus Oka, told me: "If I am working on both a Rangda and a Barong it is like a fight within myself!"[83]

Sacred masks are always made with traditional paints, made from ground horn or bone, *ancur*, and ground natural pigments. The decorations on these masks are very elaborate and often require quantities of real gold leaf and highly polished precious and semi-precious stones. As well as the painted wooden mask, which features a moveable jaw (or, occasionally, tongue and ears), the Barong requires an intricately-tooled crown or collar made of gilded rawhide leather *(sekar saji)* inlaid with small mirrors and polished stones. If it is a *Barong Ket,* a beard of human hair is attached to the chin.[84] It has been suggested that the *Barong Ket* mask is a relatively recent innovation, designed in the late nineteenth century by Cokorda Gde Api of Singapadu.

> According to his grandson, Cokorda Raka Tisnu, who is one of the few carvers of sacred Barong on the island today, the chief of Srongga village went to Cokorda Api, then a young carver, and asked him to come to Srongga and create a mask with the likeness of Banaspati Raja, Lord of the Forest. . . . He did not know what Banaspati Raja looked like, so he meditated, accompanied by the temple priest, . . . and asked Siwa, the god of the temple, to send him a vision of the masks' persona. Soon after, a pale, translucent, cloudlike image appeared, and Cokorda Api dutifully re-created it with a stick on the earthen floor of the temple.[85]

This story, however, is just one of many regarding the origins of the Barong Ket—nearly every village has one. There are several different kinds of Barong which have been noted by scholars including: *Barong Macan* (tiger),

---

[83] Interview, 14 April 1997.

[84] Often this is hair taken from a pre-pubescent, and therefore pure, girl.

[85] Slattum, p. 100.

Barong Bangkal (boar), *Barong Singha* (lion), *Barong Manjangan* (deer), *Barong Lembu* (bull*), Barong Kedingkling* (monkey), *Barong Kebo* (buffalo), *Barong Naga* (dragon), *Barong Djaran* (horse), *Barong Kambing* (goat), *Barong Tjitjing* (dog) and *Barong Puuh* (quail).[86] Some of these types are rarely seen today, though the *Barong Bangkal* and *Barong Macan* are fairly common. However, the Barong who appears in conjunction with the Calonarang dance-drama is almost without exception the *Barong Ket*. Bandem and de Boer imply that the Calonarang play of the widow of Girah and the *Barong Ket* mask developed at the same time in the late nineteenth century.[87] It is tantalising to consider the possibility that the incursions of the Dutch colonisers prompted the development of this exorcistic drama and the powerfully sacred, healing mask of *Barong Ket*.[88] However, that is highly unlikely. The association of the Barong, in whatever form, with healing and exorcism has a long history that pre-dates by several centuries the arrival of the Dutch on Bali.[89] It is much more likely that the *Barong Ket* is simply a more abstract version of this ancient figure following the iconography of the protective *Bhoma* and the masked figures of Balinese *Wayang Wong*.[90]

---

[86] de Zoete and Spies, p. 113, Slattum, pp. 104–111. Slattum provides photographs of several of the named examples.

[87] Bandem and de Boer, pp. 105–106 and 113–114.

[88] Emigh (1996, pp. 97–99) suggests that the self-stabbing of the '*kris* dancers' in Calonarang may have been encouraged or given greater resonance by the *puputan* of 1906. On the other hand, Vickers notes that there are Dutch records of *puputan* incidents dating as far back as 1849 and earlier (Vickers, p. 34).

[89] Slattum (p. 76) says that "Calonarang drama first appeared in fourteenth century Java". Vickers (p. 51) traces the story of the drama to the Majapahit era of the fifteenth and sixteenth centuries and Lovric (p. 310) cites evidence of Barong's perceived healing and exorcistic powers from the eleventh century.

[90] Dr. Angela Hobart points out that evidence exists of the Balinese Barong mask as early as the fourteenth or fifteenth century and that East Javanese examples have been documented from the thirteenth century. She suggests that both (Rangda and Barong) masks may derive from Tantric practices brought to Java and Bali from South-eastern India and Sri Lanka (personal communication). See also W. F. Stutterheim *Indian Influences in Old Javanese Art* (London: The India Society, 1935) p. 14.

The Performers

Because of the sacredness and supernatural power of the Rangda and Barong masks, those who wear these masks must be ritually pure and, particularly in the case of the Rangda mask, spiritually strong. Dr. Wayan Dibia, who has performed in both masks, described some of the necessary preparations:

> Performing Barong is very challenging, because there not only are you dealing with the heaviness of the Barong, but the spiritual elements [as well]. In my case, when I studied performing Barong, my fellow villagers conducted a ritual for me, a blessing and purification ceremony. Because you are dealing with a sacred object, you have to do this kind of purification ceremony so when you dance with that sacred object, your body is also in that kind of state. So if you touch [the mask], or your leg moves higher than the head of the Barong, nobody will mind. Nobody will feel you will hurt the sacredness of the mask because you are already purified in that ritual process.
>
> It's not necessary for you to be *sakti* [spiritually powerful] personally to perform Rangda, but that you believe that Rangda can protect you from outside attack. . . . When you are dealing with a community where people are practising black magic then you need, yourself as a human being, a protection, because as Rangda you will have to recite all of that black magic formula. So, then to test how good you are in that, people will try to attack you from outside. But if you know that Rangda will protect you from that, you don't need this kind of protection. I myself, I don't need that, but before I enter the Rangda mask I always pray and spiritually ask Rangda for protection.[91]

---

[91] Interview, 11 March, 1997.

Stories abound of dancers who, because their faith in Rangda was insufficiently strong, became ill and died after performing in the Rangda mask. Whereas those who perform in the Barong mask must have highly developed dancing skills, those who perform as Rangda are often persons who feel they have been 'called' into her service (for example, the mask might have appeared to them in a dream); they are regarded as specialists but are not necessarily dancers. The strongly mediumistic associations of the Rangda mask mean that it is the god in the mask who animates the performer, rather than the performer who animates the mask. Those who wear the masks of Barong and Rangda are usually unpaid and perform as a service to the temple and the god.[92]

The Costumes

Like the Topeng dancer's costume, the costumes of Rangda and Barong function as extensions of the mask. This 'body-mask' redefines the performer's physical dimensions, alters his relationship to space and affects the character and quality of his movement in space. The costumes are hot and heavy, restrict vision and breathing and thus set up the physiological conditions in which altered states of consciousness are more likely to occur. Each Rangda and Barong, while adhering to the same iconographic template, is unique. With both characters the costume and mask function together as a unit, creating a figure that has a particular character and spiritual significance for the community.

The Rangda performer wears long trousers with stripes in the sacred colours of black, white and red. His upper body is tightly wrapped in several meters of canvas webbing, similar to the Topeng performer's *sabuk*, but covering the entire area from chest to hips. One purpose of this garment is to provide some protection for the performer against the *kris* blades with which he is likely to be attacked during the course of the performance, in case the ritual purifications and

---

[92] Nyoman Catra insisted: "We never, ever accept the money, the payment for this, we just do it for *ngayah*." (*Ngayah* is unpaid work performed as a service, particularly in relation to temple ceremonies. It is considered an act of worship.) Interview with I Nyoman Catra, 24 March, 1997.

his own spiritual strength prove insufficient. Like the Topeng dancer's *sabuk*, it also serves to constrict the ribs, requiring the performer to support the voice from the diaphragm. Over this binding he may wear padding that enlarges his figure and provides additional protection. On top he wears a long-sleeved tunic, striped like the trousers and hung with large, pendulous breasts and tubular appendages representing the entrails of Rangda's human victims. The performer, who is invariably male,[93] is thus further alienated from his own persona by taking on prominent sexual characteristics of the opposite gender. He wears white gloves with long, pointed fingernails made of buffalo horn, which may be five or six inches long and significantly alter the expressive use of the hands. Many Rangda performers wear a skullcap or kerchief on the head to help cushion the mask and ensure a secure fit. The mask itself consists of two connected parts: the face, with its bulging eyes, jointed jaw and long, mirrored tongue, and the basket-like 'skull' to which the long tendrils of Rangda's hair (made from palm fibre or horsehair or both) are attached. The mask is heavy, perhaps weighing as much as two kilograms, and must be carefully fitted so that the mouth of the mask can be manipulated by the performer's jaw when necessary. Like other Balinese masks, the mask of Rangda has slits beneath the eyes through which the performer can see, but it is likely that he will have as much or more vision through the mask's nostrils or mouth. The mask is much bigger than Topeng masks and fits more loosely on the performer's face, with no strap to attach it firmly, so that sometimes the 'skull' of the mask is stuffed with cloth to make it fit more securely to the performer's head. The hair hangs down to the ground unifying the mask and costume so that the figure appears as a single body. In the case of the Barong, the entire outfit is a mask of which the wooden face is simply a constituent part. The face of the Barong and its elaborate gilded collar is attached

---

[93] Young women training at STSI (the performing arts academy) in Denpasar (ISI, formerly STSI) apparently now have the opportunity to appear as Rangda in performances at the school. However, all of my informants have indicated that it is considered highly 'dangerous' for a woman to appear as Rangda in a ceremonial context, the argument generally being that they are not 'strong enough".

to a long shaggy body, which may be made of palm fibre, feathers or cloth. It is operated by two dancers who are concealed under baskets inside the body, disguised on the outside by elaborate ornaments of gilded rawhide set with precious stones and small mirrors (Figure 10). The front performer dances and manipulates the mask while the rear performer dances in conjunction with him and manipulates the Barong's tail, which extends vertically from the ornament at the back and usually has a small bell attached. The performers wear striped trousers like those of the Rangda performer, along with thick ankle bracelets of bells that jingle with each step. Since only their legs are visible in the costume, the dancers usually wear nothing to cover the torso. Inside each 'basket' is a padded, domed area for the performer's head. The costume is exceptionally heavy and difficult to manipulate, but most performers have practised since childhood as members of children's Barong troupes and are well accustomed to its physical challenges. A chief difficulty in manoeuvring the Barong is that, once inside the costume, the performers are virtually blind. The performer in the rear can see nothing at all unless he looks directly down at his own feet. The performer at the front, who manipulates the mask, holds it at waist height most of the time and so cannot see through it. Occasionally he can lift the mask and see straight forward through the open mouth, but opportunities for this manoeuvre are few. Exteriorisation of focus is essential for the Barong dancer who can only make the mask expressive by imagining it from the outside.

> **Nyoman Catra:** "When you perform Barong, you never know what you look like, even more than in [Topeng] masks, because inside [all] you can see [is] the basket holding the glamour decoration of the costume of Barong. From outside it's very glamorous, from inside you can see the basket, the holder and you can see the handle of the Barong's head and you can see how

people sewed things. . . . It's totally the opposite way from the inside, but we have to understand from outside.[94]

Both performers must live through the mask in order to bring the Barong to life. Each must re-think his relationship to his body becoming part of a whole, a creature that is non-human, essentially an animal, and one that uses the feet as expressive instruments. They must also take into account the character of the Barong mask to determine the character of the choreography that they will follow:

> **Wayan Dibia:** "When I perform Barong, I try to look at the face of the Barong—whether this Barong is a little bit sweet or wild or maybe demonic. So if it's sweet, then I have to locate a certain set of choreography, a certain set of music to fit this kind of character. . . . But if the mask is so wild and demonic I will pick different sets of choreography. . . . The face of the Barong from place to place is slightly different. In one village you have very sweet kind of Barong, very friendly, and for that you need a very sweet kind of movement, very sweet music. You go to the next village, and it's completely different and that requires a different set of music and choreography."[95]

So the Barong performers must study the mask carefully before entering the costume because, once inside, their movement must be consistent with the mask's characteristics. Blind inside the costume, the performers can only determine their placement on the stage in relation to the sound of the gamelan orchestra. Yet in spite of these hindrances, they must make the mask come alive and make the creature seem a unified, independent intelligence, fierce but loveable, a demonic, yet protective god.

---

[94] I Nyoman Catra, interview, 24 March, 1997.

[95] I Wayan Dibia, interview, 11 March, 1997.

Calonarang at the Pura Dalem, Bona Village, Gianyar[96]

The Setting

Bona is a fairly prosperous village in south-eastern Bali about 15 kilometres from Ubud. It is famous as a centre for basket weaving and for its performances of the *Kecak* (sometimes called the 'Monkey Chant')[97] and trance dances for tourists. It is a village known to have been plagued by epidemics that, some inhabitants believe, have been kept in check by the regular performances of these exorcistic dances.

The *Pura Dalem* stands adjacent to the cemetery, a place of dangerous magical forces. There is not always a Calonarang given at the *odalan* here—it happens only if the 'god wants to dance'. *Ratu Ayu,* the goddess of this temple, makes her wishes known through a priest-medium at a late-night ceremony held a few weeks before the *odalan* and, if she indicates that she 'wants to dance', a performance of the dance-drama is arranged. This was the third and final day of the temple anniversary ceremony and my companions and I arrived at the temple at about nine o'clock at night. Outside the main temple walls were stalls selling food and drinks and huddled groups of men and boys playing gambling games by the light of oil lanterns. In the outer courtyard a stage area had been set up where painted cloths had been hung from bamboo scaffolding to create a curtained entrance. The playing space was defined by a low bamboo fence and a piece of carpet (about ten by fourteen feet) and was roofed with bamboo scaffolding and palm leaves. The gamelan orchestra was already in place beside the stage but was

---

[96] Documentary photographs are not provided for this performance because it is regarded by many as very dangerous to photograph certain sacred masks, especially Rangda.

[97] For a detailed description, see I Wayan Dibia, *Kecak: The Vocal Chant of Bali* (Denpasar, Bali: Hartanto Art Books, 1996) p. 6. The chant derives from that used for some sacred ceremonial trance-dances and imitates the sounds of the gamelan. The version performed for tourists (which both the villages of Bona and Bedulu claim to have created) accompanies a dramatisation of an episode from the *Ramayana*. A modified version, created by Walter Spies for a 1931 German film made in Bali called *Insel der Dämonen,* has inspired many subsequent Kecak groups. See also Picard, pp. 150–151; Bandem and de Boer, pp. 127–131; de Zoete and Spies, pp. 80–85.

still playing the ruminative, non-dramatic pieces that serve as a more or less continual musical backdrop to a Balinese temple ceremony. We entered the temple with our offerings and flowers, prayed to the Hindu trinity of Brahma, Siwa and Wisnu and were purified with holy water. Next we proceeded into the inner sanctuary and prayed before the two Rangda masks in their special shrine, which was filled with offerings of fruit and flowers and lit with candles and weak electric light. Both masks, one red and one white, represent the local deity *Ratu Ayu* which, roughly translated, means 'Beautiful Goddess'. The masks were made at a time when there was an epidemic in the village; as my informant put it: "Many people, little bit sick, then die; little bit sick, then die". The sickness was deemed to have come as a result of black magic practised by persons unknown. The *pemangku* of the *Pura Dalem* had a dream in which he heard the voice of *Sang Hyang Durga* (the goddess Durga) who said they must make a *pratima* in the shape of *Ratu Ayu*, and so these Rangda masks were made. *Ratu Ayu* has another *pratima*, in the shape of a beautiful woman, but when she wishes to dance, she descends into these masks. The white mask is *Ratu Ayu* herself while the red serves as her *'Patih'* or minister and, in accordance with traditional iconography, the white mask is more *halus* in behaviour, the red more *keras*. According to my informant, the masks will protect people from black magic if they properly honour *Ratu Ayu* and, in keeping with the dualism of Balinese Hindu philosophy, the masks can also aid those who wish to study black magic. Those who wear the masks of *Ratu Ayu* must be ritually purified *(mawinten)*, for if they are not spiritually clean they will become ill and might even die as a result of wearing the mask. Those who become entranced or possessed in the presence of the mask may also be allowed to wear it, but it is unclear whether they must *mawinten* in these circumstances.

The Performance
Preliminary dances
After honouring the goddess at her shrine, we proceed to the stage area to wait for the performance to begin. Just before ten o'clock, the gamelan strikes up a lively

theme and a Barong appears through the curtain. He looks rather scruffy; the mirrored panels on his back and sides are dull and his shaggy, palm-fibre coat is somewhat dishevelled, but the mask, a *Barong Ket,* is very jolly and full of life. He does not belong to this temple, since to honour a Barong mask here would be considered an insult to *Ratu Ayu,* so it has been borrowed from another temple in the village. As he dances about the stage area, the small boys sitting at the front grab at his coat hoping to snatch a bit of his 'fur' which is believed to have magical, luck-bestowing powers. This sort of dance is sometimes referred to as *'Bapang',* an introductory, non-narrative dance unrelated to the drama that follows. It is an opportunity for the members of the *seka Barong* (Barong club) to show off their skills and is a popular entertainment. The appearance of Barong before the Calonarang drama creates a mood of happy excitement among the audience. They are gathered not only to see the enactment of stories of the mythical past, but also to witness tangible evidence of the workings of the *niskala* (unseen) world of black magic in their own community, the ill effects of which the performance is meant to reveal and control.

The Barong dances about the stage area snapping his jaws at the audience and showing off, but after about five minutes, he exits through the curtained doorway. On his departure, the music for the *Baris* dance begins. This is an unmasked dance of a young warrior preparing for battle, performed as a virtuosic solo. The dancer, a boy from the village, performs brilliantly and is applauded fulsomely by an appreciative audience. When he has completed his dance and departed, Barong returns, animated by two new dancers performing a lively, energetic choreography featuring skilful jumps and well-executed *agem* (a straight-legged 'pose' that is a feature of many Balinese dances) with the mask held high, trembling slightly to communicate Barong's excitement and anticipation. The audience is delighted, but this appearance is also brief, and after about five minutes of dancing he departs once again. There is a brief pause, and then Barong returns once more, animated by a third set of dancers. This time he wears a length of black and white checked cloth called *poleng* around his neck.

This patterned cloth is used in a number of ceremonial contexts and symbolises the polarity and interrelationship of black and white magic. The cloth signals that the play is soon to begin. These are clearly the best of the Barong dancers in the village. There is perfect co-ordination between the front and the back as Barong executes quick, complicated footwork, jumping down and wriggling like an excited puppy. His tail wags provocatively and the mask tries to bite it, but then he becomes bored and lies down while the gamelan plays a quiet, gentle tune. Barong seems to be asleep and his head, resting on his front paws, moves up and down with his breath. The picture is very convincing, but it is hard work for the front performer who must sit with his legs splayed in front of him, supporting the basket and its heavy ornamentation with his head while he manipulates the mask with his hands and arms. Suddenly, Barong wakes, stretches his right front leg and waves to the audience with his foot then he does the same with the left and gets up, shaking himself awake. He looks as if he is going to exit, but then the *suling* (bamboo flute) begins to play and he turns back, curious. He rushes at the audience again and again, as if looking for the flute, then rushes at the gamelan, snapping at the flute player. He feigns dizziness and falls to the ground; the *suling* stops. He rouses himself, licks his foot then looks at the audience and flirtatiously kicks at a girl in the front row who moves away with excited giggles. Then Barong gets up and makes as if to climb over the bamboo barrier in order to kiss the girl, much to the delight of the audience. Soon bored with this, he trots to the steps leading up to the narrow doorway of the inner temple and sits facing the audience, his hind legs on a lower step, while the front dancer sits a few steps above. He wags his tail as if to show his delight in his own cleverness, then stands and trots back to the stage. After a last promenade and a bit of jaw-snapping centre-stage, he exits. This virtuosic display has lasted about twenty minutes and will be the last we see of Barong this evening.

The drama
After a pause, the gamelan strikes up a new tune and four girls with flower headdresses and strange, old-fashioned costumes enter. These are the *sisya,*

students of black magic who dance sinuously and chant magic formulae in Kawi. Sometimes they wave their bodies side-to-side as if entranced like the *Sang Hyang Dedari,* (trance-dancing pre-pubescent girls said to be possessed by 'celestial nymphs'[98]) and sometimes they execute squatting hops in the manner of Rangda and Sidha Karya. A voice is heard from behind the curtain, its shrieking tone characteristic of those dangerous god-demons who possess magical powers. At this, the *sisya* exit. The next person to enter the stage is the sorcerer whom the *sisya* serve, but it is not the widow-witch familiar from the Calonarang plays performed for tourists. Instead, the figure that emerges from behind the curtain is indisputably male and sports an enormous painted moustache and a fierce expression. He announces that he is a *sakti Brahmana,* Balian Batur (that is, a spiritually powerful member of the Brahmana caste with magical healing powers who comes from the village at the edge of the volcano, Mount Batur). Apart from the moustache, his makeup is otherwise very similar to that worn by those who play the Widow of Girah, with white dots at the temples and between the brows and a line of white dots below the eyes (see Figure 36). All unmasked performers in a Calonarang are decorated with spots of white placed at significant points that are believed to protect them from possible attack by black magic. It is necessary because the performance is a challenge to black magic practitioners in the village to try their powers against the god.[99] The *sisya* return, their headdresses removed and their hair hanging loose over their shoulders.[100] Balian Batur walks among them issuing instructions in Kawi as the girls dance, waving white cloths over their heads. The Balian has told them to spread pestilence throughout the kingdom and, under their magical cloths that render them invisible, they go off to

---

[98] This exorcistic trance dance is still regularly performed in Bona village both within the temples and for tourists. For descriptions of various versions see Bandem and de Boer, pp. 11–14; see also de Zoete and Spies, pp. 70–74.

[99] Bandem and de Boer, p. 120.

[100] Bandem and de Boer (p. 113), in their discussion of this dance, cite Claire Holt who pointed out that the dance of the *sisya* "is an inversion of classical Balinese dance. The extended arms,

do his bidding. The Balian performs a wild dance in the *keras* style, cries out with Rangda's demonic laughter and then exits. The person who plays the role of the sorcerer, though he must demonstrate some characteristics of Rangda, will not appear later in the Rangda mask. That privilege is reserved for persons selected by the temple—*wong sakti*—individuals whose spiritual power has been proven.

There is a brief pause, and then two *Leyaks* enter, one dressed in a pink *kain* the other, red. These are the first masked characters to appear and they are quite terrifying, with enormous fanged mouths, and heads bald except for a tonsure of long, scraggly white hair. (Figure 11 shows an example of this type of mask, also known as *Celuluk*.) Their pendulous breasts indicate that these creatures must be female (though they are played by men), but they are horribly ugly, very much in contrast to the lovely *sisya* we saw dancing only a moment ago. The audience knows that the *sisya,* as students of black magic, have the power to transform themselves into *Leyaks*. The lesson here is that, however normal or even beautiful a person might appear to be by the light of day, it is entirely possible that they could actually be a *Leyak*. Interestingly, although the masks are hideous, the characters are comic. They dance about provocatively, flirt with the audience, and then exit. There is another brief pause, then a young man enters wearing a *poleng* saput, a packet of cigarettes tucked into his waistband and carrying a copy of today's *Bali Post*. In a moment, he is joined by an older man, dressed in similar fashion. The audience swells as gamblers leave their games and others who have been milling about gather to watch, for the comedians are the most popular part of the show. The two farmers speak to one another in low Balinese, making jokes about local people and current events and establish for the audience the story so far: a mysterious plague has fallen on the village, many are sick and dying and it is clear that black magic is to blame. These two have been sent to guard the village and watch for *Leyaks*, but it is frightening to

loose hair, immodest and uncontrolled gestures, and nakedness are all antithetical to the deepest essential sensibility of classical Balinese dancing".

be out in the ricefields all alone at night. The young man casually lights a cigarette to show he's not afraid while the old man swaggers about brandishing an absurd wooden machete to prove his bravery. Then, suddenly, there is a howl in the distance; the farmers fall silent and exchange a frightened look. One of the *Leyaks* appears upstage, unseen by the two comics, and curls up in a corner to go to sleep. Shortly thereafter, the old man lies down for a little nap, while the young man kneels in prayer. A second *Leyak* appears behind them, upstage. The first *Leyak* wakes and gets up to urinate (in male fashion) on one of the umbrellas that marks the stage entrance, then he 'urinates' over the young man, who is still praying so fervently that he notices nothing. The second *Leyak* lies down next to the old man, and he cuddles up to the monster not realising just what kind of creature he's hugging. The audience are hugely amused as the *Leyak* and farmer become affectionately entwined. The first *Leyak* gently strokes the young man's back with her long fingernails but he brushes the hand away as if it were a mosquito. At the third stroke, however, he turns, sees the *Leyak* and leaps up, terrified. He wakes the old man who is horrified to discover that he is entangled with a *Leyak*. (This kind of broad comedy and sexual humour is typical of Calonarang performances.) There is a good deal of slapstick as the farmers and the *Leyaks* chase one another around the stage. The *Leyaks* block their exit and perform a macabre, flirtatious dance. The young man cleverly trips one of them and this allows the old man to escape. Then the young man, too, takes to his heels as the *Leyaks* dash furiously offstage after them.

After another brief pause, the *Penasar* is heard singing behind the curtain. He enters and greets the audience and then calls to the *Wijil* (equivalent to *Penasar Cenikan* in Topeng), his younger brother. They are costumed in the same manner as Topeng performers, but wear make-up instead of masks. The *Penasar* has a large painted moustache and thick black eyebrows; the *Wijil* has a tiny, pencil-thin moustache and, instead of the velvet *baju* worn by his higher-ranking brother, he wears a short-sleeved white shirt. Both have spots of black and white at the temples, between the brows and below the nose, to protect them from the *buta-kala*. The *Penasar* struts about the stage making self-important gestures indicating his rank (lifting his gilded saput, touching his headdress and so on) while his brother mimics him, making faces. There is a good deal of slapstick play at fighting and chasing. Eventually they begin to discuss the business that has brought them: the King has called upon a famous holy man to drive out the evil affecting the kingdom and the two *Penasar* are to be his servants.

Another voice is heard from behind the curtain, singing in Kawi. The Holy Man appears, wearing the ceremonial crown of a *Pedanda* and a huge rope of beads of the sort that high priests wrap around their bodies when performing certain rituals. After the two servants have made their obeisance to the priest, all three turn to address the curtain, calling for the source of the evil to come forth. Balian Batur enters with a white cloth decorated with magic symbols over his head. The Holy Man draws his *kris* and tries to attack the sorcerer, but misses because the magic cloth has made him invisible. Balian Batur shouts challenges to the Holy Man, which the *Wijil* translates, mockingly, for the audience. This infuriates the Balian, who attacks *Wijil* and, in the process, reveals himself. The Holy Man attacks him again with his *kris*, but the Balian escapes up the stairs into the temple.

Rangda
There is an announcement over the PA system from inside the temple and the audience kneels. The Holy Man runs into the temple and out again. Then, from inside the temple there is a howl—it is Rangda. The Holy Man enters the temple once more and emerges backwards, slowly, as the Red-Faced Rangda appears followed by the White-Faced Rangda. Both are clearly in trance and are supported by temple attendants. Other attendants hold umbrellas over the two Rangdas, an indication of the community's veneration for the masks and for *Ratu Ayu*. The Red-Face wears purple garments and a leather apron inlaid with tiny mirrors that glitter as she moves. The White-Faced mask is clothed almost entirely in white. As the Holy Man approaches the Red Rangda with his *kris*,

several people standing nearby go immediately into trance, leap to protect Rangda and have to be pulled away by temple attendants. The Holy Man, *Penasar* and *Wijil* exit, their work finished. One of the trancers begins to shout and his entire body trembles convulsively before he falls to the ground. The White-Faced Rangda seems unperturbed and dances alone in a stiff, vacant manner. Then the Red Rangda begins to speak, presumably in Kawi, but the words, interspersed with shrieks and laughter, are incomprehensible. The music of the gamelan is fast, loud and insistent, not only providing an accompaniment for what is going on but also heightening the already charged atmosphere. The Red Rangda becomes increasingly worked up and suddenly bolts away towards the graveyard followed, at a run, by umbrella holders, attendants and many of the audience. The trancers remain, hanging limply in the arms of attendants. The White Rangda also stays, supported by two priests; she seems somnolent and somewhat bewildered, but soon rouses herself and resumes her gentle dance. In the distance the Red Rangda's shrieks are heard from the graveyard. One of the trancers begins to dance with the White Rangda then kneels at her feet.

After about five minutes, the Red Rangda returns and seems calmer. The trancer at the feet of the White Rangda begins to dance again, then falls to the ground and clings to White Rangda's leg. A moment later, the Red Rangda begins to go wild again, rushes towards the temple but stops on the steps, turns and speaks to the congregation (for it is now certainly a congregation of worshippers rather than an audience). She descends the steps and dances briefly, then goes into the temple, followed by the White Rangda.

Completion
It is midnight. Along with many of the congregation, we follow the two Rangdas into the *jeroan,* the innermost part of the temple. Here a group of worshippers is chanting and singing quietly. Both Rangdas stand, supported by attendants, facing the *pemangku*. A small chick is prepared and a tray with bottles of holy water and

arak-brem[101] is standing by as the Rangdas are led to the shrine of *Ratu Ayu*. From my vantage point it is not possible to see what is done, but, based on other accounts,[102] it is likely that, after the masks are removed, the wearers drink the blood of the chick and perhaps some *arak-brem* to bring them out of trance and they are then splashed with holy water for purification. Once the masks have been replaced in the shrine, the singing stops and some women of the temple prepare special offerings and incense. It is relatively quiet, some people chat to one another while the Rangda performers, now out of the masks, are helped out of their costumes.

The person who wore the white mask turns out to be a very distinguished looking old man with a white beard. He is Mangku Ketut Puger, a black magic *balian* aged approximately seventy-five years. According to my informant, if someone comes to him for medicine he contacts *Ratu Ayu* through prayer. Because of his power and sacred status, Mangku Puger cannot be near sick people, though it is not clear whether it is the sick or his magic that would be thus endangered. He is both a temple priest and a practitioner of black magic, yet he is not regarded as either dangerous or evil, and he is deeply respected in the community.[103] The wearer of the red mask is younger, between thirty-five and forty, stocky, with shoulder-length hair. He is Ketut Brata, described as '*sudah mawinten, sakti sekali*', that is, he is already purified and spiritually very powerful. Because he had a dream in which *Ratu Ayu* appeared to him, he is believed to have been chosen to wear the mask. It is extraordinary how relaxed they both seem after all of the frenzy only a few minutes before. The two descend

---

[101] A mixture of palm brandy and rice wine used for various ritual purposes, most often poured on to the ground to placate the *buta-kala*, but also given to trancers to help them recover. See Eiseman, 1990a, pp. 233–234 and pp. 307–308, also Belo, 1960, *passim*.

[102] Belo, 1960; Eiseman, 1990a.

[103] It is likely that Mangku Ketut's black magic practice consists mainly of providing advice and/or charms to persons who seek his services. People may come to him for protection from 'black magic' curses or they may wish (for any number of reasons) to find the means of bringing bad luck on others.

from the *balé* where they changed their clothes. Mangku Puger is led out of the temple by attendants while Ketut Brata sits and chats with some of the people who are milling about. A few people sit and pray before the shrine of *Ratu Ayu*, where the masks now sit, as the *kul-kul*,[104] the wooden temple bell, gently sounds.

Presently, the gamelan strikes up again, in Balaganjur mode—a brisk, noisy tune in which the small cymbals, onomatopoeically called *ceng-ceng*, feature prominently. It seems to signal that the performance, and the ceremony, are now finished and people begin to go home, secure in the knowledge of *Ratu Ayu's* protection.

Trance and The Masked Performer

While this performance of *Balian Batur* was unique to this particular place and occasion, it is in many ways typical of the Calonarang dance-drama genre. Like Topeng, a Calonarang usually includes preliminary dances which are non-narrative 'character studies' not necessarily related to the drama which follows. As well as (or instead of) *Baris*, these might include the comic masked dance of the demon *Jauk* (Figure 16) and the appearance of a group of masked dancers called *Telek* or *Sandaran* who are guardians or companions of Barong (Figure 37).[105] The dance of the *sisya* and the comic scenes of simple farmers confronted with supernatural beings are also typical of Calonarang. Most importantly, the drama is inconclusive. The moment Rangda appears, the drama breaks off and is not 'resolved' because Rangda cannot be killed. Instead, the event becomes an occasion for the demonstration of the god's power through trance and mediumistic trance-possession. Those in the community who are purveyors of

---

[104] The *kul-kul* is used as a signal to call the community for meetings, worship, working parties or for emergencies.

[105] The *Telek* or *Sandaran* are ascribed mystical significance in some communities and various versions of *Jauk* are sometimes associated with Rangda. See Lovric, p. 311, Bandem and de Boer, pp. 106–107; Eisman, 1990a, pp. 295–297 and 317–321; de Zoete and Spies, pp. 99–101 and 174–177.

negative black magic are challenged to test themselves against the god. Finally, Rangda's apotropaic power is reaffirmed and the community is once more set in balance.

What is interesting about this performance is the difference in the performance states of the various masked actors. The Barong performers may have enjoyed a heightened state of awareness which enhanced their performance, but the Rangda performers were clearly in an advanced state of hypnotic trance, perhaps even trance-possession. To what can this be attributed? Both the Barong outfit and the Rangda masks were *tenget,* (spiritually charged) so it cannot be simply the spiritual power or religious significance of the mask that is the source of the performer's state. Several additional factors come into play including the circumstances of performance, the preparation rituals, the function of the mask figure in the performance, the expectations of the audience and the nature and predilections of the performers. Those who wore the masks of Rangda were chosen especially because they had already demonstrated a sympathetic identification with the mask and/or the deity the masks are believed to represent. It is also possible that these individuals have a psychophysiological susceptibility to hypnosis and trance.

In all ceremonial performances of Calonarang that I have observed, the individual or individuals wearing the Rangda mask have exhibited evidence of being in an altered state of consciousness. Sometimes this manifests itself as a somnambulistic state (as with Manku Ketut Puger) and on other occasions as a violent, convulsive seizure. Often, as in the case described above, it is not only the masked performer who becomes entranced, but also members of the congregation. In the case of the so-called '*Kris* Dancers', (the followers of Barong) described by Belo, de Zoete and Spies and others, it is the sight of the Rangda mask that appears to trigger the change in consciousness. In commercial performances for tourists it may often be observed that those who wield the *kris* avert their eyes from the Rangda mask to avoid falling into trance. One example is the Sadha Budaya Troupe who perform a 'Barong and Kris Dance' (a truncated version of the Widow of Girah story) for tourists every Friday evening at the *Puri Saren* in Ubud.[106] The masks used by this group, controversially, have been sanctified and are *tenget,* thus there is always a danger that the power which resides in the masks will be made manifest. The leader of the company explained why the risk is taken:

> In Bali we believe it is the same, the spirits are there, the gods are watching in the temple and it is the same for the tourists. We make offerings for the masks before and after the performance. . . . They [the '*kris* dancers'] do not want to go into trance, but it has happened. When we performed in Finland one of the *kris* dancers went into trance and fell off of the stage. People in the audience thought he was sick, that he was dead, they came backstage afterwards to find out what was wrong, but he was all right, because he was in trance, Rangda protects him. The spirits come with us from Bali when we travel. It also happened in Japan that some of the dancers were in full trance in the performance.[107]

Even masks that have not been subjected to the appropriate ceremonies, and are therefore not considered *tenget,* may still have a powerful effect upon performers. Dr. Wayan Dibia told of an occasion when he was himself stricken in a performance given by the STSI (now ISI) (Academy of Performing Arts) Calonarang group:

> I went into trance in Jogjakarta when I performed Calonarang there. I don't know what happened. I was performing the Prime Minister that had to stab Rangda at that time. For some reason, although I brought not a sacred Rangda and not a sacred Barong, but for this performance, I asked someone to make complete

---

[106] Indeed, the company, augmented by professional comedians and local performers, also performs Calonarang in its full version for ceremonies at various temples in the Ubud area.

[107] I Madé Sadiya, interview, 10 March, 1997.

offerings. So that must have somehow invited the spirit to enter the body of Rangda and when I, as the Prime Minister, was about to stab Rangda, I was just out of control. And the electric power just cut off like that—for no reason. All the lights [went out] just *pah, pah, pah, pah*—like that. The power was there, but for some reason the lights just blacked out. I went into trance and I realized later on I was lying down in the dressing room.[108]

Here, it would seem, is powerful evidence of the power of the Rangda mask. It is impossible to discover *why* these individuals fall into trance since they themselves claim that they do not seek to do so. When questioned, those who fall into trance at the sight of the Rangda mask and attack her consistently speak of being overtaken by a great rage. Dibia, for example, speaking of the incident described above said: "I was in great anger at the time, wanting to stab Rangda badly, so that means I was driven by that power". Belo's subjects, too, spoke of 'bad thoughts' and a desire "to attack Rangda".[109] The power that drives them is the power that resides in the mask, which is the visible *(sekala)* representation of an invisible *(niskala)* force.

But what of those who wear the mask? What is the source of their altered state of consciousness? Sometimes it is necessary for the performance that those who wear the mask are already entranced before they put it on, most particularly in the case of Rangda. The case is rather different for Barong. The Barong performer is most active when performing the *Bapang*; it is an opportunity to demonstrate his skill. Prior to Barong's first appearance, the performers pray and are purified with holy water, but are unlikely to be subjected to trance-inducing techniques because a focused concentration is required to successfully manipulate the mask. Should the Barong appear later in the drama (usually to revive those who have fallen into trance) the mask is not characterised, or 'danced' to any

---

[108] Interview, 11 March, 1997.

[109] Belo, 1949, pp. 54–56.

significant degree since it appears only as a representation of the god. There are times, however, when a trance state is not sought but nonetheless imposes itself upon the performer as a result of both tangible and intangible factors relating to the circumstances of performance. Dr. Dibia related a particularly striking experience he had performing Barong in conjunction with a ceremony in his own village:

> At that time it was a process of purification ceremony for the new Barong. In my village and in many places here, there is a tradition for repainting the Barong, replacing the hair of the Barong. When that happens you have to cut the mask off the body and put the mask in a very sacred place and replace whatever part of the body of the Barong should be replaced and when it's ready, you bring the mask and the body together. While you are cutting the mask from the body, you are sending the spirit of the Barong out from the body. When it's ready you put [it] together. You are inviting [the spirit] to reside in the Barong. During that process... [while dancing], I felt that the Barong was kind of heavy at first, so heavy, but then it was kind of lighter, lighter and lighter. It felt so strange [I thought], "This thing is getting lighter, it must be something . . ." So, hearing stories from my seniors in my village, [I realised] that is one of the signs that the spirit of the Barong is entering the Barong. So if you're there, you will go into trance. At that time I was not ready yet; I didn't want to. I called somebody, "Could somebody replace me please!" And as soon as I stepped out and this person went in—Wah! He went into trance. Just 30 seconds.[110]

---

[110] Interview, 11 March, 1997.

On this occasion, no trance induction procedure had been performed for any of the Barong dancers, neither Dibia nor those who followed. Nevertheless, Dr. Dibia became aware of an ineffable sensation of lightness which he (correctly, as it turns out) took to be the harbinger of trance. Interestingly, having extricated himself from the Barong, he was no longer subject to the sensation. Yet, the power which he identified as "the spirit of the Barong entering" had an immediate effect upon the dancer who next put on the mask. Whether this trance occurred as a result of supernatural forces or a combination of the circumstances of the ritual, the atmosphere of excitement, the heat, the crowd, the rhythmic, percussive music of the gamelan orchestra and sincere belief of the participants is hardly important. The efficacy of Barong's power was demonstrated.

In the case of Rangda, a number of procedures may be followed to induce trance including inhalation of smoke from a brazier of incense, meditation and ritual offerings. These may be accompanied by chanting, singing or strongly rhythmic music from the gamelan. Madé Djimat described the preparation thus:

> First they must have water, clean water, *air suci*, from the priest. Then, together with the dress, with the headdress—before do[ing the] costume—he must do offering first, *sambahayang* [pray], ask the god to help him, not make problem.[111]

The preparation of the Rangda player is somewhat secretive and frequently takes place in a small, specially constructed bamboo hut on stilts about ten feet above the ground with a ramp leading to the playing area.[112] The performer is taken to the hut at some point during the performance, accompanied by a *pemangku* and attendants with bottles of *arak-brem* and holy water. When Rangda's characteristic howls and laughter emanate from the hut it is a signal that

---

[111] Interview, 19 April, 1997. The offerings will always include incense smoke for purification and to waft the essence of the offerings to the gods. See also Belo, 1960 *passim*.

[112] This was not the case at the performance in Bona because of the special circumstances of that temple, but was the case in ceremonial performances in Pengosekan, Penestenan, Lodtunduh and Silungan.

she is ready to appear. Whatever action is taking place on the stage quickly adjusts to prepare for Rangda's entrance. (Since Calonarang, like Topeng, is essentially improvised on the basis of a loosely constructed scenario, this is a simple task.) Then, whoever has been sent to destroy her draws his *kris* and calls for Rangda to appear. Evidence of the performer's altered state is often demonstrated even before the entrance by great shaking and terrible cries from the hut. When the performer does appear, he might collapse immediately and require the assistance of others to make his way down the ramp. On other occasions Rangda may proceed into the playing space in a fury, fighting off her attackers with seemingly superhuman strength and challenging all comers. Because of the very real danger of injury to participants and audience, there are usually a number of temple attendants on hand to try to keep things under control. Over-enthusiastic trancers who vigorously and repeatedly stab Rangda with their *kris* are pulled away after a time (but will usually attack again or attempt to stab themselves in their frenzy). The audience will be instructed to clear the way for Rangda to run or dance wherever she chooses. Since the Rangda performer is considered to be the embodiment of the god, it is imperative that nothing should hinder her.

There is a distinct movement vocabulary for the Rangda performer, though she does not engage in formalised dance steps of traditional choreography. Rangda's 'dance' consists mostly of running and jumping not unlike that of *Sidha Karya*, though much more vigorous, with legs bent and feet raised high. A striking feature of Rangda's movement, which is also displayed by other trance-dancers like the *Sanghyang Dedari,* is an arching of the body forward and backwards, with the head nearly touching the ground. In the case of Rangda this action is accompanied by terrifying, screeching laughter. These trance-postures are also sometimes performed by the *'kris* dancers' who have been 'possessed' by Rangda and mimic her movement and laughter. Occasionally, a Rangda performer who is particularly confident in the god's protection may even remove the mask and continue to challenge the knife-wielding attackers, still in the character of Rangda but without the protection of the mask.[113] Most often, however, the removal of the mask signals the end of the trance episode and the performer is revived with *arak,* and holy water.

My interviews with Rangda performers indicate that the altered state of consciousness which they experience is amnesiac and they are unable to recall any details of the performance or their behaviour, even in cases in which the Rangda seemed relatively articulate and controlled. A Calonarang performance given in conjunction with an important ceremony at the Pura Dalem in Pengosekan village[114] provides an interesting example of a more extreme manifestation of trance. Here, the renowned dancer I Madé Djimat performed as *Jauk Keras* in the preliminary dances and later appeared in the role of Rangda. I was able to observe some of his preparations, which began in a large enclosure that had been set aside for all of the performers to put on costumes and make-up. After his initial dance, there was a period of rest and socialising before he began to prepare for Rangda. After prayers and meditation, he was helped to don the costume, then taken inside the temple to collect the sacred mask and finally he was conducted to Rangda's hut at the far end of the playing area. In an interview a few days later he described what he remembered of the preparation:

> Before we enter inside the Rangda mask I do an offering first. I tell the god help me because I am just normal, I want god help me without problem. Then I do offering; then we do a little bit yoga before. Before offering we do yoga, *meditatasi* [meditation] a little bit. Inside the temple with the Pemangku, *sambahyang* [pray], then after I don't know, because already inside.[115]

---

[113] When this occurs in the course of the 'Legong Trance Dance' performed by the *Seka Andir* of Tista, Kerambitan, the Rangda mask remains displayed hanging from a tree in the performance space. Trancers occasionally break off from their attack on the person who embodies Rangda to embrace the mask, hugging its long hair to their bodies.

[114] 23 April, 1997.

[115] Interview, 27 April, 1997.

By 'already inside' Djimat meant he was already in an altered state, which left him unable to remember what occurred. It is interesting that he does not speak of being 'entered' by the god or 'possessed' or 'overtaken' but of himself going 'inside'. Belo's subjects, too, 'forget everything' while under the mask's influence, as if the subjective consciousness of the performer is not absent, but simply forgotten, denied. (The Balinese term for becoming unconscious, *engsap* also means to forget; to return to consciousness is *inget,* remember.[116]) In other words, the soul or self of the entranced does not depart to make room for an outside force or presence, but is simply set aside. The subject does not deny his behaviour, but does not bear responsibility for it. Falling into trance and the capacity for entrancement are regarded positively by Balinese society and, as a number of commentators have noted, these events provide a useful, socially acceptable outlet in this rigid, highly controlled society.[117]

Djimat is well known as a dancer and teacher both in Bali and internationally. He is a charming, well-mannered person, gentle and soft-spoken, but his appearance as Rangda was a complete transformation. He entered the playing space in a fury, easily throwing off his *kris*-wielding adversary, and was guided out of the performance area to the adjacent graveyard where a small altar had been erected. There a number of offerings were made, including the sacrifice

---

[116] See Eiseman, 1997b, p. F-17 and 1997a, p. I-3.

[117] Lenora Greenbaum 'Possession Trance in Sub-Saharan Africa: A Descriptive Analysis of Fourteen Societies', in *Religion, Altered States of Consciousness, and Social Change* edited by Erica Bourguignon (Columbus: Ohio University Press, 1973) p. 59:

"The hypothesis is offered that in a rigid society, that is, one where the social structures deny the individual freedom for achievement and personal control over his daily life activities, possession trance is likely to be widespread. Conversely, under more flexible systems, possession trance is likely to be either absent or a rare phenomenon. The rationale is that, under rigid systems, simple decision-making is fraught with danger from internal and external social controls. Possession trance relieves the individual of personal responsibility in the decision-making process by temporarily changing the identity of a human being into that of a spirit." According to psychiatrist Denny Thong in *A Psychiatrist in Paradise: Treating Mental Illness in Bali*, translated by Bruce Carpenter (Bangkok: White Lotus, 1993), p. 83: "In my opinion, these repressed emotions find an outlet in the dance and drama–an outlet the culture has provided for the Balinese to let off steam, either vicariously or directly". See also Belo, 1949, p. 12, Bateson and Mead, p. 188.

of a live chicken and a small pig. During this time, Djimat spoke in a kind of glossolalia (which may have been taken to be Kawi) and made extraordinary noises of pigs and chickens. When this ceremony was completed, he was led back into the arena where he began to 'dance' in an ever more frenzied fashion using Rangda's typical movement vocabulary. This frenzy increased in intensity until Djimat grabbed a bamboo pole demarking part of the playing area and began to scream in a furious, high-pitched wail, thrashing about violently. Six or eight temple attendants rushed forward trying to subdue him and were finally able to carry the still-screaming Rangda into the temple. Of this, Djimat remembered nothing. However, in describing his state he said: 'It is very difficult for me to tell you about this because it's the god, *the god comes inside the mask*—not *inside me*, inside *the mask*'. The power of the god is perceived to reside in the mask rather than in the performer, who is merely a vehicle, a puppet, animated by the mask.

When he was taken into the temple, the mask was removed and he was gradually revived with holy water. It took some time however, to bring Djimat out of his trance and his state of consciousness was tested by pinching his foot to see if he responded to pain. Having been revived, he felt elated and energised:

MC: How do you feel after an experience like that? It must be very tiring.
DJIMAT: After I am very happy, not tired, very happy.
MC: Can you go to sleep afterwards? [The performance ended at about 3 am.]
DJIMAT: No. I go to Batubulan [his village], maybe a few hours. I go to sleep maybe about half-past 5 in the morning. I talking with husband of my daughter maybe 2 hours more. Not yet sleep. I sleep about 6.00 or 5.30 until midday. I'm not tired afterwards.[118]

---

[118] Interview, 27 April, 1997

It is clear that this trance is substantially different from the rather more controlled but still altered state of consciousness of the Topeng performer or Barong dancer. While sharing many aspects of that heightened performance state, chief among them dissociation and automaticity, this experience is in every way more intense. What is also clear is that the mask is an essential element in the process of transformation and trance. I asked Djimat about the difference in sensation between masked and unmasked performance, he said:

> Oh yes, different. When we play *Gambuh* [unmasked court dance-drama], never trance. Maybe this trance come from the mask. Because magic comes inside the mask. Like Rangda that stays in the temple, Barong that stays in the temple then the god stays inside the mask.

The masks, as is clear in the example from Bona above, are powerful in themselves. Those who wear them are placing themselves in the hazardous position of lending their bodies to the gods, making themselves subject to dangerous, unseen magic powers from which—they hope—the gods will protect them. If the performer is spiritually strong enough to wear the Rangda mask, the god that inhabits the mask will protect him. What is essential for the ritual, and for the performer, is the mask. Napier has pointed out that:

> Some particularly powerful demonic parts are too dangerous to play without masks. In such cases, the mask object is not only a vehicle for the demon to become manifest but also some assurance that the actors can divest themselves of personalities that they might otherwise have had to live with.[119]

When the Rangda or Barong performer removes the mask, he is given holy water to revive and purify him, but he is not affected negatively by having worn a demonic mask. The performance will have left him energised and elated,

---

[119] Napier, p. 222.

while the powerful and dangerous forces that have been made manifest in his performance remain with the mask.

Conclusion

While many of the same principles apply to performers of Topeng and performers of Rangda and Barong, there are some important differences. In both cases performers work within a traditional movement vocabulary, must interact appropriately with the musical accompaniment, and must subject themselves to the requirements of the mask. However, although they are subject to similar physical constraints with regard to vision and breathing, the physical requirements of Rangda and Barong are in many ways more intense and demanding and are more likely to lead to dissociation and trance. The combination of these elements with the supernatural powers ascribed to the masks, the preparations designed to induce trance, the driving quality of the music that accompanies the appearance of the masks, the atmosphere of the performance and the ritual activities required of the masks can lead performers from simple dissociation to states of deep trance. This radical dissociation can involve loss of consciousness and memory and might, in some circumstances, be characterised as 'trance-possession'.

Table 1. Periods in Japanese history[1]

Ancient Period	
Yamato	300–710
Nara	710–794
Heian	794–1192

Medieval Period	
Kamakura	1192–1333
Muromachi or Ashikaga	1333–1568

Early Modern Period	
Azuchi-Momoyama	1573–1600
Edo or Tokugawa	1600–1868

Modern Period	
Meiji	1868–1912
Taishô	1912–1926
Shôwa	1926–1989
Heisei	1989–present

---

[1] Adapted from Benito Ortoloni, *The Japanese Theatre: From Shamanistic Ritual to Contemporary Pluralism* (Revised edition. Princeton, NJ: Princeton University Press, 1995) p. xv.

Diagram 1: The "Efficacy-Entertainment" Braid applied to Noh and Balinese Topeng.

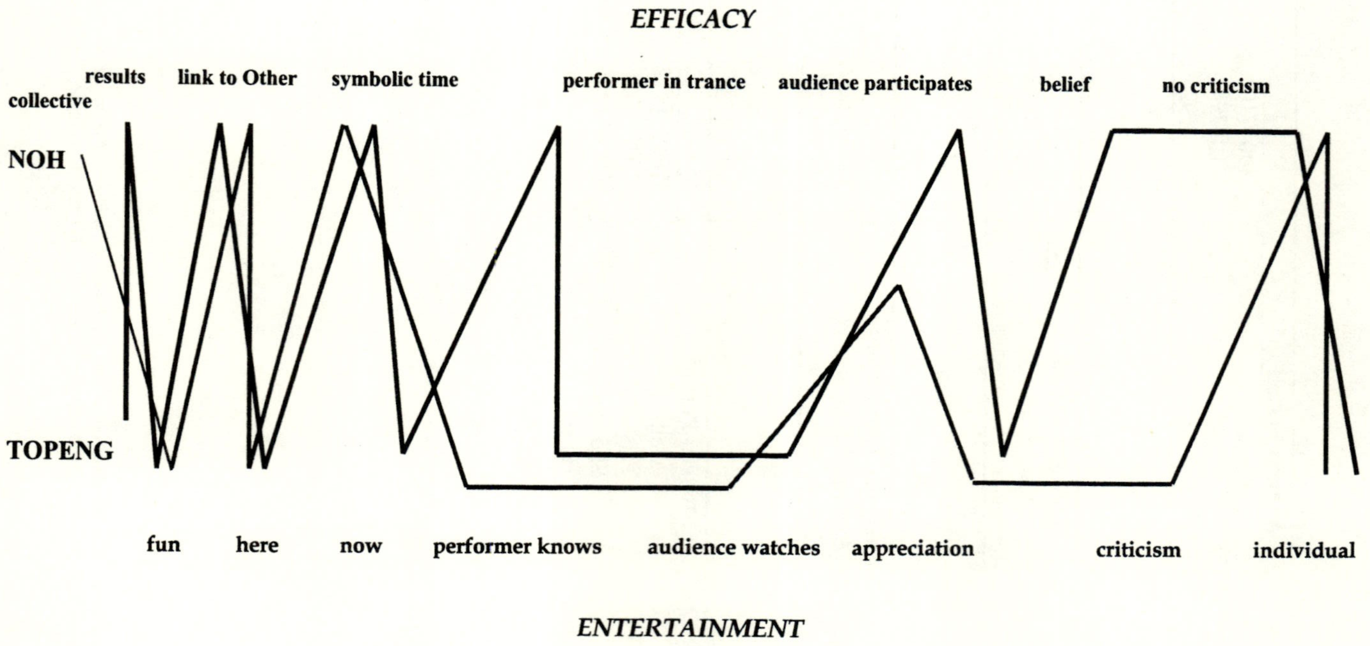

Diagram 2: The Noh Stage

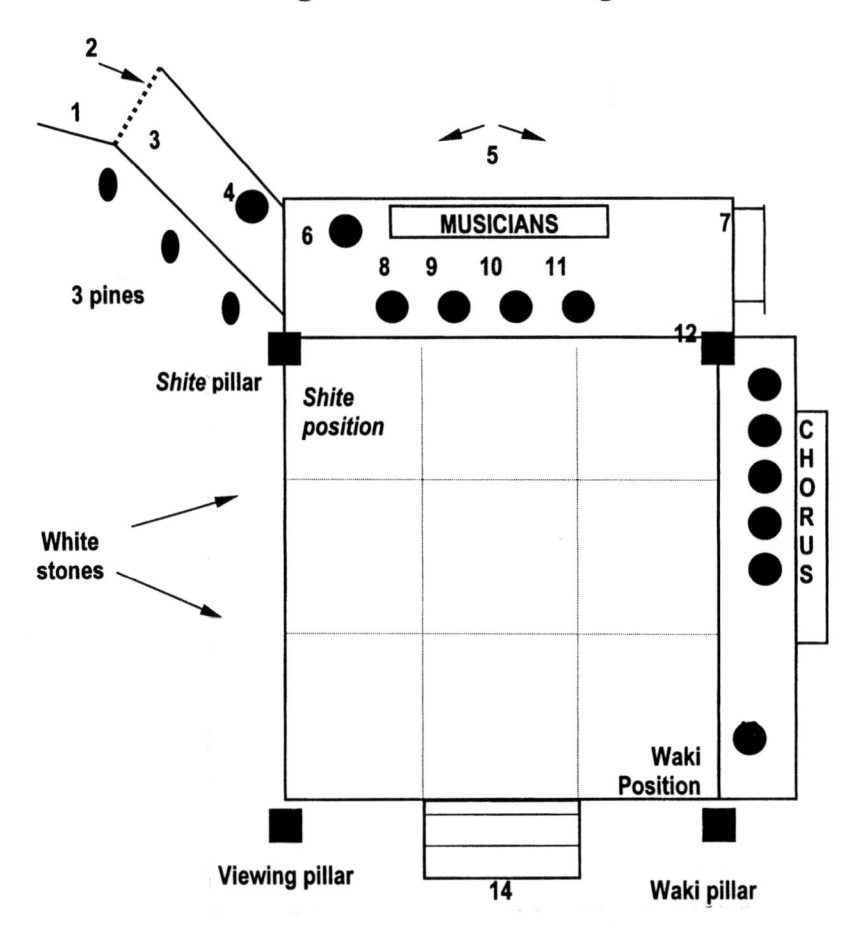

1 *kagami-no-ma* (mirror room)
2 *age-maku* (curtain)
3 *hashigakari* (bridge)
4 *kyôgen* (seat)
5 *kagami-ita* (mirror board)
6 *kôken* (stage assistants)
7 *kiri-do* (low entrance door)
8 *taiko*
9 *ôtsuzumi* (hip drum)
10 *kôtsuzumi* (shoulder drum)
11 *fue* (flute)
12 flute pillar
13 Waki seat
14 steps (used only in *Okina*)

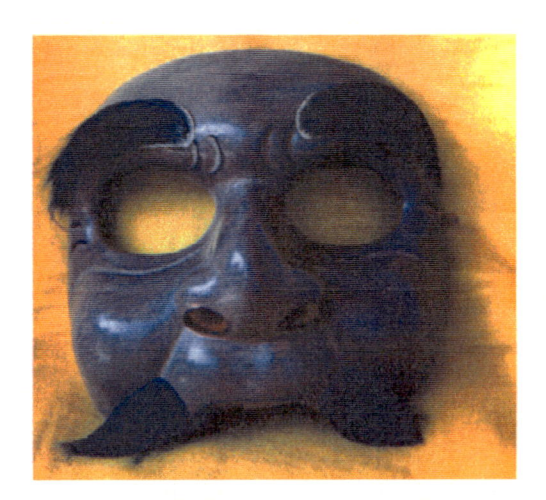

Figure 1: Penasar Kelihan

Figure 2: Penasar Cenikan

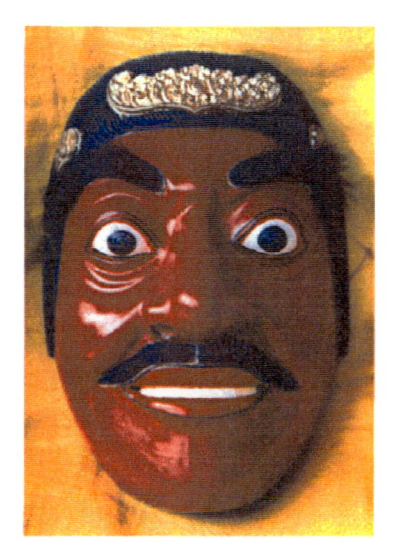

Figure 3:
Patih (Topeng Keras)

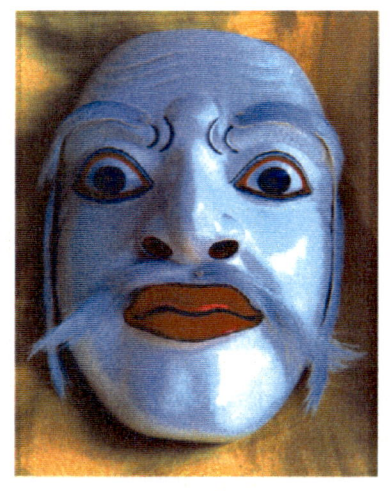

Figure 4:
Topeng Tua

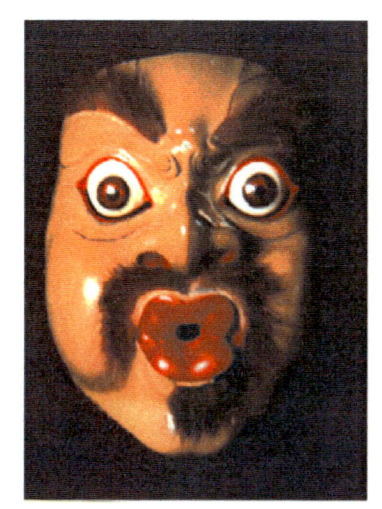

Figure 5:
Patih Lucu (comic Patih)

Figure 6:
Dalem (refined king)

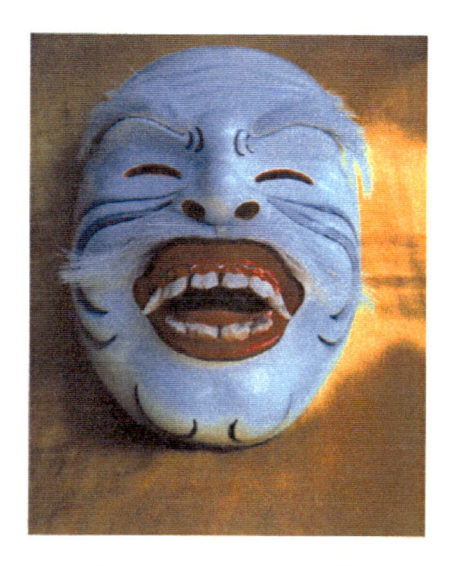

Figure 7:
Sidha Karya

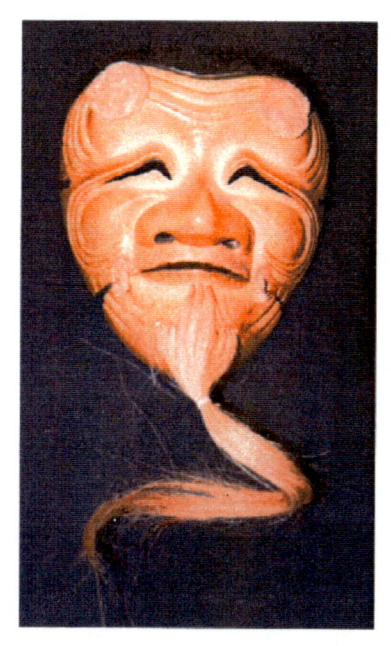

Figure 8:
Okina

Figure 9:
Rangda

Figure 10:
Barong Ket

Figure 11:
Leyak

Figure 12:
Balinese carving tools: (from left) hand ax, mutik (flat knife), pangot (curved knife), curved and flat pahat (chisels), ebony mallet.

Figure 13:
Anak Agung Gede Ngurah measures an unpainted Dalem mask against a new block

Figure 14:
Children's Barong Macan (Tiger Barong).

Figure 15:
One of Barong's attendants.

Figure 16a: Jauk Manis ("sweet")

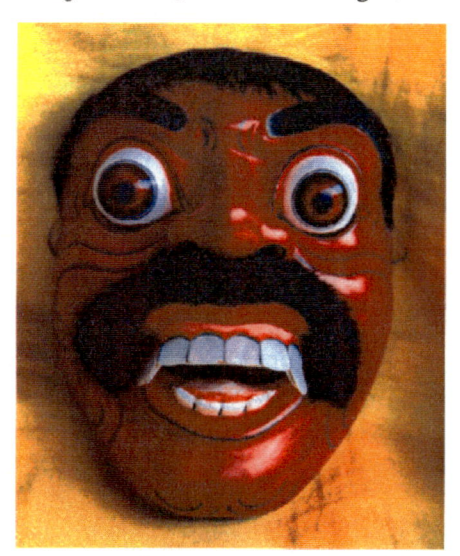

Figure 16 b: Jauk Keras ("rough")

Figure 17
Nagayama Toyo Saburo wears the Aku-Jo mask as the goblin in *Kurama Tengu*

Figure 18:
Folk mask of Shi-shi from
the Shi-shi Kaikan in Takayama, Hida Prefecture.

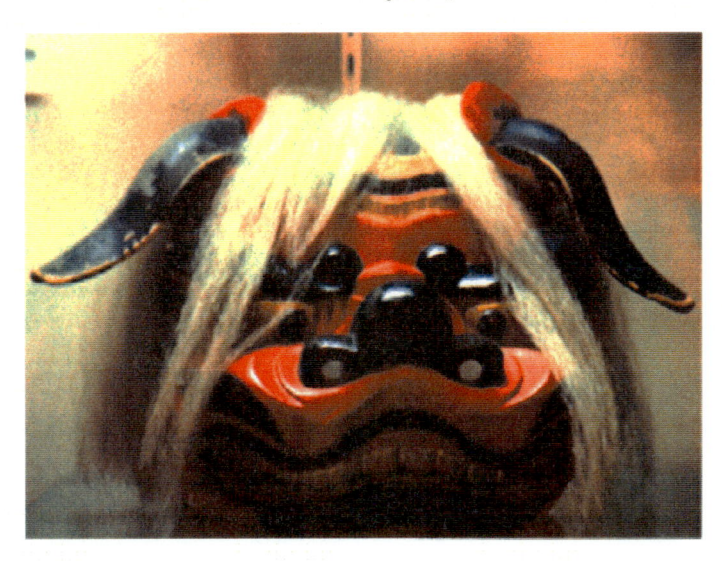

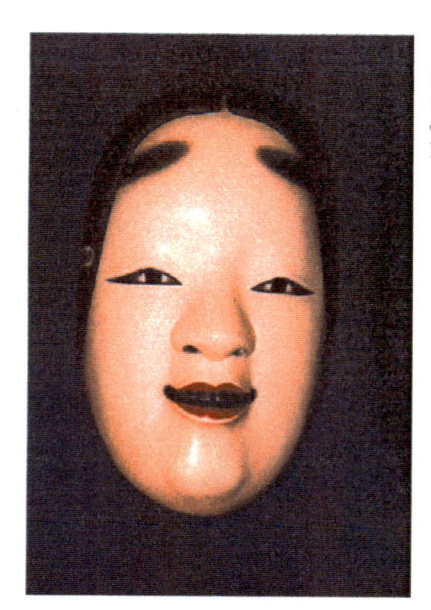

Figure 19:
Ko-omote
carved by
Hiroyuki Yamamoto

Figure 20:
Hannya
carved by
Hiroyuki Yamamoto

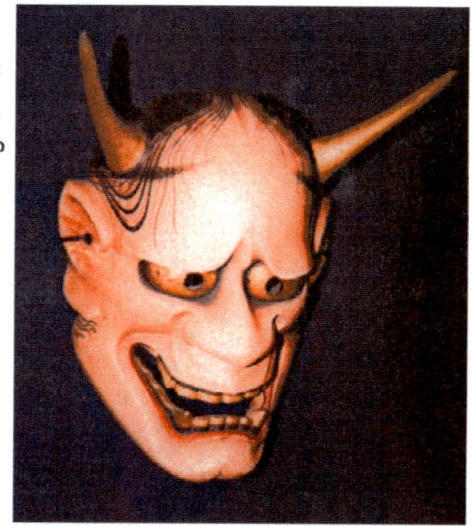

Figure 21:
Contemporary Noh mask of
Shishi-Guchi
carved by Udaka Michishige

Figure 22:
A goblin appears "disguised"
as a Yamabushi priest in
KURAMA ZOH

Figure 23:
The goblin in his "true form"
wearing the O-Beshemi mask.

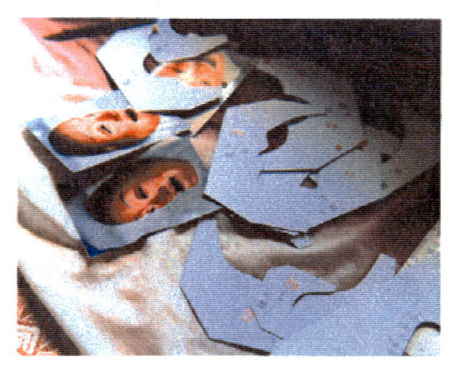

Figure 24: Templates for Noh masks.

Figure 25: Testing a mask with a template.

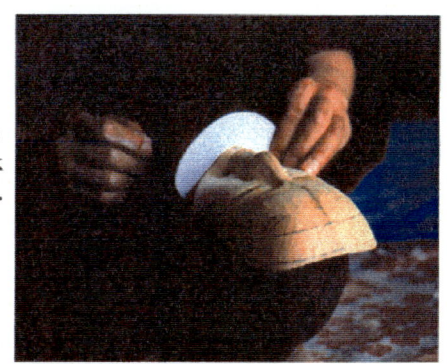

Figure 26:
Some of the tools used for carving Noh masks.

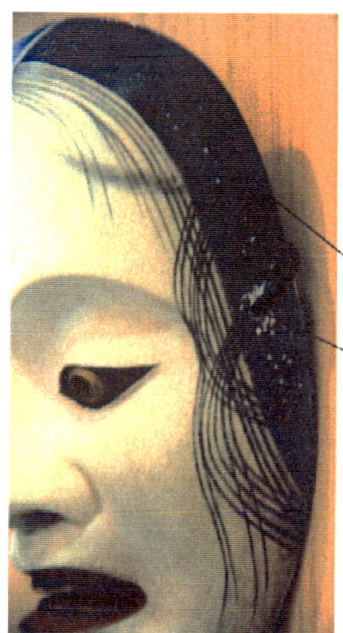

Figure 27 a & b:
New Noh masks deliberately damaged to give the impression of age and use.

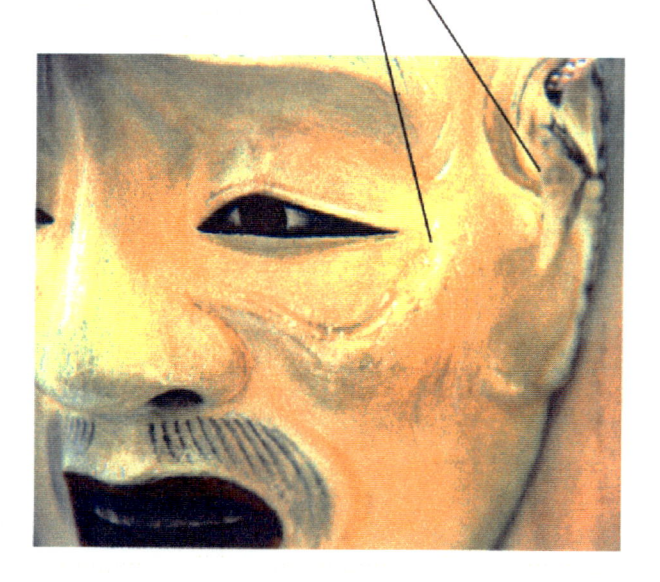

Figure 28: Ida Bagus Alit recites mantras before
a performance of Topeng Pajegan while his assistant,
Gusti, waits to open the box of masks.

Figure 29: Gajah Mada,
created by Ida Bagus Alit.

Figure 30:
I Wayan Balik as Patih Jelantik

Figure 31:
Patih Demming Bues ("Lucu")

Figure 32:
Topeng Tua carved
by Ida Bagus Alit

Figure 33:
Cristina Wistara as Dalem.

Figure 34:
Ida Bagus Alit as Pedanda.

Figure 35:
Balinese high priest

Figure 36:
The Widow-witch in Calonarang. Note the white spots to protect the performer from black magic.

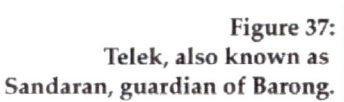

Figure 37:
Telek, also known as Sandaran, guardian of Barong.

Figure 38:
Rehearsal of KIYOTSUNE at Suwa Jin-Ja on Sado Island. Note that both the shite and the tsure wear Ko-omote masks.

Figure 39:
Hôshô school masks of Ko-omote and Chujo displayed for actors in the mirror room.

Figure 40:
Haori Tadao as the ghost of the warrior Kiyotsune.

Figure 41:
Fujima Satomi in
Hagoromo
at the Kanze Noh Theatre,
Tokyo.

Figure 42:
Kongô Hisanori as the
Heavenly Maiden at the
Yamato-Ya Noh Theatre,
Matsuyama

Figure 43:
Attendants dress the
Heavenly Maiden in
her feather robe.

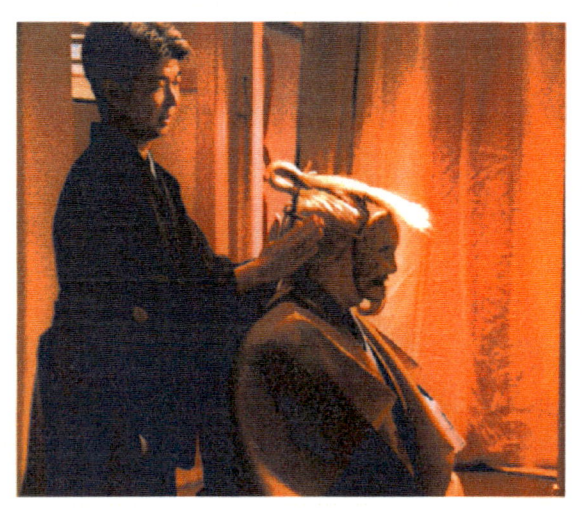

Figure 44:
Udaka Michishige is assisted with fitting the Sanko-jo mask for the first act of TÔRU

Figure 45:
The Old Man remembers Tôru's magnificent house and gardens

Figure 46:
The young nobleman Minamoto no Tôru dances to express his joy in the beauty of nature.

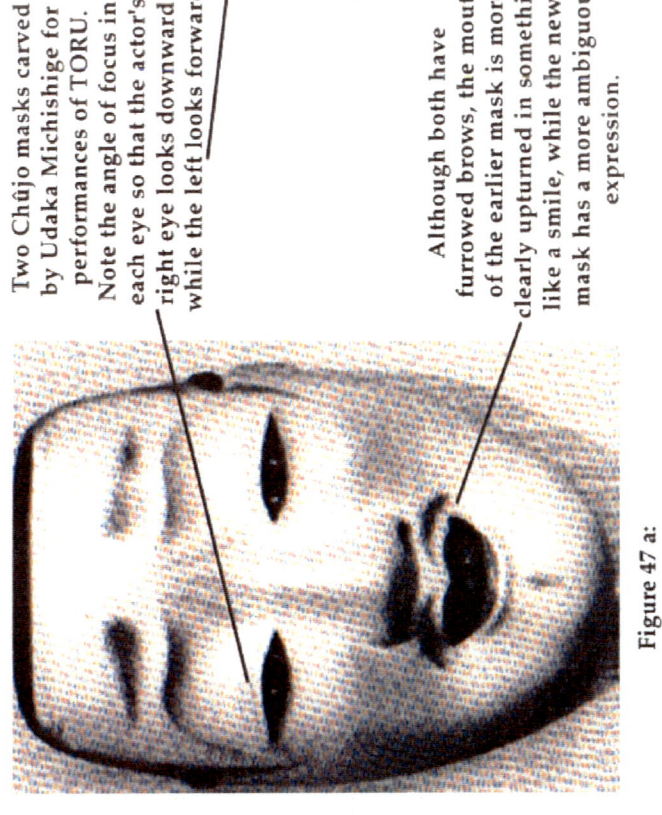

Figure 47 a:
photograph by Rebecca Teele

Figure 47 b:

Two Chūjo masks carved by Udaka Michishige for performances of TORU. Note the angle of focus in each eye so that the actor's right eye looks downward while the left looks forward.

Although both have furrowed brows, the mouth of the earlier mask is more clearly upturned in something like a smile, while the newer mask has a more ambiguous expression.

Chapter 6: Noh Masks in Performance

It is difficult to convey the power of a Noh performance seen live. Filmed and videotaped performances can give a vague impression of what goes on in a Noh play, but cannot capture the sheer intensity of the experience in the theatre. Without question Noh is an acquired taste: its highly ritualised stylistic elements, physical and emotional restraint and the often tediously slow pace of the action can make a rather dull theatrical experience for the uninitiated spectator. Yet the dramas themselves are powerful, the costumes and masks spectacular, the music haunting and evocative, so that occasionally, within this ancient form, a gifted group of artists can create a spectacle that is extraordinary and electrifying.

A number of factors come into play in considering Noh performance including the play, the masks, the rank of the leading actors, the nature of the performance space and the audience. Each Noh performance is unique; a particular group of actors and musicians may come together only once. Thus, there is no 'typical' Noh performance, yet they all have many elements in common. The performances discussed in this chapter were selected because collectively they provide something of an overview of the variety of circumstances of Noh performance and individually they provide an opportunity to examine the ways in which some of the same mask types are used in different plays by different actors. In most instances, these are performances in which I was able to observe backstage preparations and speak with the players about their work. While I have found that each performer's response to the mask is in some way unique, I have also observed, perhaps not surprisingly, that the physical process of using the mask and its effect on the performer are parallel in most cases.

Two programmes will be analysed in detail. The first is similar in some ways to the circumstances of provincial *sarugaku-nô* in that it happens at a temple, is sponsored by the local community and performed by members of the Noh school based in the area. The second is very different: a special performance in a commercial venue given by the *Iemoto* of the Kongô school and his colleague, one of the very few Noh actors who is also a master mask maker. My purpose is to give as full a picture as possible of the process of a Noh performance, focusing particularly upon the activities and responsibilities of the masked performers.

Takigi Noh at the Suwa-Jin-Ja, Sado Island

On June 7, 1997, a *Takigi* (torchlight) Noh performance of *Kiyotsune* was given at the Suwa-Jin-Ja Temple near the main port of Ryotsu on Sado Island. June is known as 'Takigi Noh Month' in the tourist literature for Sado—once a place of exile but now a popular resort—and throughout the month Noh plays are performed on many of the outdoor Noh stages *(nô-butai)* that adjoin temples all over the island. This performance was an event sponsored by the local community through the Ryotsu city cultural department. Unlike performances given in the large indoor Noh theatres in Tokyo, where wealthy aficionados come together to witness a rarefied cultural artefact, this had the feel of a traditional festival that is a vital part of the lives of the people. Although, unlike some Takigi Noh, the performance was not given in conjunction with a religious ritual, the setting and the sense of community participation gave one the impression that this might be something like provincial Noh performances given in earlier times.

The temple and its Noh stage are set among giant cedar trees on a hillside overlooking Lake Kamo-ko and the mountains beyond; it is an atmosphere at once peaceful and majestic and entirely appropriate for the drama which was to be enacted. *Kiyotsune,* by Zeami, is the moving story of a defeated warrior (Kiyotsune) whose unhappy spirit visits his wife in her dreams. He has come to chide her for rejecting the lock of his hair that he had sent to her with a messenger bringing news of his suicide. Surprisingly, she responds with anger telling him that by choosing to drown himself he has deserted her. The chorus laments:

> *In bitter rancor they blame each other,*
> *Their tears, stringed pearls, fall on their arms, pillowed on them,*
> *Side by side they should be lying this night, and yet,*
> *With rancor bound, in solitude they sleep,*
> *Separated from each other, how sad*[1]

Kiyotsune tells his wife the story of his travail and death and his battles in hell. As he completes his final dance, the chorus relates that Kiyotsune's last prayer before dying has won Buddha's mercy and redeemed his soul.

Kiyotsune is an unusual play in several ways. The *waki* is a servant rather than a Buddhist priest and he leaves the stage before the *shite* arrives. As a result, the bulk of the play consists of the meeting between the ghost of Kiyotsune and his wife (the *tsure*) in her dream. Thus the drama, although it serves to reinforce important Buddhist precepts, remains a powerfully human story of love and loss. There is only one act so, unlike many other plays of this type, there is no change in the protagonist from an apparently human disguise to his true form as the warrior's ghost. With no break in the action, the performance increases in intensity until the very last moment. Unlike most Noh programmes, for this event only one play was performed, without even a Kyôgen comic interlude. Another unusual feature of this particular performance (by members of the Hôshô school based on Sado) was that the *tsure* role of Kiyotsune's wife was played by a woman, Ms. Nakagawa. The title role of Kiyotsune was taken by Houri Tadao.

---

[1] Shimazaki, *Battle Noh*, p. 148.

The Rehearsal

When I arrived, some four hours before the performance, the chorus, musicians and actors were already gathered on the stage and busy with a rehearsal. Noh plays are not rehearsed in a manner familiar to Western theatre practitioners; this is partly because actors begin to train in the Noh repertoire from a very early age so that the 'lines' *(utai)* and 'moves' *(kata)* are already well known to them. There is no place for a 'director' in Noh performance tradition since the interpretation of the text and stage movement are in accordance with the tradition of each particular school, handed down through generations of families in the form of the highly secret *katazuke* (choreographic manuals). A leading actor may, of course, practice his part alone, sometimes for several months before a performance, but there is generally only one brief run-through with the entire cast, chorus and musicians even though the members of the company may never have worked together before. Because the leading actor *(shite)* is likely to perform a particular role only once in his or her lifetime, this single rehearsal, just an hour or two before the performance is significant.

For this particular rehearsal, the chorus and musicians were dressed in ordinary street clothes, as was the *shite;* the *tsure* wore a simple kimono. Both the *shite* and the *tsure* wore masks and, interestingly, both wore the female *Ko-omote* mask (see Figure 38). The use of masks for a Noh rehearsal is not required but at the player's discretion. Certainly rehearsing in a mask serves a practical purpose in that it gives the actor the opportunity to adjust to the space and the particular demands of the mask. Vision is severely limited in the mask, and the resulting disorientation can lead to problems with placement; for example, the actor might come dangerously near the edge of the stage or even collide with stage properties, musicians, chorus or other players. However, it seemed unusual that the *shite* in this case should choose to rehearse with a woman's mask for a male role. After the rehearsal, I questioned him about it:

HOURI: I have practised for 3 months for this part. I have my own *Ko-omote* mask and so whatever the play is, I practice with *Ko-omote*. Today the mask is *Chûjo*.

MC: Have you had the chance to work with that [*Chûjo*] mask?

HOURI: No, but *Chûjo* is very similar to *Ko-omote*. The audience sees the different face but for me it is almost the same. Both masks have square holes and the point of the eyes is the same. I've never seen this *Chûjo* mask but *Ko-omote* is very important for Noh archetypes.[2]

Although familiar with the *Chûjo* mask type, the actor had never seen the mask he was to wear for the performance (it was brought later by the leader of the school) and he certainly had no opportunity to rehearse with it. The two masks, *Ko-omote* and *Chûjo*, are somewhat alike in that they are both young and beautiful, but the differences are significant. Mr. Houri was surprised to learn, once he had seen the *Chûjo* mask, that the eyes are not at all similar to those of *Ko-omote*. Whereas *Ko-omote* does indeed have square eyeholes, *Chûjo's* eyeholes are round, creating a rather different field of vision for the performer. The spirit of each of the masks is also distinctive. Of course the most obvious distinction is that the masks represent opposite sexes, though they both share a certain quality of androgynous innocence. On the other hand, although *Chûjo* represents a youth, the mask is nonetheless definitively masculine with a hint of maturity evidenced by a faint moustache and facial hair under the chin. Perhaps more importantly, the expression of the *Chûjo* mask is troubled and anxious whereas *Ko-omote* is calm, even cheerful, with her lips upturned in a shy smile. The *Ko-omote* is regarded by many as the "epitome of the Noh mask—the ultimate symbol of beauty as defined in Noh"[3] The subtlety of these masks is such that very fine distinctions in age and

---

[2] Interview, 7 June, 1997, translated by Shigeki Takahashi.

[3] Pulvers, 1978, p. 206.

character may be discerned, particularly among the various 'woman' masks. Of these, *Ko-omote* is not only unquestionably feminine but also clearly girlish rather than womanly. Mr. Houri finds *Ko-omote* a useful tool in rehearsal because its simplicity and 'intermediate' expression may be put to use in so many varied dramatic contexts. A later interview with the Kita school actor Ryoichi Kano, revealed that he, too, practices with a *Ko-omote* mask:

> It's not a special mask, but it's just a mask that is often worn by the *tsure* because it is already less good, perhaps, than that of the *shite,* or a mask that is not really well made. It is not a mask that is specially made for practice, but it is not as good as the masks used on stage.[4]

So, the 'practice mask' is generally one of slightly inferior quality, which nonetheless serves to accustom the performer to the general requirements of working in a mask. Performer and carver Rebecca Teele suggests that the ubiquity of the *Ko-omote* mask as a practice device may simply have to do with its availability:

> Most actors do not have many masks for their personal use. Often an actor may have only one, probably one which he might have the greatest occasion to use: the *Ko-omote*... It might also be the easiest to procure, being common in the repertory of mask carvers, as it is both a *tsure* and *shite* mask (depending on the particular mask's qualities), and probably not too expensive.[5]

Thus it is not unusual for performers to practice with masks but since it is primarily for practical reasons that they are used, whether the mask represents the appropriate character does not appear to be an important consideration in such cases.

---

[4] Interview, 12 June, 1997.
[5] Personal communication, 2 February, 1999.

The rehearsal was a 'start-and-stop' run-through of the most difficult portions of the play with musicians and chorus. The atmosphere was cheerful and relaxed, yet concentrated. When it finished, the players retired to consume the contents of their bento[6] boxes and, after a short rest, they began the next phase of preparation.

The Costumes

Dressing for a Noh performance has a complex ritual all its own. The large, modern, purpose-built Noh theatres like the Kanze or the National Noh Theatre in Tokyo have enormous backstage areas with several *tatami* lined rooms to accommodate many groups of performers. In addition, every Noh theatre has a *kagami-no-ma* (mirror room) near the curtained stage entrance where the leading actor sits with the mask before a large mirror for meditation prior to his first entrance. The Noh stage attached to a temple, however, is a more modest affair. At the Suwa Jin-Ja, the space available for the company to dress consisted of a single room at the end of the *hashigakari*. This served as dressing room, *kagami-no-ma* and storage space for props and supplies. The musicians and chorus dressed first, since their costuming is much simpler than that of the principal actors, and then the room was made available for the *shite, tsure, waki* and their assistants. The backstage atmosphere was busy and occasionally almost chaotic as six assistants helped the three performers into their elaborate costumes.[7]

Each costume consists of a number of layers, beginning with lightweight white undergarments followed by an *ōkuchi,* (divided skirt-like pantaloons) for men or a *surihaku* (light silk inner kimono) for female roles. In this case the outer garments were fairly simple, but highly ornamented. The *waki* ('witness', the secondary character, in this case Kiyotsune's servant) wore a *kitsuke* (inner kimono) with a cross-hatched pattern

---

[6] Japanese box lunch.

[7] For a description of preparation and performance in a more 'conventional' setting, see Bethe and Brazell, 'The Practice of Noh Theatre', in *By Means of Performance*, Schechner, Richard and Willa Appel (eds) (Cambridge: Cambridge University Press, 1990) pp. 178–184.

in blue, white and brown and over it he wore a short dark blue, unlined robe patterned with white cranes and an *otoko-gasa* (man's low, broad, conical hat). The *tsure* wore a magnificent *karaori* (shorter-sleeved brocade robe) of shimmering orange silk with a delicate pattern of flying cranes. Her long black wig was tied in a simple ponytail with a band around the crown matching the colour of the outer robe. According to tradition the *shite*, Kiyotsune, should be dressed "in the costume representing the military attire of a young Heike nobleman".[8] In this instance this consisted of an *atsuita karaori kitsuke* (a thick, brocade, short-sleeved kimono), predominantly blue, with a vivid gold, red and green pattern resembling armour. Over this he wore a short, unlined robe of gold brocade with one arm outside the sleeve to reveal the more elaborate kimono beneath. The arm of the outer robe was tucked into the belt in the style of a warrior, ready for action.[9] He wore a long black wig with the hair hanging loose over his shoulders, a warrior's hat and a white band around his brow. In the case of the *shite* and *tsure,* the wigs, hairbands and hat serve to disguise the edges of the mask; for the *waki,* who is unmasked, the hat hides his face until he reveals himself to Kiyotsune's wife.

A Noh actor requires the services of at least two trained assistants in order to dress for a performance and these are generally *shite* actors of the same school. Each costume element must be properly placed and securely fixed: this, in practice, often means that an actor must actually be sewn into the costume. It is interesting to note that the deliberate pace and symbolic gestures, which are regarded as characteristic of Noh performance, are dictated not only by the aesthetic principle of *yûgen* but in a fundamental way by these outer accoutrements. The many layers of bulky clothing distort the actor's body, at once diminishing and augmenting the person within. In observing the preparation

---

[8] Shimazaki, *Battle* Noh, p. 135.

[9] See Monica Bethe, 'Nô Costume as Interpretation' in *Nô/Kyôgen Masks and Performance,* p.150.

process it becomes evident that the stately, controlled movements of Noh are made necessary by these heavy and restrictive costumes. Significantly, the quality of stillness that results heightens the effect of the masks. The performer, through this preparation, gradually comes to inhabit a drastically altered physical frame. Within this he is aware that the body inside the costume is as it is accustomed to be, while still cognisant of his responsibility for manipulating a larger physical self in a way that will seem appropriate to the spectator. Craig's term 'Übermarionette' comes to mind, for the Noh mask and costume become very much like a giant puppet manipulated by the actor inside. Thus the actor is the puppeteer in both a physical and metaphorical sense. His body animates the mask and costume, just as his consciousness, *kokoro,* animates the spirit of the character.

To adjust both mentally and physically to the world of the Noh play, an actor needs time, space and intense concentration. In the hectic and noisy atmosphere of a tiny room crowded with busy, nervous people, how can the actor find the necessary calm, meditative state of mind that can help to effect the transformation from ordinary person to legendary warrior spirit or tragic young widow? Rebecca Teele pointed out that, however hectic, the process of dressing for the character forms part of the actor's psychological and spiritual preparation:

> I think once you're backstage in the Noh, there are those various distractions but people also—the ones who are doing the dressing and so on—are creating the outer form of the character. It is the responsibility of the actor to be accepting those outer layers manifesting the physical presence of the character but also the actor himself finding that soul of the character inside.[10]

So there is a simultaneous process of transformation, both inner and outer, each reinforcing the other. In spite of the noise and the rather anxious atmosphere, the

---

[10] Interview, 4 June, 1997.

actors appeared to become calmer and more still as the process of preparation continued. When she was finally sewn into her costume, Ms. Nakagawa sat quietly on a stool, eyes shut, her evident concentration a still centre in the whirlpool of activity backstage.

The Masks

Once costumed, the leading performers are presented with the masks they are to wear and have some time to study them before putting them on and entering the stage (Figure 39). After a few moments, the actor (the *tsure* first, in this case, because she must be in place before the play begins) salutes the mask and carefully places it over her face, adjusting it so that she can see through the eyeholes. With the Noh mask the actor quite literally sees through the eyes of the character, because the eyeholes are carved into the iris of the mask's eye. The performer is helped to tie the braided silk cords that hold the mask in place, and these must be completely secure, for if the mask should slip during the performance the actor might not be able to see at all. The actor then spends some time before the mirror, apparently looking at the reflection of the character. Yet, what seems apparent to the observer is not quite what is seen by the actor. The masked actor cannot actually see the mask that he is wearing without raising his head to an unnatural position because the eyeholes are cut in such a way that the actor's field of vision is downward, towards the floor. The practical necessity for this is obvious, since it is of primary importance for the performer to be aware of where his feet are going and of any possible obstructions. Therefore, what the actor sees as he gazes into the mirror is not the whole figure and certainly not the face of the character.

> Usually the actor is seated about a meter from the mirror when he is given the mask and it is put on for him. . . . Seated in this way before the mirror the actor should be able to see himself reflected from the nose down as far as he can, depending on the distance from the mirror. If the actor sees above his nose, he is looking up

too much, his head is tilted too far back. The actor must always be aware of the angle of his head and keep the same posture when he is standing and moving on stage as when he is sitting.[11]

The actor will, of course, need to raise his head to check the placement of the mask on his face, but it is not possible to see the whole figure while wearing the mask. How, then, does the actor get a complete impression of the character's outer form, its face and body? First, of course, there will have been a long study of the role, the text, and the movements, probably since childhood, working with a teacher and observing performances by others. The costuming process, during which the actor is clothed in the character's garments, re-defining his own body, helps the performer to adjust to the new sensation of the character's physical form. Finally, in the time given to studying the mask before it is put on, the actor has the opportunity to contemplate the face of the character, imagining it as his own. Once the actor has donned the mask, he must seek to become one with the character through a more internal process. As Nakamura Yasuo puts it:

> The actor's attitude toward the mask is aptly expressed in the admonition, "The mask is not put on the face, but the face should be thought of as being pulled into and clinging to the mask."[12]

Like the legend of the *Fudô* mask that 'sticks to the flesh', the mask becomes part of the actor or, perhaps more appropriately, the body of the actor becomes fused with the mask. From inside the mask, the actor must deepen his concentration so that he is able to visualise the whole figure of himself as the character. Here it is important to note that the limited vision afforded by the mask's eyeholes actually assists this process:

> The narrow slits for the eyes . . . hold the inner concentration by literally impeding the actor's view of the external world. Cut off

---

[11] Kongô Iwao, 'Recollections and Thoughts on Nô', *op. cit.* p. 78.
[12] Nakamura, 1971, p. 214.

from his immediate surroundings, the actor can have a more intense vision of the imaginative role he is called upon to live and act.[13]

Performers unaccustomed to the discipline imposed by the Noh mask find this one of its most striking characteristics. I have frequently observed how participants in Noh and other mask workshops are immediately struck by this feature of the mask.[14] The University of Hawaii engaged in a substantial, year-long project on Noh theatre employing Noh masters from Japan to train university students to perform Zeami's masterpiece *Matsukaze*.[15] The students trained for months using traditional methods, and for the performance they used authentic Noh masks. One student who participated in the project and played the title role commented:

In all the Western theatre I've done, I've never felt the character as strongly as when I wore the mask. The mask cut off what was outside, so I could internalize everything.[16]

The mask turns the actor's focus inward, not upon himself, but upon the character he is to play. Yet if the actor is not gazing at the character's reflection in the mirror but sees only part of the body, what then is the purpose of sitting before

---

[13] Akhtar Quamba *Yeats and the Noh* (New York: Weatherhill, 1974) pp. 52–53.

[14] In 1996, I designed and made Western-style (open-eyed) masks for a performance of Yeats' Noh play *At the Hawk's Well*, performed by undergraduates studying Noh Drama at Royal Holloway, University of London. Noh master Umewaka Naohiko then took these students through a workshop using traditional Noh masks for the same roles. They were astounded by the difference in perception and concentration afforded by the Noh masks. I subsequently conducted workshops using Copeau-style masks alongside Noh and Balinese masks with students at the Krishnamurti school and with professional actors at Interchange Studios in 1998. In these instances also the masks had the same effect.

[15] The title means 'pining wind' and the play tells of two sisters who were loved and abandoned by the poet Ariwara no Yukihira. Two young-woman masks are used: *Waka-onna* and *Ko-omote*.

[16] Robert Ito, student from University of Hawaii, Manoa in a 1989 interview quoted by J. R. Brandon in 'The Place of Noh in World Theatre', *International Symposium on the Conservation and Restoration of Cultural Property: Nô–Its Transmission and Regeneration* 1991 (Tokyo: Tokyo National Research Institute of Cultural Properties c. 1994) pp. 12–13.

the mirror? Practically speaking, as Kongô Iwao indicated above, the actor is able to check his reflection for correct posture and alignment in spite of his limited vision. In a spiritual, or a metaphorical sense this circumscribed reflection, which fails to reveal that definer of identity—the face—allows the actor to free himself from the limitations of personal identity and selfhood. This leaves his mind clear for the performance he is about to give.

> The appearance of the *shite* has been described as similar to a famous painting by the Chinese artist Liang K'ai depicting the descent of Sakyamuni (the Buddha) from the mountain immediately after his enlightenment. The comparison is appropriate because the proper state of mind for a *shite* is the total emptying of all thoughts and feelings from the mind and complete concentration like the state required for Buddhist enlightenment.[17]

Thus, putting on the mask is the final act of self-obliteration in order to take on the role; it is the moment in which the actor is able to leave his own persona behind, and become available as a vessel for the character.

The Performance

The audience, made up of local people of all ages as well as a few holiday-makers from the mainland, have gathered on tarpaulins spread on the ground on two sides of the Noh stage. Some enterprising individuals have brought low folding chairs or pillows to sit on as well as flasks of hot drinks and bags of snacks. A festival atmosphere prevails. Then, all grows quiet as two local women, dressed in the style of *miko* (temple priestesses) come from the temple to light the large braziers standing on the ground before the two front corners of the stage. Since the performance is taking place at night (and it is already dark) the stage is also illuminated with electric lights, though not the powerful stage lights familiar in Western theatres. Behind the curtain the musicians are heard quietly playing the

---

[17] Nakamura, 1971, p. 214.

oshirabe, "a brief formalized warm-up".[18] This 'overture' not only gives the musicians the opportunity to check the tuning of their instruments,[19] but also sets the mood for both performers and audience. The curtain is raised and the musicians walk silently, formally, along the *hashigakari* to take their places at the back of the stage. The chorus (numbering eight) come through the low door at stage left and take their places, kneeling along the side of the stage in two rows. The curtain is raised again and the *tsure* moves along the *hashigakari* with the distinctive sliding steps *(suri ashi)* that are "the essence of Noh movement".[20] She moves slowly across the stage to the *waki* position where she kneels, facing the central stage area. The flute and drums play the *shidai,*[21] a musical introduction, while the *waki* enters and stands near the *shite* pillar. He turns towards the pine painted on the back wall and sings the first three lines of the text after which the chorus repeats the last two lines in a quiet chant.

> *O'er the eight-fold briny way, with sea waves,*
> *O'er the eight-fold briny way, with sea waves*
> *To the nine-fold Capital I now return.*[22]

The *waki* then turns to face the audience and speaks the lines he has just sung. He announces that he is Awazu no Saburô, servant to the warrior Kiyotsune who was defeated in battle and, in despair, threw himself from the ship near Willow Bay. The servant says that he has found a lock of his master's hair that his master left behind and he is now making his way back to the capital. The next section,

---

[18] Bethe and Brazell, 'The Practice of Noh Theatre', p. 182.

[19] The drums are made of traditional materials with 'coltskin' on the shoulder drum and 'ox or horsehide' on the knee drum. These drumheads need to be warmed and moistened to bring them up to pitch before the performance and require tuning during the performance as well. See Keene, 1966, p. 78.

[20] Richard Emmert, 'Expanding *Nô's* Horizons: Considerations for a New *Nô* Perspective' in *Nô and Kyôgen in the Contemporary World,* edited by James R. Brandon (Honolulu: University of Hawaii Press, 1997) p. 26.

[21] The name refers both to the three-line introductory song and the instrumental music, which precedes it. See Shimazaki, *Battle Noh,* p. 220.

[22] *Ibid.,* p. 136.

michiyuki, is a travelling song. The actor moves a few steps, singing of his journey and, when he stops, he announces that he has arrived at his master's house in Kyoto. At his call, the *tsure* responds telling him to enter; she moves to sit at centre stage and asks why he has come. In the course of their conversation, Awazu reveals that Kiyotsune is dead, but not in battle:

> *Late on a moonlit night, from the ship he threw himself and was lost*[23]

The *tsure* replies in a kind of recitative form called *kakaru*. She is in anguish; had he died in battle or as a result of illness she could be reconciled to his fate, but his suicide seems to her a repudiation of their marriage vows. The chorus chants of the transience of earthly life and the misery of loss. The *waki* presents the keepsake and, as she takes it, the *tsure* sings lines from the classical epic that inspired the play:

> *When I look at it, my heart aches in deep sorrow, so this lock of hair*
> *Sadly I give back to Usa, the holy place whence it came.*[24]

The *waki* takes the lock of hair and exits; the *tsure* moves back to her previous position. The chorus sings of how she has gone to bed, weeping, but cannot sleep. Then, summoned by the cries of the drummers *(kakagoe)*, the *shite* appears and makes his way along the *hashigakari* to the stage. He stops beside the *shite* pillar and begins to sing (Figure 40):

> *For the sage, there is no dream . . .*
> *On such a thing as a dream*
> *I have come to hang my hope"*
> *How now, dear one,*
> *Kiyotsune has come to you.*[25]

---

[23] *Ibid.*, p. 140.

[24] *Ibid.*, p. 142. Usa is the name of the shrine which Kiyotsune's party visited with offerings, only to receive a message from the god that defeat was inevitable. This dark oracle prompted Kiyotsune's suicide. The epic is the *Heike Monogatari*, which tells of the rise and fall of the Tiara family.

Upon hearing his voice, the *tsure* looks up, and the effect of this gesture is extraordinary. The face of the mask, which was downcast and clouded with misery, is suddenly suffused with joy and light and utterly transformed. How can this be? It is, after all, only made of wood, yet with this small movement the features seem to have changed completely. The effect is created by a simple technique that is one of the most fundamental *kata* of mask use in Noh. When the mask looks down, the position is called *kumorasu*, 'clouded'; the face is shadowed, the eyes appear half-closed and the expression on the mouth is slightly obscured. When it is tilted upward slightly, position is called *terasu*, 'shining', small indentations carved in the surface of the mask catch the light, the eyes appear to open and look up, the smiling mouth is revealed. This tiny shift in position has a powerful effect from the audience point of view, and is executed with minimal but concentrated effort on the part of the performer. Zeami instructs that for all movement on the Noh stage, "what is felt in the heart is ten, what appears in movement, seven".[26] In other words, the performer must produce maximum internal energy and concentration throughout the performance, but should reveal only a portion of that energy in his actions. This gives each gesture, however subtle, a powerful resonance. The slight movement of the *tsure's* mask is remarkably potent, revealing an intensity behind the gesture that is greater than the gesture itself. My copy of the translated text includes few indications of stage movement so I do not know whether the mask's movement is part of the choreography or if it might be a conscious interpretative choice on the part of the performer.[27] When I asked Ms. Nakagawa about this moment after the performance, her reply was surprisingly subjective:

---

[25] *Ibid.*, p. 144.

[26] Rimer and Yamazaki, p. 75.

[27] Although printed scripts and translations sometimes make note of movements required at certain moments in the text (stage position, standing, sitting, turning to face a character or the audience) details of dance choreography and *kata* are recorded only in the *katazuke,* the secret choreographic manuals held by each Noh school. Examples of the kind of material recorded therein may be seen in Naohiko Umewaka's, unpublished PhD dissertation: *The Inner World of*

MC: There was a moment when Kiyotsune first appeared and you see him in your dream. I felt, at that moment, that the mask seemed to smile and I wondered what was going on in your mind at that point?

TSURE: The Noh mask looks sometimes sad, sometimes happy. You thought that the mask of his wife looks like it's smiling. I'm very happy if you saw that. My feelings are just as if I was Kiyotsune's wife. It was wonder. I just couldn't believe that he'd died. I was just in wonder.[28]

Her response indicates a powerful identification with the character but, when questioned closely about the *kata,* she had no particular memory of the action she performed. It was not a 'conscious decision', but neither was it accidental. Since the movement from *kumorasu* to *terasu* is specific, a known choreographic device, the performer's response indicates that, in this case, the technique had been completely assimilated resulting in what in Stanislavskian terms might be referred to as an 'organic' performance.

The wife's initial joy at seeing the figure of her husband turns to hurt and anger at his suicide. He, in turn, reproaches her for rejecting his keepsake. The chorus comments as above, then Kiyotsune tells his story: how they were defeated in battle and fled by sea; how they consulted the oracle at the temple only to learn that there was no hope. At this Kiyotsune cries:

Alas!
Buddhas and gods, beings divine,
Forsake us completely[29]

---

the Noh: The Influence of Esoteric Concepts on the Classical Theatre of Japan, as Evidenced Through an Analysis of the Choreographic Manuals of the Umewaka Family, Royal Holloway College, 1994.

[28] Interview, 7 June, 1997.

[29] Shimazaki, *Battle Noh,* p. 152.

As the chorus continues the narrative, he performs the *kata* of weeping, slowly bringing his hand up towards the mask as his head is inclined downwards. Then he rises and performs a rather stately dance while the chorus continues the story. They tell of the Imperial party's continued flight, of Kiyotsune's despair and how, at last, standing in the ship's prow, he played his flute, sang a song, recited a poem and then, calling on *Amida,* the merciful Buddha, he leaped to his death. The movements of the dance are not a pantomime of the events related in the text, but they subtly convey Kiyotsune's confusion and despair. Throughout the dance the mask moves very little, and when it does so it is a movement of the head (or of the head in conjunction with the torso) that is clearly part of the overall choreography. As in Balinese dance-drama, the movements of the mask are not separate from the movement of the body but, rather, are an integral part of the puppet-like whole. Thus it is possible and necessary to view the entire figure as a mask, for indeed costume and mask function as one and are perceived so by the performer.

The *shite* dances to the end of the *kuse* (the song the chorus sings of his despair and death), then stops and crouches beside the *shite* pillar for an exchange with the *tsure* in which she bemoans their suffering and he replies: "An infernal place is life". The conversation reflects Buddhist pessimism about the trials of earthly life and reveals Kiyotsune's unenlightened attachment to the wife and the world he has left behind. Even in death his suffering is not over:

> *To Shura-do-o I've fallen, where, here and there*
> *Stand trees, so many enemies, the rain the arrow heads,*
> *The earth planted with sharp swords, mountains are iron forts,*[30]

As the chorus sings of the terrors of *Shura-dô,* the warriors' hell, the *shite* performs the *shura-nori,* a dance depicting his fight with the demons and apparitions that torment him. In this powerful and fast-paced choreography the

---

[30] Shimazaki, *Battle Noh,* p. 158.

mask is used actively to show Kiyotsune's fear and fierceness with quick side-to-side movements called *kiru,* (literally 'cutting', it is a movement frequently used in demon plays of the fifth group). The movement is precise: the head snaps to one side, pauses briefly, and then to the other as he draws his sword against the shadowy enemies that beset him. The sense of intensity of both physical strength and emotion is powerful and made more so by the clarity and control in the movement. The dance is accompanied, at a steadily accelerating pace, by the drums, flute and, most importantly, the cries of the drummers, which become more frenzied as the action of the dance intensifies. Then, quite suddenly, the atmosphere becomes calm as the chorus sings:

> *In truth, at the last moment of his life,*
> *Ten Prayers having duly offered, now on board the Law's boat,*
> *His prayer fulfilled, beyond any doubt,*
> *True to his name, pure-hearted Kiyotsune, . . .*
> *The Holy Fruit obtained; oh, what bliss!*[31]

With that, there is a single high-pitched cry on the flute, a last, sharp beat on the drums, and the play is ended. The *shite* folds his fan, turns, and slowly, silently moves up the *hashigakari;* the curtain lifts before him as he goes offstage. The others follow, the *tsure* first, then the musicians, and finally the chorus, who exit through the *kiri-do.*

After the performance, activity backstage is brisk and matter-of-fact. Musicians, chorus and actors change out of their elaborate costumes as quickly as possible and the atmosphere is not much different from any theatrical dressing room after a show. Assistants are on hand to help the leading actors to unfasten and fold each element of costume. The masks are carefully placed into silk pouches and then into wooden boxes to be returned to the school's collection. Although the night air is quite cool, the *shite* and *tsure* are sweating profusely as

---

[31] *Ibid.,* p.160.

they shed their bulky costumes. Tired but exhilarated, they are unable to remember specific moments of the performance, but are aware that it pleased the audience.

Secular Entertainment or Sacred Art?

Takigi Noh performances such as this prompt questions about the essential nature of Noh performance and whether it is entirely secular or fundamentally a sacred genre. Such distinctions, predicated as they are upon Western assumptions of a strict division between sacred and secular, are probably out of place, but must nonetheless be addressed if we are to consider the mask's association with shamanism and mediumship. The performance takes place in the temple precincts partly because of historical associations and partly because this particular temple stage provides a magnificent setting, especially for this play. Are these sacred or secular considerations? Given that an appreciation of the beauties of nature is central to the spiritual ethos of Japanese life and is the most distinctively Japanese aspect of religious thought here, such considerations go beyond merely superficial concerns about attractive surroundings and go to the heart of a definitively Japanese spiritual experience. The *waki* sings the *shidai*, offering the performance to the unseen *kami* seated in the painted representation of a pine at the back of the stage. Is this a matter of performance tradition or a sincere gesture to the abiding spirit of the place? 'Temple priestesses' appear to light the braziers, but they do not enter into mediumistic trance. Instead, the *shite*, conjured by the cries of the drummers, appears in a mask as the ghost of Kiyotsune to tell his story. In other words, the heroic ancestor appears from the realm of the dead to teach moral lessons to the living by the example of his life and death and, at the end, the chorus sings a hymn to the merciful Buddha. Has this been a shamanistic ceremony or merely an evening's entertainment? For the audience, it is clearly an entertainment, an enactment of an episode taken from a famous epic of old Japan. Yet, like Balinese dance-drama, the entertainment serves as a socially binding affirmation of culture and values in which the setting, the theme of the play and the ritualised nature of the performance work together to address the audience in a profoundly spiritual way. For the performers it is primarily a fulfilment of professional responsibility, utilising the skills they have developed since childhood. They see themselves not as priestly mediators between gods and human beings, but as highly trained craftspersons practising their art. Contemporary Noh (with the exception of the sacred *Okina* ritual discussed later) is avowedly secular and does not associate itself with shamanism or possession, in spite of its historical legacy. Yet there are still resonances with an older tradition and a certain reverence for the spiritual aspects of the genre among both performers and audiences. The themes of the plays, the deliberate, highly ritualised movement and the rhythmic vocal and musical accompaniment impart an atmosphere of liminality to the proceedings so that the performance seems to inhabit a higher plane.

Hagoromo and Tôru in Matsuyama

Matsuyama, on the island of Shikoku, is reached by ferry across the Inland Sea from Hiroshima. The island has close associations with the Shingon sect of esoteric Buddhism and pilgrims still make the circuit of eighty-eight temples on the island that were selected by the sect's founder, Kûkai. To the east of the town is a well-known hot-spring, Dôgo Onsen, and here a fully equipped Noh theatre was built as part of the Yamato-ya, one of the many luxurious hotels which serves the area. On November 8, 1998, a special Noh performance was given at this theatre by members of the Kongô School from Kyoto.

The two plays selected for this performance were *Hagoromo* (*The Feather Mantle*), which is among the most famous of Noh plays, and *Tôru*, a celebratory play sometimes designated as a fifth-group play and sometimes as a play of the first or fourth group.[32] The two plays are thematically linked by their use of moon

---

[32] Yasuda, Kenneth. *Masterworks of the Nô Theatre* (Bloomington and Indianapolis: Indiana University Press, 1989), pp. 460 and 463. There is also some confusion regarding the classification of *Hagoromo,* which began as a fourth-group (miscellaneous) play but is now

images and references to the dance of Heavenly Maidens around the Palace of the Moon.

The *shite* in *Hagoromo* was the new *Iemoto* of the Kongô school, Kongô Hisanori, and the title role in *Tôru* was taken by the actor and mask maker Udaka Michishige, a native of Matsuyama. Among the audience were members of the local university Noh club for whom Udaka occasionally gives master classes. (Today many Noh scholars and sometimes even performers are drawn from the ranks of university Noh clubs.) The rest of the audience consisted mostly of Noh aficionados who followed the performance with their *utai-bon* (copies of Noh plays with rhythmic indications, used by those who study Noh chant). It is a rare privilege to see a Noh programme given by performers of such stature and even more so in a provincial city like Matsuyama.

Preparation

If the Takigi Noh performance on Sado Island was a bit like provincial *sarugaku-nô*, then the atmosphere at this performance bore some similarity to court performances given for the Edo aristocracy. The audience was knowledgeable, cushioned seats were provided for all and diners in the expensive restaurant adjoining the theatre could also watch the play. Despite being on the fourth floor of the hotel, the roofed stage is in an open courtyard, so that natural daylight reflects up from the white stones surrounding it. A large tatami-lined room adjoining the *kagami-no-ma* and the stage was made available to the performers and there a large low table was placed, laden with trays of food and materials for making tea.

The special feather mantle and lotus crown used in this performance of *Hagoromo* are items reserved exclusively for the use of the Iemoto of the Kongô School. The mask that he has chosen is a *Zo-onna* mask made in the seventeenth

---

classified as a third-group 'wig' play by all but the Hôshô school, who place it in the fifth group. *Ibid.,* p. 134.

century. At that time, the early Edo period, symmetry had become fashionable as an aesthetic ideal (replacing the earlier, medieval preference for asymmetry in art) and this mask represents an example of the style. It is therefore considered to be particularly well-suited for use in roles of goddesses and heavenly beings since a symmetrical, unambiguous expression is more appropriate for characters who have already attained enlightenment and exist on a higher plane. Before preparations began I was allowed to examine the mask, which showed only a few signs of its age. That it has been repaired at least once was clear when the mask was viewed from the back: a triangular piece at the top had been broken off and glued back into place, though there is no evidence of this on the mask's face where the paint remains unmarked. At the bottom of the mask, under the chin, three hundred years of handling have worn away the paint to the bare wood and there are a few small scratches on the mask's cheeks. Inside the mask, pads were glued to the forehead and cheeks to hold the mask approximately one-half inch away from the actor's face. In the early days of Noh, actors were not allowed padding to cushion their faces from the often uncomfortable and certainly unyielding wooden masks, but now they are widely used. Each *shite* will have his own collection of pads for various masks since every face and mask is different. The pads are glued to the inside of whatever mask is being used with a mixture of rice flour and water or some other natural paste, and are removed after the performance. These not only cushion the mask but also allow the actor's mouth and jaw to move freely, allowing for greater clarity in articulation and vocal expression. At the corners of the mouth and beneath the nose on the inside of the mask, small pieces of muslin are attached to absorb perspiration and saliva.

Three leading actors assist in dressing the *Iemoto* for the role of the Heavenly Maiden, while others stand and watch, ready to assist if necessary. After being securely bound into the kimono, the *Iemoto* sits in front of a large mirror while the wig is fitted, dressed and secured with a white band that fits snugly over the eyebrows. Now fully dressed, he remains seated at the mirror, attempting to gather concentration, but he is frequently interrupted by visiting dignitaries (the local mayor, for example) and admirers who come to pay their respects and bring gifts. Presently, he moves to the *kagami-no-ma* where his dressers attire him in the mask and the lotus blossom crown. The ornaments hanging down from the crown disguise the edges of the mask and contribute to the otherworldly quality of the Heavenly Maiden. The *Iemoto* coughs and blows through the mouth of the mask to check for obstructions, then lifts his head so that he can check the placement of mask and headdress in the mirror. The musicians are seated behind him and begin to play the *oshirabe* while he prepares. When the musicians have finished and begin to move along the *hashigakari* towards the stage, the backstage atmosphere becomes charged with excitement and anticipation. The most senior attendant (in this case today's other *shite*, Udaka Michishige) stretches the *shite's* arms and adjusts the sleeves of the kimono, the *shite* rises and the stool on which he was seated is taken away. After final adjustments, the *shite* stands before the curtain; he makes a half-turn to the left and then to the right (a ritual gesture to the *kami*), then gives a low murmur, and the curtain is raised.

Hagoromo

This play, generally attributed to Zeami, is among the most popular and highly regarded in the Noh canon. The story is a simple and moving version of one of the 'bird woman'[33] myths that are found in many cultures. A fisherman discovers a feather mantle hanging on a pine branch beside the seashore and decides to take it home with him. Suddenly, a beautiful heavenly maiden, who has been bathing nearby, appears. She claims that the robe is hers and asks him to return it. At first he refuses, but seeing her distress he relents, on the condition that she will dance for him the 'dance of the angels'.[34] She happily agrees to perform a dance "which

---

[33] For a detailed discussion of *Hagoromo* in relation to other 'bird woman' myths see Poh Sim Plowright, *Mediums, Puppets and the Human Actor in the Theatres of the East*, Mellen Studies in Puppetry, Vol. 4 (Lampeter: Edwin Mellen Press, Ltd., 2002).

[34] *Hagoromo, ibid.,* p. 179.

we dance about the Palace of the Moon above"[35] but in order to do so she says that must have her feather robe. The fisherman is suspicious that she will take the robe and fly away without fulfilling her promise, but she reassures him: "Doubt exists only among you mortals. In heaven there can never be deceitfulness".[36] Shamefaced, he returns the robe, she puts it on and dances joyfully for him and then flies away, disappearing into the mist.

This *Hagoromo* is a *kogaki*, or variant performance version, in which the *shite* makes the costume change (putting on the feather robe) seated on a stool centre stage *(shogi-no-monogi)*, rather than in the usual place at the back of the stage *(koken-za)*. It is also a shorter version that leaves out the first, slow dance *(jo-no-mai)* and moves immediately to the quicker *ha-no-mai*.

It is interesting to compare this to an amateur performance of the play that I observed at the Kanze Noh Theatre in Tokyo only a few days before.[37] The *kogaki* version in Matsuyama was shorter and the staging used by the Kanze and Kongô schools differed in a number of ways. However, the most interesting contrast was the effect of the mask (Zo-onna in both cases)—particularly since the *shite* in the amateur performance was a petite and slender woman, while in the Kongô performance the Heavenly Maiden was played by a stocky, middle-aged man. The contrast between Figures 41 and 42 is striking. The mask fits the face of the female *shite* nearly perfectly and the illusion of an otherworldly being is beautifully realised. The male *shite* looks bulky by comparison and his jaw is clearly visible behind and below the mask. It has been argued that such jarring

---

[35] *Ibid.*, pp. 179–180.

[36] *Ibid.*, p. 180.

[37] After many years of study, and if they are wealthy enough, amateur students of Noh may perform a *shite* role. Usually several will club together to give a full programme of 3 or more Noh plays along with several dance excerpts. The chorus and musicians (and Kyôgen players, if there are any) are professionals hired for the performance and the students rent costumes and properties from the school. The performances are generally open to the public. The cost of such an enterprise is likely to be in excess of £5000 for each *shite* in a full-length play and rather less (but still a substantial amount) for those who perform only a dance excerpt.

incongruity, especially evident when a delicate feminine mask is worn by a stocky, male performer, is an essential element of Noh. It is felt that the apparent contradiction, like the Zen *koan,* serves as a spiritual challenge forcing the spectator to see beyond superficial attempts at illusion to a deeper truth, a higher reality. As appealing as this view might be from the philosophical point of view, the disparity of fit between face and mask is more likely to have been the result of historical accident. Zeami's few notes about masks mostly concern practical matters, especially the proper fit of the mask, and he discusses in detail the relative advantages of trimming the tops of certain masks to accommodate particular headgear.[38] His concern seems to be with the perfection of the image of the character as perceived from the audience point of view. Evidence of surviving masks indicates that Noh masks were generally larger in Zeami's time and it is accepted that the average size of individuals in medieval Japan was rather smaller than today. The imperfect illusion, the mismatch between mask and wearer apparent in this instance, is an anomaly Noh learned to live with as it became increasingly subject to regulation by its elite patrons. Interestingly, what emerges from observing these two performances is not the disparity in the illusion, but an appreciation for the skill of the performer whose mastery of *monomane* overcomes his apparent physical inappropriateness for the role. In spite of the incongruity of masculine jowls behind the face of the Heavenly Maiden, Kongô Hisanori is able to create a performance of extraordinary feminine grace and lightness that is especially impressive in such a large man. His success in this indicates an affective dissociation from his own physical identity and a strong identification with the mask. Each simple movement— raising a hand to indicate weeping, for example, is executed with a seemingly innate delicacy and that quality is realised by the entire body, informing each step, each turn, each movement of the head. The mask is fundamental to this capacity for transformation, as Kanze Hisao observed:

---

[38] Rimer and Yamazaki, pp. 230–231.

> He [the actor] must somehow subjugate his natural physicality and do away with all consciousness of showing his body and abilities. . . . The Nô actor depends upon the mask to lead him into the realm of mindlessness, while also struggling with it and throwing his energy against it, in the work of giving birth to true Nô acting. The mask is an equal partner with the actor in accomplishing this purpose.[39]

The mask is the spur to the actor's process of transformation and the apparent disparity between mask and wearer serves to heighten the spectator's appreciation of the performer's art.

An additional incongruity between mask and wearer, which a comparison of these two performances highlights, is the tone and timbre of the voice. Techniques of vocal production do not vary for male and female Noh performers, thus even women produce a deep, resonant tone in *utai,* though the range of pitch for women is usually more limited and not so low. However, the very deep, powerful voice of the *Iemoto's* Heavenly Maiden presents a substantial contrast with the delicacy of the mask.[40] Here again, however, the physical realisation of the character along with the beauty of tone and carefully nuanced expression in the singing help to persuade even a sceptical Western observer that this figure is, indeed, a beautiful and feminine heavenly being. For the performer, these incongruities are not an issue; he or she will have studied the *kata* and the mask and, in performance, will chiefly be concerned with the successful execution of the choreography in a manner that is consistent with the characteristics of the Zo-onna mask. Specialised physical discipline and training since early childhood

---

[39] 'Life with a Nô Mask', p. 71.

[40] No effort is made to alter the pitch of the voice for female characters as, for example, in Kabuki where the *onnagata* (male actors who impersonate women) produce a refined falsetto. This convention is so ingrained that in Noh it is the sound of a woman's voice that is regarded as unnatural.

make it possible for the professional Noh performer to create the qualities of *yûgen* required for the role without particular conscious effort.

Returning to the story: the *waki*, a fisherman called Hakuryô, and his two friends *(waki-tsure)* have already entered and found the robe hanging on a pine[41] when the Heavenly Maiden speaks her first lines from the curtained entrance to the *hashigakari*: *"That robe is mine! Why are you taking it?"*[42] The *shite* appears wearing a brilliantly patterned orange kimono hanging from the waist with a white kimono above, indicating symbolically that the Heavenly Maiden is only partially clothed, having come directly from bathing in the sea. Her tone of command changes to one of despair when the fisherman refuses to return the robe: *"Alas! Without my robe I cannot soar along the pathways of the sky nor climb the air to reach my heavenly home. Oh, I pray you, give it back to me."*[43] Eventually the fisherman, seeing her distress, relents and returns the robe to her, having extracted her promise to dance. He moves to the *waki* position and sits. The stage attendants bring a lacquer stool for the *shite* who sits as the attendants dress the Maiden in her feather robe. (Figure 43) The *shite* cannot make the costume change himself since he must maintain the integrity of the character's image for the audience. The limited vision of the mask and the physical restrictions required to keep mask and costume (the 'body-mask') in consistent relation to one another mean that alterations in posture and movements of the head that would be necessary to effect the change would shatter the illusion of the stage figure. So, the *shite* remains still, a static image of the Heavenly Maiden, while the feather robe is arranged on her shoulders. The process takes some time, during which there is no music or chanting, but at no point does the *shite* 'break character'; an atmosphere of concentration and anticipation is maintained.

---

[41] The pine is a chest-high prop held in a bamboo frame placed downstage centre. In the Kanze version, the robe is hung on the first pine in front of the *hashigakari*.

[42] *Hagoromo*, translation from the Nippon Gakujitsu Shinkokai Collection.

[43] *Ibid.*, p. 24.

This special feather robe is breathtaking; it is woven from threads of shimmering gold and patterned with a white peacock whose wings cover the sleeves of the garment. As soon as the costume is secure, the *shite* rises, the stool is taken away and the music begins for her dance. As he rises, the *shite* tilts the mask upwards slightly to the *terasu* position, registering the Maiden's joy in being garbed in her magical robe once more. As the chorus describes the celestial dance around the Palace of the moon, the Heavenly Maiden begins to dance, occasionally stopping to interject a few lines of sung verse. This is merely the *kuse*, and not the dance proper, but when she sings to praise the Prince of the Moon, there is a change in pace:

Thee I do adore,
O Prince of the Moon, Thine be glory and praise,
O Bodhisattva Seishi![44]

In contrast to the even-paced, ritualistic movements of the *kuse*, the choreography now becomes more detailed and complex. The head is kept quite still, however energetic the movement of the feet, so as not to disturb either the mask or the lotus crown. The three-dimensional, moving 'picture' of the Heavenly Maiden must never be in disarray. Gradually, the Maiden's dance quickens and the chorus chants its description of her dance and flight:

The maiden in her feather robe
In the gentle sea-breeze streaming,
Soars above the pines of Mio, ...
And now is lost amid the mist of heaven.

At this point the Maiden stops beside the *shite* pillar and stamps twice. The play is ended. The *shite* folds his fan, turns and moves off along the *hashigakari*.

---

[44] The Shinto deity, the Prince of the Moon, is directly associated here with one of the bodhisattva (one who has achieved enlightenment) who resides with Amida Buddha in the Western Paradise. *Ibid.*, p. 30.

Transition

The *shite* is the first offstage and he sits before the mirror in the *kagami-no-ma* where attendants are waiting to help remove the lotus crown and mask. He is given a damp cloth to wipe his face and the inside of the mask, both of which are bathed in perspiration. As the members of the company come off the stage, *waki, waki tsure,* and musicians, one-by-one they kneel at the *Iemoto's* feet and bow deeply to him and to one another. The *Iemoto* bows to each of them in return, thanking them for their work in the performance. (This is a ritual that is also repeated in every Noh lesson, as the student kneels at the feet of his *sensei* (teacher) and bows with his forehead to the floor in obeisance.) After the long preparation it is startling to see that the *shite* has shed his costume in less than five minutes. As the Kyôgen play begins on the Noh stage, the *Iemoto* is able at last to have his lunch.

Meanwhile, Udaka Michishige is getting into his costume for the *shite* role in *Tôru*. With the help of attendants he first puts on lightweight white silk underwear consisting of leggings with stirrups and a sleeved vest to which strips of towelling are attached for padding. Next comes a skullcap to cover his own hair to accommodate the wig of the old man whom he will play in the first act. At this point he also prepares the mask, a *Sanko-Jo* mask from the Kongô collection, attaching the pads and testing the fit. The second layer of costume consists of a white, knee-length coat, topped with a false collar that is placed like a shawl over his shoulders. On top of this is a full-length kimono of dark blue. Each successive layer must be adjusted and fastened in place so that each element is properly placed, carefully aligned and completely secure. A long wig of beige horsehair is fitted over the skullcap, tied in front and then dressed by the attendants. Over the blue kimono he wears a light-weight brown muslin *hito-happi* (a short robe with wide sleeves) and, over this, a hemp apron indicating that the character is a salt-gatherer. Once fully dressed, the *shite* and his attendants move to the *kagami-no-ma*. Here Udaka spends a short time studying the face of the mask, then salutes it and an attendant helps to put it on (Figure 44). By this time, the Kyôgen play has ended, the musicians have resumed their places and the *waki* has already entered.

Tôru, Part One

This plotless but poetically sophisticated play, attributed to Zeami, is essentially a celebration of the faded magnificence of a great house and gardens built by the Minister Minamoto no Tôru in Kyoto. In the first act the *waki*, a priest, announces that he has just arrived in the capital (Kyoto) and stops to rest at a place called *Kawara-no-in* (Kawara villa). An old man appears carrying a yoke with water pails and sings of the beauty of the Bay of Shiogama in the autumn moonlight. When questioned by the priest, the old man says he has come to draw salt water. The priest replies: *"How odd! This is not the coast, yet you mistake yourself for one who draws salt water, old man?"*[45] The *shite* replies that in this place the nobleman, Minamoto no Tôru, built his estate and there created a replica of the beach on Shiogama Bay:

> *From the Mitsuno beach in Naniwa he had salt water brought every day, and here he burned off the salt for his pleasure for the rest of his days. But as there was no one after to inherit and enjoy it, the Bay, left as it was, became a dry bed.*[46]

The old man shows great sophistication and refinement in his knowledge and understanding of beauty and poetry. He tells the story of Tôru, how he reproduced "the scenic view of Shiogama" and its salt kiln here in the capital, miles from the sea. He sings of the beauty of the moonlight on the water and how he longs for the past (Figure 45). At the *waki's* request, he identifies and describes the mountains that can be seen from this spot and celebrates the beauties of nature. The movement throughout is slow and stately, with an air of mournful reminiscence. The mask is used subtly, often in the *kumorasu* position, but also

---

[45] *Tôru*, unpublished translation by Rebecca Teele, p. 2.
[46] *Ibid.*

raised, apparently seeing the distant mountain peaks. For the performer this 'seeing' is a real effort of imagination, since the angle of the eyeholes does not allow him to see much above floor level. To create the illusion of seeing the moon or the mountains, the actor must imagine seeing them through the mask's eyes and visualise his own figure in the mask from the point of view of the audience in order to determine the scope of the movement required. This activity requires a subjective response to the imagined beauty of the scene that can only be achieved through the objectification of the actor's physical apparatus. The masked figure appears to see and respond to the beauty of the moon and the mountains while, in reality, the performer who manipulates this 'body mask' must achieve verisimilitude through a combination of technical mastery and imagination.

Eventually the old man recalls that he has come to draw salt water and goes to collect his pails. The *shite* mimes drawing water from the sea and makes his way across the stage. He stops at the *shite* pillar, puts down the pails and then stands "as though he has faded away".[47] After a pause he turns and slowly exits while the chorus sings:

> *But under the cover of the*
> *Salt sea mist*
> *He fades, no trace left to be seen.*[48]

Transformation

Once the curtain has descended upon the old man, the *shite* and his attendants must set to work quickly. Onstage, the Kyôgen player is telling the *waki* the story of Minamoto no Tôru and suggests that the old man seen by the priest must have been Lord Tôru himself. Backstage, within thirty seconds of his arrival, Udaka

---

[47] Yasuda, *Tôru*, in *Masterworks of the Nô Theater*, p. 475. Yasuda relies upon the Kita school *utai-bon* for his stage directions, which differ from the Kongô staging in several instances; here, however, the action is the same.

[48] *Tôru*, Teele, p. 4.

has shed the mask, wig and costume used for the first act and is being helped into an orange brocade kimono for his appearance as the young Tôru. Next comes the white *ôkuchi,* a bulky, pantaloon-like divided skirt worn over the first kimono and tied at the waist. Another divided skirt in pale green is fitted over the first *ôkuchi* and a sash is added and tied at the front while attendants pleat the kimono at the back. Over all of this is another large garment in yellow and grey with a linked-diamond pattern. One of the attendants brings a bottle of water for Udaka while others adjust, fasten and sew various elements of the costume into place. There is an air of controlled panic as the Kyôgen player comes offstage and the call of the flute signals the start of the second act. The entire party moves to the *kagami-no-ma* where Udaka sits before the mirror while an orange and gold brocade headband is fitted low over his brow. He then takes up the *Chûjo* mask that he has made himself especially for this performance and finished only days before. Once the mask is secured, the headress is added and tied under the chin. Udaka tests his fan (the essential hand prop which serves a multitude of purposes in Noh) and then, after a few final adjustments, takes his place before the curtain as the vigorous young nobleman, Minamoto no Tôru.

This complicated costume change has been effected in less than ten minutes, but it has not been easy. There has been no opportunity for the *shite* to engage in even the briefest moment of calm meditation to make the shift from agéd peasant to youthful nobleman, and this is not an unusual state of affairs for the Noh performer. Indeed, some transitions are a good deal more difficult since they must be performed onstage, shielded only by a large prop or even (as in *Hagoromo* earlier) in full view of the audience. How does the Noh actor accomplish such a complex transformation in these circumstances? Like the performer of Topeng Pajegan, he will have had the benefit of disciplined kinaesthetic training from an early age so that much of what is required by the role can be accomplished simply through 'muscular memory' rather than through conscious determination. A vital component is the inevitable physical and psychological dissociation imposed by the mask and costume. Whatever the performer's personal feelings or anxieties, this 'body-mask' enforces its own requirements upon the performer. Kanze Hisao described the sensation:

> His face is hidden, his movements are restricted and the singing and the dialogue are so set that he is not even allowed to breathe as he pleases. In other words, all normal desire to perform and express one's own individuality is closed off and denied to the Nô actor.[49]

The performer is thus completely subject to the requirements of the role, and more particularly, of the mask. However, some conscious effort must be required to reach a state of sufficient concentration to be able to perform with skill and sensitivity. After the performance, I asked Udaka whether he had a meditation system that helped him maintain concentration through such difficult transitions. He admitted to practising daily meditation, but not necessarily in conjunction with performances. Like other Noh masters, he felt that training and discipline over many years had made it possible to snap into a 'performance state' whenever it was required: "It's like jumping in a river; you just have to go with it. I don't feel I have to do anything, I just go with it".[50]

Tôru, Part Two

After the Kyôgen player's exit, the *waki* sings that he will now sleep *"among the rocks/ . . . to await a dream/ In pilgrim's sleep"*.[51] After a musical introduction,

---

[49] Kanze Hisao, 'Life with a Nô Mask', in Teele, 1984, *op. cit.*, p. 70.

[50] Interview, 8 November, 1998. Umewaka Naohiko and Ryoichi Kano both voice similar views. According to Umewaka: "You just have to have that quality, all the time. Day to day. Capable of getting that state. I think in Noh theatre, you have to go into the state immediately. So there is no breathing preparation before you react. It's just sudden, just there. Inside you, it has to be. It's an immediate reflex and it's more than a reflex. [. . .] In the Noh theatre, you have to go into that state of mind immediately without any difficulty; you can't have 5 minutes extra to get into the state". (Interview, 27 May 1997). Ryoichi, a younger and less experienced performer, said: "It's really hard to get all of these worries out of one's mind and I am not yet able to clear my mind totally. But it's very important not to worry, because then the kind of spiritual energy, which is very important for the performance, will go down". (Interview, 12 June, 1997).

[51] *Tôru,* Teele, p. 4.

the *shite* enters as Minamoto no Tôru. He makes his way to the *shite* pillar and sings:

> *Forgotten are all the*
> *Many years that have passed.*
> *Again, as in days long ago,*
> *The waves return,*
> *Rising at Shiogama...*[52]

He identifies himself as Tôru and sings of the beauty of the moon, the dance of the Heavenly Maidens and the joy of drinking rice wine in the moonlight (Figure 46). He then begins the *haya-mai,* (fast dance) as the chorus sings of music and dancing in the light of the harvest moon. Even within the stylistic restraints of Noh, the transformation of the performer from a fragile old peasant to a youthful aristocrat full of virile vitality is palpable and impressive. The vast, many-layered costume makes the actor look like a gigantic doll that comes to life in this vigorous dance that is full of complex interweavings, sharp side-to-side movements of the head and resounding stamps that seem to make the ground tremble. This performance is another *kogaki* variation in which 13 movements of the energetic *haya-mai* are performed then repeated, placing enormous physical demands upon the *shite*. Tôru's dance, according to Teele, is "an expression of his enjoyment of the scene".[53] The audience is meant to enter imaginatively into the priest's dreamlike vision of Tôru dancing his delight in the moonlight. The character here is not really a ghost, but more akin to a Shinto *kami,* a resident spirit of the place who dances in celebration of the beauties of nature which he sought to recreate through artifice within these grounds. The Noh performer uses his own art to draw the spectators into this celebration. Although the *waki* is a Buddhist priest and the *shite* nominally a secular, human figure, the play nonetheless has many of the attributes of the more obviously religious plays

---

[52] *Ibid.*
[53] *Ibid.*

based upon Shinto legends found among those of the first group. However, the manipulations of the mask, using rapid *kiru* (side-to-side movements), confirm that this is a play of the fifth group that may have been based on an earlier 'demon' play.[54] The cock crows, moon begins to set, the *shite* completes his dance as the chorus sings:

> *In the moonlight he seems drawn*
> *To the Moon Capital*
> *And he seems to enter there.*[55]

At the *shite* pillar, he turns to the *waki*, gives a final stamp, closes his fan and moves off along the *hashigakari*. There has been no conflict; he has neither sought nor achieved either revenge or redemption and the character has not altered as a result of his visit to the temporal world. The play is regarded as a masterpiece not because of its dramatic qualities, but because of its literary refinements and evocative imagery.

Given this lack of conflict, the choice of mask for this play seems rather odd. *Chûjo* is primarily associated with defeated warriors like Kiyotsune whose spiritual torment may be read in the mask's furrowed brows. However, it is also associated with the poet Ariwara no Narihira whose nobility and sensitivity are reflected in the delicacy of the features.[56] It is interesting to note that Udaka already possessed a *Chûjo* mask that he had made for a performance of Tôru some fifteen years before, but while preparing for this performance, he felt that the older mask no longer seemed appropriate to the role. In comparing figures 47a and b one can immediately see the difference in expression between the two masks. The newer mask looks more troubled and regretful, less sure. The previous mask appears to be almost cheerful, with a distinctly upturned mouth.

---

[54] Yasuda speculates that Zeami may have based his play on an older demon play performed successfully by his father, Kanami (Yasuda, p. 462).

[55] *Tôru*, Teele, p. 6.

[56] Pulvers, 1978, p. 201.

There is a dichotomy between the furrowed brow and almost smiling mouth of 47a, which makes the mask's expression difficult to read. Of course, the *Chûjo* mask requires an ambiguous expression but, whereas Figure 47a appears to be worried yet cheerful, 47b seems more profoundly anguished but at the same time, visionary. The question that comes to mind is, why should Udaka choose to create a mask for Tôru that is so sad? Is this not meant to be a celebratory play in which Tôru dances for joy at the beauty of his garden? The answer may lie in the last lines of the play:

> *sweetly touched by parting sorrow*
>
> *appears his visage,*
>
> *touched by parting sorrow*
>
> *seems his visage.*[57]

In Tôru we have a figure of one who has loved life and things of the material world and returns to earth to express his joy and sing with longing of past pleasures. This delight in earthly joys is incompatible with Buddhist principles of non-attachment, but is entirely in keeping with Shinto materialism. Yasuda contends that Tôru does not ask the priest to pray for him because he has already achieved enlightenment and "dwells among the heavenly hosts".[58] Udaka's new mask suggests a different interpretation. Elements of the carving, particularly the troubled expression, indicate that this Tôru has not entirely succeeded in overcoming his attachment to worldly pleasures, and the dance may represent a working out of these obsessions. In examining Figure 47b closely, one can see that the stage right eye of the mask is focused downwards, towards the earth, but that the stage left eye (which is apparent to the audience as the *shite* exits) is focused forward, towards enlightenment. Although this asymmetry is also visible

---

[57] Yasuda, p. 484.

[58] *Ibid.*, p. 462.

in Figure 47a, the smiling shape of the mouth serves to make the overall expression of the mask less clear.

In performance the mask in 47b communicates many things including youth, charm, concern and joy. Although the expression of the mask at rest seems fixed, when animated by the performer there is extraordinary variety of subtle shifts of mood, so that at times the mask even seems to breathe. The performer creates this impression not just through movements of the head, but also through movements of the body and feet, shifts in weight, gestures of the hands and use of the fan. The actor himself is unconscious of much of what is communicated through the mask because what is perceived by the audience is an interaction of mask, body and costume as the performer executes the choreography coloured by the physical and emotional responses of the actor (both conscious and unconscious) to elements of the text. Some movements and gestures will have been self-consciously performed as part of the choreography (since the *kata* include not only movements of the feet, but of the hands, head and costume as well), while others may be more serendipitous, coming as a result of the imaginative response of the actor to the meta-text: story, words, music and choreography.

Post-performance
When the curtain falls behind him, the *shite* is hot and tired but exhilarated and, with the help of assistants, he has soon changed from his costume into normal street clothes. A number of students and admirers come backstage to greet him while the entire company busies itself with packing up masks, costumes and properties to be transported back to the Kongô Noh Theatre in Kyoto where they are based. The *shite's* exhilaration lasts for several hours; at a banquet held later in the evening Udaka was still buoyant and energised, but said that he would undoubtedly be exhausted on the following day. The eight-shows-a-week pattern

of Western commercial performance is quite incomprehensible to the Noh actor, who may only perform once a month or even once a year.[59]

Within the world of Noh these leading actors are indisputably 'stars'. In performance, every element depends upon and revolves around the *shite* and, outside the performance, they are treated with (and expect) enormous respect and adulation from other performers and their public. They are not so ostentatious or high-profile as their counterparts in, for example, Kabuki, but they do regard themselves as the guardians of Japan's greatest classical theatre tradition. In spite of all this there is a striking humility and simplicity about these performers when speaking of their art and one sees little of the self-obsessed egotism that may be found among their counterparts in the West. I suspect that this is attributable, at least in part, to the use of the mask and the negation of self that it requires.

Performing in the Noh Mask

Most of the fundamental elements of Noh performance relate in some way to the use of the mask and each in its way contributes to the masked actor's performance state. In Chapter 4 it was noted that the architecture of the stage and the fixed positions of the musicians, chorus and secondary characters are arranged to allow freedom of movement for the leading, masked actor. In performance it becomes evident that there are other subtle yet essential elements of the leading actor's physical and spiritual orientation that are determined or influenced by the demands of the mask.

The basic, 'earth-centred' posture *(kamae)* with knees bent and abdomen thrust slightly forward gives the Noh performer dynamic power and extraordinary control of movement. Energy is focused at a point just below the navel, which is

---

[59] Udaka Michishige is busier than most Noh actors and performed the *shite* role in the 'demon' play *Shessho-seki* only one week later. Matsuda Kanji, of the Kanze school (the largest school with the largest number of leading actors), is able to perform a *shite* role only once a year.

regarded as the centre from which all movement and spiritual strength emanates.[60] The *suri ashi* (sliding step), which requires that the feet never fully leave the floor, provides a secure base for both forward and backward movement and allows turns to be executed with smooth precision. Because the mask severely limits vision, the performer can easily become disoriented, thus the posture and walk help the masked actor to maintain balance and keep movement controlled even in very rapid dance passages. The *suri ashi* has the added advantage of allowing the actor to feel the stage beneath his feet and to know whether he has reached the edge or if there is an obstacle in his path. This style of movement also ensures that the mask is not disturbed by any extraneous action; as in Balinese dance-drama, the mask is kept as still as possible unless and until a specific movement or gesture is required. The bulky, precisely arranged costume also contributes to this stillness and control.

Another feature of some Noh masks, most particularly the frequently-used *Ko-omote*, is that the wearer has the sensation of seeing through a single eye-hole. Although in actuality the performer sees through both eyes equally, the eye-holes are cut in such a way as to create a kind of tunnel-like stereoscopic effect. Certainly for some performers the effect of this 'single-vision' is to create a sensation of single-mindedness in the performance. It is a subjective atmosphere of focused concentration which allows the performer to 'tune-out' possible distractions lending clarity and precision to the execution of the role's requirements.[61]

As both puppet and puppeteer, the human being who wears this 'body-mask' cannot rely merely upon his own internal sensations to make a successful and appropriate rendition of the role; he must also have some idea of the

---

[60] See D. Suzuki, *Zen and Japanese Culture* (Princeton, NJ: Princeton University Press, 1973) p. 185; also Eugenio Barba and Nicola Savarese, *A Dictionary of Theatre Anthroppology: The Secret Art of the Performer* (London: Routledge for the Centre for Performance Research, 1991), pp. 74–88.

[61] Interview with Umewaka Naohiko, 29 November, 1995.

impression he gives as he performs. This dual perception is the subject of an aesthetic concept called *riken-no-ken*. Put simply, the principle holds that the actor must be able to perceive his performance both subjectively and objectively, having a clear internal conception of the character while simultaneously visualising his performance from the point of view of the audience.

> *Riken* means objective judgement, and Ze-Ami is advocating an objective appraisal of one's own work and performance which should allow one to see oneself as others do, from the side, from behind and so on. . . . In dancing he particularly recommends a technique called *mokuzen-shingo*, eye front, mind behind, which suggests the same kind of objectivity, seeing one's performance in the round.[62]

It is not merely a matter of having a generalised sense of whether or not a movement 'works', (in the manner of the Western actor who depends upon the objective view of the director to determine the success of his performance), but a clearly defined impression of the appropriate physical shape and orientation of all elements of the 'body mask' manipulated by the actor as he moves about the stage. This process of maintaining a simultaneous internal and external conception of one's performance is translated by Rimer and Yamazaki as 'Movement Beyond Consciousness':[63]

> This expression *[mokuzen shingo]* means that the actor looks in front of him with his physical eyes but his inner concentration must be directed to the appearance of his movements from behind. . . . The appearance of the actor, seen from the spectator in the seating area, produces a different image than the actor can have of himself. What the spectator sees is the outer image of the actor.

---

[62] Sekine, p. 97.

[63] This is a translation of the term *buchi*, which means 'understanding the dance'. Rimer and Yamazaki, p. 261.

> What an actor himself sees, on the other hand, forms his own internal image of himself. He must make still another effort in order to grasp his own internalised outer image, a step possible only through assiduous training.[64]

What is called for is a dual consciousness, at once subjective and objective, that will inform the physical realisation of the performance.

> Thus while the actor identifies, subjectively, with the part he is playing he should also keep a part of his mind free, alert to the effect which he creates, watching his own performance as others see it. Thus an actor juggles with both the intensity of his subjective emotions and the objective clarity of his critical mind. Two levels are at work.[65]

The effect of maintaining this dual consciousness is to lead the performer further into the dissociative state into which each element of preparation for the performance has been designed to take him. In this, the state of the masked actor in performance is not unlike the Buddhist state of *satori:*

> The contrast he [Zeami] makes between riken no ken and gaken, literally 'ego perception', is illuminating. If riken no ken is an 'objective, self-less and detached' mode of seeing; gaken is a 'subjective, self-centered and attached' mode of seeing, colored by various preconceptions and feelings and limited in scope. As the actor transcends his ego-bound mode of being, his gaken gives way to the more universal riken no ken, which objectively embraces the subjective view point as well as the hitherto

---

[64] *Ibid.*, p. 81.
[65] Sekine, p. 97.

objective viewpoints . . . riken no ken is ultimately the satori-mind adopted and enacted in the art of Noh.[66]

So, every element of Noh—the kinaesthetic, non-analytical training from childhood, being dressed for the character, and meditation with the mask—leads the masked performer away from an integrated relationship with self and towards a detached, dissociated state in which the performer's self is set aside in favour of the internal concentration on character and the external requirements of the performance. The physiological manipulations discussed in relation to Balinese Topeng performance are also found in Noh: sensory deprivation, restricted breathing and reduced oxygen intake, rhythmic auditory stimuli and powerful 'driving' elements in the accompaniment to the climactic dances. The combination of these factors has a powerful physiological and psychological effect upon the mask wearer inducing an altered state of consciousness which, in spite of the myriad physical impediments imposed, allows the actor to present an integrated performance.

The Noh Performer as Medium

What of the notion of the Noh mask as a tool or means of mediumship? In proto-Noh performance genres the mask was frequently considered to be the representation and residing place of the god or spirit it depicted and the performer who animated the mask was seen to be the conduit for this act of visitation. Is such a concept simply irrelevant in contemporary Noh performance? Certainly some of my informants found the idea of identification with the character (and the kind of 'possession' that implies) completely incomprehensible; as one put it: "A player cannot be another character, he is himself".[67] Yet this seems rather at odds

---

[66] Michiko Yusa, '*Riken no ken:* Zeami's Theory of Acting and Theatrical Appreciation', *Monumenta Nipponica*, 42, 3, pp. 335 and 344.

[67] Interview with Matsuda Kanji, translated by Yasuko Igarashi 30 May, 1997.

with the legends and literature of a tradition which speaks of the mask becoming one with the actor's flesh. Noh scholar Monica Bethe explained:

> There is a real tendency among Japanese, and Noh actors in particular, to de-mystify or avoid mystical connections regarding elements of culture. Also it is a matter of ego, the actor doesn't want to say that the mask controls him. As far as the actor is concerned the mask makes no difference to what he actually DOES—it is for the audience.[68]

This is true enough; the choreography of the role is learned before the performer ever sees the mask he is to wear and does not alter in any fundamental way once he has put it on. The mask, then, might be viewed by some as merely symbolic of the character and the actor who wears it as one who simply performs traditional gestures and choreography as a representation, rather than an embodiment of the character. Yet there is more to the actor's work than mere repetition of choreographed movement. One young Noh performer asserted:

> **Ryoichi Kano**: I think it's important to think about the role and to get an image. . . You should not get too close, to try to become the person. I don't try to become the role. If you try to do that it will get into some kind of ... it would become too close to, for instance, Kabuki. It is not necessary to really become the role—not [in] a realistic way of showing this character, but more symbolic. I have this image and I go from the image.[69]

While Kabuki theatre would hardly be considered 'realistic' by modern Western or Japanese standards, what seems to be at issue here is a portrayal of character that is inconsistent with the essentially symbolic nature of Noh. In the canon of Noh drama, plays about living human beings are very much in the minority and

---

[68] Interview, 2 June, 1997.
[69] Interview translated by Arnoud Rauws, 12 June, 1997.

the sufferings of Noh protagonists are not really the stuff of everyday life. Thus an identification with the role is not, perhaps, so useful as an understanding of what the character represents and how the character should be perceived by the audience. Again the concept of *riken no ken,* a self-less and detached understanding, becomes essential. The performer must be able to give himself over to the role completely while still maintaining an objective perspective on his own performance. Umewaka Naohiko suggested that the image of the character comes partly from the external promptings of the mask's visage and partly from an internal, imaginative understanding of the underlying qualities of the character:

> Playing the role of a snake, for example, the most effective way of being a snake is not wearing the Noh mask only, trying to think your mask, but actually trying to act like a snake or a serpent. Acting is not good enough. Most important is to be a snake, you believe that you become a snake. It's a trance situation, but controlled.[70]

Here the complexity of the Noh actor's process begins to become clear. First the actor learns the choreography of a role by rote to perfection, without knowing anything of the story or the character. At the same time he will learn the *utai,* but again without reference to the meaning of the words he sings. Eventually he is informed about important aspects of the character, in the case of *Dōjōji,* for example, that the dance is one of a young woman transformed by jealousy into a fire-breathing serpent. When he sees the mask (*Hannya*, Figure 20), though it is a recognisably human and female image, it has an unmistakable demonic cast made more obvious by the horns that protrude from its forehead. In addition, the costume is diamond-patterned, like the skin of a snake. The actor must now take these elements into account in his performance of the fixed choreography he has

---

[70] Interview, 27 May, 1997.

learned since childhood. At this point he may begin to understand certain aspects of the choreography more clearly and find ways of bringing a snake-like quality to the movement. Since the 'steps' and the text have already been learned and cannot be altered, the actor must allow the image of the snake to work in his imagination and subtly find its way into his physical interpretation of the role. The mask aids him in this process both physically and imaginatively since it frees him from the necessity of finding facial expressions that are consistent with the character's snake-like persona. More importantly, perhaps, it cuts him off from outside distractions allowing him to focus upon his inward image of the character. The actor's contemplation of the mask itself will teach him more about the role, since the particular subtleties of the mask's expression reveal a number of characteristics. With the *Hannya* mask, for example, the fierceness of the mouth is in contrast to the anguished expression of the eyes and forehead, indicating both torment and fury. The 'trance' to which Umewaka refers is the actor's state as he performs complex *kata* automatically through muscular memory while simultaneously concentrating upon both his inward image of the character's persona and the outward image of the character seen from the point of view of the audience. The actor in this case is both in control and entranced by the image of the character. Is this mediumship? In a purely religious sense, perhaps it is not. Yet in a broader sense the performer who animates the mask sets his own personality aside and concentrates his conscious and subconscious efforts upon bringing the character to life. While he is not 'possessed' in the sense that a *Kagura miko* or Balinese Rangda performer might be, he nonetheless becomes the medium for the mask's expression.

Chapter 7: The Consciousness of the Masked Actor

Humankind has a neurobiological as well as a spiritual need for myth and ritual in order to explain the ineffable. Traditional theatrical performance genres, like those studied here, are often concerned with the fundamental myths of their societies. Because of their relationship to spiritual life and religious practice, traditional performances such as these often call for ritualised activities and meditation on the part of performers in the course of preparation and performance. We have already seen how such practices are utilised in Noh and Balinese dance drama as the performer seeks to clear his mind of external distractions (in Zen terms, seeking *mushin*), denying his own ego in order to take on the persona of the mask. This chapter will discuss the ways in which ritual behaviours and meditation, which are an integral part of the transformation process, engage neurophysiological changes in the organ of the brain that manifest themselves in an altered state of consciousness. One important aspect of this altered state of consciousness is a sense of union with an exterior force or 'other'. In the case of a religious trance this is reflected in a feeling of oneness with a god or the cosmos. In the case of the masked actor, however, what is achieved is a sense of unity with the mask character. The analysis that follows will show that the consciousness of the masked performer can be characterised in scientific terms as a trance state. Moreover, it will become clear that this trance develops through the process of transformation and is fundamentally connected to the relationship of the actor to the transformational mechanism of the mask.

Transformation, Consciousness and the Mask

In Japanese Noh and Balinese dance-drama, the mask serves as a means by which the performer transforms from his own persona to that of a character and then from one character to another. By donning the costume and placing the mask over his face, the performer clearly effects an objectively observable change in his outward appearance, but how does this process bring about an internal change in the actor's consciousness? By 'consciousness' I refer to that phenomenon which is at once both mind and brain; an entity that encompasses awareness, sensation and thought and is at the same time an organ of the body, subject to physical, biological and chemical processes. The evidence that emerges from the examples discussed in the preceding chapters indicates that a number of elements of performance in each genre, which are directly or indirectly related to the mask, contribute to an alteration in the state of consciousness of the masked performer. To clarify these issues, it will be necessary to investigate the nature of the altered states of consciousness to which the masked performer may be subject and the means by which such states are effected. I shall refer to my own experience as a performer of Balinese Topeng as a 'case study' to illustrate the unfolding of the transformation process and the nature of the altered state of consciousness that is evoked.

It is evident that several elements come into play in the transformation process including the relationship of these genres to religious ritual, the circumstances in which performances take place and the ritualised nature of the performances themselves. The methods by which performers are trained and the nature of the musical accompaniment with which they must interact also significantly affect the performer's state. However, fundamental to this change in consciousness is the mask itself and the requirements that it makes of the wearer. Although all actors may be subject to 'performance states' that differ from normal consciousness, my research indicates that the performance state of the masked actor is particular, unique and distinct from that experienced by the unmasked performer and that alterations in consciousness occur as a direct result of the performer's relationship with the mask.

Elements of the Transformation Process

Let us review what has already been established regarding Noh and Balinese masked performance:

- The movements of the characters and the dances that they perform are learned kinaesthetically through imitation and physical manipulation. This enables the performer to execute the required movement or choreography automatically, through muscular memory rather than by conscious effort.
- Preparations for performance involve fixed rituals of a sacred or semi-sacred nature including meditation, mantras and/or prayer. These serve to empty the performer's mind of distractions and separate him from ego.
- The actor seeks to become one with the mask in which he performs through studying its iconography, the character it represents and the way in which the mask moves most expressively. He then must adapt his face, body and movement to that which is most appropriate for the mask.
- The body is distorted by a bulky, multi-layered costume that restricts movement and, in some cases, breathing.
- The mask covers the performer's face, obscuring his identity and expression, limiting vision and impairing respiration.
- Performance occurs in a special, often sacred space.
- The content of the performance relates to fundamental myths of each culture and the characters represent gods, heroes and idealised figures rather than ordinary human beings.
- The performer interacts with rhythmic musical accompaniment with which he must be perfectly co-ordinated and intimately attuned.

Each of these elements has some effect upon the performer. The kinaesthetic training, meditation, mantras and invocation of gods, spirits or ancestors serve to dissociate the actor from the act and implicitly or explicitly indicate that the performer is a vessel for the performance rather than its instigator. The distortion of the body through costume and the negation of the face by the mask obscure, even obliterate, the performer's persona placing him at the service of the body-mask. The necessity to be in concert with the musical accompaniment also requires the performer to set aside his own ego and subject himself to an outside force. Thus, all of these aspects of performance require the performer to abnegate himself and objectify his performance. The consciousness engendered by these various factors must embrace duality while striving for a unity with the character and performance. The cultural and religious significance of the performance—the occasion, the space and the subject matter—demands an attitude of mind that is serious and respectful and creates an atmosphere of portentousness around the performance. All of these are givens; it now remains to examine whether these elements of mind have an effect upon the organ of the brain and the organism that is the actor.

Ritual, Theatre and Consciousness

It is accepted that myth and ritual serve an important purpose in the successful functioning of societies and have a place, in some form or other, at the core of all cultures. Art, poetry, literature, music, theatre and philosophy have emerged in relation or response to myths and rituals which we regard as significant, whether or not we still endorse their religious dimension. (For example, contemporary artists in the West may still make reference to classical myths, although Olympian polytheism is no longer practised. The dilemma of Oedipus still has resonances, even without belief in oracles.) D'Aquili and Laughlin have argued that myth and ritual have developed in all societies not merely as a cultural adjunct but, rather, as a result of neurobiological necessity related to the fundamental nature of the human organism:

Given an organism in which the neural mechanisms for abstract thought have evolved, which require causal and antinomous thinking as a highly adaptive trait, that organism must necessarily use these mechanisms in an attempt to explain his existential situation. Such explanation involves the obligatory structuring of myths, complete with the organization of the world into antinomies and with the positing of initial causal termini of strips of observed reality that man calls gods, spirits, demons and the like. These mechanisms are not a matter of choice but are necessarily generated by the structure of the brain in response to the cognitive imperative. . . . Ritual behavior is one of the few mechanisms at man's disposal that can possibly solve the ultimate problems and paradoxes of human existence.[1]

Thus, myth and religious ritual provide a framework within which humankind can confront and explain the ineffable, reconciling apparent opposites or contradictions. These are created out of organic necessity 'generated by the structure of the brain'. One can see how this operates in the rituals of Western civilisation. In the Christian church, for example, the theatrical ritual of the Eucharist confronts the communicant with prospect of his own mortality and offers, through an efficacious enactment (imbibing the communion bread and wine symbolic of the body and blood of Christ), the possibility of salvation and 'eternal life'. Similarly, the enactments of ritual theatre are not merely entertainment but are necessary to the psychological health of society. The Balinese are reassured by a performance of Topeng because it honours the deified ancestors and protects the priest's ritual while the blessings of Sidha Karya ensure that the ceremony is completed appropriately. Perhaps even more vividly, the appearances of Rangda and Barong visibly challenge and exorcise dangerous

---

[1] Eugene d'Aquili, Charles D. Laughlin, 'The Neurobiology of Myth and Ritual' in *The Spectrum of Ritual: A Biogenic Structural Analysis*, d'Aquili, Laughlin and John McManus, editors (New York: Columbia University Press, 1979) p. 179.

black magic in order to protect the community. Noh drama, while nominally secular, nonetheless serves a similar function by presenting supernatural beings *(Hagoromo)* or departed souls *(Kiyotsune* and *Toru)* who honour the *kami* or impart teachings concerning enlightenment and salvation.

It is also generally accepted that theatrical performance constitutes a kind of ritual itself in that it is "a customarily repeated act or series of acts".[2] Barbara Meyerhoff provides a definition of ritual that coincides even more closely with conventional notions of theatrical performance:

> Rituals are communicative performances that always provide a sense of continuity and predictability. They must be reasonably convincing, rhetorically sound, and well-crafted, but do not require an alteration in individual belief at the deepest level, though that is often highly desired.[3]

Thus, Noh and Balinese theatre, quite apart from their connection with religious ceremonies, can both be seen to be rituals (that is, formally repeated acts) whether or not they involve "individual belief at the deepest level". Moreover, like religious rituals, these theatre forms require performers to engage in fixed patterns of behaviour ('customarily repeated acts') and, significantly, these behaviours often include meditation. What is important about this, particularly in the case of masked performers, is that ritualised activity and meditation function on a deep level to bring the participant to a state in which apparent contradictions are reconciled and a sensation is imparted of oneness with the divine, the universe or, in this case, the mask:

> It appears that, during certain meditation and ritual states, logical paradoxes or the awareness of polar opposites as presented in myth

---

[2] *Merriam-Webster Dictionary* (New York: Pocket Books, 1974) p. 604.

[3] 'The Transformation of Consciousness in Ritual Performances: Some Thoughts and Questions' in *By Means of Performance: Intercultural Studies of Theatre and Ritual*, in Schechner and Appel (eds), 1990) p. 246.

appear simultaneously, both as antinomies and as unified wholes. This experience is coupled with the intensely affective 'oceanic' experience that has been described during various meditation states, as well as during certain stages of ritual.[4]

The Noh performer meditating with his mask in the *kagami-no-ma* and the Topeng performer reciting his mantra before the box of masks at the edge of the stage are engaging in activities designed to focus concentration. These preparation activities, which form a fundamental part of the transformation process, coincide with the kinds of practices known to bring about alterations of consciousness in ritual practitioners. The performers' efforts to attain *mushin* (in Noh) or *taksu* (in Balinese dance-drama) prompt a series of physiological changes. D'Aquili and Laughlin's observations indicate that the performer's sense of one-ness with the mask character is achieved as a result of alterations in the brain and nervous system brought on by these preparation activities.

> We note what appears to be a different neurophysiological approach to essentially the same end state following meditation and ritual behavior. In both cases the end point appears to be the unusual physiological circumstance of simultaneous strong discharge of both the ergotropic [sympathetic] and trophotropic [parasympathetic] systems and involving changes in the autonomic system[5] and the onset of intense and unusual affective states coupled with the sense of union of logical opposites, usually the self and a personified force or god.[6]

---

[4] d'Aquili and Laughlin, 1979, p. 176.

[5] The *autonomic* system controls involuntary bodily activities. It encompasses both the *ergotropic* system, which stimulates muscles and reduces activity in the internal organs—the 'fight or flight' mechanism, and the *trophotropic* system, which brings on relaxation of muscles and increased activity of internal organs.

[6] *Ibid.*, p. 176.

The performer feels at one with the mask not only because he *wishes* to do so, but also because his preparation activities have triggered chemical changes in the brain evoking the desired sensation. Furthermore, the physical processes which precede these activities, (kinaesthetic training and even the act of putting on the costume), because of their ritualised nature, also contribute to this shift from normal consciousness. Performers interviewed in the course of my research agreed that the immediate process of transformation begins with changing clothes—donning the costume of the character. This shift in consciousness is then deepened and enhanced through a period of concentration, however brief, with the mask.

In my own experience of masked performance, I found that the purely physical, non-analytic method of learning the dances had already inculcated a routine of 'emptying' the mind before embarking upon the work. It seems necessary for the mind or ego to be set aside to allow the body to perform actions that are stored in a sub-conscious 'muscular memory'. Next, the business of putting on the costume actually alters the body, transforming not only the way one looks, but also the way one feels. In the case of the Topeng costume, the restrictive *sabuk* which binds the chest, the *stewel* fastened tightly around the calves and the weight and bulk of the various layers of decorative pieces distort one's posture and movement as well as the body's outward shape. The relationship to self is fundamentally altered by this change. Having reached this point, one then studies the face of the mask—an act that is something like looking into a mirror, in that one looks at a face with which one must identify as if it were one's own. In finally donning the mask the performer makes a leap of faith, abandoning the 'self' entirely and entering a new phase of consciousness which is driven by the music and by the mask.

Altered States

It is difficult to find appropriate terminology to describe the 'performance state' of the masked actor. One hesitates to use the term 'trance' because it is so loaded with connotations of somnambulism on the one hand and frenzy on the other. Many performers object strongly to the use of the term 'trance' to describe the performance state especially when (as in Bali, for example) the term has particular ritual and religious connotations in the culture. Emigh points out:

> In talking with men who undergo trance possession, or visitation, while performing with masks in Papua New Guinea, Bali and India—many of whom have experience as character actors—it is clear that they regard these two modes of performance as discrete. Ritual performers familiar with the process know whether or not they have been acting or in trance, just as accomplished actors have a clear sense as to whether or not they are pretending. In other words, though there may be degrees of accomplishment within each mode of performance, a quantum leap seems to be required to get to the next mode along the 'continuum'.[7]

While acknowledging the distinction between theatrical performance and trance-possession I would contend, with Emigh, that the performance state is one of the stages along the same 'continuum'. The stages of this 'continuum' might be delineated as follows:

1. objective observation rendered as simple indication or imitation ('me')
2. conscious enactment, 'pretending' ('me-plus')
3. identification with character ('me/not me')
4. transformation with altered cognition and perception ('not-not me')
5. trance-possession ('not me')

In spite of the negative connotations of trance, neurobiological evidence indicates that this term, properly defined, may be the most appropriate to characterise the performance state of the masked actor. Barbara Lex, in her essay 'The

---

[7] Emigh, 1996, p. 30.

Neurobiology of Ritual Trance', points out that: "Although not all rituals evoke states of trance, rhythmic stimuli and fixed interaction tend to produce these states".[8] Both Noh and Balinese dance-drama, as well as being ritual activities associated with fundamental myths of their cultures, entail fixed interaction and rhythmic stimuli. Considered in conjunction with the use of meditation and repetitive mantras, it seems clear that if performers in these genres operate in an altered state, such a state might justifiably be characterised as trance.

What is Trance?
Suriyani and Jensen, in their study of *Trance and Possession in Bali,* give the following general definition of the trance state:

> Trance is an altered state of consciousness (ASC) characterized by changes in cognition, perceptions, and/or physiologically based sensibilities. In these aspects it is identical to hypnosis, which produces a state in which cognition and perception are altered. Brown and Fromm (1986) have stated that "dissociation is part of many hypnotic experiences" . . . The terms 'trance' and 'hypnosis' overlap and can be used interchangeably to refer to the same biophysiological state.[9]

According to this definition, it appears that the actor's process of transformation may be a kind of spontaneous hypnosis or self-hypnosis. Although actors themselves do not use these terms, the process of clearing the mind through mantras or meditation combined with concentration upon rhythmic music and the mask in order to more skilfully execute kinaesthetically acquired choreography would seem to have some relationship to such an activity. The connection with

---

[8] Barbara Lex, 'The Neurobiology of Ritual Trance', in *The Spectrum of Ritual: A Biogenic Structural Analysis* edited by Eugene d'Aquili, Charles D. Laughlin and John McManus (New York: Columbia University Press, 1979) p. 120.

[9] Luh Ketut Suryani and Gordon D. Jensen, *Trance and Possession in Bali* (Kuala Lumpur: Oxford University Press, 1993) p. 28.

dissociation is significant because it helps to explain several phenomena of the performance state which link it with trance.

> Dissociation is a psychological mechanism which operates in the everyday life of normal people and in abnormal mental states as well. Psychiatry has defined it as an unconscious 'defence' mechanism through which emotional significance and affects (feelings) are split off, separated, or detached from an idea, situation, object, or person.[10]

It should be noted that dissociation is not a strictly pathological phenomenon, but is also apparent in everyday life. Dissociative experiences may include such common occurrences as, for example, being so involved in reading a book on the bus that one misses one's stop, or the simple 'absent-mindedness' which causes one to mislay the house keys.[11] Dissociation often occurs in the performance of habitual or repetitive activities, for example working out in the gym or working on an assembly line. This may explain the apparent detached quality of Balinese dancers, which led Artaud to describe them as 'animated hieroglyphs', and the similarly remote demeanour of Noh performers as they execute their dances as if by rote. Suiryani and Jensen point out that "dissociation involves a fragmentation of consciousness and automaticity".[12] These characteristics, which in everyday life might be regarded as undesirable or indeed pathological, serve a positive function in the case of the masked performer. The 'fragmentation of consciousness' provides a mechanism which allows the performer to operate on two different levels of consciousness simultaneously—as both character and

---

[10] *Ibid.*, p. 20.

[11] "Studies of dissociation using the DES [Dissociative Experiences Scale] in normal subjects revealed that over 25 per cent reported a substantial number of dissociative experiences (Ross, Joshi, and Currie, 1990)". Suryani and Jensen, p. 23.

[12] *Ibid.*, p. 20.

performer or, as Zeami suggests, as puppet and puppeteer.[13] Furthermore, the 'automaticity' of dissociation enables the performer to execute complex choreography and other physical activities subjectively as the mask character, while at the same time maintaining a critical and objective consciousness of his performance. Both of these characteristics of trance—'fragmentation of consciousness' and automaticity—appear to coincide with Zeami's concept of *riken no ken*, 'The Detached Eye'.[14]

Such altered states of consciousness are achieved by various means. According to I. M. Lewis:

> As is well known, trance states can be readily induced in most normal people by a wide range of stimuli, applied either separately or in combination. Time-honoured techniques include the use of alcoholic spirits, hypnotic suggestion, rapid overbreathing, the inhalation of smoke vapours, music and dancing.... Even without these aids, much of the same effect can be produced, although usually in the nature of things more slowly, by such self-inflicted privations as fasting and ascetic contemplation (e.g. 'transcendental meditation'). The inspirational effect of sensory deprivation...has also been well-documented in recent laboratory experiments.[15]

Preparations performed by actors in each genre include several of these additional trance-inducing stimuli. The Noh actor's period of meditation with the mask, the Topeng performer's mantra and prayers or the Rangda performer's inhalation of

---

[13] "This constructed puppet, on a cart, shows various aspects of himself but cannot come to life of itself. It represents a deed performed by moving strings. At the moment when the strings are cut, the figure falls and crumbles. *Sarugaku* too is an art that makes use of just such artifice. What supports these illusions and gives them life is the intensity of mind of the actor". Rimer and Yamazaki, p. 97.

[14] See Chapter 6.

[15] I. M. Lewis, *Ecstatic Religion: A Study of Shamanism and Spirit Possession* 2nd ed. (London and New York: Routledge, 1989) p. 34.

incense—each of these activities contributes in some way to an alteration in consciousness. Perhaps even more efficacious is the highly rhythmic and repetitive music that accompanies the performance that the actors are able to hear during this period of preparation and with which they must interact in performance. Equally significant is the sensory deprivation to which the masked actor is inevitably subject from the moment he dons the mask: vision is significantly restricted to the point that the performer is virtually 'blind' and breathing is inhibited in such a way as to induce hyperventilation.

This effect is evident when performers remove the mask and reveal themselves sweating and breathless, but the process begins at the moment the mask is placed on the face. From my own subjective experience I know that the moment of donning the mask marks a significant change in the performer's consciousness. When the mask goes on, it presses against the face and vision is immediately restricted.[16] One's own breath creates heat and condensation on the inside of the mask and one is sharply aware that less air—less oxygen—is available. Breathing becomes laboured as one strives to overcome the light-headedness that accompanies oxygen deprivation. These sensations, combined with the weight and constrictions of the costume, force one to concentrate that much harder on the music and its rhythms. There is an intense desire to transcend the limitations of costume and mask or to somehow find a way to live within them comfortably. In order to accomplish this the only recourse is to focus one's concentration on the character, taking on the appropriate physical postures and moving the body in concert with the mask. One is aware that the mask has expressions and that it must live as part of the body, but also that it does not follow the movements of one's own face. How then does the performer make the mask expressive? It becomes essential to create a mental picture of the outside of the mask, and not of the mask alone but also of the costumed body of the

---

[16] Although the Noh mask is usually padded to hold it slightly away from the actor's face, it is still tied tightly enough that the heat and restrictions upon breathing are not much different from the sensations experienced by Balinese masked performers.

character—the body-mask. As one executes the choreography this image, an 'objective' view of the mask character, is always present to some degree.[17] Zeami's concept concerning *riken no ken*—imagining one's performance from the outside—is an essential and, perhaps, inevitable consequence of wearing the mask. So, having reached a state of dissociation through various preparatory activities, one's consciousness is forced to become further fragmented by the restrictions imposed by the mask. The subjective sensation is rather difficult to describe since one is aware of being somehow both inside and outside the experience. One's concentration is focused on the body-mask and the music as the character's movement is executed seemingly without conscious thought. All that happens during the performance seems to take place in a heightened present. One is a part of the performance as it is executed and yet apart from it. The experience is certainly one of an altered state of consciousness.

The Physiology of Trance

When stimuli combine to evoke a trance state, there are measurable physiological changes in the affected individual. Trance "arises from manipulation of universal neurophysiological structures of the human body"[18] in which biological rhythms are synchronised by environmental stimuli. This process is referred to as 'entrainment'. The stimuli might include fasting, inhaling incense or hyperventilation and, "combined in the context of a ritual, effectually generate stimulus bombardment of the human nervous system".[19] To be specific, the trance-inducing stimuli simultaneously excite both the sympathetic nervous system (the *ergotropic* system which stimulates muscles and reduces activity in the internal organs) and the parasympathetic nervous system (the *trophotropic* system which brings on relaxation of muscles and increased activity of internal

---

[17] This sensation was also noted by Topeng performer Dr. Wayan Dibia: "I try to visualise the combination of myself with the mask to dancing with the character . . . that picture comes again and again during the process of performance". Interview, 4 March, 1997.

[18] Lex, p. 118

[19] Lex, pp. 120–124.

organs) producing paradoxical physiological effects. Whether this excitation is driven by active ritual behaviour (dancing, chanting etc.) or quiet meditation, the final effect is the same.

> It appears that during meditation one begins by intensely stimulating the trophotropic system. There is a marked decrease of sensory input, the attempt to banish all thought and desire from the mind, and the attempt to maintain an almost total baseline homeostasis state with only enough intrusion of the ergotropic system to prevent sleep. The spillover in the case of meditation is from the trophotropic to the ergotropic side with the eventual result in strong discharges from both systems. Ritual behavior apparently starts from the opposite system. . . The rhythm of the prayer or chant, by its very rhythmicity, drives the ergotropic system independent of the meaning of words. If the ritual works, the ergotropic system becomes, as it were, supersaturated and spills over into excitation of the trophotropic system, resulting in the same end state as meditation but from the opposite neural starting point.[20]

Noh and Balinese masked performers engage in both meditation and ritual behaviour and may be subject to neurophysiological stimulation from one or both activities. The important elements of trance induction which correspond to the circumstances of Noh and Balinese performers include on the one hand the "marked decrease of sensory input" (restrictions of mask and costume) and, on the other, the rhythmicity of prayer or chant used in performance or pre-performance ritual. In this altered state the chemical changes in the brain and nervous system are accompanied by certain measurable physical and chemical changes in the body. These have been outlined by Felicitas Goodman, whose

---

[20] d'Aquili and Laughlin, 1979, pp. 176–177.

doctoral research dealt with the phenomenon of glossolalia, or 'speaking in tongues' (a feature of religious trance/possession), and who has continued to examine the trance experience from a biophysiological point of view with subjects in non-religious circumstances. Her more recent experiments have required subjects to "assume ritual postures known from native art, certain stereotypical ways of standing or kneeling and holding their arms and hands".[21] When trance was induced through rhythmic stimulation, the subjects experienced physical symptoms consistent with those of religious trance/ecstasy:

> The heart rate of the subjects increased dramatically and blood pressure simultaneously dropped considerably below preexperimental levels. In the blood serum the stressors, namely adrenalin, noradrenalin, and cortisol, initially rose slightly, then dropped below normal levels, while beta-endorphin, the brain's own painkiller and opiate, made its appearance and stayed high even after the conclusion of the experiments, accounting for the euphoria so often reported after a religious trance experience.[22]

Interestingly, some of these so-called 'trance postures' correspond to the basic performance postures for Noh and Balinese performers.[23] However, more startling evidence that physiological changes corresponding to those described by Goodman are experienced by the masked actor may be seen in a 1989 documentary made for the Japanese television network, NHK. Programme makers measured heart and respiration rates of Noh master Umewaka Naohiko both in rehearsal and during a performance of the powerful and challenging

---

[21] Felicitas D. Goodman, "A Trance Dance with Masks: Research and Performance at the Cuyamungue Institute', in *The Drama Review*, Vol. 34, no. 1, Fall 1990, p. 105.

[22] *Ibid.*, p. 106.

[23] These postures were also the subject of Grotowski's experiments examining performance and altered states of consciousness conducted with a multi-cultural group of performers. See I Wayan Lendra, 'Bali and Grotowski: Some Parallels in the Training Process' in *The Drama Review*, Vol. 35, no. 1, Spring 1991, pp. 113–128.

demon play *Dôjôji*.[24] The performer's heart rate at the play's climax is over 200 beats per minute—a rate that might be regarded as life-threatening in a normal individual even in the course of intensive exercise. Yet, at the conclusion of the performance, the subject felt no ill effects. During the performance the actor was unaware of the profound physiological changes that were taking place in his own body, so fully taken up was he with executing the necessary activities.

The biochemical changes that occur in trance are interesting enough in themselves, but there are other physiological aspects of this process that emerge from inquiries into the subjective experience of performers. One difficulty that has arisen in the course of my research is the seeming inability of performers to give detailed descriptions of their experiences and sensations. Jane Belo encountered the same problem when she sought detailed information about trance states from her Balinese subjects:

> In the course of our study we were careful to collect as many introspective statements of the Balinese principals in these trance performances as it was possible to glean, by interviewing them ourselves or by sending our specially trained secretaries to do so. The non-verbal character of the Balinese made these statements relatively unrevealing. It was, apparently, almost impossible for a Balinese trance subject to put into words what he had experienced, even though the acting out, the attitudes and gestures had been most eloquent.[25]

Subsequent investigations have revealed that it may not simply have been the characteristic reticence of the Balinese which prevented Belo from eliciting articulate analysis from trance subjects, but rather the physiology of trance itself. Information regarding the different functions of the right and left hemispheres of

---

[24] For the science series *The Universe Within*, 'The Heart: A Supple Pump System' written and directed by Masakatsu Takao, produced by Katsuhiko Hayashi and Bo G. Erikson, 1989.

[25] Belo, 1949, p. 54.

the human brain and the interplay of these factors in the ritual trance process sheds light upon a possible explanation for these difficulties while providing even stronger evidence for the element of trance in the performance state.

> Briefly stated, in most human beings the left cerebral hemisphere functions in the production of speech, as well as in linear, analytic thought, and also assesses the duration of temporal units, processing information sequentially. In contrast, the specializations of the right hemisphere comprise spatial and tonal perception, recognition of patterns—including those constituting emotion and other states in the internal milieu—and holistic, synthetic thought, but linguistic capability is limited and the temporal capacity is believed absent.[26]

This last point bears re-emphasis: because of the predominance of the right hemisphere in these activities, the altered state is evidenced by a diminution of linguistic and temporal capacities. The Noh and Balinese performer's ability to execute elaborate choreography and interact with complex musical patterns indicates the predominant influence of the right hemisphere. In addition, the reticence of actors in describing their experiences during performance can be explained by that hemisphere's limited linguistic capability. Ritual behaviours engaged in to evoke trance "place in pre-eminence right hemisphere functions and at the same time inhibit or hold constant the capacities of the left hemisphere".[27] The recitation of mantras, a ritual shared by both Noh and Balinese dance-drama, is noted particularly in this regard:

> For example, in certain meditation techniques reduction of sensory inputs by means of repetition of a *mantram*, . . . has the effect of monopolizing the verbal-logical activities of the left hemisphere,

---

[26] Lex, p. 125.

[27] *Ibid.*, p. 126.

leaving the right hemisphere to function freely. Conversely, response to the rhythms of chanting and singing, dancing, handclapping and percussion instruments engages right hemisphere capabilities, concomitantly evoking the 'timeless' quality of the attendant experience.[28]

From this it appears that the inability to describe trance/performance experience is due to the inhibition of left hemisphere verbal function combined with predominance of right hemisphere functions demanded by the ritual activities of the performance (singing, dancing and interaction with rhythmic, percussive music). Even my own experiences of masked performance are difficult to articulate in spite of my best efforts to record impressions. I am able to envision and imaginatively 'feel' the sensations but they are virtually impossible to describe in precise detail through words. The 'timeless' quality to which Lex refers is also an important symptom of ASC exhibited by masked performers. This is demonstrated in the intense paroxysmal trance episode experienced by I Madé Djimat at the Calonarang performance in Pengosekan (see Chapter 5) in which he was unable to remember any of his activities from the onset of the most intense stage of trance and unable to estimate the amount of time required for his recovery. These symptoms are also manifested in less spectacular circumstances, even when the performer may be unaware of operating in an altered state of consciousness. An incident observed at the performance of a Noh dance sequence *(shi mai)* provides an illustrative example.

Temporal disorientation and verbal/analytical dysfunction in performance
A leading Noh performer, Umewaka Naohiko, was to give a 25 minute 'demonstration' performance of the final dance sequence from the Noh play *Dôjôji*[29] in full costume with a *Hannya* mask from the actor's own collection.

---

[28] *Ibid.*

[29] The performance was given for an invited audience at the Noh Studio at Royal Holloway, University of London, in the autumn of 1995.

Because it was to be only a brief excerpt, a tape recording was used to accompany the performance rather than live musicians and chorus. The performer spent approximately two hours before the demonstration rehearsing and becoming accustomed to the space, then retired to the *kagami-no-ma* to dress and prepare. In the course of his rehearsal he had marked out the choreography and indicated the point in the dance at which his assistants (of whom I was one) should raise the curtain for his exit. During his preparation, as in a typical Noh performance, he was able to hear, albeit on tape, the sounds of the musicians and the *kakegoe* of the drummers. The tape recording was being played as the audience took their seats in the theatre and, as the volume and tempo of the accompaniment intensified, the performer took his place before the curtain, which was then raised at his signal. The performance was vigorous and concentrated and the performer executed the complex choreography with skill and precision in conjunction with the music and with no signs of disorientation. It was therefore surprising to see the performer reach the stage position that was the signal for his exit after only about ten minutes had elapsed (I was timing the action); the curtain was raised just in time. When the performer asked me about the performance immediately afterwards, I replied that it had been 'very quick'. When he learned that the dance excerpt had lasted less than half the allotted time, he was quite shocked and found it difficult to believe that he could have miscalculated to such a degree. Because the program had been so brief, he was asked if he might take some questions from the audience, which he readily agreed to do. However, when he was asked detailed questions about the dance he had just performed, the performer was uncharacteristically unforthcoming. This particular performer is an accomplished English speaker, articulate and knowledgeable, particularly in this, his area of expertise. Yet on this occasion he was unable to speak in any detail about the performance he had just given, nor was he able to give an analysis of aspects of the play or the genre. At a reception after the performance, however, his mood was buoyant, exhibiting the post-performance 'high' often experienced both by performers and trance subjects.

Driving mechanisms and mediating elements

Some important questions arise from this example. How could such an experienced performer 'lose track' of his actions to such an extent that he performed a piece of set choreography in less than half the normal performance time? Why is it that an articulate individual accustomed to analysis found himself 'speechless' when asked to describe and analyse his performance? With regard to the first question, it is important to note that in this case the performer lacked the 'anchor' of having other performers present with whom he could interact. A Noh performance involves a complicated communication between musicians, chorus and leading actor, especially in the fast-paced final dance. The tempo is determined both by the drummers and the dancer and is mediated by the chorus. It is well-known that the speed of Noh performances slowed substantially during the Tokugawa period so that a contemporary Noh performance can last as much as four times longer than it would have in Zeami's time. Thus it is possible for a performer to execute the fixed choreography for a given dance quickly or slowly depending upon the circumstances of the performance and his interaction with the drummers. Because in this case the performer had to rely upon a recording, there could be no interaction. Although the accompaniment is rhythmic, the choreography is not fixed to precise 'counts' in the music so it is possible for a dancer to perform at double or at half the speed of the musicians while still being 'in time' with the music. The accompaniment to final dances in Noh also employs what Goodman refers to as 'driving mechanisms',[30] manifested in the intensification of rhythmic stimuli in the music such as short, rapid *kakegoe* and quick tempo drumming. (Similar driving mechanisms are also apparent in the accompaniment to trance-possession portions of the Rangda-Barong enactments with increased tempo and percussiveness in the gamelan orchestra.) Lex points out that "intense rhythmic, photic and auditory stimulations generated by dancing

---

[30] So called after the 'repetitive photic stimulations' similar to strobe lights, used to test susceptibility to seizures. See F. D. Goodman, *Speaking in Tongues: A Cross-Cultural Study of Glossolalia* (Chicago: University of Chicago Press, 1972) p. 74.

to particular musical tempos and instruments appear to be sufficient synchronizers to effect entrainment of brain rhythms".[31] In Noh, the increasingly urgent tempo of the drumming and the increased speed, volume and urgency of the *kakegoe* combine with the rhythms of the dance to drive the *shite* ever more powerfully into an altered state of consciousness, but the performance is controlled by the interaction of (unmasked) musicians and chorus with the leading actor. In a Noh performance the *shite* can abandon himself to the dance, trusting in his fellow performers to moderate the tempo if necessary. In this case three factors drove the *shite* (Umewaka) to a state which he was less able to control: the performer's concentration upon the intensely rhythmic accompaniment; the necessity to perform the climax of the piece without having built up to it through the rest of the play; and the lack of mediation by other performers. This altered state of consciousness rendered the performer temporally unaware during his dance and subsequently unable to analyse his actions, even though he was able to execute the choreography perfectly.

Sensory deprivation

The second question, about the performer's seeming inability to articulate his experience immediately after the performance, also finds its answer in the nature of this altered state of consciousness. As has already been indicated, the activities of the Noh and Balinese masked performer, including mantras, meditation and interaction with rhythmic stimuli, engage the functions of the right cerebral hemisphere to the detriment of the left. However, aspects which are specific to these performance genres, in particular the mask/ body-mask, also make a significant contribution to this alteration in consciousness. Experiments to determine the effects of various sorts of sensory and perceptual deprivation on humans have been conducted since the nineteen-fifties and effects reported by subjects include some of those at issue here, in particular temporal disorientation

---

[31] Lex. p. 123.

and deterioration in logical thinking. In seeking a neurological explanation for these symptoms, G. F. Reed indicates that hemispheric specialisation may hold the key:

> The RH [right hemisphere] operates in a holistic, intuitive manner, utilizing configurational relationships and imagery, it is inferior in analytical, verbal and logical operations and in time-sequential functions. *And this list includes exactly those characteristics which we observed to be typical of SD* [sensory deprivation] *effects.* [32]

The masked actor, as we have noted above, must function in an environment of sensory and perceptual deprivation in which he is physically dissociated from his body by the costume and visually impaired by the mask. Furthermore, it is evident that these physical and perceptual restrictions have an effect upon the actor's consciousness, particularly combined with other aspects of these performance genres such as rhythmic music, dancing and so on. Reed concludes that:

> SD [sensory deprivation] conditions may in some way facilitate activity of the right hemisphere whilst inhibiting that of the left. . . .
> SD conditions drastically reduce meaningful input, whilst discouraging or excluding verbalization. The former restriction may encourage the imaginal mode of cognitive processing, whilst the latter may simultaneously inhibit the verbal mode.[33]

Thus if sensory deprivation contributes to the state of the masked performer, such a contribution is likely to manifest itself in temporal disorientation and verbal/logical inhibition indicating a right-hemispheric predominance consistent with a trance state. As indicated above, the sensory deprivation imposed by the mask, inhibiting vision and breathing, has a tangible effect upon the performer.

---

[32] G. F. Reed, 'Sensory Deprivation' in *Aspects of Consciousness*, Vol. 1, edited by Geoffrey Underwood and Robin Stevens (London: Academic Press, 1979) p. 170.

[33] *Ibid.*, p. 174.

"Imaginal modes of cognitive processing" are evident as one attempts to cope with the mask's restrictions by envisioning the performance as if from the outside. The subjective effect of this shift in cognitive operation is to place all activity into a kind of dissociated present. The sensation in performance is timeless and dreamlike.

Charting the Trance Process
It is by now clear that there are a number of elements of these performance genres which contribute to an altered state of consciousness for the masked Balinese or Noh performer. Although culture, custom and belief systems certainly have a part in this process, it is essentially a neurophysiological alteration created by physical stimuli. Whether or not the performer acknowledges that a transformation in consciousness takes place, these elements of performance set in train certain unavoidable biophysiological processes that affect perception and cognition.

Body, Mind and Mask

We have already seen that the mask is one among several elements of performance which contribute to the masked performer's altered state of consciousness, but is it the essential component of this process of inner transformation? Much has been made of 'the power of the mask' in terms of visual impact and spiritual resonances, but few have examined whether the mask object itself has any discernible effect upon the wearer as opposed to the viewer. Certainly the mask has a physical effect upon the wearer in covering the face, limiting vision and inhibiting respiration. An additional element, essential to the Noh mask and applicable to Balinese full-face speaking masks like Pedanda, Sidha Karya and Rangda, is the effect of the performer's voice behind the mask that he wears. The vibration created inside the mask between the face of the performer and the back of the mask is another element that may contribute to the performer's dissociation. However, beyond these physical effects, which certainly facilitate alterations in consciousness, it is apparent that the body-mask itself has a transformational effect upon brain process through what Laughlin and Laughlin have termed 'Symbolic Penetration':

> the process by which an initial image or sensation evokes (triggers, activates, excites) a field of multiple somatic (perceptual, cognitive) associations that are its meaning. ... 'Penetration' refers, therefore, not only to relations between an object in the world (for instance, a mask 'out there') and a brain, but also between initial sensory activity (e.g., an initial sensory image of an object that becomes known as 'a mask') and the totality of neurocognitive processes arising as a consequence (e.g., the entire field of associations, or meaning, within consciousness of the mask). Depending on the extent of penetration and the exact range of neural entrainment, a variety of experiences may be evoked by masking.[34]

In other words, the cultural and mythopoetic significance of the mask object, its iconography and the character it represents all have a perceptible effect upon the human organism. Moreover, while *looking* at the mask certainly affects the viewer, the process of studying and, ultimately, embodying the mask has an even more profound effect upon the wearer.

> The field of entrainments mediating motor activity, affect, perception, metabolic activity, and cognition is expanded and reorganized to produce a far greater range of entrainments than those previously possible within a more limited set of habitual patterns associated with a mundane body image.[35]

---

[34] Charles D. Laughlin and Judi Young-Laughlin. 'How Masks Work, or Masks Work How?' *Journal of Ritual Studies*, 2/1, 1988, p. 74.

[35] *Ibid.*, p. 75.

Whereas the viewer perceives the face of the mask (and the body of the performer) as an object, it remains objectified, separate, outside. For the wearer, however, the body-mask is both objectified as a separate entity and, simultaneously, embodied as the subjective face and body of the performer. This apparent contradiction is resolved by entrainment of brain processes that favour activities of the right hemisphere. It has already been demonstrated that the performer's preparations, his ritualised behaviours and particular elements of performance can lead to right hemisphere predominance. Neurobiological evidence further indicates that the capacity for recognition of facial expression (as opposed to facial form) is located in the right hemisphere, which is also concerned with emotion.[36] In studying the mask and visualising the image of the body-mask during performance, the actor forms an emotional relationship with his other face (the mask) and, in emulating its expression, takes on the 'emotions' of the mask. Since it comes about through activities of the right hemisphere, this relationship, although powerfully felt, cannot be articulated and resists logical analysis. Laughlin and Laughlin contend that:

> The disciplined donning and the dramatizing of particular masks is causally linked to predictable and distinct experiences (Webber, Stevens and Laughlin 1983). And these experiences are causally linked to the simultaneous blending of conventional, ego-identifiable imagery, affect, and somaesthesis, and alternative (frequently reversed or contrary) imagery, affect and somaesthesis produced via penetration by the mask and associated imagery and activities. The presence of these variant phenomena, simultaneously operating within the sensorium of an actor, sets the stage for a transformation of initial experiential dualisms by means

---

[36] Napier, pp. 204–205.

of a reorganization of operating neurocognitive and neuroendocrinal structure mediating two sets of experiences.[37]

Thus the mask provides the causal link to a number of neurophysiological changes in the consciousness of the performer. It is the agent of the actor's outward and inward transformation, a physical and neurophysiological transformation mechanism. Because of the mask and through it, the actor is simultaneously aware of himself as 'puppeteer' manipulating the body-mask and as puppet, the masked figure he embodies. The two entities are distinct, yet unified in the mind and person of the performer. The mask can be understood in psychological terms as a transitional object which, in Winnicott's description, occupies the "potential space between the subjective object and the object objectively perceived, between me-extensions and the not-me".[38] Schechner has described this state as 'not-not me', a simultaneity of self and other which the masked performer is able to sustain because of the neurophysiological alterations in consciousness set in train by donning the mask.

Sacred Masks

In the preceding analysis the performer's experience of the mask has been discussed only in practical, secular terms applicable to 'theatrical' use. However, certain masks exist in both traditions which have important spiritual significance and bestow upon the wearer the status of a god. Because such significance must have some bearing upon the actor's process of transformation, it is necessary to give special consideration to two very similar masks of these two traditions: Sidha Karya and Okina. The correspondences between these masks are curious and remarkable. They are both mysteriously unrelated to the dance-drama forms with which they are so closely associated and yet, interestingly, those aspects which make them uncharacteristic of Topeng and Noh are precisely the things

---

[37] Laughlin and Laughlin, *op. cit.* p. 77.

[38] D.W. Winnicott, *Playing and Reality* (London: Tavistock Publications, Ltd., 1971) p. 100.

which they seem to have in common. In spite of these apparent anomalies, each of these mask figures is held to be absolutely fundamental to its genre and culture, perhaps representing some essential ancestral connections.

Most importantly, both masks are regarded as abodes of gods, and therefore those who wear them are regarded as embodiments of the gods during the performance. In neither genre is much attention given to physical or psychological interpretation of the mask since, as Kenji Matsuda put it: "the mask is a god, not a character".[39] No other mask in either genre carries with it such a strong sense of mediumship and visitation. Both require special and elaborate preparation ceremonies that include fasting as well as special prayers and rituals. Interestingly, however, performers who wear these masks do not believe that they are possessed by the god within the mask when they perform. The instructions regarding the Noh Okina are unequivocal and clearly state that the moment the actor dons the Okina mask he "becomes the god".[40] However, performers insist that they are not possessed by an outside spirit but instead find the god within themselves. According to Takabayashi Kôji:

> The actor who performs Okina must become himself *(jibun ni narikiru)*. This is a different self from the self who enters the stage and bows down before donning the mask. I walk onto the stage as my everyday self. Once I wear the mask I am in communion with the god inside me, with the universal part that transcends the mundane. That part of me which is godlike dances and that same

---

[39] Interview, 30 May, 1997.

[40] Documents held at the Centre for Noh Studies at Hosei University include manuscripts of certain choreographic and performance manuals, including one for *Okina*. In an interview, 28 May 1997, Noh scholar Dr. Haruo Nishino pointed out that the manuals indicate that it is not simply a matter of the actor 'pretending' or 'impersonating' the deity–the language clearly states that upon donning the mask the performer 'becomes the god.' It is regarded as a true act of transformation.

universal god resides in the mask; therefore both mask and performer are god.[41]

Balinese performers, too, speak of working in partnership with the god in the mask rather than being possessed. Ida Bagus Alit spoke of the interaction between the performer and the Sidha Karya mask:

> Whenever I take the Sidha Karya mask to dance, I feel something really great, an extra power, an extra energy. If I'm tired and weak from dancing, when I touch the Sidha Karya mask and dance it I feel a new energy, a new life. ... Sidha Karya is a very sacred & powerful mask and when you dance it, you have to be able to chant the mantra very well, because it's a very different mantra that has to be chanted quickly. . . . You have to be sure that you have fully devoted yourself to the god, the ritual. If you concentrate you feel sure that you are doing your job, confident and centred and full of WILLINGNESS, the god of Sidha Karya comes down and is sitting on you. You have to be strong to accept that power within your self, it comes down into your body and you have to be sure and willing.[42]

So, the god inhabits the mask and the mask is given life by the performer, but while the performer is a 'medium' for the god, he is not 'possessed', simply augmented. In becoming one with the god in the mask, he does not lose himself but is, rather, a willing participant. Without the mask, however, he could not embody the god since the god resides only in the mask. This all would seem to imply that the mask object itself possesses some special power beyond human consciousness. There are a few obvious differences in the preparation process required for using these masks as compared to other, non-sacred masks, but the

---

[41] Takabayashi Kôji, p. 96.
[42] Ida Bagus Alit, interview, 5 April, 1997.

pattern of activity, from the point of view of neurophysiological stimulation, is essentially the same. The special powers attributed to these masks by performers may be the effect of 'symbolic penetration'. The performer, already in an altered state of consciousness, introduces the image of the sacred mask, which is replete with symbolic significance. This image and the power it represents may act upon the performer like a post-hypnotic suggestion so that he feels imbued with the god-like powers associated with the mask, which are nonetheless recognised as powers of the mask and not of the performer. The same duality of consciousness that operates with non-sacred masks seems to operate here so that the performer is able to maintain a simultaneous subjective-objective view of the performance.

Whether the same holds true of performances of Rangda and Barong is another matter. Responses of performers were mixed. If, as was suggested above, states of consciousness may be seen to occupy a continuum and the masked performer is, in any case, subject to an altered state of consciousness, then the paroxysmal 'trance-possession' sometimes observed with these masks may be simply another step on that continuum. The state, whether one of 'trance' or 'trance-possession' is achieved through a process in which the mask functions as a transformational mechanism altering consciousness by means of its physical demands and symbolic penetration of the mask image.

Conclusion

Whether characterised as *yasuki kurai* ('Perfect Fluency'[43]) or *taksu*, the state to which the masked performer in Noh or Balinese Topeng aspires is one in which he possesses the perfect subjective fluency of being one with the body-mask which he inhabits while able to maintain objective control of his performance. In order to achieve this simultaneous duality and unity, he must cultivate an altered state of consciousness. Specific elements in the process of transformation in each performance genre contribute to the creation of this state including methods of

---

[43] Rimer and Yamazaki, pp. 135–136.

training, the circumstances and content of the performance as well as costume, rhythmic musical accompaniment and dancing. However, by far the most important element and the engine of the actor's transformation is the mask which, while visibly transforming the actor's outer aspect, becomes a trigger for his inner transformation of consciousness. It functions as a transformational mechanism not only metaphorically and psychologically but also in a tangible, physical manner.

The mythopoetic associations of the masks, and the preparatory rituals using meditation and mantras which they require, set in train certain chemical changes in the brain which stimulate ergotropic and/or trophotropic activity. The actor's conscious effort to 'become one with' the mask accelerates this process. Placing the mask over the face leads to a psychological state of dissociation, fragmenting the performer's sense of self, causing his behaviour to become automatic, 'unconscious'. The masked actor's concentration is turned inward as he simultaneously tries to imagine the figure of the character he embodies from the outside. The physical effects of the mask involve a significant degree of sensory deprivation: vision is impaired enhancing the sense of dissociation and breathing is inhibited leading to oxygen deprivation and hyperventilation. These physical and psychological effects also entrain biological rhythms, increase heart rate and enhance right hemisphere function leading the performer to a holistic, intuitive and imaginal mode of cognitive processing in which spatial and rhythmic activities are to the fore while logical and analytical processes are inhibited.

Based upon my own experiences in performing Balinese Topeng, the state described here seems an accurate reflection of that subjective reality. Dissociated from ego and self, one's focus is upon the rhythms of the music and the effort to bring the mask to life. Somehow the choreography is executed, seemingly without conscious effort. Since it is almost impossible to see through the mask, one relies upon hearing and an extended sense of touch, a sort of 'sixth sense', in order to stay within the appropriate performance area, but one must at the same time 'think' through the mask's eyes so that they seem to see. To do this one must imagine the face of the mask as viewed from the outside while directing one's 'vision'—movement that indicates 'sight'—from behind the mask, adjusting for the disparity between outside perception and inner reality. The costume is hot, heavy and restrictive, and the physical effort required in executing the choreography is tremendous. Inevitably one finds oneself breathless and perspiring by the time the mask is removed. The relationship to the mask itself is complex. It is outside oneself, covering one's own face but it also becomes a second face, a face 'once removed' which must be manipulated appropriately. One feels at the same time a part of the mask and apart from it. Viewed subjectively or objectively the tantalising question remains: is it the performer who controls the mask or the mask that controls the performer? The 'answer', if one is needed, is that the two work in concert—the mask is brought to life by the actor whose movements are dictated by the mask. Leaving aside notions of mediumship and possession, it is clear that the mask has a powerful physical and psychological effect upon the performer who wears it. Regardless of whether the performer seeks a 'mystical communion' with the character or god depicted in the mask, human physiology dictates that the performer is likely to experience an altered state of consciousness as a result of wearing the mask. This has important implications for masked performers in other genres and for contemporary acting pedagogies that make use of masks for actor training.

Chapter 8: The Mask and Transformation

What happens to the actor who puts on a mask? He is cut off from the outer world. The night he deliberately enters allows him first to reject everything that hampered him. Then, by an effort of concentration, to reach a void, a state of un-being. From this moment forwards, he will be able to come back to life and to behave in a new and truly dramatic way.[1]

Any mask can be an agent of transformation for the performer who wears it. The relationship is a complex one in which the mask acts on the performer as the performer enacts the mask. This examination of Noh and Balinese masked dance-drama, which places the two genres within the contexts of both theatrical performance and sacred ritual, reveals much about the fundamental nature of the process of theatrical transformation and the interaction of mask and performer. In exploring the responses of those who use masks, rather than the effect of masks upon observers (audience), I have sought to shift the focus of performance studies research to centre on the experience of the performer, rather than on the perceptions of the audience. This work provides the first direct comparison of Balinese and Noh masks and the circumstances of their performance within each culture touching on some of the iconographic and functional similarities between certain significant mask types in both genres. What a comparison of these individual performance practices reveals is something fundamental about the

---

[1] Jean Dorcy, quoted in Johnstone, p. 187. Dorcy was a student of Copeau at the Vieux Columbier.

effect of masks upon performers in both secular, theatrical circumstances and in sacred, consciously mediumistic applications. The systematic analysis of common elements of masked performance and the neurobiological and psychophysiological symptoms discernible in masked performers (derived both from objective observation and subjective accounts from performers) clearly indicates evidence of altered states of consciousness engendered by the use of the mask.

How does the mask influence the performer? It covers the face, abnegates personal identity, focuses concentration and directs the action of the actor-puppeteer. The psychophysiological effects of the mask drive the performer to a dissociative state in which a dual consciousness operates. In this state the performer is able to visualise his/her own masked figure from the outside while manipulating the body-mask from the inside. As a practitioner myself, I can attest that it is an experience utterly distinct from unmasked performance. Can these findings be applied to the experiences of mask performers in the West? I believe it is possible since, even without the spiritual and religious underpinnings (which are, of course, fundamental to the genres examined here), many aspects of the physical process of mask use are the same. These physical processes are the source of the psychophysiological changes that lead to altered states of consciousness. Western performers who enter into mask work without the benefit of a culturally embedded spiritual explanation for the physical sensations experienced with the mask often find themselves troubled (or sometimes inspired) by their experiences. As a result, the encounter with the mask becomes subject to various sorts of mystical speculations. Noh and Balinese performers, on the other hand, have important ritual functions to carry out and cannot indulge themselves in this way. The mask in these cultures is not a tool for 'self-realisation'. Theatrical practitioners in the West who use masks in their work would do well to be aware of the psychophysiological implications of mask use so that they and their students can understand and maintain some perspective on the work.

Here we find a fundamental difference in perception between Eastern and Western mask users that illuminates the gulf that appears to exist between Eastern and Western approaches to performance, theory and analysis. On the surface, the Western approach seems to be self-conscious and analytical, whereas that of the East is more pragmatic. However, there is more to this apparent pragmatism than meets the eye. The Western researcher, with his or her analytical bias, seeks to find the 'deeper meaning' of performance activity and is hampered in this by the Eastern practitioner's reticence in discussing sacred matters. Eastern philosophies tend to emphasise the importance of secret knowledge imparted orally to trained initiates and hold in great reverence those things which cannot be analysed. The Western analyst attempts to probe deeply but, from the point of view of the Eastern practitioner, such an approach misses the point. Analysis implies dissection of a problem yet in Eastern philosophy understanding comes not from breaking the subject down into component parts, but by grasping the whole. Western theory tends to be somewhat suspicious of this holistic view. Dr. James H. Austin, a neurologist and a student of Zen, provides an anecdote from his apprenticeship in meditation that illustrates the problem. Here Austin is trying to come to an understanding of the *koan* his teacher has set for him:

> "How is it", I ask, "that emptiness—this central Buddhist concept—can exist if supposedly, at the same time, everything in the universe is all linked together? Doesn't the latter imply that there is a very high degree of fullness?" "You are getting diverted", he answers. "You have to *know* emptiness", he replies. "You must stop splashing along the surface with all your words and concepts. You cannot understand emptiness with words or with ideas."[2]

---

[2] Austin, pp. 108–109.

Too often the Western researcher's attempts at analysis—usually in the form of asking what seem to be 'intelligent' questions—are, in effect, just 'splashing along the surface'. In the course of his study, Austin discovers that he must come to understand 'emptiness' through experience, and that his finely honed analytical tools are of no use to him in these circumstances—in fact, they are a hindrance. A kind of knowing that is not based on theory, hypothesis or analysis is also what is required of the performer in these masked dance-drama genres. The deeper meaning reveals itself without analysis. Throughout my field research my 'analytical' inquiries were met with amusement or mystification from my informants. My gradual understanding of the experience of the masked performer came through my own experience of the processes of training and performance. This realisation has revealed, to me at least, the fundamental contradiction of any notion of 'Performance Theory' since performance, by its very nature, is practical rather than theoretical.

The Path Ahead

A number of fascinating topics have emerged in the course of this research that merit further investigation. Certainly more work needs to be done to try to discern the links between the folk mask traditions of Japan and the evolution of the Noh mask, for it is clear that masked dance-drama has been part of Japanese culture for a very long time. In the course of such research, much might be revealed about links between various Asian mask traditions. Is the speculation of Napier and others indicating the possibility of powerful interconnections between the theatrical cultures of Ancient Greece and India an example of European chauvinism or could it be (as Takabayashi Kôji suggests) that all of these mask traditions derive from a single source?

Certainly there is much to be gained by further investigations into the differing relationships of performer to mask in various cultures. The neurophysiological processes discussed here would seem to apply universally, but practice and belief systems differ widely and each genre deserves to be explored as a discrete entity. In particular, a number of relatively ancient European folk mask traditions still exist and warrant further study and documentation before globalisation subsumes all communities and cultures into a single undifferentiated, homogenised corporate entity.

What about the new traditions of mask use in the West? Should they be related to traditions of the past? If masks are increasingly used in performer training, will new mask theatres emerge? I wonder, too, about the relationship of theatre and ritual and whether some of the new, self-conscious masking traditions might give rise to new religious belief systems rooted in ecstatic experience and trance-mediumship.

The Power of the Mask

On reflection, this study may seem rather coldly rational—a precise clinical dissection of events—while these performance traditions are extraordinary, inexpressibly wonderful theatrical experiences. Although these traditions are very old and their subjects often obscure, the power of these masked dance-drama genres to excite and delight has not diminished—even after years of research I remain in awe. There is something very special that happens in masked performance. Whether it is the power of *Taksu* or *hana,* somehow a brilliant performance makes itself apparent as a physical sensation grasped not only through vision and hearing, but as a tangible response to 'something in the air'. For both the performer and the audience something miraculous happens, an inexplicable atmosphere of electricity that may manifest itself as goosepimples or breathlessness or heightened perception. When one looks at a mask on the stage and that piece of carved wood appears to breathe, one is aware of being in the presence of something beyond mere skill, perhaps something beyond human power. There is a peculiar alchemy affecting performer and audience alike, binding all in a communal apprehension of the ineffable.

In performance, those who animate these masks inhabit a liminal realm, somewhere between the gods and humankind; through them, and through the mask, something extraordinary is communicated. It cannot be achieved through logical thought or careful planning but depends entirely upon the willingness of the performer to allow this communication to take place. The great Topeng performer Kakul observed: "The power of the mask, its spirit, will speak only if the actor is devoted and in a state of total receptivity".[3] It is that ultimate selflessness required of the masked actor that enables this act of transformation.

---

[3] Daniel, p. 112.

Glossary 1: Balinese Terms

alus or halus	Refined; a term referring to characters, usually of high caste, whose mask is white or light coloured indicating refinement, gentleness and purity. Contrasted with *keras*.
baju	In Indonesian and Balinese the term refers to a shirt or dress; it is the term used to refer to the velvet jacket worn by the Topeng performer.
buta-kala or bhuta-kala	Mischievous elemental spirits who may cause accidents or interfere with ceremonies. They must be fed with small offerings frequently, especially before an important event or performance.
canang	Small offering in a palm-leaf basket consisting of flowers, shredded pandandus leaf, fruit and the components of betel chew.
dalang	Master of the *wayang kulit* or *wayang lemah* shadow puppets who manipulates the puppets and provides dialogue and narration. A great *dalang,* whatever his caste, has status equivalent to that of a high priest in Balinese society. They are very learned and able to recite from memory the great epics and other sacred poetry. They are very physically skilled as well, able to perform for many hours at a time, speaking and singing over the gamelan accompaniment while at the same time manipulating each character according to its appropriate movement vocabulary.
Kajeng Kliwon	A day on which the Triwara (3 day) week and the

	Pancawara (5 day) week of the Balinese calendar coincide and which occurs every 15 days. On this day the buta-kala, or elemental spirits, are held to be particularly active and require propitiation.
kamben	Also referred to as *kain* and (inaccurately by Westerners) sarong, it is the standard garment for both men and women of the region. It consists of a piece of cloth usually about 2.5 meters long and 100–110 cm wide generally worn wrapped around the body at the waist. In the male costume for Topeng and other dance dramas it is wrapped around the chest.
kanda empat	The four sibling spirits, which accompany every child into earthly life, manifested in elements of the birth process. They are: amniotic fluid *(yeh nyom);* blood *(getih);* vernix caseosa *(lamad,* the membrane covering the foetus' skin); and the placenta *(ari-ari).*
Kawi	A literary language of Javanised Sanskrit in which most of the classic literature of Bali is written. It is the highly formal language spoken by high-caste characters in Topeng dramas and is also said to be the language spoken in trance by performers of Rangda.
keras	Rough or strong; a term used in reference to characters whose mask is coloured in reddish or brownish tones with strong features. Contrasted with *alus* or *halus*.
kris	Ceremonial dagger, often with a wavy blade which is part of the costume of male characters in Balinese dance drama.
manusia yadnya	Life cycle rituals fundamental to Balinese Hindu tradition.
ngayah	Unpaid work performed as a service, particularly in relation to temple ceremonies. It is considered an act of worship.
niskala	The invisible world; that which is beyond the five senses; the realm of spirit and the occult. Contrasted with *sekala*.
odalan	Temple anniversary ceremony.

pedanda	Brahmana high priest.
pemangku or *'manku'*	Village temple priest, usually of the Sudra caste-group.
poleng	Black and white checked cloth representing the polarity of black and white magic, used in a number of ceremonial contexts, for example to clothe sacred trees, as an ornament for shrines and as a garment for trancers in the Calonarang drama.
pratima	An object that acts as a seat for the god which usually is brought out when the gods descend for a temple anniversary. A *pratima* may be a small figure in the shape of a human being or an animal but may also be a mask.
pura	Balinese-Hindu temple which consists of two or three enclosed courtyards.
Pura Dalem	Temple located near the graveyard and thus often referred to as "The Temple of Death" but a more accurate translation would be "Temple of the Interior" or perhaps "Temple of Mysteries" since *"dalem"* means deep, interior or mysterious. It is often the location for ritual performances of Calonarang.
sabuk	A length of canvas webbing wrapped around the Topeng performer's upper body to secure the *kamben*.
saput	In the Topeng costume, the gilded and multicoloured cape worn over the *kamben*. Also a piece of fabric worn over the *kain* in certain ceremonial circumstances. Members of a Barong club might wear a *saput* of the black and white checked fabric called *poleng* indicating their membership of the group and their involvement in magic rites.
sekala	The visible world; that which can be perceived by the senses; the seen. Contrasted with *niskala*.
stewel	Highly decorated leggings, part of Topeng costume.

Glossary 2: Japanese Terms

bugaku "Dance entertainment"; a masked dance genre of the court which succeeded and gradually supplanted *gigaku*. It is still performed for certain ceremonial occasions.

Dainichi The "cosmic Buddha" or "universal entity" of Esoteric (Shingon) Buddhism in Japan.

dengaku "Rice-field entertainment"; a medieval performance genre popular in provincial Japan and later with the Court after Zeami's fall from favour.

fue Flute in the Noh instrumental ensemble.

furubi A soot-based liquid used to add character to a newly carved and painted Noh mask.

gigaku "Elegant entertainment"; a court art imported from China and Korea between the sixth and eighth centuries which featured masked dances.

hana Literally, "flower"; a term used by Zeami to convey mastery of technique; novelty; inspiration in performance.

hashigakari Bridgeway connecting the backstage area to the main playing area on a Noh stage.

hinoki Japanese cypress wood used to make Noh masks and Noh stages.

honmen	Masks by the old masters used as models for subsequent masks.
hôshibara	Entertainers in medieval Japan who dressed as monks and performed at temple festivals.
Iemoto	The leader of a Noh "school" who owns all masks, costumes and properties of the company and decides which plays shall be performed and by whom and which masks may be used. He is also responsible for financial matters, ranking of performers and awarding diplomas.
jo-ha-kyû	Beginning-development-climax; a term applied to the structure of a Noh play, the ordering of a Noh programme or the elements of a Noh performance.
kagami-no-ma	Mirror room; place adjacent to the Noh stage with a large mirror where the leading actor makes his final preparations and dons his mask.
kagura	Entertainment performed for the visiting spirits in Shinto religious festivals.
kakaru	Recitative form of Noh chant used in conversational scenes.
kakegoe	The cries of the drummers who accompany Noh drama, thought to be based upon ancient ritual calls summoning the gods.
kamae	Noh posture with knees bent, lumbar spine tilted to thrust the abdomen slightly forward and arms held in a strong, slightly bowed position a few inches from the sides.
kamakura	Pillar on which the visiting *kami* are believed to alight to watch entertainment during a Shinto religious festival.
kamen	Original word used to designate a mask meaning "substitute or provisional face".

kami	Gods or spirits of people, animals, plants, objects or places; the objects of worship in Shinto.
kamigakari	Divine trance-possession, which may be part of the entertainment of the *kami* in Shinto religious festivals.
kata	"Form" or "pattern" of movement in traditional performance, including both gestures and dance movements or patterns.
katazuke	Secret choreographic manuals of movement, gestures and dances passed down through families of Noh performers.
kiri-do	Low door on the stage left side of a Noh stage through which the chorus and attendants enter and exit.
kiru	Quick side-to-side movements of the mask.
koan	A kind of riddle used as a concentration device in Zen Buddhist meditation.
kogaki	Variant performance of a Noh play in which some aspect of staging, costume or text is different from standard practice.
kokata	Child player in Noh.
koken	Stage assistant in Noh, always a performer of equivalent rank to the performer whom he assists.
kokoro	"Heart"; the inner emotional/spiritual core; the actor's consciousness.
kotsuzumi	Drum held against the shoulder played as part of the ensemble that accompanies Noh performances.
kumorasu	"Clouded"; downward inclination of a Noh mask indicating sorrow.

Kyôgen	Literally "wild words"; a comic theatre tradition which developed with Noh and continues to be performed in conjunction with Noh plays either as an interlude between acts of a single Noh drama or as separate plays between Noh dramas in a full programme.
matsuri	Shinto religious festival, literally "service to the *kami*".
metsuke bashira	"Sighting pillar"; downstage right used by the main masked actor to orient himself on a Noh stage.
michiyuki	Travelling song.
miko	Shinto priestess/medium.
mokuzen-shingo	"Eyes in front, mind behind"; a technique in which the Noh performer strives simultaneously to see in front of himself while imagining his appearance from behind and the side.
monomane	"Imitation"; the term is made up of the elements *mono*, meaning "things", *ma*, meaning "pure" or "true" and *ne*, meaning "resemble", thus: resembling the real thing.
nô-butai	Noh stage.
omote	Term for mask, meaning "front" or "face", which replaced the earlier word *kamen;* made up of the elements *omo*, meaning "recollect" and *te,* meaning "from all directions".
Oni	Demon
Oni Daiko	Literally "demon drum": a folk mask tradition featuring a performer in an *Oni* mask who performs a frenzied dance while beating on a large drum. Probably once a trance dance, it is now performed as an entertainment.
oshirabe	Musical "warm-up" or introductory music played backstage before the beginning of a Noh play.

Oto	Comic female mask used in Kyôgen and folk performances, possibly based on earlier Shinto ritual masks of the dancing goddess *Ama no Uzume*.
otsuzumi	Knee drum played as part of the musical ensemble that accompanies Noh performances.
riken-no-ken	"Objective judgements"; a concept which requires the Noh performer to imagine his performance from the outside, from the perspective of the audience.
sake	Rice wine.
sangaku	Entertainments imported to Japan from the Chinese mainland including acrobatics, juggling and magic acts.
sanjo	Special ghetto reserved for outcasts of Japanese society, particularly during the medieval period. Those who were consigned to the *sanjo* included entertainers, prostitutes, butchers and undertakers.
sarugaku	"Monkey Music"; a medieval performance genre popular in both the provinces and the court, probably not unlike *dengaku*. *Sarugaku-no* was the precursor of contemporary Noh drama.
Shi-shi	Large mask of a mythical animal most frequently characterised as a lion or dog, which derives from ancient folk tradition and associated with ritual purification. The mask resembles the "Chinese Dragon" and is the model for masks in later genres of Gigaku, Noh and Kabuki.
shidai	Introductory music and song in a Noh play.
shite	The main character or leading actor who plays the central role in Noh drama.
suri ashi	"Sliding step"; unique Noh walk in which the whole foot slides along the floor, raising the toes slightly at the end of each step.

taiko	The largest drum of the Noh musical ensemble played with two sticks.
takigi	Torchlight, "Takigi Noh" is Noh drama performed by torchlight.
Tengu	Goblin.
terasu	"Shining"—tilting a Noh mask upward to indicate joy or happiness; to make the Noh mask "smile".
tsure	"Companion" to the shite or waki.
utai, utai-bon	Noh chant; books of Noh chant with rhythmic markings.
utushi-men	Copies of *honmen,* the model masks of the old masters.
waki	The "witness" or secondary character in Noh drama.
Yamabushi priests	Ascetics associated with an indigenous mountain worship who frequently entertained at Shinto festivals. In several Noh plays goblins appear in the guise of *Yamabushi* priests.
yûgen	A profound grace, mysterious elegance.

Works Consulted

Books
Albery, Nobuko. *The House of Kanzê: A Saga of Fourteenth Century Japan*. London: Century Publishing, 1985.
Appel, Libby. *Mask Characterization: An Acting Process*. Carbondale: Southern Illinois University Press, 1982.
Archer, William. *Masks or Faces?* New York: Hill and Wang, 1957.
Artaud, Antonin. *The Theatre and Its Double*. Translated by Mary Caroline Richards. New York: Grove Press, 1958.
Austin, James H., MD. *Zen and the Brain: Toward an Understanding of Meditation and Consciousness*. Cambridge Massachusetts and London, England: The MIT Press, 1998.
'Babad Dalem Sidakarya'. Unpublished document, translated into Indonesian from the sacred Balinese Lontar, 1992.
Bablet, Denis. *The Theatre of Edward Gordon Craig*. Translated by Daphne Woodward. London: Eyre Methuen, 1981.
Ballinger, Rucina. 'Dance in Bali: The Passing on of a Tradition'. *Dance as a Cultural Heritage*, Vol. 2, edited by Betty True Jones. Selected Papers from the ADG-CORD Conference 1978. New York: Congress on Research in Dance, 1985.
Bandem, I Made and Fredrik de Boer. *Balinese Dance in Transition: Kaja and Kelod*. Kuala Lumpur: Oxford University Press, 1995 [1981].
Bandem, I Made and Emigh, John. 'Jelantik Goes to Blambangan: A Topeng Pajegan Performance by I Nyoman Kakul (as recorded at Tusan, Klungkung, Bali on February 6, 1975)' *The Drama Review,* 23, number 2, June 1979, pp. 37–48.
Barba, E. and Savarese, N. *A Dictionary of Theatre Anthropology: The Secret Art of the Performer*. London: Routledge for the Centre of Performance Research, 1991, pp. 74–88.
Barth, Fredrik. *Balinese Worlds*. Chicago and London: The University of Chicago Press, 1993.

Barthes, Roland. *Empire of Signs*. Translated by Richard Howard. London: Jonathan Cape, 1983 [1982].
Bateson, Gregory and Mead, Margaret. *Balinese Character: A Photographic Analysis*. New York: New York Academy of Sciences, 1942.
Belo, Jane. 1949 *Rangda and Barong* (Monographs of the American Ethnological Society). New York: J. J. Augustin.
——1960 *Trance in Bali*. New York: Columbia University Press.
——1970 *Traditional Balinese Culture*. New York: Columbia University Press.
Bharucha, Rustom. *Theatre and the World*. London and New York: Routledge, 1993.
Bloch, Susanna. 'ALBA EMOTING: A Psychophysiological Technique to Help Actors Create and Control Real Emotions' *Theatre Topics* Vol. 3, number 2, September, 1993, pp. 121–138.
Bourguignon, Erica (editor). *Religion, Altered States of Consciousness, and Social Change*. Columbus: Ohio University Press, 1973.
Brandon, James (editor). 1997 *The Cambridge Guide to Asian Theatre*. Cambridge: Cambridge University Press.
——1997 *Nô and Kyôgen in the Contemporary World*. Honolulu: University of Hawaii Press.
Brandon, James 1993 'Performance Training in Japanese Nô and Kyôgen at the University of Hawaii' *Theatre Topics* Vol. 3, number 2, pp. 101–120.
——1991 'The Place of Nô in World Theater'. *Nô: Its Transmission and Regeneration. International Symposium on the Conservation and Restoration of Cultural Property*. Tokyo: National Research Institute of Cultural Properties, pp. 11–15.
Catra, I Nyoman. *Topeng: Mask Dance-Drama as a Reflection of Balinese Culture; A Case Study in Topeng/Prembon*. (Unpublished Master's thesis) Boston, Massachusetts: Emerson College, 1996.
Coast, John. *Dancing Out of Bali*. London: Faber, 1954.
Cole, Toby. *Playwrights on Playwrighting*. New York: Hill and Wang, 1960.
Comaraswamy, Ananda K. *Hindus and Buddhists*. London: Senate, Studio Editions 1994.
Covarrubias, Miguel. *Island of Bali*. Kuala Lumpur, Singapore, Djakarta: Oxford University Press/P.T. Indira, 1972.
Craig, Edward Gordon. *On The Art of the Theatre*. London: William Heinemann, Ltd., 1911.
Csikszentmihalyi, Mihalyi. *Beyond Boredom and Anxiety*. San Francisco: Jossey-Bass, 1975.
Daniel, Ana. *Bali Behind the Mask*. New York: Alfred A. Knopf, 1981.
De Marinis, Marco 'The Mask and Corporeal Expression in 20th-Century Theatre'. Translated by Betsy K. Emerick in *Incorporated Knowledge* (*Mime Journal* 1995) edited by Thomas Leabhart. Claremont, CA: Pomona College, pp. 14–37.

De Vale, Sue Carole. 'Symbolism in Design and Morphology of Gamelan in Java'. *Essays on Southeast Asian Performing Arts: Local Manifestations and Cross Cultural Implications.* Kathy Foley, editor. Berkeley: University of California Center for Southeast Asia Studies, 1992, pp. 54–95.

De Zoete, Beryl and Walter Spies. *Dance and Drama in Bali.* London: Faber and Faber, 1938.

Dibya, I Wayan, 1995 'Nopeng atau Napel dalam Seni Patopengan Bali'. *WRETA Cita*, Nomor 4, 11 Juni, pp. 2–3.

——1996 *Kecak: The Vocal Chant of Bali*, Denpasar, Bali: Hartanto Art Books.

Diderot, Denis. *The Paradox of Acting.* Translated by Walter Herries Pollock. New York: Hill and Wang, 1957.

Dumoulin, Heinrich. *Understanding Buddhism: Key Themes.* New York and Tokyo: Weatherhill, 1994.

Dunn, Charles. 'Religion and Japanese Drama.' *Drama and Religion. Themes in Drama 5.* Translated by Joseph S. O'Leary. James Redmond, editor. Cambridge: Cambridge University Press, 1983, pp. 225–237.

Dunn, Deborah. *Topeng Pajegan: The Mask Dance of Bali.* (PhD dissertation, 1983) Ann Arbor: University Microfilms International, 1987.

Eisman, Fred B. 1990a *Bali: Sekala and Niskala (Vol. 1: Essays on Religion and Art).* Singapore: Periplus Editions.

——1990b *Bali: Sekala and Niskala (Vol. 2: Essays on Society, Tradition and Craft).* Singapore: Periplus Editions.

——1997a *Balinese-English Dictionary*, second edition. Jimbaran, Bali: Fred B. Eiseman.

——1997b *English-Balinese Dictionary*, second edition. Jimbaran, Bali: Fred B. Eiseman.

Eldredge, Sears. 1975 *Masks: Their Use and Effectiveness in Actor Training Programs* (PhD dissertation, Michigan State University). Ann Arbor, Michigan: University Microfilms International.

——1996 *Mask Improvisation for Actor Training and Performance: The Compelling Image.* Evanston, Ill : Northwestern University Press.

Emigh, John. 1979 'Playing with the Past: Visitation and Illusion in the Mask Theatre of Bali'. *The Drama Review* 23, number 2, pp. 11–36.

——1996 *Masked Performance: The Play of Self and Other in Ritual and Theatre.* Philadelphia: University of Pennsylvania Press.

Emmert, Richard. 'Nô in English: Nô's Contemporaneity and Universality'. *Nô: its Transmission and Regeneration. International Symposium on the Conservation and Restoration of Cultural Property.* Tokyo: National Research Institute of Cultural Properties, 1991, pp. 165–169.

Ernst, Earle. 'The Influence of Japanese Theatrical Style on Western Theatre'. *Educational Theatre Journal* 21, number 2, May 1969, pp. 127–138.

Foley, Kathy. 'Artaud, Spies and Indonesian/American Artistic Exchange and Collaboration'. *Modern Drama* 35, number 1, March 1992, pp. 10–19.

Geertz, Clifford. 1959 'Form and Variation in Balinese Village Structure'. *American Anthropologist.* Vol. 61, pp. 991–1012.

——1973 *The Interpretation of Cultures*, New York: Basic Books.
——1980 *Negara: The Theatre State in Nineteenth Century Bali.* Princeton, New Jersey: Princeton University Press.
Geertz, Hildred. 'A Theatre of Cruelty: The Contexts of a Topeng performance'. *State and Society in Bali: Historical, Textual and Anthropological Approaches.* Leiden: KITLV Press, 1991.
George, David E. R. 1992 'Performance as Paradigm: the Example of Bali'. *Modern Drama* 35, number 1, March pp. 1–9.
——1991 *Balinese Ritual Theatre.* Theatre in Focus Series. Cambridge and Alexandria, Virginia: Chadwyck Healy, 1991.
——1989 'The Tempest in Bali'. *Performing Arts Journal*, 33/34, Vol. XI number 3/Vol. XII, number 1, pp. 84–107.
Goodman, Felicitas D. 1990 A Trance Dance with Masks: Research and Performance at the Cuyamungue Institute'. *The Drama Review*, Vol. 34, number 1, p. 105.
——1990 *Where Spirits Ride the Wind: Trance Experiences and Other Ecstatic Experiences.* Bloomington and Indianapolis: Indiana University Press.
Grimes, Ronald L. 1982 *Beginnings in Ritual Studies.* Boston: University Press of America.
——1992 'The Life History of a Mask'. *The Drama Review* 36, number 3, pp. 64–70.
Haga, Hideo and Dr. Gordon Warner. *Japanese Festivals.* Osaka: Hoikusha Publishing Co., Ltd., 1970.
Harding, Francis. 'Actor and Character in African Masquerade Performance'. *Theatre Research International* 21, number 1, Spring 1996, pp. 59–71.
Hare, Thomas Blenman. *Zeami's Style: The Noh Plays of Zeami Motokiyo.* Stanford California: Stanford University Press, 1986.
Herbst, Edward. 1992 *Voices, Energies and Perceptions in Balinese Performance.* (PhD dissertation, 1990) Ann Arbor: University Microfilms International.
——1997 *Voices in Bali: Energies and Perceptions in Vocal Music and Dance Theater.* Hanover and London: Wesleyan University Press.
Hobart, Angela, Urs Ramseyer, Albert Leemann. *The Peoples of Bali.* Oxford: Blackwell, 1996.
Hookyas, C. *Religion in Bali.* Leiden: E.J. Brill, 1973.
Hunter, Thomas M., Jr. 'Desa-Kala-Patra: Space, Time and Person in Bali'. *Balinese Traditions, Balinese Dilemmas, an LCS Reader, Volume I.* Unpublished manuscript: Thomas M. Hunter, 1996.
Immoos, Thomas. *Japanese Theatre.* Translated by Hugh Young. London: Cassell and Collier Macmillan Publishers Ltd., 1977.
Innes, Christopher. *Directors in Perspective: Edward Gordon Craig.* Cambridge: Cambridge University Press, 1983.
Jenkins, Ron. 1978 'Topeng: Balinese Dance Drama'. *Performing Arts Journal,* Fall 1978, pp. 39–52.
——1979 'Becoming a Clown in Bali'. *The Drama Review* 23, number 2, pp. 49–56.

Johnson, Martha. 'Reflections of Inner Life: Masks and Masked Acting in Ancient Greek Tragedy and Japanese Noh Drama'. *Modern Drama* 35, number 1, March 1992, pp. 20–34.
Johnstone, Keith. *Impro: Improvisation and the Theatre*. London: Methuen, 1981.
Keene, Donald 1966 *Nô: The Classical Theatre of Japan*. Tokyo and Palo Alto: Kodansha International, Ltd.
——1970 *Twenty Plays of the Nô Theatre* (editor and translator). New York: Columbia University Press.
Kirby, E. T. 1972 'The Mask: Abstract Theatre Primitive and Modern'. *The Drama Review* 16, number 3, September, pp. 5–21.
——1975 *Ur-Drama: The Origins of Theatre*. New York: New York University Press.
Kiyota, Minoru. *Kendô: The History and Means to Personal Growth*. New York: Kegan Paul International, 1995.
Knappert, Jan. *Indian Mythology: An Encyclopedia of Myth and Legend*. London: Diamond Books, 1995.
Komparu, Kunio. *The Noh Theatre, Principles and Perspectives*. New York, Tokyo and Kyoto: Weatherhill/Tankosha, 1983.
Lansing, J. Stephen. 1977 *Rama's Kingdoms: Social Supportive Mechanisms for the Arts in Bali*. PhD dissertation, Ann Arbor, Michigan: University Microfilms International.
——1995 *The Balinese*. San Diego: Harcourt Brace College Publishers.
Laughlin, Charles D. and Eugene d'Aquili (editors). *The Spectrum of Ritual: A Biogenic Structural Analysis*. New York: Columbia University Press, 1979.
Laughlin, Charles D., Eugene d'Aquili, John McManus. *Brain, Symbol and Experience: Towards a Phenomenology of Consciousness*. Boston and Shaftsbury: New Science Library Shambhala, 1990.
Laughlin, Charles D. and Judi Young-Laughlin. 'How Masks Work, or Masks Work How?'. *Journal of Ritual Studies*, 2/1, 1988, pp. 59–86.
Lendra, I Wayan. 'Bali and Growtowski: Some Parallels in the Training Process'. *The Drama Review*, 35, number 1, Spring 1991, pp. 113–128.
Lévi-Strauss, Claude. *The Way of the Masks*. Translated by Sylvia Modelski. Seattle: University of Washington Press, 1982.
Lewis, I. M. *Ecstatic Religion: A Study of Shamanism and Spirit Possession* 2nd edition. London and New York: Routledge, 1989.
Lex, Barbara W. 'The Neurobiology of Ritual Trance'. *The Spectrum of Ritual*, Eugene d'Aquili and Charles D. Laughlin, editors. New York: Columbia University Press, 1979 pp. 117–151.
Lommel, Andreas. *Masks: Their Meaning and Function*. Translated by Nadia Fowler. London: Ferndale Editions, 1981.
Lovric, Barbara. *Rhetoric and Reality: The Hidden Nightmare. Myth and Magic as Representations and Reverberations of Morbid Realities*. Unpublished PhD dissertation, University of Sydney, 1987.
Lucas, Heinz. *Japanische Kultmasken: Der Tanz der Kraniche*. Kassel: IM Erich Röth-Verlag, 1965.

McPhee, Colin. *A House in Bali.* London: Victor Gollancz, Ltd., 1947.
Mack, John (editor). *Masks: The Art of Expression.* London: British Museum Press, 1994.
Maruoka, Daiji and Tatsuo Yoshikoshi. *Noh.* Translated by Don Kenny. Osaka: Hoikusha Publishing Co. Ltd., 1969.
Mason, Anthony and Goulden, Felicity with Richard Overton. *Bali.* London: Cadogan Books, 1989.
Mason, R.H.P. and J.G. Caiger. *The History of Japan* (Revised edition). [1973] Singapore: Charles E. Tuttle Company, Inc., 1997.
Mead, Margaret. *Letters from the Field 1925–1975.* Ruth Nanda Ashen, editor. New York: Harper and Row, 1977.
Masselos, Jim, Jackie Menzies and Pratapaditya Pal. *Music and Dance in Indian Art.* Sydney: The Art Gallery of New South Wales, 1997.
Merittinen, Jukka O. *Classical Dance and Theatre in South-East Asia.* Singapore: Oxford University Press, 1992.
Mershon, Katharine Edson. *Seven Plus Seven: Mysterious Life-Rituals in Bali.* New York: Vantage Press, 1971.
Meyer-Dinkgräfe, Daniel. *Consciousness and the Actor.* European University Studies; Series 30, Theatre, Film and Television; Vol. 67. Frankfurt am Main: Peter Lang, 1996.
Moerdowo, R.M. *Ceremonies in Bali.* Jakarta: Bhrataru, 1973.
Nakamori, Shozô and Akira Iwata (photographs). *Nô: Design Aesthetics.* Osaka: Toho Shuppan, 1995.
Nakanishi, Toru and Komma, Kiyonori. *Noh Masks.* Translated by Don Kenny. Osaka: Hoikusha Publishing Company, 1983.
Napier, A. David. *Masks, Transformation and Paradox.* London: University of California Press, 1986.
Nearman, Mark J. 1978 'Zeami's *Kyûi:* A Pedagogical Guide for Teachers of Acting'. *Monumenta Nipponica* 33.3 pp. 299–332.
——1980 '*Kyakaraika:* Zeami's Final Legacy for the Master Actor'. *Monumenta Nipponica* 35.2, pp. 153–197.
——1982 '*Kakyô*: Zeami's Fundamental Principals of Acting'. *Monumenta Nipponica* 37.3, pp. 333–374 and 1983, 38, 1, pp. 49–71.
Nishikawa, Kyôtarô. *Bugaku Masks.* Translated by Monica Bethe. Tokyo and New York: Kodansha International Ltd. and Shibundo, 1978.
Nogami, Toyoichirô. *Zeami and His Theories on Nô.* Translated by Ryôzô Matsumoto. Tokyo: Tsunetarô, Hinoki Shoten, 1973.
Noh Masks from the Negoro-Ji Collection: 1996 Exhibition Catalogue. Tokyo: National Noh Theatre, 1996.
Nosco, Peter (editor). *Confucianism and Tokugawa Culture.* Honolulu: University of Hawaii Press, 1997.
Nunley, John and Cara McCarty. *Masks: Faces of Culture.* New York: Harry N. Abrams Inc., 1999.
O'Neill, P. G. 1953 *A Guide to Nô.* Tokyo: Hinoki Shoten.
——1958 *Early Nô Drama.* London: Lund Humphries.

——1974 'The Nô Schools and their Organisation'. *Bulletin*, 73, London: Japan Society of London, pp. 2–7.
Ono, Dr. Sokyo and William P. Woodard. *Shinto: The Kami Way*. Rutland, Vermont and Tokyo, Japan: Charles E. Tuttle Company, 1962.
Ornstein, Robert E. *The Nature of Human Consciousness*. San Francisco: W.H. Freeman and Company, 1973.
Ortolani, Benito. *The Japanese Theatre: From Shamanistic Ritual to Contemporary Pluralism*. (Revised edition. Princeton, NJ: Princeton University Press, 1995.
Otto, Rudolf. *The Idea of the Holy: An Inquiry into the Non-Rational Factor in the Idea of the Divine and Its Relation to the Rational*. Translated by John W. Harvey. London: Oxford University Press, 1950.
Oxford English Dictionary. 2nd edition. J. A. Simpson and E.S.C. Weiner, editors. Oxford: Clarendon Press, 1989.
Pernet, Henry. *Ritual Masks: Deceptions and Revelations*. Translated by Laura Grillo. Columbia, South Carolina: University of South Carolina Press, 1992.
Picard, Michel. 1990 'Cultural Tourism in Bali: Cultural Performance as Tourist Attraction'. *Indonesia* (number 49, April 1990) Cornell: Cornell Southeast Asia Program, pp. 37–74.
——1996 *Bali: Cultural Tourism and Touristic Culture*. Translated by Diana Darling. Singapore: Archipelago Press.
Pilgrim, Richard B. 'Some Aspects of *kokoro* in Zeami'. *Monumenta Nipponica* 24, 4, pp. 393–401.
Plowright, Poh Sim. *The Classical Noh Theatre of Japan*. London: Chadwyck-Healey, Ltd., 1991.
Pound, Ezra and Fennollosa, Ernest. *The Classic Noh Theatre of Japan*. [1917].New York: New Directions, 1959.
Pollman, Tessel. 'Margaret Mead's Balinese: The Fitting Symbols of the American Dream'. *Indonesia* (number 49, April 1990) Cornell: Cornell Southeast Asia Program.
de Poorter, Erika. *Zeami's Talks on Sarugaku*. Amsterdam: J.C. Gieben, 1986.
Price, Raymond (editor). *Trance and Possession States: Proceedings of the Second Annual Conference of the R.M. Bucke Memorial Society*. Montreal: R.M. Bucke Memorial Society, 1968.
Pulvers, Solrun Hoass. 1978 *The Noh Mask and the Mask Making Tradition*. Unpublished PhD dissertation, Australian National University.
——1982 'Noh Masks: A Legacy of Possession'. *The Drama Review* 26, 4, pp. 82–6.
Quamba, Akhtar. *Yeats and the Noh*. New York: Weatherhill, 1974.
Reynolds, Peter. *Unmasking Oedipus*. London: Royal National Theatre Publications and NT Education, 1996.
Rix, Roxanne. 'Comments on Process: ALBA EMOTING: A Preliminary Experiment with Emotional Effector Patterns. *Theatre Topics* Vol. 3, number 2, September, 1993, pp. 139–145.
Robinson, Geoffrey. *The Dark Side of Paradise*. Ithaca: Cornell University Press, 1995.

Rodowicz, Jadwiga. 'Rethinking Zeami: Talking to Kanze Tetsunojo'. *The Drama Review*, 36, number 2, Summer 1992, pp. 97–104.
Roederer, Juan G. *Introduction to the Physics and Psychophysics of Music*, second edition. Heidelberg Science Library, v. 16. New York: Springer-Verlag, 1975.
Rolfe, Bari.*Behind the Mask.* San Francisco: Persona Products, 1977.
Rouget, Gilbert. *Music and Trance: A Theory of the Relations between Music and Possession*. Translated by Brunhilde Biebuyck. Chicago and London: The University of Chicago Press, 1980.
Rudlin, John and Paul, Norman H. (editors) *Copeau: Texts on Theatre*. London: Routledge, 1990.
Saint-Denis, Michel. *Training for the Theatre,* edited by Suria Saint-Denis. London: Heinemann, 1982.
Scambler, Graham. *Epilepsy.* The Experience of Illness Series. London: Routledge, 1989.
Schechner, Richard. 1985 *Between Theatre and Anthropology*. Philadelphia: University of Pennsylvania Press.
——1988 *Performance Theory*. London: Routledge.
——1993 *The Future of Ritual: Writings on Culture and Performance*. London: Routledge.
Schechner, Richard and Willa Appel, editors. *By Means of Performance: Intercultural Studies of Theatre and Ritual*. Cambridge: Cambridge University Press, 1990.
Sekine, Masaru. *Ze-Ami and his Theories of Noh Drama*. Gerrards Cross: Colin Smythe, 1985.
Sekine, Masaru and Christopher Murray et al. *Yeats and the Noh: A Comparative Study*. Gerrards Cross: Colin Smythe, 1990.
Sellin, Eric. *The Dramatic Concepts of Antonin Artaud*. London: University of Chicago Press, 1968.
Shimazaki, Chifumi. *The Noh, Volume II: Battle Noh*, Tokyo: Hinoki Shoten, 1987.
Slattum, Judy. *Masks of Bali: Spirits of an Ancient Drama*. San Francisco: Chronicle Books, 1993.
Smith, Susan Harris. *Masks in Modern Drama*. London: University of California Press, 1984.
Snow, Steven. 1983 'Rangda: Archetype in Action in Balinese Dance-Drama'. *Drama and Religion. Themes in Drama 5.* James Redmond, editor. Cambridge: Cambridge University Press, pp. 273–291.
——1986 'Intercultural Performance: The Balinese American Model'. *Asian Theatre Journal*. Vol. 3, number 2, pp. 204–232.
Sorell, Walter. *The Other Face: The Mask in the Arts*. London: Thames and Hudson, 1973.
Stutterheim, W. F. *Indian Influences in Old Javanese Art*. London: The India Society, 1935.

Suradnya, I Nyoman. *Karya Agung Penyegjeg Bumi, Memungkah, Ngenteg Linggih, Tawur Agung Pedanan, Ngusaba Desa lan Ngusaba Nini*. Ubud, Bali: CW Printing, 1997.
Suriyani, Luh Ketut and Jensen, Gordon D. 1992 *The Balinese People: A Reinvestigation of Character*. Singapore: Oxford University Press.
——1993 *Trance and Possession in Bali: A Window on Western Multiple Personality Possession Disorder and Suicide*. Kuala Lumpur: Oxford University Press.
Swellengrebel, J.L. *Bali: Studies in Life, Thought and Ritual*. W. F. Wertheim et. al., editors. The Hague and Bandung: W. Van Hoeve, 1960.
Takayama, Shigeru. 'A Study of a Noh Play 'Okina': Its Early Aspects and 'Tototarari' *Progress Reports in Ethnomusicology*, Vol. 1, number 5. Baltimore, Maryland: SEMPOD Laboratory, Department of Music. 1984.
Teele, Rebecca (editor). *Nô/Kyôgen Masks in Performance*. Mime Journal, number 10. Claremont, CA: Pomona College, 1984.
Tenzer, Michael. *Balinese Music*. Singapore: Periplus Editions, 1991.
Thong, Denny. *A Psychiatrist in Paradise: Treating Mental Illness in Bali*. Translated by Bruce Carpenter. Bangkok: White Lotus, 1993.
Thornbury, Barbara E. *The Folk Performing Arts: Traditional Culture in Contemporary Japan*. Albany: State University of New York Press, 1997.
Thornhill, Arthur H. III. *Six Circles, One Dewdrop: The Religio-Aesthetic World of Komparu Zenchiku*. Princeton, N. J.: Princeton University Press, 1993.
Turner, Victor. *From Ritual to Theatre*. New York: Performing Arts Journal Publications, 1982.
Tyler, Royall (editor and translator). *Japanese Nô Dramas*. London: Penguin, 1992.
Umewaka, Naohiko. 1992'The Inner World of the Noh'. *Contemporary Theatre Review 1992*. Vol. 1, pp. 29–38
——1994 *The Inner World of the Noh: The Influence of Esoteric Concepts on the Classical Theatre of Japan, as Evidenced Through an Analysis of the Choreographic Manuals of the Umewaka Family*. Unpublished PhD dissertation, Royal Holloway College.
Underwood, Geoffrey and Robin Stevens, editors. *Aspects of Consciousness*. Vol. 1: *Psychological Issues*. London: Academic Press, Inc., 1979.
Underwood, Geoffrey, editor. *Aspects of Consciousness*. Vol. 3: Awareness and Self-Awareness. London: Academic Press, 1982.
Varley, Paul H. *Japanese Culture* 3rd edition. Honolulu: University of Hawaii Press, 1984.
Vickers, Adrian. *Bali: A Paradise Created*. Hong Kong: Periplus Editions, 1996 (1990).
Wavell, Stewart (editor) with Audrey Butts and Nina Epton. *Trances*. London: George Allen and Unwin Ltd., 1966.
Willett, John. *The Theatre of Bertolt Brecht*. Rev. ed. London: Methuen, 1977.
Winnicott, D.W. 1971 *Playing and Reality*. London: Tavistock Publications.
——1975 *Through Pediatrics to Psycho-Analysis*. London: Hogarth.

Yamazaki, Masakazu. 'The Aesthetics of Transformation: Zeami's Dramatic Theories'. Translated by Susan Matisoff. *Journal of Japanese Studies* Summer, 1981, pp. 218–257.

Yasuda, Kenneth. *Masterworks of the Nô Theatre*. Bloomington and Indianapolis: Indiana University Press, 1989.

Young, Elizabeth F. *Topeng in Bali: Change and Continuity in a Traditional Drama Genre*. (PhD dissertation, University of California at San Diego, 1980) Ann Arbor: University Microfilms International, 1980.

Yousef, Ghulam-Sar War. *Dictionary of Traditional South-East Asian Theatre*. Kuala Lumpur: Oxford University Press, 1994.

Yusa, Michiko. '*Riken no ken:* Zeami's Theory of Acting and Theatrical Appreciation'. *Monumenta Nipponica* 42.3, pp. 331–345.

Zarrilli, Phillip B. 1988 'For Whom is the 'Invisible' not Visible? Reflections on Representation in the Work of Eugenio Barba'. *The Drama Review* Vol. 32, number 1, Spring pp. 102–110.

—— 1995 (editor) *Acting (Re)Considered*. London and New York: Routledge.

—— 1999 'Negotiating Performance Epistemologies: Knowledges "about", "in", and "for"'. Plenary address to PS 5 Performance Studies Conference, University of Wales, Aberystwyth. 10 April, 1999.

Zeami. *Kadensho* Translated by Chûhie Sakurrai, Shûseki Hayashi, Rokurô Satoi, Bin Miyari. Kyoto: Foundation of Sumiya-Shinobe Scholarship, 1970.

Zeami. *On the Art of Noh Drama: The Major Treatises of Zeami*. Translated by J. Thomas Rimer and Yamazaki Masakazu. Princeton NJ: Princeton University Press, 1984.

Zurbuchen, Mary. *The Language of Balinese Shadow Theatre*. Princeton, New Jersey: Princeton University Press, 1987.

Films

Acting Techniques of Topeng. Directed by Larry McMullen. Performed by John Emigh. Department of Theatre, Michigan State University in association with Instructional and Public Television, Michigan State University. 1980.

Adapting Topeng, the Masked Theatre of Bali. Directed by Larry McMullen. Performed by John Emigh. Department of Theatre, Michigan State University in association with Instructional and Public Television, Michigan State University. 1980.

Bali Beyond the Postcard. Executive producer, Nancy Dine. Produced by Peggy Stern. David Dawkins, cinematographer. Filmmakers Library. 1991.

'The Heart: A Supple Pump System'. Written and directed by Masakatsu Takao, produced by Katsuhiko Hayashi and Bo G. Erikson, from the NHK science documentary series *The Universe Within*. 1989.

Taksu: Music in the Life of Bali. Directed by Jann Paster. UCLA Extension Center for Media and Independent Learning. 1991.

Tari-Tarian Tradisional di Bali. Film Forms International, Singapadu, [Bali] 1975.

Trance and Ritual in Bali. BBC, distributed by Xerox Films. 1972.

Index

Airlangga. *See* Erlangga
Alit, Ida Bagus, 70, 94, 99, 170, 171, 172, 175, 176, 177, 178, 179, 180, 181, 182, 184, 185, 186, 187, 188, 192, 196, 199, 315
Ama no Uzume, 104, 113
Amaterasu, 113, 115, 117, 129n75
Anom, Ida Bagus, 70n58, 90n111, 92, 94, 99, 192, 196–97
Aoi no Ue, 137
Appel, Libby, 26, 28
Artaud, Antonin, 12–13
Austin, James H., 321–22
automaticity, 156, 238, 297–98

Babad, 68, 179
Badung Regency, Bali, 53, 56
Bali:
   calendar, 58, 79
   history and culture, 49–57
   masked drama, 7, 18, 59–62, 65–69
   religion, 57–62, 75. *See also*
   Buddhism in
Balian Batur, 209, 225, 228
Banaspati Raja, 204–206, 211
Bandem, I Madé, 22, 70, 71, 76, 91, 92, 95, 179, 181, 197, 208,
Barba, Eugenio, 17, 21
Baris, 86, 87, 220, 228
Barong, 22, 55, 66,67, 72, 74–78, 80, 82, 84, 85, 86, 87, 95, 96, 103, 104, 109, 170, 201, 228, 230, 231, 307, 316
   and trance, 206 200–201
   compared to *Shi-Shi*, 103
   costume, 212, 247-250
   mask, 78–84, 201–209, 210–12
   performance, 219–21
   performers, 213–14, 229, 238
Bateson, Gregory, 21, 201, 204
Batubulan, 208 237
   "Barong Dance", 216
Belo, Jane, 21, 72, 74, 75, 88, 95, 201, 202, 203, 204, 229, 231, 236, 303
Bethe, Monica, 22, 105, 284
Bharucha, Rustom, 34
Bhoma, 103, 203, 212
Blahbatuh:
   masks, 66
Bloch, Susannah, 47
Bona
   Rangda masks, 202, 238
   Village, Bali, 210, 218
Brahmana Kling or Keling, 70
Brecht, Bertolt, 4
Brook, Peter, 17
Buddha, 113, 123, 125, 243, 253, 258
   Dainichi, 125
Buddhism, 115, 122–27, 139, 203, 261
   "esoteric" (Shingon), 123, 124–25, 127, 139, 156, 261
   "sixty-six entertainments", 113
   and *Gigaku*, 108, 116
   and images, 139
   and Noh, 117–18 156, 203

and Noh masks, 219
and Shinto, 127
in Bali, 70–71, 75, 90n111, 124–25, 185
in *Kiyotsune*, 242, 258
in *Tôru*, 292
satori, 282
terminology and Noh, 157, 294
Zen, 7, 22, 116, 125–27, 128, 153, 154, 266, 287, 321
and Shingon, 123, 127, 261
Bugaku, 108, 116, 119

Calonarang, 72–75, 202–203
Caste
in Bali, 62, 63–65
in Balinese dance-drama, 62–65, 180, 182
in Japan
the sanjo, 110–12
Catra, I Nyoman, 17, 90, 195, 216
Celuluk
Leyak mask, 224. *See also* Leyak
Cokorda Gde Api, of Singapadu, 211
Commedia dell'Arte, 3
consciousness, 127
altered states of (ASC), 2, 16, 45, 46, 127, 156, 157, 165, 166, 192, 200, 214, 229, 231, 235, 238, 283, 287, 288, 289, 290–94
and music, 200
and ritual, 293–96
and the actor, 17–19, 20, 23, 27, 35–40, 156, 165, 231, 238, 290–94, 317
fragmentation of, 297
in Vedic psychology, 36, 43
kokoro, 165–8, 249
mushin, 42, 287, 293
riken no ken, 42, 44, 282, 283, 285, 298, 300
Copeau, Jacques, 13–16, 26, 27, 48
Craig, Edward Gordon, 10–12, 13, 14, 44, 160, 249

Cupak, 209

d'Aquili, Eugene, 35, 46, 290, 293
Daniel, Ana, 21, 93
Decroux, Etienne, 16
dengaku, 108–10
Dibia, I Wayan, 194, 195, 197, 213, 230, 231, 232, 233
dissociation, 19, 40, 69, 157, 193, 238, 239, 266, 273, 297, 298, 300, 310, 317
Djimat, I Madé, 179, 198, 233, 236–38, 305
Dôjôji, 285, 303, 305
Dorcy, Jean, 16
driving elements, 239, 283, 307–308
Dunn, Deborah, 22, 64, 86, 91, 97, 98, 177, 183
Durga, 75, 79, 201–202, 206, 219. *See also* Uma Dewi

Edo. *See* Tokugawa
Efficacy-Entertainment Braid, 31–4. *See also* Diagram 1
Eiseman, Fred J., 21, 76, 92
Eldredge, Sears, 26, 27
Emigh, John, 23–25, 71, 76, 198, 203, 295
ergotropic (sympathetic) nervous system, 293, 300–301, 317
Erlangga [Airlangga], Balinese Prince, 74, 202
Ernst, Earl, 106

Fenollosa, Ernest, 86, 179, 238

Geertz, Clifford, 21, 181
Gianyar Regency, Bali, 45, 48, 188
Gide, André, 14
Gigaku, 108–109, 116
glossolalia, 237, 302
Goodman, Felicitas, 47, 301, 302, 307
Granville Barker, Harley, 14
Grimes, Ronald, 33

Grotowski, Jerzy, 35, 302n23

Hagoromo, 261–69, 273, 292
Hall, Sir Peter, 4, 6n7
Hata no Kôkatsu, 113
Hôshô School, 136
    Sado, 242
Houri, Tadao, 243, 245, 246
hypnosis, 229, 200, 296

Japanese folk masks:
    Oni, 103
    Oto, 103
    Shi-shi, 104, 105, 109
    Tengu, 103
Jimbaran village, Bali, 209
Johnstone, Keith, 26, 28, 36, 45

Kagura, 119, 286
Kakul, I Nyoman,198, 324
Kanami, 105, 108, 111, 136
kanda empat, 204–205
Kano, Ryoichi, 246, 284
Kantan, 14
Kanze:
    Hisao, 44, 136, 141, 143, 166, 168, 247, 266, 274
    Noh Theatre, Tokyo, 247, 265
    School, 136, 268
Kawi, 64, 69, 72, 99, 179, 180, 181–82, 222, 225, 226, 237
Ketewel
    masks, 66
Kirby, E.T., 115
Kirtimukha, 225 203
Kita School, 136, 246
Kiyotsune, 257–58, 259, 260, 276, 292
    performance, 260
Komparu School, 120, 136, 142
Kongô:
    Hisanori, Iemoto, 262, 263, 266
    Iwao, actor, 151, 252
    Magojirô Hisatsugu, maskmaker, 150
    Noh Theatre, Kyoto, 261, 278

    School, 136, 242, 261, 262, 265
    costumes, 278
    masks, 137
    Ujimasa, actor, 140
Kurama Tengu, 103
Kyôgen, 104, 119, 120n52, 130, 133, 243, 270–74

Lansing, Stephen J., 21, 76, 94, 205
Laughlin, Charles, 35, 46, 290, 293, 311, 312
Lecoq, Jacques, 16, 26
Lex, Barbara, 46, 305, 307
Leyak, 73, 224

Mahendradatta, 73, 201, 202, 208
Majapahit dynasty, 52, 176, 179
masks:
    and Christianity, 4–6
    in actor training, 1, 14–16, 26–29, 323
    in Western theatre, 4–5, 9–11, 12–17
Matsukaze, 252
Matsuyama, Shikoku, 261–62, 265
mawinten, 90–91, 227, 219
McManus, John, 46
McPhee, Colin, 21
Mead, Margaret, 21, 201, 204
Mershon, Katharine, 204
Meyer-Dinkgräfe, Daniel, 35
Meyerhoff, Barbara, 292
Michishige, Udaka, 145, 150, 264, 270,
miko, 115, 119, 253, 286
Mnouchkine, Ariane, 17
Muromachi Period, 133, 136, 144, 145. *See also* Table 1

Narasimha, 204
Nearman, Mark, 22
Noh (Nô), 5, 22, 23, 26
    aesthetic, 22, 157–68
    contradictory elements, 128, 246
    hana, 162–63
    jo-ha-kyû, 158–60

kokoro. See consciousness
kokoro vs. *kotoba*, 165
monomane, 160–62
yûgen, 164–65
and religious ritual, 50, 107, 116–26, 288–92
costumes, 241, 259, 278
hierarchy, 136–39
history, 105–16
influence on Western theatre, 5, 9–19
music, 135–36
plays, 133–35
scholarship on, 22
stage, 118, 129–32. *See also* Diagram 2
training, 59, 125, 89–92, 151–57
Noh mask use, 256, 313–19
Noh masks, 139–43, 280
books about, 23, 24
carver-actors, 150–52
compared to Balinese, 8, 194
maskmaking, 144–49
types:
 Aku-jo, 104
 Chûjo, 245–46, 273, 276, 277
 Fudô, 139, 140
 Hannya, 140, 285–6, 305
  prototype, 109
 Kantan-otoko, 121
 Ko-omote, 16, 147, 154, 244–46, 280
 Okina, 71, 109, 140
  compared with *Sidha Karya*, 313
 Sanko-Jo in *Tôru*, 270
 Shi-shi Guchi, 109
 Tenjin, 140
 Zo-onna
  in *Hagoromo*, 262, 265, 267

O'Neill, Eugene, 5
Oka, Ida Bagus, 211
Okina, 116, 261

Pengosekan Village, Bali, 235, 305

Pengrebongan, 77, 209
Pound, Ezra, 106
Prince Koripan story, 209
puputan, 54–55

Ramayana, 67, 218n97
Rangda, 55, 67, 72, 73, 74, 75, 76, 77, 206, 207, 208, 235, 239, 307, 310, 316. *See also Calonarang*
costume, 214–17
mask, 78–85, 170, 186, 209–11, 229, 231, 235
performance, 210, 298
performers, 213
rasa, 81
rhythmic stimuli, 47, 200, 283, 296, 298, 300, 307–308, 310
Rolfe, Bari, 26, 27–28
Royal Court Theatre, 28

Sado Island, 103, 131, 141, 242, 262
Saint-Denis, Michel, 15, 16, 26, 27
sangaku, 108, 109, 110, 111, 112, 116
sarugaku, 109, 110–14, 115–16
Schechner, Richard, 2, 30–34, 36–41, 45, 46, 313
sensory deprivation, 200, 283, 298, 299, 308, 309, 317
Shinto, 104, 105, 113, 115, 117–22, 123, 127, 132, 139, 275, 276, 277
and Buddhism, 122–23, 127
Shiva, 57. *See also* Siva and Siwa
Shôtoku, Prince, 114, 123
Siva:
 and Durga, 75, 206. *See also* Shiva and Siwa
Siwa, 57, 62, 75, 78–79, 185, 186, 187, 206, 207, 211, 219. *See also* Siva and Shiva
Slattum, Judy, 24, 71, 202
Stanislavski, Konstantin, 28, 35, 257
Suriyani, Luh Ketut, 21, 296
Suzuki, D.T., 42
symbolic penetration, 311, 316

Takabayashi, Kôji, 314. 322

Takasago, 120
Takigi Noh, 7, 130, 242–61
Taksu, 45, 81, 89, 92–99, 100, 163, 176, 199, 200. 204, 206, 293, 316
Taniko, 5
Teele, Rebecca, 22. 23, 240, 249, 275
temporal disorientation, 305–306, 308, 309
Tenget, 76–78, 80, 229, 230
The Tale of Genji, 7
The Tale of the Heike, 7
Tokugawa, 131, 136
    aesthetic, 227
    Period, 102, 106, 107, 133, 142, 307. See also Table 1
    Shogunate, 101, 106
Topeng, 22, 32, 53, 64, 66, 69, 70, 71, 72, 74, 79, 80, 82, 83, 89, 91, 93, 96, 98, 99, 200, 208, 214, 215, 216, 224, 228, 234, 238, 239, 273, 283, 288, 291, 293, 294, 313, 317, 324
    and *Taksu*, 93–94
    carver-dancers, 195–96
    definition, 65–66
    masks
        Bedahulu, 83
        Bondres, 69, 182
        Dalem, 68–70, 83, 98, 99, 180–82, 190–91, 210
        Patih (Topeng Keras), 68, 69, 74, 99, 176, 177–78, 181
        Pedanda, 58, 62, 63, 69, 90, 171, 182–84
        Penasar, 69, 74, 191, 224–26
        Sidha Karya, 65, 68, 71, 116, 170–88, 192, 222, 234, 291, 310, 315
        Topeng Tua, 69, 178, 186,
    use, 170–71
    music in, 166–67
    performance state, 199–201, 238
    ritual requirements, 78–80
    Sidha Karya (character), 65, 68, 69, 70–72
    training, 75–78

Topeng Pajegan, 65, 69, 170–71. See also *Topeng Sidha Karya*
    performance description, 147–63
Topeng Panca, 65
Topeng Prembon, 65
Topeng Sidha Karya, 65, 68, 71, 116, 172, 179
Topeng Wali, 59. See *Topeng Sidha Karya*
Tôru, 272, 273, 292
    performance, 274–79
trance, 1, 11, 19, 21, 23, 97, 103, 119, 120, 127, 200, 222, 226
    and possession, 26, 96, 115, 119, 120, 200, 305
    in Japan, 237
    and the mask, 28
    and transformation, 19
    definition, 2
    in Bali, 23, 65, 74, 76, 77, 78, 79, 157, 201, 206, 207, 212, 229, 233
    example, 228–39
    physiology of, 300–310
    ritual, 23, 46–47
transformation, 2, 6, 15, 17, 168, 175, 176, 203, 236, 238, 249, 266, 273, 275, 287, 289–90, 293, 294, 296, 310, 311, 312, 313, 316
    and the mask, 319–22
    and trance, 306
    definition, 2
    process, 41, 42–44, 45, 320–23. See also "transitional object"
    vs. "transportation", 37–40
transformational mechanism, 321–23, 40–41, 44, 289, 317
transitional object, 15, 40–41, 313
trophotropic (parasympathetic) nervous system, 293, 300–301, 317
Turner, Victor, 21, 29

Übermarionette, 10–12, 44, 249
Uma Dewi, 75, 78–79
Umewaka:
    family, 114, 136

Minoru, 106, 114
Umewaka, Naohiko, 13, 43, 285, 286, 302, 305

Vieux Colombier Theatre, 14
Vishnu, 57, 204. *See also Wisnu*

Waley, Arthur, 14, 106
Winnicott, D.W., 19, 31, 35, 271
Wisnu, 50, 57, 105, 187, 205, 219. *See also* Vishnu

Yeats, W.B., 12, 106, 160
Yoshimitsu, Ashikaga, 105
Young, Elizabeth, 22, 91, 92, 96
Zeami, 42, 44, 46, 105, 106, 108, 111, 112, 113, 126, 128, 131, 133, 134, 136, 140, 141, 142, 152, 153, 156, 157, 158, 159, 160, 161, 162, 165, 166, 167, 243, 252, 264, 266, 271, 282, 298, 300, 307
Zenchiku, Komparu, 142, 148, 156, 167

STUDIES IN THEATRE ARTS

1. J.R. Dashwood and J.E. Everson (eds.), **Writers and Performers in Italian Drama From the Time of Dante to Pirandello: Essays in Honour of G.H. McWilliam**
2. David P. Edgecombe, **Theatrical Training During the Age of Shakespeare**
3. Bryant Hamor Lee, **European Post-Baroque Neoclassical Theatre Architecture**
4. Diane Hunter (ed.), **The Makings of Dr. Charcot's Hysteria Shows: Research Through Performance**
5a. Jan Clarke, **The Guénégaud Theatre in Paris (1673-1680): Volume One: Founding, Design and Production**
5b. Jan Clarke, **The Guénégaud Theatre in Paris (1673-1680): Volume Two: The Accounts Season by Season**
6. James Strider, Jr., **Techniques and Training for Staged Fighting**
7. Steve Earnest, **The State Acting Academy of East Berlin–A History of Actor Training From Max Reinhardt's** *Schauspielschule* **to the** *Hochschule für Schauspielkunst "Ernst Busch"*
8. Calvin A. McClinton, **The Work of Vinnette Carroll, An African American Theatre Artist**
9. Linda Mackenney, **The Activities of Popular Dramatists and Drama Groups in Scotland, 1900-1952**
10. Kazimierz Braun, **Theater Directing–Art, Ethics, Creativity**
11. Jerry Rojo, **An Acting Method Using the Psychophysical Experience of Workshop Games-Exercises**
12. Tony Williams, **The Representation of London in Regency and Victorian Drama (1821-1881)**
13. Lloyd Anton Frerer, **Bronson Howard–Dean of American Dramatists**
14. Roy Connolly, **The Evolution of the Lyric Players Theatre, Belfast: Fighting the Waves**
15. Bonnie Milne Gardner, **The Emergence of the Playwright-Director in American Theatre, 1960-1983**
16. Thomas H. Gressler, **Theatre as the Essential Liberal Art in the American University**
17. Thomas Riccio, **Reinventing Traditional Alaska Native Performance**
18. Mira Wiegmann, **The Staging and Transformation of Gender Archetypes in** *A Midsummer Night's Dream, M. Butterfly,* **and** *Kiss of the Spider Woman*
19. Michael Balfour, **The Use of Drama in the Rehabilitation of Violent Male Offenders**
20. Anthony Hostetter, **Max Reinhardt's Großes Schauspielhaus–Its Artistic Goals, Planning, and Operation, 1910-1933**
21. Kazimierz Braun, **A Concise History of Polish Theater from the Eleventh to the Twentieth Centuries**
22. Frederick Paul Tollini, **Scene Design at the Court of Louis XIV–The Work of the Vigarani Family and Jean Berain**
23. Jerry D. Eisenhour, **Joe Leblang's Cut-Rate Ticket Empire and the Broadway Theatre, 1894-1931**
24. Joel D. Eis, **A Full Investigation of the Historic Performance of the First Play in English in the New Workd–The Case of** *Ye Bare & Ye Cubbe,* **1665**
25. Scott L. Root, **An Examination of Robert Beadell's (1925-1994) Four Major Works for the Lyric Stage**
26. Michael Anthony Ingham, **The Prose Fiction Stage Adaptation as Social Allegory in Contemporary British Drama: Staging Fictions**

27. Mark Medoff, **The Dramaturgy of Mark Medoff–Five Plays Dealing with Deafness and Social Issues,** compiled and with an introduction by Samuel J. Zachary
28. Michael Taub (ed.), **An Anthology of Israeli Drama for the New Millennium**
29. Kevin Bradshaw, **The Curriculum, Training Methods, and History of a Competitive Improvisational Comedy Company**
30. Margaret Coldiron, **Trance and Transformation of the Actor in Japanese Noh and Balinese Masked Dance-Drama**